THE
CADAVER
GAME

THE CADAVER GAME

Kate Ellis

piatkus

PIATKUS

First published in Great Britain in 2012 by Piatkus

A CIP catalogue record for this book
is available from the British Library.

ISBN 978-0-7499-5367-6 (HB)
ISBN 978-0-7499-5372-0 (TPB)

Typeset in Baskerville by M Rules
Printed and bound in Great Britain by
Clays Ltd, St Ives plc

Papers used by Piatkus are from well-managed forests
and other responsible sources.

MIX
Paper from
responsible sources
FSC® C104740

Piatkus
An imprint of
Little, Brown Book Group
100 Victoria Embankment

For Ruth and David

Chapter 1

Run as fast as you can, because captivity means certain death. Oblivion. No mercy is ever shown to those who fail and no second chances are given. That is The Game.

Barney has played The Game over and over again in the cocooned comfort of his room, but the real thing is different. In the real thing your feet squelch and skid on mud and stinking cow pats. In the real thing your muscles throb with tearing pain, adrenalin pumps through your body and makes your heart thump like a drum. In the real thing your burning legs are filled with molten lead, slowing you down as the hounds close in.

In the moonlit darkness everything is in half-seen silvery shadow and the familiar landscape is transformed and twisted into a fearful alien world – the world of The Game.

He can hear the throaty roar of quad bikes and the eager barking of hounds in the distance, a little louder with each passing second. They are getting closer and closer and if he doesn't run they'll catch him.

He has to move quickly. He has to outrun them. It is all uphill now, through the glowering trees and then across a stream. But he needs to rest, so he stops and bends double, catching each breath. With the confidence of youth he'd thought he was invincible. He'd thought this would be easy. No problem.

'I can't go any further. Wait for me. Hang on.'

He turns, and in the light of the full moon he can see Sophie's slender body quite clearly, her pale flesh glowing like alabaster. She has slumped down on to the grass a few yards behind him, her head bowed in defeat over her splayed knees, and he feels a stab of anger because she should have waited until they reached the shelter of the trees. He knows that when they are still, they're vulnerable. This is no time to take a rest, not while they're exposed to the enemy.

'We've got to get a move on or they'll catch us. Can't you hear them?' When there's no reaction he barks an order. 'Get up.'

Sophie shakes her head slowly. She looks utterly exhausted and her fine, fair hair is plastered to her forehead with sweat.

'My new trainers are ruined,' she whines. 'Whose idea was this?'

'Just shut up, will you.'

'Where's Dun?' He sees her look round anxiously but there's no sign of the other boy. 'Maybe he's been caught. Maybe the dogs have got him.'

She sounds close to tears and he knows that involving her was a big mistake.

'You're talking crap. Dun went off in the other direction. He'll be fine.' He feels like slapping her but that would never do.

'I want to go home,' she moans, like a tired child.

'No way. We carry on. Just try and keep up. It's not far to the stream now – me and Dun reccied it yesterday. Come on.'

He retraces his steps and holds out his hand to her. His hand is scratched and filthy but she snatches it and he hauls her to her feet. Then he hears the shot, sharp and sudden, exploding in the night air.

'What was that?' He can feel her body tense with fear.

'It'll be some farmer after vermin. Come on.'

'They've got guns. You never said they'd have guns.'

There is panic in Sophie's voice now and he knows she's losing it. He grabs her wrist and she cries with pain as he drags her forward. The sheltering trees are close now and if they can get to the stream there's a chance that the water will put their pursuers off the scent.

'Of course they've not got guns, you stupid bitch.'

'You told me this was meant to be a game.'

He doesn't answer as he pulls her onwards. They have to keep going and once they cross the stream maybe they can relax a little.

They stumble on, making for the cluster of trees looming ahead against the grey, starry sky. Sophie tries hard to keep up but somehow she always falls behind. She is a liability, and all the desire Barney ever felt for her is evaporating. He can hear her breathing, wheezy as though her lungs are about to burst. He'd asked her here because he thought it would be a chance for them to be alone. Stupid idea.

'What was that?'

Sophie has stopped again and she's standing quite still, frozen as if she's been turned to stone by some magic spell. If she carries on like this, he knows he'll have to abandon her . . . leave her to the mercy of the hunters. 'What are you on about?'

'That noise. There's someone here. One of them's caught up with us.'

'You're imagining things. Come on or I'll have to leave you behind.'

As she starts to move towards him, he hears it. A crack, like a foot on a rotten twig. Sophie was right. There is someone there.

'Dun,' he calls. 'Is that you?'

No answer. Of course it isn't Dun. He headed off half an hour ago, making for the chalets to fool their pursuers. Dun ran for the school; he was fast and knew what he was doing. Maybe they should have ignored instructions and stuck with him.

Suddenly Barney wants to be out of there. He grabs Sophie's hand and pulls her towards the trees, ignoring her squeaks of protest. But as soon as they reach the wood, he hears the sound again – a rustling and soft footsteps somewhere ahead of them. And something else. The distinctive double click of a gun being cocked.

Then comes the light – so bright that it dazzles his eyes. He hears Sophie gasp as he puts a defensive hand between himself and the beam. It is focused on him, blinding him, so that he can't make out what or who is behind it.

'Stop it!' he hears Sophie shout with a new found boldness. 'Stop messing about, whoever you are. We surrender, OK? You've won.'

4

But there is no answer and the merciless beam still burns into their eyes.

'Please,' Sophie whispers, her grip tightening on Barney's arm.

Then two shots echo through the woods – and two bodies hit the cold undergrowth.

Chapter 2

The Jester's Journal

18 May 1815

It is said that I am the last of my kind. The Last Fool in Devonshire – or should I say, the last to accept the rank of Fool as my calling in life. As the last of my ilk, I feel it necessary to set down an account of my deeds for generations yet to come, generations that might scoff at Fools and neglect to take account of their skills. For Foolery is a trade like any other. Fools have served kings since the Conqueror and were valued and respected as the only honest men at court; the only men able to tell the truth without resorting to flattery and politics.

They call me Silly John. Other men may take this title as an insult, but I do not, for I know there is no truth in it. Silly John is a mere mask, a role I play. When I am alone with my thoughts, or lying with a willing maidservant, I am John

Tandy; small of stature, with a hump upon my back, yet wise as any squire, parson or magistrate in the county, and with more cunning than any man of authority. Yet it suits my purpose that the Squire is unaware of my true nature.

In three days' time the Squire's cousin Henry will visit. He is a man of rare and violent tastes and the Squire has requested that there should be another hunt. I have given orders that the hounds should not be fed before they are released, for it gives better sport if the quarry is afraid of the hungry jaws of his pursuers. I like to see the fear in the quarry's eyes, for it brings to mind the power that I hold over life and death in this place. I anticipate Henry's arrival with glee. What sport we shall have.

Chapter 3

The entrance hall was neat and clean with nothing out of place. Only the rotting flowers standing in a vase of brown water by the telephone, the pervasive smell of decay and the distant hum of buzzing flies suggested that something was amiss.

'What did the caller say?'

'Just that there was a dead woman at this address. He hung up without giving his name, but the call was from a mobile so we might be able to trace who it's registered to.'

The man who stepped into the hallway was tall, black and smartly dressed, with handsome features and intelligent eyes. He was followed by an older, slightly smaller man, well-built with grizzled hair, and a girth that suggested a love of the wrong type of food. Both men instinctively put their hands to their faces. They knew the signs from long experience. Death was present, hiding somewhere in this unpretentious Victorian cottage in a quiet Morbay suburb.

'You go first, Wes.' Both men knew from the constable's initial report what they were about to see. A woman, dead a week or so; her discoloured flesh crawling with maggots and flies. The constable had gone upstairs and peeped into the bedroom before slamming the door and throwing up in the bathroom.

DI Wesley Peterson was reluctant to move. 'Maybe we should wait for Colin and the team. They'll be here any minute.'

'Could be natural causes.'

Wesley knew that it was in his boss's nature to be optimistic.

'Sad that she's been dead so long and nobody's missed her.'

DCI Gerry Heffernan nodded. 'Yeah. All the lonely people, eh. According to the neighbours, she was probably in her late thirties but they hardly saw anything of her. They didn't even know her name. Lived next door and never spoke to her. Should be a law against it.'

'If the house is rented the landlord should be able to provide her details.'

Before Gerry could say anything else, there was a commotion outside the front door. The circus had arrived.

They opened the door wide to admit their colleagues before struggling into their crime scene suits. There were procedures that had to be followed.

The pathologist, Dr Colin Bowman, came into view, pushing past the forensic officers and photographers. He was a tall, thin man with an aquiline nose and hair that had receded over the years, leaving a monk-like fringe around his shiny pate. 'Good to see you Gerry ... Wesley. What have you got for me today?' he asked, shaking hands as if they were attending a pleasant social gathering.

'A woman . . . in her late thirties according to the neighbour.' He paused. 'I'm afraid she's been there a while.'

'I might be getting on a bit, Gerry, but I haven't lost my sense of smell,' said Colin as he donned a surgical mask.

The pathologist climbed the stairs and Wesley and Gerry followed behind. They waited on the landing while he disappeared into the room at the end. Ten minutes later he emerged, closing the door behind him and yanking off his mask so that it dangled around his neck.

'Because of the state of decomposition, I'm afraid I can't give a final verdict until I've done the post-mortem, and maybe not even then if I have to wait for toxicology tests and all that.'

'But you can make an educated guess?' Gerry said with a hint of impatience.

'There are some signs that it could be strangulation but, as I say, I can't know for certain until—'

Gerry slapped the pathologist on the back. 'Thanks, Colin. That's all I need to know. Mind if we have a quick shufti?'

'Be my guest. But watch out for the insect life.'

Wesley watched his boss's eyes light up with the excitement of the chase. Gerry put a chubby hand on his arm and steered him towards the scene of all the activity. The door stood open now and Wesley could see the team inside going through their well-choreographed routine, illuminated by the photographer's flash bulbs.

As Wesley took a deep breath, he realised that he'd grown accustomed to the smell of death. He let Gerry enter the room first, hanging back a little, bracing himself for what he was about to see.

Once inside the room, he forced himself to look at the

thing that had once been a woman. She was lying on the bed, hands neatly folded across her chest, face upwards, staring at the ceiling, mouth gaping. The first thing that struck Wesley was that the victim looked surprised. But then her face was distorted and bloated so it was hard to tell.

Putrification and maggots had done their grim work and, at first sight it wasn't obvious how the woman had met her end, but Colin's theory of strangulation seemed as likely as any other. She was fully dressed, wearing a very short skirt; too short perhaps for a woman beyond the age of thirty. Or perhaps she was only in her twenties; given the state of the body, it was impossible to tell. The thin blouse she wore was low-cut, but you could see worse on any high street. Wesley could see an embroidered, red push-up bra through the diaphanous black material and he turned away. It somehow seemed disrespectful to notice something like that. But he knew his wife Pam wouldn't wear such a bra under a blouse like that. Badly groomed, perhaps. Or just blatantly sexual.

There was an intricate silver knot ring on the swollen middle finger of the dead woman's right hand and another delicately crafted ring with a large red stone on her left little finger. Wesley had seen similar rings, individually designed and hand-made, in local jewellers and upmarket gift shops, so there was always a chance that they might help in her identification.

'We'll need to get this place searched thoroughly,' said Wesley quietly. 'We need to find out who she was and what she did for a living. What do you think of her clothes?'

Gerry snorted. 'Who do you think I am? Fashion correspondent of the *Tradmouth Echo*?'

'I meant, do you think she was all dressed up for a date?'

'Undoubtedly. There's a man in this somewhere and we need to find him.'

'Our anonymous caller?'

'Probably.' He stared at the woman on the bed. 'Do you reckon it could be a domestic? She invites her fella round, they have a row and he ends up strangling her in the bedroom?'

Wesley considered the possibility for a few seconds. 'You could be right. After all, it's the oldest story in the book. All we've got to do is find out is who he is and where we can lay our hands on him.'

Gerry sighed. 'If my theory's right it shouldn't be difficult.'

'Our man waited a while before reporting it.'

'He might have been wrestling with his conscience.' Gerry spun round and began to stride towards the door. 'I'm going to have another word with the neighbours,' he called over his shoulder. 'With any luck someone might have been watching through the net curtains and seen the killer visiting the house.'

Wesley followed him out, glad to get away from the flies and the stench of the grave.

Friday the thirteenth hadn't been DC Trish Walton's best day. She had visited the supermarket first thing because supplies of bread, milk and ready meals in the cottage she shared with DS Rachel Tracey were running perilously low, and when she'd gone to pay, found that she'd lost her credit card.

In the panic that followed she'd made several frantic phone calls before finding the card nestling in the dark depths of her handbag. She'd felt a fool. But she often felt like that. At least her boyfriend DC Paul Johnson had been sympathetic. She really didn't know why she wasn't nicer to him, but sometimes he reminded her of a faithful dog.

She looked up and when she saw Paul hovering beside her desk, she tried to smile. 'Anything new?'

'That suspicious death in Morbay. The boss says it's probably murder but there's a chance it could be a domestic.'

'Let's hope it turns out to be straightforward then.' She saw he was frowning, as though there was something on his mind. She hoped he wasn't going to go on about their relationship again. She wasn't in the mood and if DCI Heffernan found out that they'd brought their personal life into the office, they wouldn't hear the end of what passed for his cutting wit. 'Anything else?'

'I've had a call from . . . from someone. It's already been reported to Uniform but . . . '

'What is it?' She knew from the expression on Paul's face that it was bothering him.

'A girl's gone missing. She went out last night and didn't come home.'

'A girl? How old?'

'Eighteen. Just finished her A-levels.'

Trish sighed. For one moment she'd feared he was talking about a missing child . . . and that was something she didn't like to think about. 'What's her name?'

'Sophie Walter. Her mum says she was meeting her boyfriend.'

'Touch of the Romeo and Juliets then. Her parents are probably panicking. I got up to all sorts when I was that age. Didn't you?'

Paul shrugged. She knew he hadn't had a particularly

13

adventurous youth, preferring to dedicate himself to athletics. 'Her parents are worried.'

'Parents always worry. It's their job. If they've just left school they've probably decided to go off somewhere; a music festival maybe. Has the boy been reported missing too?'

'Not officially, no. But he isn't at home and his mother hasn't been able to contact him.'

'They'll turn up when they run out of money and condoms.'

'Sophie's parents said she was very secretive about what they were up to.'

'There you are then. They'll have been planning this for a while. Nothing to worry about.'

Paul looked unconvinced as he cleared his throat. 'There's something I haven't told you.'

'What's that?'

'Sophie's my cousin. Her mum's my mum's sister. She rang me after she reported Sophie missing. She's in a bit of a state.'

Trish looked into his eyes. This wasn't just another missing person; this was family – one of his own. She tried to find the right words, something that would convey her concern, but her mind went blank and she cursed her own inadequacy. 'I'm really sorry,' she said after a few moments. 'But you know as well as I do that most kids that age who go missing turn up safe and sound after a couple of days.' She knew this was the sort of routine phrase the police used day after day, probably true but not much real comfort to an anxious relative. 'I'm sure she'll be back after the weekend, but if she isn't we'll mention it to the boss, eh.'

'If you think so.'

Trish turned her head away, wishing, not for the first time, that he wouldn't leave it up to her to make all the decisions.

Wesley was glad that Colin had agreed to fit the post-mortem in at four o'clock that afternoon. The sooner they knew what they were dealing with, the better.

As the neighbours hadn't been able to give them a name for the deceased woman, their first port of call was the agency that dealt with the letting of the house where she was found. The office of Morbay Properties was in the centre of the large resort, a couple of streets back from the seafront. It was a converted shop with wooden blinds at the windows and the company name freshly painted on the glass in cream letters, with a stylised blue seagull painted beneath – presumably the company logo. It looked fairly upmarket, which was only to be expected as the cottage was in a good area and wouldn't have come cheap. When they arrived the office was closed for lunch and they had half an hour to kill.

Wesley had almost forgotten that he hadn't eaten anything since breakfast but Gerry claimed to be hungry, so, on his suggestion, they bought fish and chips to eat on the promenade. They were lucky to find a vacant bench because the first week of the school summer break had brought holidaying families out in force. In spite of a cloudy sky, children ran about with buckets and spades, their excited cries drowning out the seagulls circling in the eternal hope of a discarded chip or pasty.

Gerry sat in the midst of this scene of mayhem with a beatific smile on his face, popping chips into his mouth one by one. He looked contented, like a man who wasn't going to allow a little thing like murder to ruin his pleasures.

Wesley, however, picked at his fish, impatient to discover the dead woman's identity. He felt he owed it to her to give her a name at least.

'I thought you were trying to lose weight,' said Wesley as he watched Gerry screwing up his empty chip paper. The chips had been good, crisp and hot, but Wesley had been unable to finish them.

'Fish is health food, Wes. Thought you'd have known that what with your sister being a doctor.'

'Not when it's fried in thick batter and served with a generous helping of chips, it isn't.' He stood up. It was half past one now and Morbay Properties should be in business again.

Gerry stretched himself and followed Wesley to the office and this time the blinds were open, giving a glimpse of a cream and sky-blue interior which matched the sign on the window. When they pushed the door open a bell jangled loudly, denying them the advantage of surprise.

A plump young woman wearing a cheap, black trouser suit and a bored expression asked if she could help them. When they showed their warrant cards she raised her eyebrows but her expression didn't change.

'We need the details of the tenant of Lister Cottage on St Marks Road,' said Gerry. 'I'm sure you know where to lay your hands on the file,' he added, leaning forward and favouring her with an encouraging smile that showed the gap between his two front teeth.

The woman stood up and walked slowly to the filing cabinet, extracted a thin cardboard file and placed it in Gerry's outstretched hand.

He handed it to Wesley who put it on the desk and opened it. 'Her name's Tessa Trencham,' he said. He turned to the woman who was watching them with wary eyes. 'Have you ever met Ms Trencham? Did she come here to pick up the keys?'

'We have a lot of properties on our books. I can't remember all the tenants.'

'But do you remember this particular woman?'

'Why? What's she done?'

'She's dead,' Gerry said.

The bluntness of his statement seemed to have some effect, because the woman's bored expression vanished and her hand fluttered up to her mouth. 'Oh my God. Why didn't you say?'

'What's going on?'

Wesley turned to see a man standing in what would once have been the door to the rear of the shop. He was dressed in an immaculate pinstriped suit, snowy shirt and perfectly knotted tie, and he had a thin moustache that reminded Wesley of a wartime spiv. Somehow he wouldn't have trusted this man with his life savings.

'Kris, these men are from the police. They're asking about the tenant in Lister Cottage on St Marks Road. She's dead.' She almost mouthed the last two words as if uttering them out loud might give them some destructive power to spread death to any listener.

'I'm sorry to hear that. If you gentlemen would like to come through into my office.'

Once they were seated, the man who'd introduced himself as Kris Kettering arched his fingers and assumed an expression of co-operation as Wesley pushed the file across the desk in his direction.

'What can you tell us about Tessa Trencham?'

'Nothing much. She took Lister Cottage about three

17

months ago. I believe she'd moved to Morbay from London and rented a flat here for a while, but she wanted somewhere bigger. I think she was intending to look around for something to buy. We get hundreds of people like that. We tend to deal with the middle to top end of the market – no benefit claimants or student lets.'

'So you actually met her?'

'Briefly, but I don't remember much about her. They all blur into one after a while.'

'Who do?'

'Tenants. We're a large agency dealing with a lot of properties. Ms Trencham never made any complaints or needed anything repairing in the house so I wouldn't have much cause to remember her.'

'Can you describe her?'

Kettering frowned, puzzled. 'Why? If she's dead haven't you—?'

'Just describe her, please, sir.'

Kettering shrugged. 'As far as I can remember she was dark-haired, average height, quite attractive, probably in her late thirties. That's about it. I only met her once when she came to sign the lease and I wasn't paying much attention. How did she . . . ?'

'We don't know for certain yet, sir,' said Wesley. 'But we're treating her death as suspicious.'

Kettering nodded solemnly as though he dealt with violent death every day and it hadn't come as a shock to him.

'Is there anything else you can tell us? Who provided her references, for instance?'

'That should be in the file.' He began to turn over the papers in the cardboard folder and Wesley noticed that his hands were shaking a little. He pulled out a sheet of paper

and handed it to Wesley. 'These are the references she provided.'

'Did you check them?'

'Somebody will have done. It's routine.'

Wesley asked for a copy of all the documents in the file
and Kettering disappeared.

'Once we know who gave her the references, we might
make some progress,' Gerry whispered once they were
alone.

Wesley just hoped he was right.

Chapter 4

The Steward's Journal

20 May 1815

It is said that Bonaparte still reigns in Paris. It is less than a year since all Tradmouth celebrated his defeat and exile to Elba with a great feast of roast beef, plum pudding and ale, and now the man is at large again, a cunning fox who has escaped his captors.

The Squire's cousin will arrive on the morrow and I have orders to prepare his usual chamber. I have observed that the Squire's manners have become coarser since his cousin's return to Devonshire, especially when he has taken too much wine, and our so-called 'jester' only encourages our master's baser instincts.

I have been acquainted with John Tandy since childhood and I know only too well that he is a sly, clever creature, although I fear he was much put upon throughout his early life and tormented because of his unfortunate deformity. It suits him well to play the role of Silly John but he cannot deceive me as to his intelligence and true nature.

I hear Henry and Tandy are bent on organising another hunt, but I pray this is not so. The last time the Squire and his cousin released the hounds and rode after their quarry, I heard that the action had unfortunate consequences, although nobody dares to speak of it.

However, I must hold my tongue for I depend upon the squire for the roof over my head and the food upon my table. Weak sinner that I am, I become blind to wrongdoing in order to preserve my station in life.

Chapter 5

Paul's cousin Sophie had always been the adventurous type, but she'd never done anything like this before and that worried him. Perhaps the boy she'd been with had led her astray. The opposite sex, in Paul's experience, could have a strange effect on even the most level-headed teenager. That was how nature worked and how the human race continued.

The disappearance of two young people was a routine matter for Uniform who had given his aunt and uncle the usual spiel about errant kids turning up with their tails between their legs within forty-eight hours. Paul had heard it all before; he'd even said it himself to parents worried out of their wits. But when it's someone close to you, somehow the words seem hollow and patronising.

He went off duty at four and he knew that the DCI and Inspector Peterson would be over in Morbay attending the post-mortem of the woman found earlier that day. If Dr

Bowman delivered a verdict of murder, the whole team would begin working flat out and spare time would be a rarity, so he decided to seize the opportunity to visit his Aunty Carole that afternoon, just to see what was going on.

Over the years Carole and Brian had risen above the rest of the family in wealth and social standing. His mother's sister had married a man with an agricultural equipment hire business, which had prospered over the years, and now they lived in some splendour – or so it seemed to Paul – just outside the village of West Talton near the road to Dukesbridge. The house was a large barn conversion with galleried landings, an indoor swimming pool, a snooker room and five bedrooms, all surrounded by an acre of well-tended garden. Sophie and her brother Jack had wanted for nothing and had been sent to what Paul's mother described as 'posh schools', while Paul had attended the local comprehensive.

Paul arrived at the house and parked his ten-year-old VW Golf on the gravel drive next to his aunt's new Range Rover. When Carole opened the door he was struck by how pale she looked, as though the worry had drained all the blood from her normally rosy cheeks. As she stood aside to let him in, he reached out to her and gave her an awkward embrace. She gave his shoulder a grateful squeeze before leading him into the massive kitchen with its hand-made oak units and central island.

'Any news?' Her anxious eyes searched his face for any tell-tale signs and he felt bad that he didn't have something good to tell her.

'Not yet. Sorry.' He looked round. 'Where's Uncle Brian?'

'He's gone to work. He said he wants to keep busy.'

23

'How long has Sophie been gone now?'

'She went out last night to meet Barney – that's her boyfriend. She promised she'd be back by midnight but . . .' She spread her hands in a gesture of desperation. 'I've tried her mobile but there's no answer. Jack's tried texting her and we've been in touch with all her friends but none of them know where she is. She always lets me know if she's going to be late. That's why I'm so worried.'

'I know. You've given Uniform a photograph and details of what she was wearing and all that?'

Carole nodded. 'Her rucksack's missing, and I think she's taken some spare clothes and one of the good towels from the bathroom.'

Paul, eager to provide some comfort, pointed out that the news about the change of clothes was promising. It meant the disappearance was planned and the pair of star-crossed lovers would probably return when they were ready.

'Have you spoken to Barney's parents?'

'His mum – she's divorced.' From the way she said it, Paul sensed that she disapproved of the woman. 'She said Barney had taken a change of clothes with him too. She didn't seem too worried.'

He leaned forward and took his aunt's hands in his. 'Look, I'm sure they'll be back. You'll keep me up to date, won't you?'

Carole nodded again. Then she burst into tears. Paul put a tentative arm around her. Eventually she took a deep, shuddering breath and retrieved a tissue from her pocket. She wiped her tears and blew her nose.

Paul was a police officer, and he felt he should be able to do something to make it right. But at that moment he was as impotent as anybody else. 'Would you like me to have a look in her room, just to see if there's any clue to where she might have got to?' At least he could do something practical, just to make her feel better.

'It's at the top of the stairs, first on the left. Her computer's in there. Maybe you could . . . '

'I'll have a look.' As he stood up he put a reassuring hand on his aunt's shoulder. She touched it, acknowledging his sympathy, and smiled bravely, her eyes still red with tears.

Sophie's room was considerably bigger than the one Paul had occupied when he was that age. Twice the size, with an en-suite shower room and a huge flat-screen TV. He'd always regarded his cousin as over-indulged but he hadn't realised the extent of the lifestyle difference until now.

It was what Paul thought of as a typically girly room. Posters of handsome film vampires on the walls, and bright beads and fluffy scarves hanging from hooks and handles. He made for the shocking-pink laptop that was sitting on the desk in the corner of the room and switched it on. It was a top of the range model – he knew because he'd bought one recently; a considerably cheaper type in austere black.

When the screen flickered into life, Paul checked for any relevant emails or messages but found nothing of interest. Whatever arrangements Sophie had made for the weekend would probably have been done by phone or text. Then he checked on the websites his cousin had been using recently and found that she had mostly been using her computer for playing games, and one game in particular. It was an Internet-based game called Blood Hunt.

And she'd played it over and over again. Almost to the point of obsession.

*

Colin conducted the post-mortem on the dead woman at Morbay Hospital. The new mortuary suite there was state of the art, or so he told Wesley and Gerry. But Wesley found himself missing the homely feel of Colin's office back in Tradmouth.

The body of Tessa Trencham was naked now, her shiny, swollen, putrefying flesh mottled under the glaring lights. Wesley avoided looking at the corpse because the sight and smell of it made him feel slightly nauseous. Sometimes he found it hard to believe that he came from a family of doctors. He focused his eyes on the trolley of instruments beside the table, listening carefully to Colin's comprehensive commentary on the proceedings. In contrast, Gerry stood closer, watching carefully, asking questions.

'Because of the condition of the body, it's hard to tell whether she had intercourse before her death but I'll take samples just in case,' Colin announced.

'I think my initial diagnosis of manual strangulation was accurate, gentlemen,' he continued, sounding rather pleased with himself. 'It's difficult to tell, given the state of the flesh, but I think you can just about make out the marks.' He placed his gloved hands around the dead woman's throat. 'Fingers, you see. Textbook pattern of bruising.'

'I take it the killer was a man,' Gerry asked.

'Probably. Although a strong woman could have done it – someone who attends the gym every day and goes in for weight-training. The victim was slightly built. And I think she was attractive once,' he added softly, gazing down at the woman's face. 'But not any more, alas.'

'Time of death?' Wesley thought he'd better ask an intelligent question.

'Now you're asking.'

'I know you always say it isn't an exact science but can you make an educated guess?'

'What is referred to now as a ball-park estimate would be around a week ago. Some time last Saturday, give or take twenty-four hours. Sorry I can't be more precise. Who reported the body, by the way?'

'An anonymous caller from a mobile. It's being traced. We're just waiting for a name.'

'Have we identified our victim yet?' Colin asked.

'The house where she was found was rented to a Tessa Trencham.'

'And you're sure it's her?'

'She fits the approximate description we have. But we can't ask anyone to identify her in that state so it'll have to be dental records or DNA. The initial search didn't turn up any photos of her.'

'That's odd.'

'Some people don't like having their picture taken.'

'What about friends and family? I take it you've checked her mobile?'

'We would do if we could find it. There's no sign of a mobile on the premises. Or credit cards. Something might come to light when we have a more thorough search but ... '

'Good luck then.' Colin stood poised to make the Y shaped incision into the dead woman's chest. 'She must be someone's wife, or sister ... or daughter. And she's certainly a mother.'

Wesley caught Gerry's eye. 'Really?'

'No doubt about it. She's given birth at least once.'

'How old would you say she was?' Wesley asked.

Colin stood back and studied the body before replying.

'Late thirties or well-preserved early forties maybe. She has good muscle tone, kept herself fit.'

'So she might have belonged to a gym.' They needed something – anything – that would give them a clue to the mystery that was Tessa Trencham's life. 'And she must have worked somewhere.'

'True. Someone's bound to miss her sooner or later. If she's got a child . . .'

'If she had it young, it could be grown up by now,' Gerry observed. 'It obviously didn't live with her.'

'He or she might live with the father,' said Wesley. 'She's not wearing a wedding ring so she might be single or divorced. Life's complicated for a lot of people these days.'

'Are the references she gave the letting agency being checked out?' Gerry asked.

Wesley nodded. 'Yes. A Sylvia Cartland and a Carl Heckerty. I asked Trish to see to it.'

They fell silent as Colin went about his business, removing, examining and weighing the internal organs, keeping up a commentary into the microphone suspended above the table. Wesley continued to study the room, looking anywhere but on the thing that had once been a woman, lying with her raw, stinking innards on show.

When the post-mortem was over and Colin's assistant was sewing up the incisions, the pathologist stood holding the dead woman's left hand tenderly, as if he was about to break bad news to her. After a few moments he spoke quietly and Wesley could tell that something was bothering him. 'There is something that strikes me as a little odd.'

'What's that?'

'If someone tries to strangle you, it's normal to put up some resistance, but when I took the usual samples from her fingernails there doesn't seem to be anything there. As you see, they're immaculately manicured, no nails broken, no obvious traces of the assailant's skin caught underneath. The only injury on her body seems to be the bruising around the neck.'

'Maybe she was drunk or drugged.'

'We'll have to wait for the toxicology report to find out,' said Colin with a sigh. 'Or perhaps he just took her by surprise.'

'She was in her bedroom so it has to be someone she knew well,' said Wesley. 'A boyfriend. Someone she trusted.'

'In that case he shouldn't be hard to find,' said Gerry with confidence.

Wesley followed Colin and Gerry out of the mortuary suite, wishing he could share his boss's optimism.

'You do agree that it's an interesting project?'

Neil Watson looked at the man standing a couple of feet away from him and nodded warily, as if he wasn't convinced. With his wild shock of snow-white hair, interesting display of tattoos snaking up his arms, bright yellow Breton smock and red combat trousers decorated with embroidered chains, Kevin Orford didn't look as if he had the means to pay the Archaeological Unit the extremely generous sum of money he was offering. But appearances can deceive, so Neil was reserving judgement . . . for the moment.

The field where they stood had recently been vacated by a herd of sheep whose droppings were still scattered on the grass. A hundred yards away, Neil could see a battered wire fence separating the field from a row of run-down holiday chalets of 1960s vintage, constructed in cedar wood and the kind of stone-cladding that went out of fashion with the space-hopper. He knew the name of the place because he had stayed there once as a kid: a cheap and cheerful holiday with happy memories. It was sad to see Catton Hall Holiday Park closed and semi-derelict.

'I did tell you that we'd fund all the work involved, didn't I? And my backers have agreed to make a substantial donation to your unit.' He leaned forward confidentially and Neil could smell peppermint on his breath. 'Since I won the Turner Prize last year, money hasn't been a problem.'

Neil was part of a team excavating an unexplored section of a Napoleonic fort which stood guarding the headland a couple of miles away to the south, but he was sure the others could manage without him for a few days. And money was money.

'So let me get this straight. Sixteen years ago a group of artists had a picnic—'

'A Feast of Life to be exact. A large trench had been dug and when a hunting horn was sounded exactly ten minutes after we'd begun to eat, we deposited everything that was left of the banquet into the ground, tables, plates and all, representing our reliance on the earth for our sustenance.' Orford had a distant look in his eyes as though he was reminiscing about some great past triumph. 'It was an awesome moment, conducted in complete silence. A lot of my work deals with our relationship with food. It's a subject I find particularly pertinent to the condition of the human race.'

Neil nodded trying to hide his scepticism. This man saw nothing ridiculous or pretentious in the fact that he and his mates had chucked perfectly good food and furniture into a big trench.

'It was my first piece of serious conceptual art since I'd left art college.'

'You didn't do it on your own?'

'Three other artists took part. I have a photographic record if you want to see it.'

'That might be useful.' Neil tried to sound enthusiastic.

'I intended to gather the same artists together again but two were busy with their own work and I've been unable to contact the third. However, I've enlisted the help of three other artists in the hope that their input will bring a new creativity to the project. It's always been my intention to disinter the artwork one day and once you've uncovered it, I'll take a cast which I shall entitle "The Decay of Mankind".'

Neil studied the man. If he'd left art college over sixteen years ago that meant he must be in his late thirties. Sometimes he gave the impression of being younger but Neil could see the hardness of experience in his eyes and he suspected that he was nobody's fool. He also sensed an underlying tension as the artist spoke, as though something was preying on his mind and kept intruding. But whatever it was, it was no concern of his.

All of a sudden he knew how to turn the situation to his advantage – or at least to the advantage of the archaeological community. He gave Orford a disarming smile. 'I think this might be an interesting exercise for some post-grad students I know from the university who specialise in the scientific side of archaeology. It'll be useful for them to see the effect of burial on different materials. I take it you've no objection to ...'

Orford considered the proposition for a while before replying. 'As long as they're willing to abide by my rules I have no objection. A few lads who worked at the holiday park next door helped to dig the original trench.' Orford paused, his eyes fixed on the crumbling buildings beyond the fence. 'It was still going strong when I was last here but it looks pretty derelict now.'

'Yes. I presume you've got the necessary permission from the landowner. You can't just go digging up land without getting the go ahead.'

'I've had written permission from his son. His name's Richard Catton and he seems to make all the decisions. He's quite keen on the project. I remember he helped out sixteen years ago but he was just a kid then.'

'Where does he live?'

'Up at Catton Hall: an old, rambling place about a quarter of a mile away. This is all his land, including the holiday park.'

'How old is the hall?' Neil's appetite was suddenly whetted by the mention of an historic pile.

'How should I know?' Orford said as though the conversation was starting to bore him. 'Look, Dr Watson – or can I call you Neil?'

'Neil's fine.'

'Before we begin, I want you and your colleagues to sign a confidentiality agreement. Anything you find or see while you're engaged in this artistic project is to be strictly controlled by myself and my PR people. I take it you agree?'

'Why?' The man was starting to annoy Neil. What could possibly be confidential about digging up some old picnic?

'I don't have to give reasons. I just expect you to agree.'

The artist's eyes had hardened. Neil had seen this look on the faces of property developers trying to pull one over on his archaeological team for a swift profit. But he hadn't expected it from a well-known conceptual artist.

But the matter was hardly likely to affect his involvement so he shrugged and gave the man the answer he wanted to hear.

Chapter 6

The Jester's Journal

22 May 1815

Tonight we shall hunt again.

I have already visited the stables where my hares are to stay until they are needed. They are two goodly hares – farm lads, strong and fast. The Squire's cousin, Master Henry, expressed a preference for a female hare but I found it hard to persuade any local maid to take on the role ... especially as Henry likes to hunt a naked quarry. I must be more persuasive.

One of the hares, a well-set lad called William, raised some objection to removing his clothing, but when I told him no fee would be paid to a disobedient servant he saw the error of his ways.

23 May 1815

The hunt proceeded well last night and, oh, what pleasure and entertainment was had! I myself presented a cup of best claret to the noble riders before their departure and I hope I do not boast when I say that I provided much wit and ceremony to the event. The Squire and Master Henry riding after the hares with the hounds in full cry was a magnificent sight to see, and yet I fear that one day such entertainment will pall and Master Henry will crave ever more violent delights. I shall set my mind to their devising.

The lad, William, suffered some injury but all the signs are that he will live and he has been paid well for his pains. I have given orders that he is to be locked in the chamber beside the stables until he is recovered and I sent word to his mother that he has been called away on my master's business. He will keep his mouth shut or I shall have to take measures to ensure his silence.

Our steward Christopher Wells asked what business the two lads he saw around the stables yesterday had at the Hall. From the way in which he purses his lips at me like a frosty old dowager, I could take him for one of advanced years rather than a handsome man in his prime. But so it is with those of the Puritan persuasion. I told him nothing but he knows of the hunt, for I saw him watching from the window when our noble huntsmen set off. I trust he will not visit the parson to set him upon the Squire again. The Squire was most vexed last time and sent the man on his way with a kicked backside. How I laughed to see that pompous man of the cloth brought down. It was as good as a play by the mummers who visit at Yuletide.

Chapter 7

A more thorough search of Tessa Trencham's house was on
Wesley's list of things to organise. It was a long list, as it
always was when a murder had been committed on his
patch. On Gerry's orders the place had been sealed off
until a detailed examination of all the dead woman's possessions could be made. And he and Wesley wanted to
supervise that search themselves so that nothing was
missed.

It was coming up to six when they arrived at Lister
Cottage and Rachel Tracey met them there. Wesley noticed
that her face was flushed and she was looking rather
pleased with herself.

'Anything interesting come up from the house to house
inquiries?' he asked.

She shook her head and her blonde pony tail bobbed to
and fro. Wesley suspected that she tied her hair back to look
more businesslike and efficient. But it suited her.

'Nobody knows much about Tessa Trencham. As you can see, the house is on the main road and it's shielded from the neighbours by high hedges. She didn't pass the time of day with any of them, but a couple did say that during the past couple of weeks there have been several cars parked outside so she must have had visitors.'

'Does she own a car?'

'A blue Toyota Yaris. But there's no sign of it.'

Wesley glanced at Gerry who was hovering impatiently by the front door.

'Right, then. Forensic have finished whatever it is they do, so it's all ours.' Gerry pushed the crime scene tape aside and the door swung open. 'Come on. Me and Rach'll take downstairs and you do upstairs, Wes. We've got a licence to be nosy – official.'

Wesley caught Rachel's eye and they both smiled. Gerry's brand of Liverpudlian humour had helped them face some dire situations in the past, as long as there were no grieving relatives around to hear.

The scent of death still hung in the air but Wesley tried to ignore it as he climbed the stairs.

He started in the second bedroom, which seemed to be serving as a store room. Here the wardrobes were crammed with clothes, and boxes of paperwork lay on the bare mattress of a single divan bed: bills, bank statements and correspondence all addressed to Tessa Trencham. Someone would have to go through them all in the hope that a clue to her death would be concealed in there. He searched through the bank statements for any indication as to how she earned her living but, although the account was fairly healthy, there was nothing to suggest where that money came from. In an old shoebox at the bottom of a wardrobe he found some photographs of an elderly couple and several of a fair-haired boy from babyhood to the brink of adulthood. But there didn't appear to be any pictures of the dead woman, old or recent.

The bathroom contained nothing out of the ordinary; just an array of expensive beauty products and some common proprietary medicines in the mirrored cabinet. When he stepped out on to the landing he knew he had to face the bedroom where the woman had died. He pushed the door open and stood for a few moments staring down at the place where her body had lain undiscovered and unmissed for all that time. The pale bedspread was discoloured with a large stain and scattered with insect pupa cases, while the tiny corpses of flies lay scattered around the room. Someone, the Forensic people probably, had been at work with insect spray and, as the place stank of mingled death and chemicals, Wesley decided to open a window to let some fresh air in before beginning his search.

There were no books beside the bed. But some people, he supposed, just didn't like reading. The double bed was still made up, immaculate with a satin throw folded across the bottom and matching scatter cushions propped up on the ornate velvet headboard, but his eyes were drawn to the dark, dinted area where the body had lain. This was a woman's room all right – his wife Pam had observed more than once that no man she'd ever known could see the purpose of the scatter cushion.

He began by turning back the bedclothes. The sheets looked freshly laundered and there was no sign of a nightdress or pyjamas beneath the pillows. He made a quick search of the bedside drawers and found a box full of tissues and several packs of condoms. There must have been a man – or men – in Tessa Trencham's life. It was just a case now of finding him ... or them. He looked in the waste-bin, but there was no sign of any used condoms that would provide them with useful DNA; the lover – or lovers – had probably flushed them down the lavatory. A pity, he thought.

Rooting through the ottoman at the end of the bed, he found several changes of bedding, all newish and smelling sweetly of fabric conditioner. The wardrobes contained more clothes and the chest of drawers was filled with lacy, luxurious underwear, mostly in red and black. The top two dressing-table drawers were given over to jewellery and make-up and he could tell that she had very expensive tastes in perfume and cosmetics. Tessa Trencham was a woman who indulged herself. The jewellery was mostly solid silver and looked as though it had been individually designed. Some of it was in a similar style to the rings she was wearing and Wesley wondered why she hadn't been wearing the matching earrings and necklace which lay in a velvet box inside the drawer.

In contrast to the second bedroom, this room was show-home neat and Wesley had the nagging feeling that it was staged somehow, rather like a film set. And the clothes here seemed different to those in the spare-room wardrobe, which had been more bohemian and far less expensive. However, many women had separate wardrobes for work and leisure.

Once his search was finished, he made his way down-stairs to join Gerry and found him standing in the middle of the living room watching Rachel complete her search of a cupboard by the fireplace.

'Well?' Gerry asked when he appeared in the doorway. 'Found anything?'

'Only what you'd expect – clothes, shoes, make-up. There's some paperwork in the spare room which will have to be gone through.'

'I found a load of bedding and a couple of towels in the washing machine,' said Rachel, looking round. 'The light was still flashing so it looks as if she was killed before she had a chance to unload it.'

'The bed's neatly made up, so perhaps she changed the sheets,' said Wesley. 'Or the killer did it and filled the washer with the dirty washing with his DNA all over it.'

'A domesticated murderer,' said Gerry. 'That's a rarity. But unfortunately most people know all about DNA these days.'

'Any sign of her passport or driving licence down here?' Wesley asked.

Rachel shook her head. 'No. But I've found the registration documents for a five-year-old Toyota Yaris. There's no sign of it but she might rent a garage somewhere nearby. Or maybe the killer took it; I've alerted all patrols to be on the lookout for it, just in case.'

'Thanks. There were utility bills upstairs, all paid and in the name of Tessa Trencham; a few photos, probably old and probably family. No recent ones of her but I'll get someone to go through them all the same. She kept all her paperwork filed and up to date but there's no clue to where she worked. Her bank statements are quite healthy but there are no regular incoming payments from an employer.'

'She might be self-employed?' Rachel suggested. 'Or ...'

'Or what?'

'Well, in view of those condoms in the bedside drawer, she might be a member of the oldest profession.'

'All that means is that there was a man in her life – maybe the man who reported the body,' said Wesley. 'But you might as well check to see if she's come to the Vice Squad's attention. You never know.'

'No problem,' Rachel said as she picked up what looked like a postcard and waved it in Wesley's direction. 'One piece of good news. This was on the mantelpiece. We've found her dentist and she's got a routine appointment for next week. Her dental records should confirm her identity once and for all.'

'Good,' said Gerry. He looked round, frowning slightly as though he'd mislaid something. 'There's no computer, and no address book or diary.'

'And where's her mobile phone?' said Rachel. 'There's no landline here so she must rely on it.'

'Whoever killed her probably took it,' said Wesley. 'He knew his number would be in it and all her calls could be traced, so he's taken it with him. Same goes for her photographs and address book. I reckon he's taken everything that could lead to us identifying him.'

Gerry nodded slowly. 'The body was here a week so he's had plenty of time to do a thorough job. All the indications are that she was killed by someone she knew. And she knew him well enough to invite him into her bedroom because there were no signs of a struggle.'

'Fingerprints?' Rachel asked.

'Lots. But none of them have a match on our database.'

'Maybe her dentist will be able to throw some light on the matter. It's hard to talk with your mouth full of drill but she might have passed the time of day with him – told him what she did for a living.'

'Maybe the dentist's our man,' said Rachel hopefully.

But Wesley didn't think it would be that easy. Murderers don't usually send appointment cards.

Paul kept telling himself what he'd told his aunt, that there was nothing to worry about because Sophie and her boyfriend, Barney Pickard, had taken spare clothes with them, which suggested a degree of planning. In spite of this he still felt uneasy and wondered whether he should pay Carole another visit and maybe contact Barney's mother too. But the DCI's briefing was in half an hour. He'd hoped to take Trish for a meal at the Tradmouth Castle Hotel but the discovery of the woman's body in Morbay meant that an evening out was off the menu.

He dialled Carole's number, hoping she wouldn't rush to the phone, heart pounding, thinking it was good news.

When she answered she sounded breathless. And disappointed. Maybe he shouldn't have called and raised her hopes.

'Have you heard anything?'

'No. Have you?'

'Sorry.' He said the word as though he meant it. It was six o'clock. Even the most inconsiderate teenager would surely have put her parents out of their misery by now. 'There's something I'd like to ask you.'

'What?'

'I had a look at Sophie's computer when I was round there and I noticed she's been playing an Internet game called Blood Hunt. There were some comments posted and she'd said she was going to reach a new level last night. I wondered

whether she and Barney might have met up with someone –
other gamers. Did she mention anything about it?'

'All that stuff's a mystery to me.'

'Do you think Barney's mother will mind if I contact her
to see if she knows anything?'

Carole hesitated for a moment. 'I don't know Barney's
mum very well. I have talked to her but she seems ... I
think she was an actress or a model or something and she's
a bit distant.' She hesitated. 'When I called her she didn't
seem very worried. She said that Barney's his own person
and she doesn't interfere in his private life.'

'She's probably right not to worry. I'm sure they've just
gone off somewhere and they'll be back soon. But if I can
have her number I might just give her a call.'

There was the sound of rustling, as though Carole was
searching through her address book. Then she recited a
number and Paul wrote it down.

When he dialled the number it was a while before he
heard a female voice on the other end of the line, bored
and slightly drawling as if she'd had one too many gin and
tonics. Unlike Carole, this woman didn't sound particularly
concerned, more annoyed at being disturbed. When Paul
explained the reason for his call, she gave a deep and theatrical sigh.

'They'll be somewhere getting pissed or fucking each
other stupid. They're eighteen, for God's sake. She thinks
they're still toddlers. I told her not to call the police but she
wouldn't listen.'

'Mrs Walter says it's out of character. And when it's out
of character, we take it seriously.'

'Weren't you ever young, Detective Constable whatever
your name is?'

'Paul Johnson.' He felt himself blushing. His teenage years weren't that far behind him and now this woman was talking to him as if he were some crusty old man. 'Has Barney ever mentioned a computer game called Blood Hunt to you?'

'He spends a lot of time in his room playing games on his laptop but I haven't a clue what they're called.' There was a pause. 'I did hear him mention a hunt the other day when he was talking on his mobile and I wondered if he'd started hanging out with those hunt saboteurs. You know how kids are about animal rights. If it's got fur it can do no wrong.'

'I take it you've tried calling him?'

'A couple of times but there was no answer.' For the first time Paul sensed an undercurrent of unease in her voice.

'Have you called any of his friends to see if they know where he is?'

'No. He wouldn't thank me for making him look stupid, would he?' The nonchalance had returned.

'Did he mention anything about where he was going? Anything at all?' This was the last throw of the dice and he wasn't getting his hopes up.

There was a long silence before the woman spoke again. 'Come to think of it, he did mention a name . . . some hall, I think. Sorry.'

'Please think.'

'Sorry. I really can't remember. Do you think it might be important?'

'I don't know. But if it comes back to you—'

At that moment Gerry Heffernan burst into the incident room, calling for attention. He thanked Mrs Pickard and put the phone down, hoping that when the drink wore off, her memory would improve.

It was almost nine o'clock and the light was fading when the black Ford Focus collided with a tractor on the A385 a couple of miles west of Tradington. When the ambulance arrived, the paramedics realised the driver would need to be cut from the vehicle.

Half an hour later, when the fire-fighters had done their work, the victim was lifted carefully from his seat and placed on a stretcher with his head and limbs immobilised to prevent further injury. Then the ambulance set off, lights and sirens blazing, to Morbay Hospital's Accident and Emergency Unit with the patient in the back being checked constantly. His blood pressure was falling, the paramedic had told Constable Jim Bold from Traffic Division who had rushed to attend the scene. The man was unconscious and it didn't look good.

Jim watched the ambulance disappear into the distance. Sad, he thought, as he took out his notebook, but these things happen when people drive too fast and don't pay attention to the road. His colleague was having a word with the tractor driver who was unhurt but shaken. It had definitely been the car driver's fault. He had overtaken a slow moving Nissan Micra on a blind bend and the tractor had been coming the other way. The Micra driver, an elderly woman, was also shocked but she had made a statement to the effect that she had seen it coming, the way he'd been driving.

When Jim called in the vehicle registration number to get an ID on the owner, he was told it was registered to a Keith Marsh who lived at a Manchester address. Once he'd made certain that it was indeed Mr Marsh who'd been driving, he'd give his Manchester colleagues a call and ask them to break the news to the victim's nearest and dearest. But he didn't want to set all that in motion until he was sure of the driver's identity. The car might have been borrowed or stolen ... anything.

He walked slowly over to the wrecked vehicle. The top had been removed by the fire service's cutting equipment and the thought that the car looked like a sardine can with its lid folded back passed through his mind.

He leaned over and opened the glove compartment. There was a folder in there containing the car's complete service history along with a map of the South Devon area and a torch.

He shone his own torch down at the floor and the broken glass glinted like diamonds in the beam and there he spotted a mobile phone, lying in the midst of the debris. He picked it up carefully and scrolled down the names in the address book, thinking how strange it was that a man's life could be encapsulated in a small sliver of metal and circuit boards. Then he suddenly felt a desire to know more about Keith Marsh – if that was indeed his name – so he flicked through the last calls made from the phone, sighing when he saw that he'd been using the instrument just before the time of the crash, trying to call someone called Barry but the call hadn't been connected. Some people would never learn.

He accessed the phone book and found a number with 'home' beside it so at least he'd have something to give to Greater Manchester Police when he contacted them. He wasn't tempted to call it himself: he'd stick to procedure and leave the breaking of bad news to others.

He accessed the list of recent calls again and, to his surprise, he saw that earlier that day Marsh had made an emergency call. 999.

And half an hour later, after he'd done some checking, he knew that the man who'd just been lifted from the wreckage was wanted in connection with a murder.

Chapter 8

The Steward's Journal

24 May 1815

One of the maidservants sought me out while I was alone in the Squire's library. When she asked if she could speak with me she looked as nervous as a harvest mouse with a cat's paw hovering over it to deliver a death blow, but I assured her that she had nothing to fear and anything she shared with me would remain a secret. I am not one, I told her, for betraying confidences.

I asked her what was amiss and she said she had been frightened by strange sounds from the tack room by the stables. She had heard a ghost, she said, moaning and crying. When I enquired whether she had entered the building to discover the origin of the strange sounds, she shook her head. She had heard Silly John talk of ghosts and demons and she had no wish to come face to face with such a being.

I had little doubt that it was her imagination but when I instructed her to return to her duties, I warned her to take care and asked if she attended church on Sundays. She said she did and I told her to speak to myself or the parson if she was concerned about anything she saw or experienced. She stared at me for a few moments, as though she was about to confide some new worry, but then she fled the room like a frightened young deer. She is a pretty girl with fair curls and the sweetest of faces. How Henry Catton would relish the corruption of such sweet and tender flesh if the opportunity were to present itself.

I felt I had no choice but to visit the stables and confront this phantom for myself.

A lad was busy sweeping the yard, doubling his efforts when he spotted me, and when I asked him if all was well he would not look me in the eye. However, I let the matter rest as I suspected that the maid had heard the horses whinnying in their stalls, and in her fevered imagination, had mistaken it for some spectre that one of the lads had spoken of to frighten her and make her cling to him for safety. In the folly of my tender years even I have played such tricks on maids.

As I turned to leave I heard a sound from the direction of the tack room. The door was locked and when I demanded the key the lad's eyes grew wide with terror, but I am the steward here and he knew he could not refuse me. I took the key from his trembling hand and placed it in the lock.

As the door opened the stench of blood and excrement assaulted my senses and when my eyes grew accustomed to the dim light, I saw a human figure sprawled upon a pile of hay. William was barely recognisable as the strong young man of my acquaintance and I rushed to the lad and felt his brow. He was hot with fever and sorely wounded with bites and cuts all over his naked flesh. Too ill to move, he lay in his own filth and I was torn between disgust and pity as I considered what course of action to take.

If William stayed there, he would surely die.

25 May 1815

With the acquiescence – I shall not say aid for fear made him an unwilling helper – of the lad, I set William upon a cart and returned him to his mother. She will nurse him now but whether he will live, I know not. I vowed there and then to put a stop to Tandy's evil entertainments . . . if it lay within my power.

I shall say prayers for William's recovery, and hope that I shall find a way to put an end to the wickedness in this place.

26 May 1815

This morning while the Squire was out with his hounds at the Home Farm, I heard the bell ring at the front door. It is my duty to open the door to visitors so I made my way to the hall and discovered that the caller was a young woman. She stood before me with a bold look, and her bright clothes were as none I have set eyes upon before this day.

And she did not speak one word of English.

Chapter 9

The next morning Wesley turned over in bed and looked at the glowing red numbers on the alarm clock. Ten to seven. Normally he'd have stayed there at least another hour on a Saturday morning, but the woman lying in a refrigerated drawer in Morbay Hospital mortuary dictated that he should rise early and investigate her death.

When Pam stirred by his side he leaned over and kissed the top of her head. She half-opened her eyes and put a hand out to touch his shoulder.

'Sorry, love, I've got to go.'

She sat up, her brown hair falling in messy morning strands around her bare shoulders. 'Are you going to be working all weekend?'

He detected a note of reproach in her voice, but that was hardly surprising. He couldn't lie – and if he tried he knew she wouldn't believe him. 'Sorry.' He knew the word was

50

inadequate. 'It's that woman in Morbay – the one who'd been there a week before she was found.'

Pam looked at him, a little more sympathetic now. 'You'd think someone would have missed her. Are you looking for a boyfriend?'

'It's a question of finding out who he is. According to the neighbours she kept herself to herself, but we know she had a child.'

Pam raised her eyebrows. 'So where is he ... or she?'

Wesley shrugged. 'I've no idea. Hopefully we'll find out sooner or later.'

He kissed her and she closed her eyes and lay back on the pillow. 'Wish you didn't have to go.'

'Me too.'

She opened her eyes again and put a hand up to touch his face, brushing her pale fingers against his dark cheek. 'I should have known what I was letting myself in for when I married a policeman.'

'I promise I'll make it up to you when we've sorted out this case. Maybe your mother can babysit and we can go—'

She hauled herself upright. 'Not my bloody mother. Not after she nearly got me killed.' When she lay down again and turned her back on him, he wished he'd never brought the subject up. Della was hardly one of his favourite people, and the way she'd led Pam into danger earlier that year still haunted him when he thought of how things might have turned out. But the rift between mother and daughter made him uncomfortable.

He went downstairs to make a healthy breakfast of toast and muesli – or bird seed as Gerry always called it. He was sipping his tea and scanning the front page of the newspaper he'd found lying in the hall when his mobile phone rang and he saw the caller was Neil. He'd imagined his old university friend would still be fast asleep at his Exeter flat and he was surprised to hear him sounding so alert.

'I wanted to catch you before you went out. Pam OK?'

'Fine.'

There was a pause before Neil continued. 'I've got a legal question for you.'

'Go on.' Wesley was intrigued. He put his half-eaten toast back on his plate and listened.

'Can an artist make you sign a confidentiality clause?'

'What?'

Even when Neil repeated the question, Wesley was none the wiser so he asked him for an explanation. But what he said didn't seem to make much sense.

'So let me get this straight – this man wants you and your team to excavate a picnic that was buried sixteen years ago.'

'Not a picnic, Wes. A Feast of Life. He's paying handsomely and I'm intending to use it as a training excavation for a select band of post-grad students. The only thing is, he wants us all to sign this confidentiality agreement. I think it's in case any rival conceptual artists pinch his idea. Or perhaps he's just being a pretentious prick.'

Wesley couldn't help smiling to himself. If only he had Neil's problems instead of a body down at the mortuary. 'If I were you, Neil, I'd sign on the dotted line and take the cash. Anyway, what can be down there that's confidential?'

'My thoughts exactly, but I thought I'd better run it by you – seeing as you're the nearest thing I've got to a mate in the law.'

'So you're going ahead with this picnic thing? I thought you were working at Fortress Point.'

'Dave's taking over there for a while – holding the fort.' He groaned at his own joke. 'The artist, Kevin Orford's making a really generous donation to the unit for my services.'

'Even Neil Watson has his price.'

'Don't be like that, Wes. We need the funds. You know how things are with all the cuts and . . . '

'I've heard of Kevin Orford.'

'Everyone has. He's the *enfant terrible* of the British art scene – although *enfant* isn't quite the word – he's probably knocking on forty.'

'So where is this great artistic masterpiece going to be unearthed?'

'It's in a field near Catton Hall Holiday Park. I went there once when I was a kid.'

'It's closed now, isn't it?'

'That's right.'

Wesley glanced at the clock above the fridge. 'Sorry, Neil. I'd better go. I promised Gerry I'd be in by quarter to eight.'

'How is he?'

'Same as he always is. See you.'

He slipped on his jacket and stuffed what remained of the toast into his mouth. It was a lovely day and the sky was a cloudless blue. He lived at the top of the town and as he walked down into the centre he could see the river sparkling in the sunlight, bobbing with boats that looked like playthings in a giant's bath. He never tired of this view when the weather was good. But in the cold, damp months when the river turned dark grey and mist shrouded the hills, it could be bleaker than his native London.

When he reached the incident room it was already half full of officers typing into computers and sorting through papers. Others were arriving, exchanging pleasantries and helping themselves to a cup of coffee from the machine before starting a day's work. Gerry was waiting for him in his glass-fronted office, feet up on his desk with a large mug of tea in his hand. He looked relaxed for somebody who had the heavy responsibility of investigating a woman's murder. But appearances can deceive.

'You're late, Wes.'

'There was a time when you used to own a malfunctioning alarm clock, if I remember right.'

'Joyce bought me a new one for Christmas.'

Wesley suppressed a smile. Before his lady friend, Joyce, arrived in his life, Gerry, a widower of long standing, had led a chaotic existence. 'How is Joyce?'

'She's gone to one of those health spa places with one of her mates this weekend. Good timing, eh?'

'Yes,' he said, recalling the reproach in Pam's voice. 'Anything new come in?'

'We've got a name. The phone that reported the body is registered to a Keith Marsh – Manchester address.'

'Manchester? Holidaymaker?'

Gerry's eyes lit up and he looked like a child desperate to recount a thrilling tale. 'We had a call first thing from Neston nick – traffic division. A car was involved in an RTA last night. Bloke overtook on a blind bend and went straight into an oncoming tractor. He's in Morbay Hospital – Intensive Care. Anyway, when the constable at the scene searched the wrecked car he found a mobile phone and he had the presence of mind to go through the recent calls. The driver had made a nine nine nine call a few hours before the crash, and when the constable checked he discovered that the anonymous call reporting that body in Morbay had come from the driver's number.' A triumphant look appeared on Gerry's face. 'The car's also registered to a Keith Marsh – same Manchester address. Looks like we've found our man. I've asked for the phone to be brought over and I gave the hospital a call first thing and they said Marsh was stable.'

Wesley knew that was hospital-speak for 'no change'. But if the patient had been in the dead woman's house, they needed him conscious and talkative.

So far Trish had had no luck contacting the two people who'd provided Tessa Trencham's references. However, she felt a little more hopeful about the other avenue she was about to explore. Tessa's dentist didn't work on a Saturday, but it had been easy to get his home address.

It was a routine matter and Trish wasn't particularly optimistic that she'd learn much about the dead woman. To him she had probably been nothing more than a set of teeth.

The dentist, Steven Bowles, lived in the village of Belsham, halfway between Neston and Morbay, in the sort of thatched cottage that had graced a thousand chocolate boxes in days gone by. It had fresh paintwork, fashionable blinds at the small windows and a glossy black front door flanked by a pair of bay trees.

Before ringing the doorbell, she looked around and saw the church on the opposite side of the road behind an extensive graveyard. She knew DI Peterson's sister was married to the Vicar of Belsham and she stared at the church for a few seconds out of simple curiosity. It was very old with the sort of pinnacle-topped tower so common in the locality. Like the cottage it was pretty, but she knew she had no time to admire the architecture.

The door was opened by a tall man in his late twenties or early thirties. He wore his dark hair fairly long, but what Trish noticed most about him was his eyes, which were a striking cornflower-blue. As she produced her ID and asked whether she could have a quick word, she found herself wishing she'd taken more care over her appearance that morning.

There was a slight worried frown on his face as he stood aside to let her in.

'It's just routine,' Trish said. 'I believe you have a patient called Tessa Trencham.'

'I have a lot of patients. I can't remember them all.'

'A woman was found dead at Ms Trencham's address in Morbay yesterday. We need her dental records to confirm her identity.'

'That shouldn't be a problem.'

'If she's a patient of yours, I wonder if you can tell me anything about her. Did she talk about her family or her job?' She took a copy of the E-fit picture out of her bag. 'This might jog your memory.'

As he took the picture from her, his hand brushed hers. She stood quite still and waited for him to speak.

'It's not very good, is it?'

'The body had been there a while so we couldn't really use a photo of . . .'

He stared at the picture for a few moments before speaking again. 'I think she said she ran her own jewellery business in a converted barn near Stoke Raphael. I'm sure I remember her saying that she was from London originally and before she started her business she'd worked in admin or accounts or something. When she was down in London I think she had quite a high-flying job but she came here because she wanted to get away from the rat race. The old story, eh.' He smiled again.

He had a lovely smile, warm and sympathetic, and Trish began to wonder how easy it was to change your dentist.

'Is there anything else you can tell me? Her date of birth? Next of kin?'

'All her details will be at the surgery. We can go there now if you like. I'm meeting someone at two but it's on my way.'

Trish felt the pull of temptation but she knew that, in the interests of operational efficiency, she should decline. 'Can you call me with the information?' She produced her card and handed it to him. 'And when I get details of the deceased's dental work to compare . . .'

'Yes, that's no problem. Her dental records are back at the surgery too. Will you come along yourself?'

'When would be convenient?'

'First thing Monday?'

'I'll be there.'

Bowles looked into her eyes. 'I'll look forward to it.'

'Me too,' she said before she could stop herself. If Rachel could see her now, she'd tell her she was being unprofessional. And that was the last thing she wanted.

An hour after she returned to the incident room, she received a call. Bowles had called into his surgery on the way to his appointment and had looked at Tessa Trencham's file. She'd given her address as Lister Cottage,

St Marks Road, her date of birth was the 1st April 1972 and she had no underlying medical conditions or elaborate dental work. He ended by saying he was looking forward to seeing her on Monday when she brought him the dead woman's dental chart for comparison with his records.

Never before, in Trish's experience, had anybody made the subject of teeth sound quite so appealing.

Kevin Orford's message had been terse – quite rude really. 'Meet me at Catton Hall at three o'clock.' He had ended the call without waiting for an answer.

As it was the weekend Neil had been looking forward to a day of leisure, catching up on his reading and leafing through some of the archaeological journals that had piled up on his coffee table. Then he'd planned to meet some post-graduates for a drink and to discuss the strange proposed excavation at Catton Hall. He'd assumed Orford would realise that the arrangements would take a day or two to finalise. But it looked as if the man didn't inhabit the same planet as lesser mortals who had to work for a living.

He toyed with the idea of sticking to his original plan and not turning up. Why should he be at the beck and call of a man he considered to be a pretentious fool? He'd looked him up on the Internet and learned that his previous projects included the pile of rotting oranges, with which he had triumphed at the Turner Prize exhibition; the hundred naked men eating takeaway pizzas on the Millennium Bridge over the Thames and his twelve-foot-tall tower of rotting apples in a field next to Heathrow Airport. Then there were his smaller works, so beloved of wealthy collectors: the plastic fruit arranged in a toilet bowl; the Union Jack made from discarded meat bones. His creations hit the news and he was taken seriously by the art establishment and notable collectors, so if Orford was a fool, he was a fool with money. The way things were in the world of archaeology at that moment, Neil's unit needed all the cash it could get so at half past one, he climbed into his old yellow Mini and set off down the A380, hoping he wouldn't get held up by the Morbay holiday traffic.

He arrived at Catton Hall at ten past three, reasoning that being just a little late would make a point. Orford had specified the hall rather than the field where they had last met, so Neil drove through gates topped by a pair of stone eagles, one missing a head, the other a wing. The drive was rough and pitted and he drove slowly, fearing for the Mini's suspension, but eventually the house came into view. It was long and low and built of a rough, brown-grey stone that blended perfectly with its surroundings. He guessed that the stone had originated at the disused quarry near Fortress Point; somehow local materials always made a building appear in harmony with its surroundings. It was hard to tell the age of the house. This was no grand fashionable dwelling to impress the neighbours. It sat solidly in the landscape and had been constructed without a thought to passing design fads. This was the timeless seat of the local gentry.

There was no sign of Orford – or anybody else for that matter – so Neil parked on a patch of weed-infested gravel in front of the house and walked up to the front door. If anyone expected him to use the tradesman's entrance, they were going to be disappointed. There was a cheap plastic doorbell beside the big oak door which looked as out of place as a Post-it note stuck on the nose of the Mona Lisa. He pressed it and waited. And when nothing happened he pressed it again.

'Sorry. It doesn't work. I keep meaning to get it fixed.'

Neil turned and saw a man standing on the drive next to his car. He was in his early thirties, Neil guessed, average height with ginger hair and freckles. He strode up to Neil, hand outstretched.

'Richard Catton. I presume you're the archaeologist.'

'Neil Watson – County Archaeological Unit.' Neil shook hands. Catton's grip was weak and his palms felt a little clammy.

He looked round. 'I'm not sure where Kevin's got to. He said he'd be here at three.' Their eyes met in understanding and Neil suspected he'd found an ally. 'What do you make of his . . . project?'

Neil considered his answer for a moment. 'It sounds mad on the surface but, archaeologically speaking, it might be quite interesting. It'll give us a chance to test the rate of decomposition of various organic materials. I've got a team working a couple of miles away at Fortress Point.'

'I've heard about that. How's it going?'

'Very well. We're looking for the foundations of the pre-fabricated barracks in a corner of the site that hasn't been investigated. We've had some interesting finds; personal possessions of the garrison and that sort of thing. I might take a couple of colleagues off that to give me a hand with Kevin's project for a couple of days but mainly I'm planning to use a few post-grad students who are interested in the scientific branch of archaeology.'

'I was afraid you'd think Kevin was wasting your time. I told him he'd be lucky if he got you to co-operate.'

'Like I said, it might be interesting. And of course my unit's always looking for funding.'

Catton gave him a conspiratorial smile. 'He's paying me rather generously too. Lord knows where he gets all his money from, but ours not to reason why, eh.'

Neil smiled. 'I expect people have done far worse things for money.'

'I see you two have met.'

The two men swung round to see Kevin Orford striding down the drive towards them. He was carrying a large patchwork bag slung across his shoulder and his calculating, determined expression seemed more suited to a business-man than an artist.

'I take it you've managed to draft in some help, Neil.'

'We can start on Monday if that's OK?'

'Not tomorrow?'

'Tomorrow's Sunday.'

'And archaeologists always observe the Sabbath? How delightfully archaic.'

Neil felt a sudden impulse to defend himself. 'It's the weekend. A lot of the students taking part will be away . . . or hung-over.'

'I would have preferred tomorrow. Some people from Tate Modern are down for the weekend and they wanted to be present when the digging begins.'

'If you'd given me more notice I might have been able to arrange something.' Orford was really starting to irritate him, but he tried to keep visualising the promised cheque. He saw Catton was looking a little wary, as though he was afraid of causing offence.

61

'Have you told him yet?' Orford's question was directed at Catton and the words were barked like an order.

Neil wondered how this jumped-up artist had the temerity to speak to the son of the landowner in that way. Here was a man who knew the balance of power. And it seemed it was in his favour.

Catton cleared his throat. 'My father's writing a book about one of our ancestors and Kevin's been talking to him about his research.'

Orford interrupted. 'I've had an idea for a new artwork linked to the history of this house. It's a piece of performance art and I plan to film it to create an installation.'

'Some sort of re-enactment, is it?'

Neil earned himself a disdainful look. 'Not a re-enactment – a visualisation. It will be my next work after Feast of Life Revisited. Richard's ancestor used to keep a jester whose journal was found in the family archives. Alfred's allowed me to read it.'

'Alfred's my father,' said Richard by way of explanation.

Orford ignored him. 'The jester was called John Tandy but he was commonly known as Silly John. When I learned about his life the concept suddenly came to me.'

'What concept?' Neil asked, curious now.

'A hunt. But we'll have no objection from the animal rights lobby.'

'Why's that?'

'We hunt human beings, that's why.'

Neil glanced at Richard Catton and he was surprised to see that he looked worried.

*

It was the height of the tourist season, so the craft workshops in the converted barn on the outskirts of the village of Stoke Raphael were open for business all weekend.

When Trish had returned to the incident room and told DCI Heffernan what she'd learned from Steven Bowles, he'd announced that as it was a pleasant day and he needed some fresh air, he'd come with her to the workshops to see if they could find anyone who knew Tessa Trencham. She forced herself to smile. The DCI's blunt approach didn't go down well with everyone, especially those of a nervous, criminal or artistic disposition.

He asked her whether she'd managed to contact Sylvia Cartland and Carl Heckerty, the individuals who'd provided Morbay Properties with Tessa's references, and she had to tell him that she'd had no luck as yet. But she'd keep trying.

She drove them out to Stoke Raphael. The roads were packed with tourists, all wanting a Saturday afternoon out in the resort of Morbay, and when they reached Stoke Raphael all the available parking spaces had already been taken by visitors who had come to gaze at the village's attractions: the thousand year old yew tree in the churchyard; the picturesque pubs and the waterfront. When Trish eventually managed to park, a wooden fingerpost directed them to the Craft Centre by way of the riverside path.

'Lovely day,' said Gerry, turning his face towards the sun.

'Not for Tessa Trencham,' Trish said softly.

'The poor woman's in a better place, Trish.'

'You believe that, sir?'

'Don't you?'

Trish didn't reply. Questions of life and death seemed

too overwhelming just at that moment. She changed the subject to something more comfortable and mundane.

'We haven't been able to trace any next of kin.'

'It's early days.'

'Didn't Dr Bowman say she'd had a child?'

'It could have been adopted. Or died. There was certainly no sign of a child in that house.'

'We don't really know anything about her life, do we?'

It was Gerry's turn to fall silent. They walked on, and as they rounded a bend the Craft Centre came into view. The agricultural origins of the building could be seen if you looked carefully but the old barn had been so comprehensively modernised that any farm hand who'd worked there back in the days of its original purpose would hardly have recognised it. Today the place was crowded with visitors in shorts and bright summer dresses flocking around the huge arched entrance. Whining children armed with ice creams were being dragged along by overheated parents and sullen men were being coaxed towards the shopping experience by their eager wives. Trish knew that similar scenes would be playing out at every shopping centre in the land, but in these normally tranquil rural surroundings, they seemed a little out of place.

'I think we've chosen a bad time,' Gerry observed. But, undeterred, he edged his way past the crowd and soon they were inside the building where small shops lined the walls, each with its own workshop space at the rear so that the public could see the items for sale being created.

'This place must be a gold mine in high season,' Trish said. 'No wonder she could afford the rent on that house.'

'I bet trade's not so good in winter though,' the DCI replied, looking round for any sign of a jewellery shop, possibly one that was closed up because its owner was lying in the mortuary at Morbay Hospital.

'I've counted five jewellery places so far. All of them open for business.'

'She might have an assistant or a business partner. We'll have to visit them all.' Gerry rooted in his trouser pocket and drew out his warrant card.

At the fourth shop they tried, Trish knew they had found the right place because the jewellery on display bore a strong resemblance to the stuff they'd found at Lister Cottage. She gave the boss a nudge and they steamed in past a pair of women who appeared to be deciding between two almost identical silver bracelets. A stick-thin, middle-aged woman was watching them, arms folded as though she suspected they were intent on foul play. Trish imagined they'd have a lot of trouble with shoplifters – especially with the prices they charged.

When the woman spotted Gerry, she fixed him with a stare as though she regarded him as a hostile invader. Even when he held up his warrant card for her to examine and whispered that he'd like a word – nothing to worry about; just routine – she gave him a look that would curdle milk.

After calling across to a girl leaning on the counter in the shop next door to ask her to keep an eye on things, she took the newcomers to one side. She stood next to the glittering display on the back wall, her eyes flickering towards the precious items on show.

'Do you own this shop?' Gerry began.

'Yes. Why?'

Gerry nodded to Trish who took out her notebook.

'What's your name, love?'

'Sylvia Cartland.'

Trish caught Gerry's eye. 'We've been trying to get hold of you,' she said.

The woman scowled. 'Is this about those shoplifters we had last week? Because if it is, you've taken your time—'

'It's not about shoplifting. We want to talk to you because you provided a reference for a Tessa Trencham. We think Ms Trencham might own one of these units.'

Suddenly Sylvia expression changed. 'Tessa's my business partner. Why? What's this about?'

Trish saw Gerry assume the sympathetic look of one who's about to break bad news. He had brought the rings the dead woman was wearing with him in a plastic evidence bag, along with the jewellery found in the dressing table. When he took the bag from his jacket pocket he handed it to Sylvia. 'Do you recognise these items?'

As she examined them it was hard to read her thoughts. After a few seconds she handed it back to him. 'Yes. They're all ours. But unless a customer's paid by cheque or credit card—'

'Does Tessa Trencham own jewellery like this?'

'She makes it, so it's hardly surprising that she wears it.'

He fished the E-fit picture of the dead woman out of his pocket and thrust it into Sylvia's unwilling hand. 'Could this be Tessa?'

She gave a snort of derision. 'It could be, but on the other hand it could be anybody. Why are you asking all these questions?'

'Yesterday a woman was found dead at Tessa's address. She's not been formally identified yet but we think it may be her. I'm sorry.'

To Trish's amazement a smile appeared on the woman's face; a smile with a hint of triumph, as though she had access to secret knowledge which was beyond their reach.

'You've made a mistake, Chief Inspector. Tessa's staying in France for a while and I assure you she's fine. She warned me that she intended to leave her phone switched off while she was over there because she didn't want any interruptions while she was working on her new designs. She's the creative one in our partnership, you see. But she popped into a nearby town to stock up on supplies and called me just to make sure everything was all right at this end. I spoke to her this morning.'

'This morning? Are you sure?'

'Are you calling me a liar?'

'So who was the woman in her house then?' Trish couldn't resist asking the question.

Sylvia Cartland shrugged. 'I really have no idea.'

Chapter 10

The Jester's Journal

27 May 1815

She arrived like a gift, wrapped in a gown of shabby, red muslin with a cloth swathed around her head in a most exotic manner. I have seen such hats in illustrations of strange and colourful people from far-away lands but I had never seen such a thing in reality. She wore a tall peacock feather tucked into the folds of her hat so that it stood erect upon her head and her gown was voluminous and most curious, like a costume in a play.

It was her attire I noted first. Then I took note of the woman within the dress. She was small and slender with a swarthy complexion and darting, watchful brown eyes which took in the drawing room as though she had never seen the like before. Upon the Squire's orders our sober steward brought her within the house but kept his distance from her as if he imagined she might corrupt him and contaminate him with her exotic ways.

Her ways, I must confess, seemed strange to me. For she treats us all as a princess would treat her minions. Her head held high, she gazed in my direction, seeing yet not seeing, as though I was beneath her attention. Her manner towards the Squire was similarly haughty and yet I could tell from the first that he had fallen under some spell the girl had cast. Was she a demon come to claim his soul? I asked myself. Or had he met her in some other life – on one of his visits to his cousin's estate perhaps? I would assume my role and question him closely – for any impertinence is tolerated if it comes from the lips of a Fool.

The young woman spoke no English but conversed in a strange tongue that even the Squire did not appear to recognise – and in his youth he had travelled to many parts of Europe. She made her desires known by giving signs, the meaning of which were quite comprehensible to all. When asked her name she merely said 'Pegassa' in a firm, clear voice. Whether it was her name or an order, I have no idea, but it became her title from that moment on. The Lady Pegassa.

Our steward behaves towards her in a circumspect manner and the Squire had to prevent him from sending word to the fort in case she was some French spy come to glean the secrets of our fortifications against Bonaparte's forces. The Squire assured him that she had no knowledge of the French tongue but this did little to assuage his suspicions.

Master Henry went yesterday to Tradmouth to call upon an acquaintance who owes him money and he told the Squire that he will stay at the inn there until tomorrow.

When he returns I have no doubt he will interest himself in our new guest.

William has vanished from the stables and the Squire supposes that he is recovered and has returned to his home.

Chapter 11

Wesley could think of better ways to spend a Sunday morning than sitting at his desk sifting through a heap of witness statements. But murder didn't keep to civilised office hours. He'd learned that years ago – as had Pam.

Sylvia Cartland's claim that she had spoken to Tessa Trencham the previous day had thrown the investigation into turmoil and caused Wesley to suspect that they could be following the wrong trail already. They were making efforts to contact Tessa in France but as yet they'd had no luck and Gerry had seemed quite despondent about it for a while. But nothing kept his spirits down for long. Keith Marsh was still unconscious in Morbay Hospital; if and when he came round, they might make some progress.

'Can I have a word, sir?'

Wesley looked up and saw Paul Johnson standing by his desk. His long, normally amiable face looked strained and there were dark rings beneath his eyes. 'Of course, Paul. What is it?'

Paul told him about his missing cousin, the computer game and the reaction of Barney's mother, the words coming out in a rush as if he was anxious not to leave anything out.

'I promised my aunt I'd have a word with Uniform and try to get the matter edged up their priority list, not that I'm expecting—'

'And you thought I might have some influence?' The young man looked so worried that Wesley felt for him.

Paul gave him a half-hearted smile. 'I thought you might know which buttons to press, if you know what I mean.'

'Uniform are probably right, you know. They might just have gone away somewhere for the weekend. Did you manage to get into that game you mentioned – what's it called – Blood Hunt?'

'No. It was password protected.'

'If the worst comes to the worst we can always get Scientific Support to have a look at the computer, but I'm sure it won't come to that.' He thought for a moment. 'I take it your aunt's contacted all Sophie's friends?'

Paul nodded and Wesley touched his sleeve, a gesture of support. 'Then all we can do is sit tight and wait for them to turn up. And if they're not back by late tomorrow we'll contact the Met in case they've decided to try their luck in London and get Uniform to look in the usual places down here.' From the expression on Paul's face, Wesley knew his words hadn't provided much comfort and, as he watched him return reluctantly to his desk, he had an uncomfortable feeling that he'd somehow let him down.

72

He was about to return to the statements when Gerry burst into the incident room. He stood in the doorway for a few seconds, looking round the room before calling for attention.

'I've listened to the tape of the nine nine nine call from Keith Marsh's phone. He doesn't say much, just that there's a dead body at the address. Then he rings off as soon as the operator starts asking for details. And apparently he'd been drinking heavily before the crash.'

Wesley considered this new information for a moment. 'So he discovered the body and reported it, then he must have gone for a drink somewhere.'

'Drowning his sorrows.'

'Or trying to blot them out. He must have had access to the house. Could he be the victim's boyfriend?'

'If he is, he might be one of many,' said Rachel sharply. 'One of the neighbours has seen quite a few men calling at the house in the past couple of weeks. I drew a blank with the vice squad, by the way. They've had no dealings with a Tessa Trencham and the address isn't known to them either.'

Gerry gave her a look of approval. 'So that's one possibility blown to pieces ... unless she's slipped under their radar somehow. We need to confirm her identity as a matter of urgency. I'm not convinced about this France story but if Sylvia Cartland is telling the truth about speaking to Tessa yesterday, we have to consider the possibility that Tessa's not our victim and that the men the neighbour saw were visiting someone else. Or Sylvia might be lying. She might have had something to do with her death.'

'We can't rule anything out at the moment,' said Wesley. 'For all we know, Sylvia might have talked to someone pretending to be Tessa. But nothing's certain till we track her down in France. We need to talk to the other referee, Carl Heckerty. He might be able to tell us more.'

'We haven't been able to get hold of him yet,' said Rachel. 'But we'll keep trying.' The telephone on her desk rang and after a brief conversation, she ended the call and stood up. 'That was Morbay Hospital. The man in the RTA – Keith Marsh. His wife has arrived.'

'We'd better have a word with her,' said Wesley. 'Maybe she'll be able to throw some light on all this.'

Gerry looked round. 'OK. You go with Rach, do the tea and sympathy bit.'

Rachel slung her handbag over her shoulder as Wesley pushed his paperwork out of the way and rose to his feet.

As soon as they left the police station the bells of St Margaret's church began to ring. Gerry was missing choir again, he thought. He liked belting out the hymns on a Sunday morning; said it set him up for the week. But murder disrupted everything.

Rachel seemed unusually quiet as they drove to Morbay. Wesley tried to make conversation, asking after her boyfriend, Nigel, a local farmer, but the answers she gave were monosyllabic and Wesley sensed the subject was off limits. There had been a time when she would have confided in him and, unexpectedly, he found himself regretting that those days appeared to be over. For the rest of the journey he talked about the case, trying theory upon theory on for size – but none of them seemed entirely satisfactory.

Once at the hospital they followed the signs to the Intensive Care Unit. Wesley hated the place; hated seeing the anxious relatives keeping wordless vigils by their loved ones' bedsides.

A young dark-haired nurse directed them to a waiting room and a few minutes later the door opened. The woman who appeared on the threshold was middle-aged but time had been kind to her. She was tall with blonde hair cut in a neat bob and she was slim, the sort of strong slenderness which results from sports and training. She wore a little make-up, not too much, and Wesley noticed that her eyeliner was unsmudged. There had been no tears.

Wesley stood up and stepped forward to greet her. 'Mrs Marsh?'

'Yes. I'm Anne Marsh,' she said as she shook Wesley's hand firmly.

'I'm DI Wesley Peterson and this is my colleague, DS Rachel Tracey. Please come in and sit down. Would you like a drink from the machine or—'

The woman shook her head vigorously. 'No thanks. I'm awash with tea. Nothing else to do at a time like this, is there?' She had a slight northern accent; Manchester probably.

'How is your husband?' he asked once they'd made themselves comfortable.

'Still unconscious. They say he's stable but I don't really know what that means. Can you tell me what happened to him 'cause I've no idea what he was doing down here or—'

'You didn't know he was in Devon?'

She shook her head. 'I thought he was going abroad for the week – Germany. He told me he was leaving the car at Manchester Airport. He rang me on Saturday night saying he was in Munich. He said he was going to a bier keller later on with some people from the firm he was visiting.'

'When exactly did he leave home?'

'The Friday before last, first thing in the morning. He said he was catching an early flight – six forty-five, I think. He was due back late yesterday evening but he never arrived and then I had a visit from the police.'

'That must have come as a shock,' said Wesley. In his mind's eye he could see the constables at the door with mournful faces; the expression of horrified disbelief on the woman's face as they broke the news.

'I was devastated. Particularly when they told me he was down in Devon. I don't understand what he was doing here.' She sounded genuinely puzzled. 'He's never mentioned Devon and I don't think he knows anybody down here.'

'Has anyone checked whether he actually travelled to Germany during the week?'

'I don't know.'

'We'll need the name of the firm he was supposed to be visiting and the hotel if you've got it.'

'Of course. It was Magborg – an engineering firm in Munich. He told me he was staying at the Emperor Hotel in the centre.'

Wesley nodded to Rachel and she wrote it down in her notebook.

'Tell us about your husband, Mrs Marsh.'

'Anne, please.'

'OK, Anne. What does he do for a living?' He almost used the past tense but he stopped himself just in time. The man was still alive . . . just.

'He's marketing manager of a car parts firm. They do a lot of business abroad so he's away quite a bit.'

'Do you have much to do with his work or . . . ?'

76

She shook her head again. 'No. I'm a teacher. Primary. I have enough on my plate with my own job.'

'I know all about the pressures of teaching. My wife teaches year six.'

She smiled. A rapport had been established. 'So you'll understand. Keith and I have our own separate interests. We lead our own lives.'

'Would you say you've grown apart?' It was Rachel who asked the question.

Anne turned to her and studied her for a few moments, as though she was unsure whether the question was impertinent or whether Rachel was sympathetic. Eventually she replied. 'I suppose you could say that we lead parallel lives. Side by side but rarely meeting. I have my running and my gym and my own friends.' She sighed. 'I've often wondered what he gets up to on his business trips. Now I've a feeling I'm about to find out. Is there a woman involved?'

Wesley could tell from her eyes that the prospect bothered her more than she would be willing to admit. They might lead separate lives but she still cared – but whether it was for her husband or for her own security and status, he couldn't tell.

'Do you think there might be?'

'I suspected there might have been someone in Munich because he goes there a lot.' She looked directly at Wesley. 'CID don't usually deal with road accidents, do they? Is there something else – something I don't know about?'

Wesley exchanged a glance with Rachel. The woman would find out the truth soon enough so they might as well get it over with.

'A woman's body was found at a house here in Morbay.

The police were alerted by an anonymous emergency call that came from your husband's phone.'

Anne sat for a while, stunned and Wesley couldn't help feeling sorry for her; sorry that she'd been drawn into this situation; sorry that her well-ordered life had been turned upside down by something of which she had no knowledge or even suspicion.

'This woman ... was he having an affair with her?' she said softly after a long silence.

'We don't know.'

'How did she die?'

'She was murdered – strangled.'

Anne sat perfectly still, her hands clasped together as if in prayer. 'And you think Keith killed her?'

'That's only one possibility among many at the moment. Does the name Tessa Trencham mean anything to you?'

'Was that her name?'

'We think so.' It suddenly struck him that with Sylvia Cartland's claim that she had spoken to Tessa since the murder, everything was up in the air again. There were no certainties now until they had a stroke of luck.

Once they had taken down details of Keith Marsh's life and work, Wesley held out his hand to Anne again.

'We'll keep you informed of any developments,' he promised before they left her in the small relatives' room with its rose-pink walls and pile of well-thumbed magazines. He hardly liked to leave her alone but there was no choice.

'What did you think?' Rachel asked as they walked to the mortuary. He had promised Trish that he'd pick up the dead woman's dental records while they were there.

'I think our friend in Intensive Care has been leading a double life.'

For the first time Rachel smiled. 'Wife in every port, you mean? Randy travelling salesman. Bit of a cliché, don't you think?'

'It may be a cliché but I believe it happens. I feel sorry for the wife, having to find out like that.'

'There's no easy way to find out your husband's cheating on you.' She paused. 'She didn't seem that upset.'

'Some people hide it well.'

'You're defending her.'

Wesley stopped in the middle of the hospital corridor. 'No I'm not, I'm—'

'You are. Nice woman. Attractive. Teacher just like Pam. Has it occurred to you that she might have followed him down here, caught them together and killed his bit on the side? Didn't Dr Bowman say that a woman could have done it?'

'A strong woman, yes, but—'

'She mentioned running and the gym. I reckon she looks capable of strangling someone, especially if the victim wasn't expecting it.'

'I don't agree,' said Wesley firmly. He suddenly felt protective towards the woman, although he wasn't sure why.

'She hadn't been crying.'

'Some people don't.'

They walked on to the mortuary in silence. Wesley had noticed before that Rachel had a tendency to come down hard on her fellow females. So much for sisterly solidarity. But on the other hand, she might be right. They had to be open to all possibilities at this stage in the investigation.

When they reached their destination there was no sign of

Colin – but then he was probably enjoying Sunday lunch in the bosom of his family, Wesley thought with a twinge of envy. However, he had ensured that the dead woman's dental details were ready for them as promised and once one of the mortuary assistants had handed them over, they made their way back to Tradmouth through the slow moving holiday traffic.

The phone on Paul's desk rang and he picked up the receiver, hoping it was Carole to say that Sophie had returned safely. He felt his heart beating fast as he recited his name.

It was Carole, but she wasn't calling with good news. 'She's still not back, Paul. I've just had a call from one of her school friends. He asked to speak to her and I had to tell him she was still missing. He said they met up on Thursday night but after that they went their separate ways. He said she was with Barney and they didn't mention anything about going off anywhere.'

'Where did they meet?'

'Somewhere out near Queenswear, I think.'

'What's this friend's name?'

'Dun.'

'Surname?'

'Her friends don't tend to do surnames.' She paused. 'I asked him about Blood Hunt.'

'What did he say?'

'That it's just a computer game and it can't have anything to do with them disappearing. He was quite definite about that.'

Paul picked up on the uncertainty in her voice. 'Too definite, do you think?'

'Do you want to speak to him?'

'We might.'

'I don't really know him but I believe his dad's a farmer. He lives just outside Morbay.'

As Paul thanked his aunt and promised to keep her posted, he was engulfed by a feeling of helpless frustration. Maybe there was more he could be doing. Maybe he should be out there looking for them.

The dogs gave Richard Catton a good excuse to walk around the estate. Not that he needed an excuse – it was his land, after all, or rather his father's – but he felt less awkward with a pair of black Labradors by his side.

He had never intended to return to Catton Hall but a few months ago his father had contacted him to say that he'd been diagnosed with a heart condition and he needed help with the running of the estate. Richard had abandoned his London life, surprised that time had blunted the antagonism he'd felt towards his father for so many years, and when he'd returned Alfred's state of health meant that he had suddenly become responsible for the manor house, estate and even the run-down holiday park. The reality of being in charge of the place at last had drawn him back and kept him there, full of tentative plans and misgivings.

The holiday park had been a money spinner in its 1960s heyday and beyond, but in recent years his father had lacked the money, enthusiasm or good health to ensure that the company running it had kept it going to a high standard. Now, like everything else on the Catton Hall estate, the holiday park had faded, crumbled and for some time it had lain semi-derelict, awaiting a Prince Charming to wake it up and give it new life. After prolonged negotiations with the bank and a couple of local backers, Richard had secured the necessary funding and soon renovation work would begin. But finances would be a struggle until the whole thing was up and running – that's why Kevin Orford's bizarre proposal had come as a welcome surprise. And that's also why he had permitted Carl Heckerty to use the land for his strange games, even though he wasn't particularly comfortable about it.

It was a perfect summer evening; warm with a gentle breeze blowing in from the sea and rustling the leaves on the surrounding trees. Richard would have liked to do something leisurely like others did on a fine Sunday evening.

Sometimes he dreamed of being with Daniel. Drinks on the terrace at the back of the house. A meal cooked from the best local ingredients bought from the farmers' market in Tradmouth. Then bed and that precious intimacy he craved but which always seemed to elude him these days. For a long time now, sexual encounters had left him feeling empty. But it hadn't been like that with Daniel. Theirs had been a meeting of souls.

He'd asked Orford whether he'd heard from Daniel but the answer had been a terse no, as though it was something the artist preferred not to talk about. Perhaps there'd been bad blood between them, although he hadn't sensed it at the time.

It was sixteen years since Daniel had gone without a word and his mother had left for a new life abroad. They'd both vanished from his life, and now the reopening of that trench in the field next to the holiday park was resurrecting memories of that summer. Perhaps he should have told Orford to get lost. But money was money.

82

The dogs ran ahead, tails wagging like windscreen wipers, making for the holiday park's empty chalets. The places would still be habitable – just – if they were cleaned up and given a coat of paint. But the chalets with their basic amenities and shabby lino floors belonged to another era; an era of make-do and mend and ferocious seaside landladies. An era when you were glad for what you were given. People these days expected more comfort for their money, especially when they were on holiday.

Carl Heckerty's people had used the chalets recently but Richard didn't ask too many questions about that. As long as Carl paid him in cash.

He heard the dogs barking as though something was bothering them. They were out of sight now but he followed the noise and found himself outside a detached chalet at the end of a row. The dirty floral curtains were drawn so he couldn't see inside but the dogs were scrabbling at the door, barking as if demanding admission.

He took hold of their collars and pulled them away. 'What is it, lads? What's the matter?' he said as he turned the door handle. When the door swung open slowly he stepped inside and followed the eager dogs into one of the rooms at the back. They were sniffing around, tails wagging excitedly, their attention focused on the clothes lying discarded on the floor. Richard pulled them away and touched the clothes with his toe. There seemed to be two sets, one male and one female, including underwear. He seized the dogs' collars again and pulled them outside.

Those things should never have been left there. Heckerty had screwed up. And he guessed it was up to him to do something about it.

Chapter 12

The Steward's Journal

27 May 1815

She calls herself the Lady Pegassa and even the Squire is
puzzled as to her origins and he is a man who claims to
know all. She speaks no English – and yet she seems to
know what is asked of her and she has no trouble in making
her desires understood. He assures me that she is not a
French spy and he mocked me for my suspicions.

There has been no talk of turning her out. Rather the
Squire has given her the blue bedroom which is kept for
honoured guests and he has instructed the maidservant,
Mary, to see to her every need.

I took Mary aside to speak some words of warning to her
privately – and to ask her to report to me daily. I must know
what manner of creature this Pegassa is, for I fear that her
arrival at the Squire's door was no accident.

The Lady Pegassa spends much time in the Squire's library taking the books off the shelves one by one and pretending to study them – although I noticed that she held some upside down, a frown of concentration on her face as though she was reading some engaging story, before replacing the books, careful to keep them in their rightful place. I stood outside watching her through the window for a good while and she never seemed to tire of this feeble entertainment, for feeble it must have been for someone unable to make sense of the volumes.

28 May 1815

It seems from what the cook has told me that word of our strange visitor has spread, and now all of Tradmouth society is curious to view the newcomer. However, the Squire's reputation may keep them from his door. I, of course, will obey his instructions and turn visitors away if necessary.

Mary tells me that this morning she met with the mother of William and the woman would say nothing other than he keeps to his bed. I have heard that the Squire instructed the doctor to visit William, paying him well for his silence. Perhaps his conscience troubles him.

29 May 1815

This morning Pegassa visited the library again. The room seems to hold a fascination for her, and I suspect that she has never seen books before in the strange country from whence she has travelled.

When I entered the library she stood up and looked boldly into my eyes. There is no maidenly modesty about Pegassa and I wonder whether all the women of her land conduct themselves thus.

She began to approach me, a smile on her full lips. She is a beautiful woman with dark eyes, full breasts and black hair like polished jet and I took a step backwards and averted my eyes from hers. When she kissed me full on the lips, for several moments I was too astounded to break away. I pray that I am strong enough to resist the temptations of the flesh.

Chapter 13

Monday was a fine morning for sailing and the breeze was warm and light as the *Justice Done* sailed round the headland making for Tradmouth harbour.

It was an ideal day to be up on deck and the owners of the *Justice Done*, a retired judge and his good lady who passed most of the summer months at their Tradmouth second home, felt the breeze on their faces as they breathed in the clean sea air; so different from the blend of traffic fumes and the stink of crammed humanity that passed for air in London. Seagulls wheeled overhead, crying like souls in torment, as the judge shielded his eyes from the sun and looked at his watch, wondering if it was too early for a gin and tonic. Probably not. It was never too early on a day like this.

He was about to call out to his wife when he spotted something at the base of the cliffs. He slowed the engine and brought the boat closer to the shore.

He could see them quite clearly now. Two pale human shapes, like naked mannequins, sprawled on the thin stretch of inaccessible sand beneath the towering cliff.

'Get onto the radio and call the coastguard,' the judge barked.

His wife obeyed without question as she always did.

Wesley ended his call and put the telephone down, looking round the room and taking a deep, calming breath before making his way to Gerry's office. He could see the DCI through the glass, feet up on desk, reading something that looked like a witness statement, away from the hum of conversation in the incident room. He opened the door without knocking. He was about to ruin Gerry's day.

Gerry looked at him as though he sensed something was wrong. 'You're going to tell me our dead woman's not Tessa Trencham? We've got to start again?'

'Worse than that. I've just had the coastguard on the phone. Two bodies were spotted by a passing boat lying beneath the cliffs a couple of miles north of Fortress Point.'

'Washed up from a boat?'

'Or a suicide pact.'

Gerry sighed. 'Or an accident – someone messing about too near the cliff edge?'

'The bodies are being taken to Tradmouth Hospital so we'll know soon enough.' He paused, wondering how Gerry was going to take the next bit of news. 'It appears that the victims were shot.'

Gerry dropped the file he was holding and leaned back in his swivel chair which groaned beneath his weight. 'Go on.'

'According to the coastguard they're both young – one

male, one female and the female has long fair hair. And they were naked. Colin's been called in.' He paused. 'You know Paul's cousin's missing from home.'

'Now let's not jump to conclusions, Wes. There's no reason to think—'

'It's just the age . . .'

Gerry picked up a pen and turned it over and over in his fingers, considering the problem. After a few moments he spoke. 'If it's a shooting, it's odds on it's drugs related; some small boat bringing stuff in and there's been a falling out. They were probably dumped from a boat and washed ashore.'

Wesley left the boss's office, shutting the door quietly behind him, hoping Gerry was right. He could see Paul Johnson sitting by the window tapping something into the computer on his desk, his face a picture of concentration. When he saw Wesley approaching he stood up.

'I thought I better let you know that two bodies have been found at the foot of the cliffs below the coastal path from Queenswear to Fortress Point,' Wesley said as he pulled up a chair to sit beside him. 'It looks like a shooting so the boss reckons it's probably drugs related. There's no reason to believe one of them's your cousin but . . .'

Paul slumped down in his seat and stared at him for a few seconds, taking in the information. Then he frowned. 'There must be a description.'

'I'm sorry.' He couldn't quite bring himself to give the details he already knew. 'Look, there's no point in worrying your aunt with this before . . . I'll let you know as soon as we have anything. Try not to worry, eh.'

He knew his last words were futile. Paul looked as if he had all the worries of the world on his shoulders.

Wesley passed Trish's desk on his way back to Gerry's office. He stopped when she asked if she could have a word, squatting down to her level so that he wouldn't have to shout.

'Paul looks upset. Is something the matter?' she said in a whisper.

He told her about the bodies, adding optimistically that it might be more the drug squad's concern than theirs. Trish didn't look convinced and he was rather relieved when she changed the subject.

'That second reference Tessa Trencham gave to Morbay Properties – Carl Heckerty. I've managed to contact him. He owns one of these paintball ranges just outside Dukesbridge – bit of a local entrepreneur by all accounts. I'm going to see him at lunchtime.'

'Did he sound worried when you spoke to him?'

She thought for a moment. 'Yes, he did a bit come to think of it. Any luck contacting Tessa in France, sir?'

'Not yet. I'm starting to think that Sylvia Cartland might have been lying about speaking to her on Saturday.'

Trish picked a file up off her desk. 'I'm going to see Tessa's dentist later. Now we've got the dead woman's dental details he'll be able to tell us for sure whether it's her or not.'

'It's about time we had something definite to go on.' He paused. 'If ... if that body does turn out to be Paul's cousin, he's going to need your support.'

Trish said nothing and hurried out of the office.

'Bad business,' were Colin Bowman's first words when he greeted Wesley and Gerry at the mortuary entrance.

Normally Colin distanced himself from the body lying on his table and maintained a cheerful and professional detachment from the horror of death. But today Wesley sensed that things were different.

'Please tell us it's suicide,' said Gerry. 'Please tell us they left a note saying "Goodbye cruel world".'

'Sorry, Gerry. Unless they developed telescopic arms and managed to shoot themselves from six feet away, suicide's out.'

'Could they have been dumped from a boat and washed ashore?' Somehow he wanted the answer to be 'yes'.

Colin considered the possibility for a few moments. 'I'm told that the tide doesn't normally reach as far as the spot where they were found, and there's no indication that they'd been in the water. In fact if I was a betting man I'd wager that the boat theory's a non-starter.'

'So what have we got?' Wesley asked quietly as they made their way to Colin's office.

'Two young people, mid to late teens. One male, one female. He was five foot ten inches tall with longish dark hair and she was five foot five inches tall with long naturally fair hair. She had two tattoos – a small butterfly on her left shoulder and a flower in the small of her back. They were found naked at the foot of the cliff halfway between Queenswear and Fortress Point. I believe the area round the coastal path has been searched but their clothes haven't been found. As far as I can see they both died of shotgun wounds. There's damage to their necks and upper chests and some of the shot spread out to their faces but they should still be identifiable.'

Wesley had obtained the photograph given to Uniform when Sophie Walter had been reported missing. The last thing he wanted was to get Paul in to identify the body unnecessarily so he handed it to Colin. 'Is this the girl?'

Colin handed the picture back. 'Yes, it's her. You know who she is then?'

'She's Paul Johnson's cousin. She's been missing since Thursday night.'

'Oh, I am sorry,' said Colin with heartfelt sincerity. 'Do pass on my condolences to Paul and his family. I don't know him well, of course but . . . Have you a name for the boy?'

It was Gerry who spoke. 'It could be a lad called Barney Pickard who was with Sophie when she disappeared. But we'll have to confirm that.'

Gerry gave Wesley a nod. There was no point in postponing the inevitable. He took his phone from his pocket and called Paul's extension in the incident room, breaking the news as gently as he could and asking if he'd mind coming to the hospital to identify the body. It would save his aunt and uncle having to do it, he said. Paul agreed. They were going to have to endure enough without that.

An hour later the body of the dead girl had been identified as that of Sophie Walter and Barney Pickard's mother was on her way.

Trish watched Paul as he left the office and saw that the colour had drained from his face, leaving the freckles standing out against his pale flesh. She stood up as he passed and caught his arm gently. She could feel the warmth of his skin though the thin cotton of his shirt.

'Is it . . . ?'

'Yeah. I've got to go.'

She stood on tiptoe and kissed his cheek, unaware of watching eyes. The thought that there had been times recently when she experienced a restlessness, a vague dissatisfaction, about their relationship, brought on a wave of guilt. He needed her now and whatever the future held, Paul was a hard man to dislike. And an easy one to hurt.

'Do you want me to contact your aunt?'

'It'll be better coming from me,' he said before hurrying out.

She slumped back into her seat and sat for a few moments, staring into space until she heard Rachel asking if everything was OK. When she broke the news, Rachel shook her head sadly and returned to her computer. No doubt they'd talk about it tonight at the house they shared together. She needed someone to reassure her that she wasn't being a bitch.

The phone on her desk began to ring, shattering the tension. When she answered it, she heard a female voice announcing that she was from the Munich hotel where Keith Marsh had told his wife he was staying. In mildly accented but perfect English the unseen German woman informed Trish that Mr Marsh had indeed been a guest at the hotel. He had stayed six nights, arriving a week last Saturday in the evening and leaving very early the following Friday morning. Trish also confirmed with the airline that he had flown out from Heathrow on Saturday afternoon and returned on the 5 a.m. flight on Friday. Keith Marsh had a day unaccounted for – around the time it was estimated the woman they still thought of as Tessa Trencham had met her death. Marsh could have stayed in Morbay on the Friday night and killed the woman before driving along the M4 to Heathrow the following day. Then, perhaps a fit of conscience had made him return to the scene of his crime a week later.

As soon as Keith Marsh regained consciousness – if he ever did – he had some questions to answer.

*

Neil decided it would be best to treat this excavation like any other. He had already briefed the post-grad students who were taking part and impressed upon them that it was a serious scientific exercise – and that it was worth a lot financially to the unit. He only hoped they'd manage to suppress their sniggers when they saw Kevin Orford and his precious artwork.

Just as Neil was directing the small mechanical digger to make the first delicate incision into the earth, the artist leapt in front of the machine shouting 'This won't do. The archaeologists should be on their hands and knees digging with tiny trowels.'

Neil turned to face him in disbelief. 'You want us to open a trench using leaf trowels? We use those for delicate work.'

'This is delicate work. It's art.'

Neil looked round his group and saw that they were seething with dissent. If he didn't handle this carefully he'd have a rebellion on his hands.

'I don't think you quite understand,' he said, keeping his voice calm and reasonable. 'We're trying to get down to the level of the, er . . . artwork at the moment. Once we reach that level we'll start to dig more carefully. I promise you we'll use the same technique to excavate something old and delicate like a Roman mosaic.' Neil paused and he saw that the artist's eyes had glazed over and his mouth was set in a stubborn line. 'Let me offer you a compromise. We'll dig out the first layer by hand with spades and then we'll start using our trowels. If we use leaf trowels we won't have gone down a foot before Christmas.'

'But the use of trowels is an artistic statement. I can't compromise my integrity—'

'And I'm telling you it won't make any difference to the

end result and it'll stop my colleagues walking out. We can use new spades if you like,' he offered as if he was coaxing a reluctant child with a promised treat. 'Nice shiny ones.'

Orford looked peeved and as he scanned the diggers' rebellious faces he appeared to consider the matter for a token few moments, obviously realising he was onto a loser. 'Very well,' he said. 'But they must be new and polished.'

Neil heard the unexpected sound of an engine and when he turned he saw a glossy, black Range Rover with darkened windows making its bumpy way slowly across the field towards them. When it stopped a few yards away, the doors opened and four people – three men and a woman – emerged from the vehicle. One of the men wore a parody of a business suit created in yellow and pink stripes and the other sported a kilt in khaki camouflage topped by a waistcoat and frilly white shirt. Next was a small, slender Japanese woman whose jet-black hair was cut at jagged angles. Then a young man with gelled hair emerged from the driver's seat. He wore an expensive dark suit with a white, open-necked shirt and he wouldn't have looked out of place in the head office of a financial institution.

The assembled archaeologists stared at the newcomers as Orford gave a triumphant sweep of his arms. 'My fellow artists have arrived so we can make a start.'

'What about the shiny spades?'

Orford ignored the question and dashed towards the newcomers, lost in a frenzy of air-kissing and mutual admiration. Neil turned to his colleagues. 'Right, let's get on with it. Spades, I'm afraid. Our digger's not artistic enough.'

Some rolled their eyes but without another word they helped themselves to the well-worn spades that were piled in the back of the minibus. As they got down to work Neil looked up occasionally and saw that the artists were watching intently. It was probably best to ignore them, he decided. Orford had left them and was in deep and serious discussion with the slick-haired young man, so perhaps their disobedience wouldn't be noticed.

After a while Neil took a break and leaned on his spade. He could see the chalets at the edge of the holiday park, separated from their field by a tall wire fence, now holed, rusty and collapsed in places after years of neglect. It was a shame the park had been allowed to get into that state, he thought. The setting couldn't be bettered: it stood in wooded countryside between Bloxham and Queenswear, a short hop over the river to Tradmouth, surrounded by rolling hills and handy for the coastal path with its dramatic cliffs and spectacular views out to sea.

He was about to resume work when he spotted Richard Catton flitting between the chalets furtively, as though he didn't want to be noticed.

Neil watched as Catton vanished into one of the chalets. When he didn't appear again Neil carried on digging.

Rachel had often wondered what it would be like to have a session at a paintball centre. War without the bloodshed, she'd heard it called, but the whole thing conjured visions of groups of young men getting over-excited, competing with each other to prove their manhood and making a terrible mess into the bargain. Pathetic really.

The centre stood on the outskirts of Dukesbridge between a petrol station and a garden centre, and the place reminded her of a toy Wild West fort her brothers had owned when they were small, all palisades and look-out towers topped with stars and stripes flags. The palings were dotted with paint splashes in bright primary colours, further emphasising the playful status of the premises. After parking the car, she made her way to the entrance. The main door stood open and as she walked in she could hear explosions and whoops of aggression – or was it pleasure?

She made straight for a door marked MANAGER PRIVATE and knocked loudly. After a few moments, it was opened by a well-built man in his early forties with closely cropped hair. He wore a checked shirt and resembled a cowboy who'd moved on into ranch management. When she produced her warrant card he took it from her hand and made a great show of examining it closely, as though he suspected she was some sort of impostor.

Once inside the office he invited her to sit down and her eyes were drawn to a large cupboard in the corner of the cluttered office, open to reveal several rows of what looked like firearms. Even though she knew they were paintball weapons, their presence still made her uncomfortable.

'So what can I do for you, Detective Sergeant Tracey?' In spite of his casual manner, he seemed a little on edge and she wondered why.

'You provided a reference for a Tessa Trencham.'

He took a deep breath and as he exhaled slowly, she was surprised to see that he looked rather relieved.

'That's not a crime, is it?'

She ignored the remark. 'You know Ms Trencham well?'

'She used to work for me.'

'Have you heard that a woman was found dead at her address last weekend?'

'I read about some woman being murdered in Morbay, but I didn't realise it was at Tessa's address.' He showed no apparent shock or curiosity, which Rachel thought was a little strange.

'We think the dead woman might be Ms Trencham.'

'Then you think wrong. Tessa's abroad. She's in France.'

'Did she tell you she was going?'

'No. Sylvia told me. Sylvia Cartland.'

'And you think she was telling you the truth?'

Suddenly Heckerty seemed a little unsure of himself. Rachel repeated the question.

'Well, Sylvia has been known to take liberties with the truth if it suits her purposes but ... surely someone's identified the dead woman.'

Normally Rachel would tread carefully at this stage but Carl Heckerty didn't look the type to upset easily. 'She'd been there a week, so the body isn't in a condition to be easily identifiable by a friend or relative. We're pinning our hopes on dental records but ... Who else would have been staying at Tessa's house?'

He shrugged his shoulders. 'Ask Sylvia. She worked with Tessa. She saw her every day.'

'When did you last see her?'

'Must be about three or four months ago. I called into the Craft Centre. She'd asked if she could give my name as a reference for the house in St Marks Road, so I thought I'd pop over and see her.'

'When did she leave your employment?'

'In February. She went into business with Sylvia. She'd made jewellery as a hobby for ages but she decided to give it a go full-time.'

'And what did she do here?'

'Admin. Accounts. That sort of thing. She moved down to Devon about eighteen months ago. She'd had some high-powered job in London and she felt she was burning out. She liked it down here. Good for my soul, she used to say. Not that admin and accounts is exactly spiritually enriching, but at least it wasn't as pressured as what she'd been used to in London. She was good at her job and I hoped she'd stay longer but she was always the creative type, I suppose. She felt she had to give the artistic stuff a try.'

'Do you know why she was going to France?'

'Sylvia said it was to get inspiration for more jewellery designs but, between you and me, I thought she might have met a bloke. Not that she'd have told Sylvia. She's got a temper, has Sylvia, and she takes things personally, and you can't do that when you're in business.'

'Would she have gone in her car?'

'Probably.'

'Could she have come back without you or Sylvia knowing?'

'Anything's possible.' His expression suddenly became serious. 'Do you really think it's her?'

'That's what we're trying to find out. Is there anything else you can tell me about Tessa? Has she ever been married?'

'She married very young and got divorced years ago – I never knew her husband; couldn't even tell you his name.'

'Any kids?'

'She'd had a son when she was in her teens. I think he stayed with his dad but she never talked about him. He'll be grown up now, I suppose.'

'What about the men in her life?'

'There have been a few of them while I've known her. Mostly losers.'

'Names?'

'Sorry. She didn't go on about her love life like some women do,' he said, scratching his nose.

Something in the way he said the words told Rachel he might be lying. 'What was your relationship with her?'

'We kept it platonic. Best way if you're working together.'

Rachel felt the blood rise to her cheeks. 'You don't have a photograph of her by any chance?'

She wasn't expecting a positive answer, so she was surprised when he opened the bottom drawer of his desk and pulled out a file. He emptied the contents onto his desk; a dozen or so snaps, mainly taken at some distant celebration – Christmas judging by the festive headgear.

He slid one of the pictures across the desk to her. 'That's Tessa,' he said, pointing at a dark-haired woman who, even though she was probably approaching her middle years, still looked slim and vivacious.

'She really hated having her picture taken – had quite a phobia about it for some reason – but I sneaked this one without her knowing.'

Rachel studied the picture. The E-fit of the woman found at Lister Cottage certainly bore a striking resemblance to Tessa Trencham. She was as sure as she could be that Sylvia Cartland was a liar.

Chapter 14

The Jester's Journal

7 June 1815

Oh, how the Lady Pegassa has the Squire in her thrall. For a woman who has no English, she knows how to make her demands clear to all. She sulks, she pouts, she throws the china if something displeases her, and behaves like some great lady who is not entrapped by manners and morals.

I asked the Squire if he thought the lady would enjoy one of my entertainments but he made no reply. Perhaps he fears her reaction if events should displease her.

I shall write to Henry Catton and suggest that he pays the Squire another visit. I long to arrange another of our hunts, but I fear that woman has caused my Master to lose his appetite for the chase. However, if anybody can overcome the power of the Lady Pegassa, it is Henry.

Today the parson came to our door, all humble and reeking of sanctity. I knew the purpose of his visit was to view the Lady Pegassa, for her presence has been the talk of idle tongues in these parts since her arrival. How the servants do spread the Squire's business abroad like muck on the fields to ensure a good crop of gossip and stories to fill their empty brains.

Our mealy-mouthed steward, Christopher Wells, invited him into the house with a display of obsequiousness that would make a cat laugh. 'Yes, Vicar. No Vicar. Shall I wipe your arse, Vicar?' How I would like to see that man kicked from the house and sent out into the lanes to beg his food.

When Wells led the parson to the library, where the lady was in the habit of spending the mornings, I secreted myself in the passage behind the panelling and listened, stuffing my mouth with a handkerchief to prevent my laughter from being heard. The clergyman attempted to speak to the lady in a number of strange tongues, and his solemnity and pomposity must have caused her much amusement, even if she did not comprehend the meaning of the words.

It was a full-half hour before he abandoned his efforts and left, his departure only to be followed by the arrival of the Misses Haddon of Neswell Court. Those two silly spinsters reminded me of a pair of hens as they clucked and fussed, looking around full of apprehension in case the Squire should appear and chase them off with a brace of whipped backsides. Once again they were shown into the Presence where they received little satisfaction as the lady addressed them haughtily in her incomprehensible tongue. The sisters, I know for certain, came out of curiosity, and now word has got out, no doubt there will be more visitors trooping up the drive in the mornings when all the district knows my master rides to view his hounds.

Perhaps I should put a stop to it. When I write to Henry, I shall tell him how these impertinent numbskulls take advantage of his kinsman.

Chapter 15

Gerry gazed out to sea, standing too near to the edge of the cliff for Wesley's liking.

Wesley edged nearer to him, trying not to look at the churning sea below. 'This must be where they went over,' he said. 'Colin said they had post-mortem injuries consistent with a fall from a cliff.'

'It's a long way down, Wes,' the DCI took a step back to the safety of the path where the crime scene tape was flapping wildly in the warm breeze and Wesley followed. 'Do you think anyone would willingly stand there on the edge, naked as the day they were born? I certainly wouldn't.'

'They might if they were being threatened with a shotgun. But the crime scene people say there's nothing to suggest they died here. No sign of any stray shot and no blood.'

'Why were they naked?'

Wesley thought for a moment. 'Could be sexual, but

we'll have to wait till the post-mortem proper to find that out. Or it could have been a matter of control or humiliation. Or to delay identification and eliminate traces of the killer's DNA.'

'We need to know where they died. And we need to find their clothes.' Gerry looked round at the woodland, stretching inland from the path. 'All this area will have to be searched. Who owns this land?'

'This coastal path belongs to the National Trust but the land and woods to our right belong to the Catton Hall estate.' Wesley was carrying an Ordnance Survey map, which he thought might come in useful. He spotted a wooden bench nearby where weary walkers could rest and enjoy the view out to sea. He strode towards it, sat down, unfolded the map and studied it closely for a few moments.

'Were you a Boy Scout, Wes?' Gerry said as he watched with a smile playing on his lips. 'You've certainly come prepared.'

Wesley looked up and smiled. 'As a matter of fact I was. And I thought the map might come in useful – give us an idea of the lie of the land.'

'Bet you got lots of badges at Scouts. My idea of being prepared was making sure I'd brought some matches and enough money for five Woodbines so we could have a smoke behind the scout hut afterwards. So what's the verdict?'

'According to this map the nearest house is Catton Hall. Didn't Paul say Barney's mum mentioned something about a hall?'

'There are lots of halls dotted around this area but we'll pay this Catton Hall a visit anyway. Someone might have seen or heard something.'

'The noise of a gunshot would carry in the night air, I suppose.'

'We're sure they were killed at night?'

'At this time of year this area's teeming with walkers during the day. If someone brought the bodies here, it would have to be under cover of darkness. Has Colin set a time for the post-mortem?'

'This afternoon at half past three.'

Wesley folded up his map carefully and stretched his arms towards the sky. He felt himself yawn. Perhaps it was the effect of all that good sea air after the muggy atmosphere of the office.

'Keeping you up, Wes?'

Wesley felt obliged to smile. He stood up and they began to walk along the path where they saw a trio of ramblers in shorts and boots that looked too heavy for the fine weather, arguing with one of the uniformed constables who'd been given the task of patrolling the perimeter of the crime scene to make sure nobody tried to get past the blue and white tape. Wesley heard the words 'public footpath' and 'right of way' spoken by a haranguing female voice, a woman who was used to being in authority, a retired headmistress perhaps. But this time she wasn't going to get her way. Her group would have to take the long way round.

Wesley's map showed clearly that there was a footpath to Catton Hall so he led the way through woodland, then past fields and hedgerows full of brambles, taking care not to get his jacket caught on the barbed tendrils that reached out to grab the unwary passer-by.

They arrived at another area of woodland and picked their way down a bracken-strewn path shaded by tall, deciduous trees. The air was filled with birdsong and the sound of unseen fluttering wings overhead: the music of the woods. They walked quite a while before they spotted the hall in the distance.

Catton Hall looked as if it had been always been there, carved out of the bedrock. It wasn't particularly large; just a rural manor house, the home of a local squire rather than some great lord. If a great lord had owned it, it would have been extended and modernised beyond recognition many years ago.

'Neil's working near here,' Wesley said as they approached the front of the house.

'I thought he was up at Fortress Point.'

'He was, but now he's taking part in some art project. Something to do with digging up a picnic.'

Gerry opened his mouth to say something but no sound came out. It wasn't often he was lost for words.

Wesley rang the bell by the hall's grand front door but there was no answer. 'Let's have a look round. The crime scene people didn't find any tyre tracks near the cliff top, and let's face it, you couldn't get a car up there, could you. That means that whoever dumped those bodies didn't take them far. There's a lot of woodland round here so we'll need a big search team. We've got to find out exactly where those kids died.'

'I've got a feeling this killer isn't going to make life easy for us. Where exactly is Neil working on this art thing?'

'Near the old holiday park.' He paused. 'He told me he stayed there once.'

'So this is a trip down memory lane for him. It used to be a nice place once upon a time.'

From the map, Wesley had worked out the route and as

he walked ahead of Gerry down a pitted driveway, then through more woodland, he kept his eyes focused on the light-dappled ground, just in case there were any tell-tale signs of a disturbance.

But there was nothing; no spent cartridges at the base of a tree; no signs of a struggle in the rotting leaves left over from last autumn; no dried blood staining the undergrowth. Soon they emerged from the shade of the trees into a large level field bordered on the far side by a rusty wire fence. Beyond the fence, Wesley could see the run-down holiday chalets with their dusty windows and peeling varnish, but the field itself was alive with activity. Wesley had studied archaeology at Exeter University and he recognised the signs at once: the trench marked out with string stretched between two points; the black plastic buckets for the spoil, the trowels, spades, mattocks and kneeling mats. The finds trays lined with newspaper waiting to receive any artefacts dug from the ground.

Four young men and a well-built girl were removing the turf and piling it beside the marked-out trench. They didn't speak and Wesley couldn't help wondering why they looked so fed up. He also wondered why they weren't using a mechanical digger for this initial stage. It would save a lot of back-breaking work, but Neil was in charge and he trusted him to know what he was doing.

He saw his friend standing a few yards away from the trench, arms folded defensively. Beside him stood a wiry man with thick white curls and brightly coloured clothes who was watching the diggers in silent fascination. Neil kept his eyes fixed ahead, and Wesley had the impression that he was doing his best to ignore his companion.

Two strangely dressed men stood behind Neil, watching

the proceedings, while a petite Japanese woman moved round the edge of the trench with an expensive-looking video camera. Her expression was one of intense concentration, as though she was engaged on serious and important business. A young man in a suit hung back a little from the rest talking on his BlackBerry, strangely out of place among such flamboyant company.

Gerry gaped with undisguised curiosity at Neil's companions. Then he turned to Wesley, with a chuckle. 'Neil looks like a nun who's just found herself in a tart's boudoir. If I were you, I'd go and rescue him.'

It wasn't long before Neil spotted Wesley and a look of sheer relief appeared on his face as he hurried over to greet him.

'Am I glad to see you,' he said, looking round to make sure he wasn't overheard. 'I've had to make conversation with that lot for the past few hours and it's not easy, I can tell you.'

'Who are they?'

'The guy in the suit is Kevin Orford's PR man and the others are his fellow artists. And a bigger load of pretentious wankers you'd never meet. Would you believe he wanted us to dig the whole trench with leaf trowels!'

'I trust you put him right.'

'We compromised on spades for the turf and the top foot or so. Our nice little mini-digger would have ruined the whole artistic ambience, and he's forbidden the use of mattocks because they represent violence.' He rolled his eyes. 'I told my colleagues to grit their teeth and think of the money.' He nodded in Gerry's direction. 'At least they're keeping your boss amused.'

'Everyone has their uses.'

'I'd heard there was something going on up by the cliffs but I assumed they'd sent the rescue helicopter out because some idiot in a boat had got into trouble.'

'Not this time. Two kids were shot, then their bodies were pushed or thrown over the cliff.'

Neil swore under his breath.

'Do you know who owns that big house just down there beyond the trees?'

'Catton Hall? I haven't met the owner but I've met his son, Richard Catton.'

'Does this land belong to the hall too?'

'The Cattons own the lot – even the holiday park, but that's been leased to a company for years.'

'Do you know where we can find Richard?'

'He's been about but I'm not sure where he is at the moment.'

'If you see him, tell him we'd like a word.' Wesley handed Neil one of his cards. 'Give him this and ask him to call me, will you?'

Neil nodded. 'Will do. I'd better get back – show willing.' He turned and walked slowly back to Orford and his companions, dragging his feet like a reluctant schoolboy.

On their return, Rachel told Wesley in a hushed voice that Paul had identified the dead girl as his cousin, Sophie. He had gone to stay with his aunt and uncle for a while, just to take them through the procedure and make things a little easier for them. If things could ever be easy for them from now on.

There was no banter in the incident room and none of the gallows humour that usually helped them get through the day. Even Gerry seemed subdued. It was as though

Paul's connection with one of the victims had brought the whole nasty business too close to home.

Rachel looked restless, as if there was something on her mind. He waited for her to continue.

'I went to see Carl Heckerty at the paintball place,' she said, leaning forward. 'Tessa Trencham used to work for him – admin and accounts. Sylvia Cartland told him the same story as she told us – that she's staying in France for a while to get inspiration for her jewellery designs. According to him, their relationship was strictly platonic and he claims he hasn't seen Tessa since she asked him for that reference.'

'You believed him?'

She tilted her head to one side, considering the question. 'I think I did.' She opened the cardboard file that was lying in front of her on the desk and pulled out a photograph. 'That's Tessa Trencham there.' She pointed to a dark haired woman. 'Think she's our mystery lady in Morbay?'

Wesley studied the photo closely. 'Probably. I'll show this to Gerry.'

'If it is her, why did she come back from France without telling anyone? And why did Sylvia Cartland lie about speaking to her on Saturday when she'd already been dead a week?'

'Maybe she wasn't lying. Maybe someone was pretending to be Tessa. We need to speak to Ms Cartland again.'

Rachel nodded. 'At the moment she has to be a suspect. Then there's Keith Marsh. It looks as though he found the body.' Her eyes lit up with the challenge of speculation. 'Marsh kills her before going off to Germany. Then when he comes back he has a fit of conscience when he remembers how he's left her lying there so he gives us a call.'

'It would make more sense if he'd gone straight home to

111

Manchester when he arrived back at Heathrow. If he knew she was dead, why come back here? Why incriminate himself?'

'Maybe he'd left something at the flat that would lead us to him.'

'What sort of thing?'

'I don't know. It could be something he had on him when he had the crash, or he might have destroyed it.'

He knew Rachel had a point. At that moment Keith Marsh was at the top of their list.

'The police want to talk to you.'

Richard Catton swung round and Neil thought he looked shocked and maybe a little guilty, like a schoolboy caught stealing sweets from a shop.

'Why?'

'Did you hear the rescue helicopter earlier?'

Richard regained his composure. 'Another sailor in trouble, I presume.'

'Not this time. They found two bodies at the foot of the cliff about half a mile from here.'

'Jumpers?'

'They were shot.'

Richard's face arranged itself into an appropriate expression of shock. 'That's awful. Dumped from a boat, I suppose. Drugs. The coastguard have a hell of a job keeping an eye on all that sort of stuff these days.'

'The police don't think they were ever in the sea.'

Richard gave a nervous laugh. 'You seem to know a lot about it.'

'A mate of mine is a detective working on the case. He wants to talk to you because it happened near your land.'

'That cliff top belongs to the National Trust,' Richard said quickly.

'The police don't think they were killed there. My mate gave me his card and asked if you could give him a call.'

Richard took the card from him. 'OK. But I don't see how I can help. How's the dig going?'

'We've not reached the picnic yet.'

'Feast of Life,' Richard reminded him with a awkward smile.

A family liaison officer had broken the news to Barney Pickard's mother. Wesley and Gerry were grateful that they hadn't had to do it.

Barney's earthly home was a substantial Georgian house on the edge of a small village not far from Bereton. The gatepost bore the name 'The Old Rectory' but, judging by the glossy paintwork, the brand-new sash windows and the immaculate window-boxes, the rector had probably moved out many years ago. The vicarage in Belsham near Neston, where Wesley's brother-in-law lived, worked and held parish meetings had a far more shabby, workaday look.

He parked the car in the gravel drive and looked at Gerry. Neither of them relished the prospect of questioning the bereaved mother, but it had to be done: a necessary evil.

The family liaison officer opened the door. She was a no-nonsense blonde who reminded Wesley a little of Rachel. She gave them a sad smile of greeting as she stood aside to let them into the hall with its polished floorboards and sweeping Georgian staircase. The place smelled of money. But no amount of money could bring Barney Pickard back from the dead.

'How is she?' Gerry asked.

'Not good,' the young woman said in a hushed voice. 'I don't think it really sank in until I took her to Tradmouth to identify the body. And now ...'

She didn't have to finish the sentence. Wesley knew they'd have to tread carefully.

'What about the boy's father?'

'They're divorced and he lives in Morbay. He's been contacted.'

'Are they on good terms?'

'I don't think so. From what I've picked up the divorce was pretty acrimonious. She used to be a model, you know. Quite famous. Patsy Lowther. Have you heard of her?'

It was Gerry who nodded. 'I remember the name. Wild parties and drug convictions, wasn't it? And didn't she have an affair with that Labour peer? And a couple of rock stars, if I remember right.'

'You're better informed than I am, Gerry,' said Wesley with a smile.

'Oh my Kathy used to love all the gossip magazines.'

It wasn't often Gerry mentioned his late wife and Wesley thought the casual way her name came up in the conversation was a good sign. Recently, since his children had both left home and gained their independence, his relationship with Joyce seemed to have reached a comfortable equilibrium – he appeared to be more contented with life these days and Wesley was glad.

He took a deep breath. 'We'd better get it over with, I suppose.'

Without another word, the family liaison officer led them to a room on the right of the hallway and knocked before opening the door.

'I'm really sorry, Patsy, but two detectives are here and

they need to ask you some questions. They'll understand if you don't feel up to talking, but it really is important.'

Wesley was standing on the threshold and he heard a voice saying 'OK. I'll see them.' It was a sexy, slightly hoarse voice, the sort that comes from late nights spent in smoky clubs. He had heard that voice coming from the lipsticked mouths of middle-aged female rock stars being interviewed on TV and, although he had never experienced that world, he was reminded of a more carefree, decadent time before Health and Safety inherited the earth.

He followed Gerry into the room and he had the opportunity to study Patsy Pickard, née Lowther, for the first time. She was perched on the edge of a brocade sofa, cigarette in one hand and a glass of some clear liquid in the other. Her hair was long, blonde and poker-straight, and her tall body was thin to the point of emaciation. She wore a pair of skin-tight jeans and a long black T-shirt. It was only the fine network of lines around her eyes that betrayed the fact that she was no teenager. She looked up, assessing the newcomers, and Wesley was struck by the beauty of her bone structure. To his surprise, he realised that her face was familiar. He must have seen it without realising in various commercials, magazines and newspapers over the years.

Gerry gave him a nudge. It was up to him to begin. 'I'm very sorry for your loss, Mrs Pickard,' he said gently.

'Thanks,' she said. 'Liz here has been great. Couldn't have got through without her. We used to call the police pigs in the old days but . . . ' She favoured the family liaison officer with a weak smile and the young woman's cheeks reddened a little.

'I'm glad you're being looked after,' Wesley said with some sincerity. 'I know it's a difficult time for you but we

115

have to ask you some questions about Barney. I'm sorry if it seems intrusive but if we're going to catch whoever's responsible for what happened . . .'

Patsy stubbed out her cigarette and pulled herself upright. 'I'm ready. Go on.'

'You last saw Barney on Thursday?'

'Yes. Around seven. I passed him in the hall and he said he was going out.'

'Did he say where he was going?'

She shook her head. 'I'd heard him on his phone earlier and I presumed he was talking to his girlfriend, Sophie.'

'Tell me about Sophie.'

'I only met her once. Well, when I say "met" I don't mean we were formally introduced. She grunted at me in the usual teenage way, then Barney whisked her off upstairs to his room.'

'Did they go to the same school?'

'Yes. Corley Grange. But they've just finished their A-levels so they've officially left.'

'I presume he had other friends at the school?'

'Sullen adolescents arrived on the doorstep from time to time. None of them speak, none of them seem to have names and most are dressed entirely in black. I'm sorry I can't help you more, but I can't really tell one from the other.'

Gerry nodded as if he understood. Wesley still had his own children's teenage years to look forward to, so he said nothing.

'I understand that he mentioned something about a hall.'

For a moment she looked puzzled. 'Hall? Oh yeah, I thought it was a hall but I could be wrong.'

'Could it have been Catton Hall?' It was Gerry who spoke.

116

Patsy shrugged. 'I don't know. What's Catton Hall?'

'It's near where . . . where he was found. There's a house there and a disused holiday park. He never mentioned it to you?'

'He never told me what he was up to and I never asked. He was an adult . . . almost.' She lit another cigarette.

'We'd like to look at his room, if we may,' said Wesley.

'Liz'll show you where it is. I haven't been able to go in there since . . . Not that he allowed me in there anyway. He valued his privacy.'

'Was he close to his father?'

'He wanted to be. It became a bit of an obsession for him – being with his father – doing father and son things. Boys outgrow their mothers when they reach their teenage years, don't you think?'

Wesley didn't answer.

'George often invites him over to his place at weekends. I presume they do – did manly things together. George was never much of a father to him when he was small and then he disappeared from his life completely for a while, but recently they've been seeing more of each other.'

'Where does your ex-husband live?'

'It's on the promenade in Morbay, overlooking the sea. A penthouse. A bachelor pad,' she added bitterly. 'Have you found Barney's phone yet?'

'Sorry. No.'

'He'd have had it with him. He took it everywhere. Surgically attached, I used to say.'

'If you can let us have his number so we can trace his calls?' Wesley passed her his notebook and she scribbled down the number. He could see tears forming in her eyes and concluded that prolonging the questioning would be an

117

act of cruelty. He caught the eye of the family liaison officer and stood up. 'We'll have a look at Barney's room now, if that's OK.'

Patsy put the cigarette to her lips and inhaled deeply. 'Help yourselves,' she said. The words were casual but the pain was there, raw beneath the surface.

Wesley suddenly wanted to get out of there. He walked to the door and the others followed. When they reached the hall, he let Liz go ahead of them up the stairs. Even if she hadn't been there to show them the way, they would have found Barney's room easily as his name was emblazoned on the door, painted in red on the Georgian mahogany. A small act of vandalism, maybe of rebellion.

They waited until Liz had returned to her charge before closing the door behind them and beginning the search. Wesley had been in missing teenagers' rooms before and always found the sight of the trivial minutiae of their lives unbearably poignant: all the mess; the unfinished homework; the posters; and the tawdry adolescent treasures. And from the expression on Gerry's face, he knew he was thinking the same.

Wesley made straight for the laptop computer on the cluttered desk. He switched it on and scrolled through the emails. There was one that caught his eye. It had been sent at four o'clock on the Thursday afternoon and it just gave a time and a place. Catton Hall. Ten o'clock.

He turned to Gerry who was watching over his shoulder. 'It is Catton Hall.'

'Who's it from?'

'It just says Game Master.'

'I hated my games master when I was at school. Maybe Barney was the sporty type – might be a team fixture.'

Wesley smiled. 'Game Master, not games. And I don't think ten o'clock at Catton Hall is a cricket first team fixture somehow.'

'Anything else?'

'Not very much in the emails. School stuff mainly, and stuff from his father. We'll have to get scientific support to sort all that out.' Wesley closed the emails and pressed a few keys.

'What are you doing?'

'Seeing if he played that game we found on Sophie's laptop. Blood Hunt.'

Sure enough it was there. It seemed that, like Sophie, Barney had played it virtually every night. He wondered whether there was any link to the email from Game Master. He'd just have to be patient until Tom, the expert from scientific support, gave his verdict.

He found the laptop case and packed the computer away. With Patsy's consent, they'd take it back to the police station for inspection. Sophie's was also being examined and Wesley hoped that it might yield some clue as to why two young people had died in that violent and terrible manner.

The search didn't turn up much else of interest and they were about to leave the room when Wesley noticed something pinned to a notice board hanging on the wall above the desk – a cutting from a newspaper, slightly yellowed by the sunlight that streamed in through the window. He retraced his steps and stood there studying it.

'What is it?' Gerry was hovering by the door, anxious to be gone.

Wesley began to read aloud. 'Manhunt. With fox hunting now declared illegal, groups of enthusiasts have taken up the sport of Hunting the Clean Boot. This involves human volunteers being hunted by riders who follow a pack of bloodhounds, rather as regular hunts used foxes as their quarry before the government ban.'

He read on in silence, Gerry now looking over his shoulder. It was a standard article, certainly nothing sinister, and the people involved seemed to belong to the normal hunting fraternity rather than any shadowy organisation. It didn't look like the sort of thing a boy like Barney would take much interest in – unless he'd volunteered to act as the quarry to earn himself a bit of extra money. Hunting was a closed book to Wesley so he didn't even know if his theory was feasible. But in this part of the world there were bound to be people who'd be able to help him. Rachel with her farming connections might know.

When Wesley unpinned the cutting from the board he saw something hidden behind it – a sheet of paper with a list of names scribbled on it. He took it down and Gerry began to read out loud.

'Dun. Jodie. Marcus. Then an email address. Game Master again. And a hundred pounds. What the hell does it mean?'

'If we pay another visit to Catton Hall we might find out.'

Trish had been looking forward to her visit to the dentist all morning. Armed with the dead woman's dental chart from the mortuary, she drove out to Morbay in the sparkling sunshine, taking the route via Neston rather than the car ferry. It was the height of the tourist season and the ferry queues were lengthening by the minute.

Steven Bowles's surgery was on the outskirts of the town,

housed on the ground floor of a large Victorian villa. She found herself staring at the sign bearing his name, clutching the file tightly in her hand. Suddenly she felt nervous. But dentists always had that effect on her.

The receptionist behind the desk was a buxom redhead whose low-cut top hardly screamed out 'medical efficiency', and the sight of her made Trish's heart sink. But the girl seemed to be expecting her and told her that Steve was between patients so she could go straight through.

When she entered the surgery he was standing by the chair in his snowy white coat, a wide smile of greeting on his face. His own teeth were perfect, as good a recommendation, she supposed, as an advertising billboard. She automatically took a step towards the chair, almost forgetting that she wasn't there for an appointment. But she needn't have worried; Steven was holding out a small brown cardboard file.

'Have you brought the records from the mortuary?' he asked.

She handed her own file to him without a word and watched while he spread both sets of records out on the counter next to the steriliser. He looked from one chart to the other and Trish saw a frown spread across his face.

Steven turned to face her. 'You're sure the chart the mortuary provided belongs to the dead woman? There couldn't have been a mix up?'

Trish shook her head. 'Our DI picked it up himself.'

'In that case, the dead woman isn't Tessa Trencham. I'm sorry.'

For once Trish was lost for words.

Chapter 16

The Steward's Journal

10 June 1815

News of our colourful guest has spread to the garrison at Fortress Point, for the Squire received a visit from two young officers who were enquiring about strangers in the vicinity. They had heard of a foreign lady, they said, and were desirous to meet her as they feared that she might be a French spy in our midst. The Squire assured them that she speaks not a word of French; rather she talks in some strange language quite unknown to him. He also insisted that there are no secrets for her to spy out at Catton Hall, a statement I feel to be far from the truth.

I met with William's mother again yesterday and she said that he has gone away to work on Henry's estate. I wonder whether this is the truth or whether some darker fate has befallen the lad – although I can think of no fate so dark as serving Henry Catton.

12 June 1815

Henry Catton has come again to visit us, riding up to the door as though he already owns the place (which is entailed to him on the Squire's demise should he die without issue). The Squire was out with his hounds so, in his absence, Henry made straight for the library where the Lady Pegassa was sitting, as is her habit in the afternoons. I feared for her welfare so I lingered for a while in the passage outside the chamber in case she should cry for help. No cry came, so after a while I returned to my duties. Perhaps the lady has tamed the wildness in my master's kinsman, for she is a woman of great beauty and strength such as I have never encountered before in the female persons of this fair county.

Since that kiss she placed upon my lips I have found myself much in her company. I beg the Lord to forgive me for she inspires feelings of desire in my breast that I know would be an abomination to all decent folk hereabouts. I have no business entertaining libidinous thoughts of a woman who is like an exotic bird of paradise compared with our English sparrows. And yet I feel I must protect her from Henry Catton and his wicked schemes.

Silly John is behaving in a most secretive manner, whispering in corners and closeted with the Squire for hours upon end. When he sees me he pulls out his tongue and insults me to my face. Hiding behind the mask of the Fool gives him licence to take liberties with manners ... and morals.

Chapter 17

'I need to see you. When can you come round?' Richard Catton pressed the telephone receiver to his ear, hoping the urgency in his tone would spur Carl Heckerty into action. He didn't want to face his dilemma alone.

He stood in the drawing room of Catton Hall, a room that had been left untouched since his grandfather's day, or maybe before, and watched dust particles dancing in the shaft of sunlight beaming in through the window, aware of nothing apart from the overwhelming problem that had occupied his every waking thought since that night.

'Calm down, Richard. They can't link anything to us.'

'They've been round asking questions. They want to speak to me.'

'I've already been interviewed.'

There was a moment of hesitation as Richard considered the implications of Heckerty's last remark. 'They're onto you?'

'No. It was about someone who used to work for me. A woman I know. It won't occur to them that there's any connection. In my experience the police aren't that bright, you know. In fact they sent me a rather pretty blonde called Detective Sergeant Tracey. She was the down-to-earth, straight-laced type but she was rather nice to look at. She asked me a few questions and then she went away satisfied ... if you know what I mean.'

Richard caught the innuendo in Carl's voice and wondered how he could joke at a time like this.

'If they find out about the hunts—'

'They won't find out. The kids will keep their mouths shut.' He hesitated for a moment. 'Anyway, what we do isn't illegal. They're all over eighteen and they gave their full consent. It's just a bit of fun.'

'I know but—'

'Just keep your head down and don't say anything.'

'I think we should meet. When the police question me we need to tell them the same story.'

'Stop panicking. You're making me bloody nervous.'

The line went dead and Richard was left staring at the phone, his hand shaking. There were times when he wished he'd never met Heckerty – and this was one of them. But there was no escaping him now.

'Who was that?'

Richard swung round and saw his father standing in the doorway. Alfred Catton had once been six foot tall and straight-backed, but now age and ill-health had made him stoop a little so he appeared smaller. His shiny, liver-spotted scalp was visible through his thinning white hair and his clothes hung loosely off his fragile body.

'Just someone trying to sell double glazing,' Richard said

125

quickly. 'I said the place was Grade Two listed – that shut them up. How are you feeling?'

'Well enough to know you're lying,' the old man said.

Richard didn't reply.

Nobody took much notice of Trish as she walked into the incident room. Everyone was engrossed in their own particular tasks: talking to potential witnesses on the phone; tracking down the school friends of the dead youngsters; and trying to trace anybody who'd known Tessa Trencham.

Trish saw that Paul's chair was empty. Then she remembered that the boss had told him to stay with his aunt and uncle for a while. At least his absence meant that she wouldn't have to watch every word she said.

DCI Heffernan was in his office, talking on the phone in an animated fashion, as though the person on the other end was beginning to irritate him. In contrast DI Peterson was sitting calmly in the visitor's chair on the other side of the desk, studying a file with a small frown of concentration on his face.

Trish gave a token knock on the door and pushed it open without waiting for a reply. Her news would send one of their investigations on a whole new course. Assumptions would be ditched; carefully taken notes would be filed away as irrelevant; and new interviews would have to be conducted.

She inhaled deeply and stepped into the office.

Wesley looked round. 'How did your visit to the dentist go?'

He looked so hopeful that Trish felt apologetic as she gave her answer. 'According to her dental records the dead woman is not Tessa Trencham.'

Gerry had just put the phone down and he half raised himself from his seat. 'Is the dentist absolutely sure?'

'I gave him that dental chart from the mortuary and he compared it with Tessa Trencham's dental records. It's definitely not her.'

'Unless there's been an administrative cock up,' said Wesley hopefully. 'Maybe the mortuary gave me the wrong chart or . . . '

Trish shook her head. 'I've checked with them. There's no mistake.'

'So Sylvia Cartland was probably telling the truth about speaking to Tessa on Saturday,' Gerry said, staring at the heap of papers on his desk. 'I'd have staked my pension on that woman being a liar. We need to keep trying Tessa's phone in the hope that she decides to switch it on again. You don't let just anybody use your house so it must be someone she knows well. Maybe she let a mate use it for a bit of extramarital hanky panky.'

Trish saw Wesley nod his head. If Gerry's theory was right, the murder of the woman at Lister Cottage *could* be a simple domestic. Maybe an enraged husband strangling his cheating wife?

'Perhaps Keith Marsh was the lover and that was why he was in Devon when he was supposed to be flying out to Germany. He found her when he returned to the house for another tryst and reported her death anonymously.'

'You could well be right, Gerry,' said Wesley. 'But we won't know for certain till Marsh regains consciousness.'

In spite of the identification setback, things were beginning to piece together quite well. Now all they had to do was to find out who the dead woman was and bring in her murderous spouse. Trish knew that most murders were quite straightforward and were often committed by the corpse's nearest and dearest.

But the two teenagers at the foot of the cliffs near Catton Hall – that was a different matter.

The afternoon sun was hot and Neil's T-shirt was drenched in sweat as he laid down his spade to take a swig from the plastic water bottle he'd left on the edge of the trench. The trench was about two foot deep now and the students were digging earnestly, piling the soil onto the ever-growing spoil heap at the side of the hole. There was a time not so long ago when he had their stamina. Now he'd almost started to prefer the hands-off supervisory or desk-based approach and he took this as a sign of creeping middle age.

He caught the eye of his colleague Dave, who had just returned from checking on the fort excavation. He had stripped off to the waist and his tanned body glistened with perspiration as he leaned on his spade, taking a much-needed rest. Dave nodded in the direction of Orford and his entourage who had obtained chairs from somewhere and were sitting in a row like a group posed for a formal photograph, watching the activity with impassive faces, as though showing any interest or excitement would mar their ice-cool image for ever.

'All right for some,' Dave whispered. 'How far down does he reckon this picnic is buried?'

'He says about six foot. Well, his actual words were "the same as a grave". He said something about it being a burial ceremony.'

'For a picnic?' Dave, a bearded doyen of the archaeology circuit who had seen most things before but nothing like this, rolled his eyes. 'Well, they're paying so we'd better get on with it. And, who knows, we may find something interesting while we're down there. Iron-age farmstead? Saxon village? Place your bets.'

'We can live in hope,' said Neil with a sigh. He shook his water bottle and found it was empty. 'I need some water. There's a drinking fountain just past the chalets in the holiday village and with any luck it'll still be working. I'll get you a refill while I'm there, if you like.'

Dave leaned over and picked his bottle up from the side of the trench, drained it, and handed it over as Neil climbed out onto the grass, aware of the watchful, earnest eyes of Orford and his fellow artists. He half expected Orford to say something, but no comment was made. Perhaps even a man like Orford understood about the dangers of dehydration. The Japanese woman with the angular hair rose to her dainty feet every few minutes and used the video camera, which, Neil assumed, was recording everything for posterity. Or perhaps it was just a pose. He couldn't be sure with these people. The PR man had gone and Neil couldn't help wondering why an artist would be in need of his services. But what did he know about the art world?

He climbed through the broken fence and walked between the chalets, thinking of that summer when he and his sister had used this site as a playground, enjoying a week of uninterrupted freedom from adult control. For endless hours he had dug for imagined buried treasure in the huge sandpit – perhaps a portent of his future career – and his sister had spent her days in the swimming pool with newly made friends. Perhaps the site had been shabby and past its best in those days too, but children never notice things like that. Only jaded adult eyes see decay and deterioration.

129

The once pristine concrete paths between the chalets were now cracked and bursting with weeds, and although a few of the chalet windows were boarded up with chipboard, most still retained their glass, dusty now from years of neglect. The drinking fountain stood in the little square in front of the dilapidated reception office, and as Neil approached it he was suddenly filled with nostalgia, so sharp and unexpected that it almost hurt. But when he spotted Richard Catton, the spell of childhood was broken.

'Hi,' he said.

Richard was emerging from one of the chalets carrying a bucket of water, leaning slightly to counterbalance its weight. In his other hand he held a plastic bag, bulging with what looked like clothes.

'Doing a bit of clearing out?'

Richard's eyes widened in alarm. 'What?'

'Didn't think you had to get your hands dirty if you were the son of the lord of the manor.'

'Some backpackers used a couple of the chalets last week and I was just checking everything was OK. No rest for the wicked, eh,' he said with forced bonhomie. 'Even the lord of the manor has to put his hand down toilets occasionally.'

'I'll take your word for it,' said Neil. 'Is the drinking fountain still working?'

'Yes ... yes it is. We're still using the place, so all the services are connected.'

'Are you planning to knock these chalets down and rebuild?'

'If everything goes to plan.' There was something nervous about his manner, as though he didn't want to be having this particular conversation, innocent though it

130

seemed to Neil. 'Look, I'd better get on,' he said, glancing around as though he was seeking an escape route.

As Richard began to hurry away, Neil called after him. 'The dig's going OK.'

Richard stopped suddenly and turned round. 'Good. Orford's paying well for the use of the land. Every little bit helps.'

'Have you called my mate yet?'

'I'm just about to do it. See you.'

Neil waited until he'd disappeared round the corner then he carried on, making for the drinking fountain. However, he couldn't resist stopping at the chalet Richard had come out of. For a cleaner, he had looked very furtive. But maybe he was embarrassed by his poverty – the lord of the manor's son and heir cleaning up after a bunch of backpackers.

He stood on tiptoe to peer through the dusty glass. The interior of the chalets hadn't changed much since the days of his childhood. But in those distant days, everything had been kept spotlessly clean and the curtains at the windows hadn't hung in tattered rags.

The sun was streaming directly through the window, and from his vantage point he could make out most of the interior. He could see that the kitchen and bedroom doors were shut and he suddenly had an irresistible urge to go inside, just for old times' sake. He put his hand on the door and pushed gently but it was locked. However, when he pushed harder the weak lock yielded to his touch and the door swung open with a creak.

The pattern on the carpet was hard to make out through the layer of grime and the place smelled musty as he crunched his way across the room, making for the

131

bedrooms – two of them in this size of chalet: one for the parents, one for the children. He opened the door to the first bedroom and when he looked round he saw that something pink had become caught under the door. On closer inspection, he realised that it was a small, lacy bra, frothy and expensive looking. Maybe it had fallen from the bag of clothes Catton had been carrying, he thought, and he stared at it for a few moments before closing the door. It was really none of his business.

'Have you contacted all the numbers in his address book?' Wesley stared down at Keith Marsh's phone, now lying on Rachel's desk.

She picked it up and started to turn it over in her fingers. 'Mmm. Some of them knew about the accident already because Mrs Marsh had been in touch, but a lot of them are business contacts. Unfortunately none of them could throw any light on what he was doing down in Devon but there was one who sounded . . . ' She searched for the word. 'Cagey. As if he was hiding something. He was OK at first, then he seemed to clam up. Couldn't wait to get rid of me. He said he was a work contact, lives in Bristol – name of Barry.'

Wesley smiled. 'He might have been in a hurry or . . . Well, we have to face the fact that some people just don't like the police, Rach.'

'He was fine at first, but when he asked me where I was based and where Keith had been found his manner changed.'

'Got his details?'

With her customary efficiency, Rachel had written it all down neatly on a sheet of paper. She handed it to Wesley.

'I've been through all Marsh's calls. Just over a week ago he made quite a few calls to a pay as you go mobile that we haven't identified. And now we know the dead woman's not Tessa Trencham, I've had one of the DCs checking through all our missing persons for anyone who matches the description.'

'Any possibilities?'

'Not really.'

'Our best bet is talking to Tessa, but if Sylvia's right and she keeps her phone switched off ... '

'Why would anyone do that?'

'Some people don't like the intrusion, especially if they're in a beautiful place seeking artistic inspiration. It's anyone's guess when she'll get back to us.'

'My money's still on her allowing a friend or relative to use the house for an adulterous affair and the irate husband walking in on a cosy little love nest. Are we taking bets on the lover being Keith Marsh?'

'All we've got to do is prove it.'

Rachel suddenly looked solemn. They could theorise all they liked but unless they had the culprit in custody and some solid evidence to hand over to the Crown Prosecution Service, all their mental efforts were as futile as a game of Cluedo.

'How are we getting on with Sophie and Barney's friends?'

'They're all being interviewed.' She pulled a face. 'Poor little rich kids from Corley Grange all off on their gap years before uni.'

The privately educated Wesley knew that Rachel had attended the local comprehensive and had a low opinion of what she considered to be the privileged classes. Less charitable men than him would have called it a chip on the shoulder. He said nothing and waited for her to continue.

'Someone's bound to know something relevant but it's a matter of getting them to admit it.' She let out a sigh. 'I can't get over the way they were both shot like that. Accurately too. It almost reminds me of a gangland killing.'

'Two kids who've just left the sixth form of exclusive school – hardly the sort who'd get on the wrong side of the criminal underworld.'

Rachel raised her eyebrows. 'You reckon?'

Perhaps, Wesley thought, she had a lower opinion of the average teenager than he had.

When Wesley arrived home at eight o'clock that evening he found Pam alone, sprawled out on the sofa with a book in her hand. It was a murder mystery, something he felt no temptation to borrow after she'd finished with it – he had more than enough of that sort of thing at work. The evening was warm and she wore denim shorts, a T-shirt and no make-up. And she looked completely relaxed. In the busy stress of term time things were so different. The scent of something appetising wafted from the kitchen and he suddenly realised he hadn't eaten since midday – and then he and Gerry had made do with a couple of sandwiches.

'The kids have gone to your sister's for tea,' she said, putting her book down. 'You hungry?'

He nodded and sat down. A taste of domestic bliss was more than welcome after the frustrating day he'd just had. He looked at his mobile and was almost tempted to switch it off and leave the landline off the hook, but he knew that would be irresponsible. What if there was some new development in the case and he was needed?

134

The meal was good – chicken in wine sauce with new potatoes and asparagus – and Wesley felt a warm glow of wellbeing as he finished off his final mouthful. He looked across at Pam and saw that she was staring at her empty plate, deep in thought. 'Something the matter?'

She gave a deep sigh. 'My mum rang earlier. She wants to see the kids.'

'But you still don't trust her?'

She looked him in the eye. 'Do you?'

'Well . . . ' He knew he should tell her to let bygones be bygones but somehow he couldn't. Della's thoughtlessness had almost cost Pam her life and both of them knew they'd never entirely trust her with their children again. 'Maybe she'll have learned her lesson,' he said, trying to sound hopeful. But he knew his words were unconvincing.

Pam didn't answer and when he reached across the table and took her hand she smiled – but he could see sadness in her eyes.

When the doorbell rang several times, he jumped up, his heart racing. He hadn't realised he was so on edge.

'That'll be Maritia with the kids,' said Pam.

He rushed to answer the door and as his sister ushered the children inside he leaned forward and kissed her on the cheek. 'Hope they haven't been any trouble.'

'Of course they haven't.' There was a secretive smile playing on her lips and he sensed she was bursting with untold news. But she carried on chattering. 'They had a good time at Sunday School, you know.'

'They told me.'

'We're having a holiday club for the kids in the parish in a couple of weeks' time and I've put their names down.' She lowered her voice. 'I did consider asking Pam to help

135

out but then I realised it might be the last thing she needed after teaching a class full of kids all term. I don't want to put her in the position of feeling embarrassed about saying no.'

Wesley nodded, glad that his sister was sensitive enough to realise that the last thing Pam needed was undertaking something akin to teaching during her precious summer break. 'You look well,' he said. Even with her dual roles as GP and vicar's wife, Maritia always seemed to be full of energy. Sometimes Wesley wondered how she did it.

Maritia's smile broadened. 'I suppose you might as well know. You're going to be an uncle. I'm expecting a baby next March.'

Wesley took his sister in his arms, surprised at how emotional he felt as he hugged her. 'Do mum and dad know yet?'

'I rang them just before I came out. They're coming up in a couple of weeks. They're looking forward to seeing you.'

'Great,' said Wesley. He saw precious little of his parents: his mother was a busy GP like her daughter and his father an eminent cardiac surgeon, so a visit to their children and grandchildren was a rare and precious treat. But he knew that if he was still involved in the investigation when they arrived, he might have to disappoint them.

The children were tired and when Amelia began to whinge, Wesley got them to go upstairs to change into their pyjamas by counting to ten and frowning like a stern paterfamilias; it wasn't a role he liked but there were times when it was necessary, and this was one of them. Maritia made for the living room to share her news with Pam and while they indulged in excited talk about the coming baby,

Wesley, feeling rather excluded, took refuge in the kitchen and put the kettle on: with Maritia pregnant and driving, a celebratory wine was probably out of the question.

When he returned to the living room he found that the conversation had moved on to murder and he wondered if he might not have preferred the baby talk.

'How's your investigation going?' Maritia asked, leaning forward as though she had some special interest in the case.

'Which one? I've got two on the go.'

'Those kids near Queenswear. Mark mentioned it last night. One of his parishioners gave him a book on local history – you know how he's interested in that sort of thing.'

'What's the connection?' His instincts told him that what Maritia was about to say might be important.

'There was a chapter about Catton Hall. One of the old squires who lived there in the early nineteenth century used to hunt naked youths on horseback, sometimes to the death. And according to legend, a ghostly pack of hounds can still be heard baying for blood around Catton Hall whenever there's a full moon. His tomb in Queenswear churchyard has an iron cage around it, allegedly to stop his spirit escaping.'

'You're not saying my murder victims were done to death by a pack of spectral hounds?' said Wesley with a smile. 'Unless the pooches were armed with shotguns, it's highly unlikely.'

Maritia tilted her head to one side. 'Your victims were found naked, weren't they?'

'Yes.'

'What if someone knows about this squire and decided to revive the tradition of his manhunts? Perhaps that's why the victims were naked.'

Wesley took a sip of tea. Over the years his sister had displayed an irritating habit of being right about a lot of things. But nobody can be right all the time.

Waiting. A murder investigation always involved waiting. For forensic reports; for vital witnesses to turn up; for all the information gleaned from house-to-house visits, and interviews to be collated into some sort of comprehensible order.

Once Maritia had returned to the vicarage, Wesley had done his paternal duty and read the children a bedtime story. Getting home at a reasonable time was a rare treat during a murder investigation but there'd been nothing more he could have done at the incident room that night. He had spent all day sowing the seed and now he was waiting to harvest the results.

It was coming up to eleven now and he was sitting on the sofa with his feet up, sipping from a glass of Chilean Cabernet Sauvignon. Pam sat in the armchair, watching the TV and when he saw that her glass was empty he got up and refilled it, disturbing the kitten who had planted herself determinedly on his knee. Moriarty, who a few months before had been a small, giddy ball of fur and energy, had now expanded into a sleek and elegant cat. And for some reason she always seemed to favour Wesley's knee over Pam's. Pam reckoned that she was probably one for the men.

Pam took a sip from her newly filled glass and closed her eyes, a beatific smile on her lips. But her peace was shattered when Wesley's phone rang.

Her eyes flicked open and she sat up as he answered it, mouthing the word 'Gerry' to Pam who rolled her eyes and sank back against the cushions. After a short conversation he ended the call.

'Sorry, love, there's been another shooting. I've only had one glass so I'm OK to drive.' He kissed her cheek and she turned away. 'Don't wait up.'

He picked up his car keys from the cupboard by the door and walked out into the summer night.

Chapter 18

The Jester's Journal

14 June 1815

Another hunt is arranged and I must recruit a pair of fine hares to provide entertainment for our gallant huntsmen. Two youths have recently begun work in the Squire's gardens and I plan to engage them in talk of money and adventure. Those two things I am certain will prove sufficient bait to lure them into my trap.

How the steward moons after the Lady Pegassa. It is better than a play to watch him making cow eyes at her. Henry has sworn that one day soon he will pluck our exotic flower and make her his concubine. Some think him a foolish and profligate young man but others, like our sober steward, consider him to be the embodiment of evil. On this matter Wells and I are in agreement: to my mind is nothing foolish about the Devil. Satan always knows what he is about and uses his poor dupes on earth with such great cunning, so that when they are committing wicked actions they imagine they act from their own free will rather than out of compulsion. I understand Satan, for I have used such tactics myself.

15 June 1815

I have uttered honeyed words to our pair of young gardeners and have tempted them from their Eden to play the quarry in our hunt tomorrow night. Henry anticipates the event like an excited child and asks me, as he always does, why we cannot have a female hare. I say, as always, that one day I will arrange it. He must be patient, for such things cannot be planned in haste.

Chapter 19

An emergency call had brought a patrol car to the spot where the young man lay, his face blasted away by lead shot. The fatal incident – for that is what it was called in the official reports to base – had occurred in a patch of woodland near the village of Whitely, three miles inland from Tradmouth.

The caller had refused to give his name but he'd spoken between sobs like a man in torment. His exact words were 'A lad's been shot in the woods near Parr's Farm. You'd better get there quick. I think he might be dead. Oh dear God . . . ' Then he'd said no more and the line had gone dead.

Wesley met Gerry at the edge of the woods where the patrol officers were waiting for them. When Wesley had first worked in the Devon countryside, after several years at the Met, he'd been struck by the impenetrable quality of the darkness. But once he flicked on his torch, everything became clearer. Colin Bowman and the crime scene team had already arrived and the two detectives followed the officers into the trees, making for the distant patch of brilliance where the floodlights had been set up.

In a clearing, brightly lit like a stage set, the corpse was lying on his back, fully clothed in jeans and sleeveless T-shirt. If his face hadn't been a bloody mass of gore, he would have looked as though he were asleep.

Colin was bending over the body and he looked up as they approached. 'He was shot from about six feet away, similar to the pair over near Catton Hall. But this time most of the shot ended up in his face, poor lad.'

'Any ID?' Gerry asked.

One of the constables produced a plastic bag with a small card inside. 'Membership of a snooker club in Morbay. He had his phone on him too.'

Wesley took the card from the man and read the name printed on it. 'Jimmy Yates. Do we know anything about him?'

'Yes, sir. He's known to us. Petty stuff. Possession of Class B drugs, shoplifting, burglary, criminal damage. He's only eighteen. Someone's gone to break the news to his mum. She's known to us and all. A few convictions for soliciting when she was younger, but nothing for the past five years.'

Wesley's eyes were drawn to the boy on the ground. He appeared younger than his eighteen years but that was probably because he was small, around five foot six, and thin. The poor lad had hardly had a good start in life – or a good finish.

'Has anyone spoken to the people in those cottages we passed down the lane?' Gerry asked.

'Yes, sir,' said the oldest patrol officer. 'One of the house-holders said he heard some shooting around 10.20 p.m. – he was certain of that because he checked the time. About five minutes later he heard the sound of a car engine. Then he heard another vehicle, and when he looked out of the window he saw a Land Rover shoot past, heading towards the village. He said it had one of those spotlights on the back. He reckons it was poachers or kids messing about shooting things. Lamping, he said. There's a lot of it about and summer evenings bring them all out for a bit of sport.'

Gerry thanked him and returned to Wesley's side. 'The shots were heard shortly before the emergency call came in.'

'Do you think this might be linked to the Catton Hall murders?'

'Do you?'

Wesley stared at the dead boy. 'The victims were the same age but that's about all they seem to have in common. This one was reported as an accident and no attempt has been made to hide his identity.'

His sister's talk about the naked manhunts at Catton Hall all those years ago suddenly leapt into his mind. But surely wicked squires and ghostly hounds were dreamed up to entertain the tourists? For a moment he wondered whether to mention it but he dismissed the idea and looked at his watch.

'Let's go home and get some sleep,' said Gerry. 'Briefing first thing tomorrow. Seven o'clock.'

It is often said that tomorrow never comes, but it came all too quickly for Wesley.

When he'd got home the previous night he'd needed to

144

unwind after encountering Jimmy Yates's pathetic corpse so he'd finished the bottle of wine. By the time he'd got to sleep it was almost one o'clock and when the alarm went off at six the next morning he fought a strong temptation to turn over and go back to sleep, or to snuggle against Pam's sleeping body and blot out the world for another couple of hours. But as he left the house and walked down the hill into the heart of Tradmouth, the fresh air on his face woke up his sleepy brain like a strong helping of caffeine, and when he arrived at the incident room he felt alert and ready to begin another day.

Gerry called the troops to attention at five past seven, armed with a selection of photographs of Jimmy Yates, dead and alive, which he pinned up on the notice board alongside the other crime scene pictures.

'James Yates, aged eighteen, commonly known as Jimmy. Address on the Winterham estate on the outskirts of Morbay. Record of fairly minor offences and the proud possessor of one of the first ASBOs in the Morbay area. No father to speak of; mother has form for prostitution. Question is, what was he doing lying in a wood with half his face shot away?'

Trish put up her hand. 'I've been thinking, sir. There's a lot of poaching about. And lamping. Doesn't Parr's Farm belong to that rock star?'

Rachel swivelled round in her chair. 'Yes. He's taken to organic farming and become a pillar of the community in his old age.'

'From drugs and rock and roll to the Parochial church council in one easy step,' said Gerry.

Rachel pressed her lips together. They were getting side-tracked. 'I do remember reading that he has a herd of deer.'

Wesley caught on fast. 'You mean Jimmy was poaching?'

'It's possible. But it's more likely he was out lamping,' she said. Being a farmer's daughter, she was the fount of all knowledge on rural matters. 'They use lamps to dazzle the animal, then the poor thing's an easy target. A lad like Jimmy would probably think nothing of shooting some unsuspecting fox or rabbit like that but serious poaching's usually done on an industrial scale these days; they even bring refrigerated lorries along to take the carcasses away and gamekeepers have been threatened. Just ask any wildlife officer.'

Wesley saw the earnest determination in her eyes. 'I know,' he said. 'It's a growing problem.'

'Then why isn't more being done about it?'

Wesley had no answer for that so he returned to the immediate problem. 'We know Jimmy wasn't out alone because someone made the call. The phone's being traced, and the location the call was made from.'

'That fits with the lamping theory,' said Rachel. 'He will have been with mates. All they'd need is an old Land Rover with a spotlight fixed to the back. There were no dead animals near the scene so they'd probably only just begun their evening when it happened.'

'Could he have been shot by accident?' Wesley asked, hoping it was a possibility. With everything they had to deal with, the last thing he wanted was another murder on his hands.

'Perhaps. Or maybe there was a falling out.'

'We need to find out whether there's any link between Sophie and Barney and Jimmy Yates,' said Gerry who had been listening with interest.

'Surely not.' It was Paul who spoke. He sounded a little

defensive, as though he was unwilling to acknowledge that his dead cousin might have been tainted by any connection with Jimmy Yates's shady world.

'There are similarities, so we've got to check, Paul,' said Wesley gently.

Paul looked away.

'We've got Tom from scientific support going through the kids' computers,' said Gerry. 'Maybe he should have a look at Jimmy's while he's at it. The lad's bound to have one that fell off the back of some lorry or other. Anything else?'

Wesley spoke. 'We need to talk to Richard Catton. He hasn't called me back so I'm wondering if he's trying to avoid us for some reason.'

Gerry pulled himself up to his full height. 'Right, we'll corner him today. And all that woodland up at Catton Hall needs to be searched.'

'Is anyone still trying Tessa Trencham's number?' Wesley asked.

Rachel raised her hand. 'I've left about a dozen messages on her voicemail but no luck yet.'

'Keep trying,' Wesley said as he looked out of the window. It was a beautiful morning. Outside he could see the ripples on the surface of the river glinting like jewels in the sun. Another visit to Catton Hall would break up the day nicely.

There was always a chance that one or more of Barney and Sophie's former classmates at Corley Grange would be able to throw light on some secret area of their lives that they hadn't been willing to share with parents or teachers.

Trish had already interviewed seven of them and she was growing a little tired of being told how 'great' and 'amazing' the dead pair were. The concept of never speaking ill of the dead had clearly filtered down through the generations. Or maybe it was something innate in all human beings. Maybe it was a primeval fear that if you angered the dead they could return and do you harm.

A few of the kids mentioned that Dunstan Price was part of the group Sophie and Barney used to hang around with and therefore Trish decided to leave him till last.

His address was Bidwell Farm and it was situated between the village of Belsham and the outskirts of Morbay where the grey industrial units of the business park nibbled away at the open countryside. It wasn't a million miles from the Winterham Estate but, driving up the muddy track away from the main road, you'd never have known.

When she drove through the gates she was surprised to discover that this was very much a working establishment. Some of the other Corley Grange students she'd interviewed had lived at addresses which had 'farm' in the title, but these had turned out to be immaculate farmhouses, improved and extended beyond recognition, with maybe a few acres attached to accommodate a paddock and spotless stables for a few pampered horses. Their owners had been incomers, mostly from London, who had come to Devon in pursuit of the rural idyll. But Dunstan's place was different. A battered Land Rover stood beside an old Nissan. No top of the range cars here. Here there was real muck, real smells, rusty farm machinery and piles of tyres. The genuine countryside experience.

She parked her car and picked her way over the muddy cobbles to the front door. The farmhouse windows hadn't been cleaned in a while; the frames looked as if they could do with a coat of paint, and Trish found herself wondering how this place went down with Dunstan's school friends. Or perhaps he didn't bring them here. Shame about lack of material possessions can be a powerful emotion at that age.

It was a while before the door was opened by a thin young man with dark, wavy hair, worn just long enough to cover his ears. He was dressed like many of his age in what looked like surfing gear – long shorts and a washed out T-shirt – and as soon as she introduced herself, he stood aside to let her in.

'Please come through,' he said like a young actor trying out the role of butler. She sensed he was nervous. But talking to the police was uncharted territory for most law-abiding kids of that age.

'I need to ask you about your friends, Barney and Sophie,' she said as she sat down on a large, shabby sofa.

'Yeah. It's terrible what happened.' He stopped suddenly and looked away. 'I've been meaning to get in touch with the police but I didn't know ... '

'What is it?' Dunstan was looking worried and she held her breath, waiting for him to continue.

'I was with them last Thursday night ... isn't that when they ... '

Trish sat forward. She'd been expecting the usual pieties but now it looked as if she'd struck gold. 'Go on.'

'We play this game online. Blood Hunt it's called. Then a couple of months ago one of my mates Marcus met a guy who was looking for someone to play it for real.'

'What's this person's name?'

'I just knew him as the Game Master.'

'Tell me about Thursday night.'

'Game Master texted and said they were organising a game up at Catton Hall Holiday Park so I went along.'

'Just you?'

'No. He said there were a couple of first-timers going too. Turned out it was Barney and Sophie. He'd tried the others but they couldn't make it.'

'Which others?'

He thought for a moment. 'Jodie and Marcus.'

'So Jodie and Marcus knew what was going on. They knew where you'd be?'

'Suppose so.'

'Most of your school friends have been interviewed and nobody mentioned anything about this game.'

Dunstan shrugged. 'Maybe they thought it wasn't important.' He didn't sound very convincing.

'Let's get back to last Thursday night.'

'OK. I met up with Barney and Sophie and Game Master was there with this other bloke. Game Master was in charge and the other guy was just there watching.'

'Have you met the other man before?'

'A couple of times.'

'Tell me what happened.'

'We were told to go into the woods, and because it was Barney and Sophie's first time the Game Master gave them all the spiel about how we'd be hunted by people with bloodhounds but it was nothing to worry about 'cause the dogs were friendly. We got paid a hundred quid each and I told them it'd be easy money.' He stopped and looked away.

'But it wasn't?' She had the feeling that the story was about to turn nasty.

'All these cars started arriving – some had trailers with quad bikes on – and we were told to go into one of the chalets and get changed. We could keep our trainers on but we had to take all our clothes off.'

150

'So you did as you were told?'

'A hundred quid's a lot of cash for a couple of hours' work. It didn't bother me 'cause I'd done it before.'

'But it bothered the others?'

'We went into the chalet and me and Barney went into one room and Sophie went into another. She didn't look happy about it but Barney kept saying it was cool. "Nothing to worry about," he said. She had a nice body and it was nothing to be ashamed of,' he added wistfully.

'What happened next?'

'The blokes were waiting outside the chalet. They had a quad bike and they took us up to the woods. They said we'd have a twenty-minute start and we were told to split up. There were meant to be three targets, you see. I thought I'd try and double back towards the chalets and I saw Barney and Sophie go off in the other direction together. I could tell she was scared so I don't suppose he wanted to leave her. I said they'd get into trouble about it but Barney took no notice. Then I went off.'

'Were you caught?'

'Eventually. It was a big bloke on a quad bike and he said something like "bang, bang, you're dead". The dog knocked me down on the ground and started licking me. He smelled at bit and slobbered all over me but, I love dogs and, like I said, I've done it before so I knew what to expect. Anyway, the bloke who caught me gave me a ride back to base on the quad bike and I went back to the chalet to put my clothes back on. Then I collected my hundred quid from the Game Master.'

'Were Barney's and Sophie's clothes still there in the chalet when you got back?'

'Yeah. I waited for them for a bit but when they didn't

151

turn up, I got fed up and drove home. I'd borrowed my dad's Land Rover to get there.'

'Did you hear any shots?'

'Yeah, but I didn't take much notice. You hear shots all the time out in the country.'

'And you can't remember what time you heard these shots?'

He shook his head. 'I wasn't taking much notice. I was too busy trying not to get caught.'

'I'll need you to describe the people who organised the hunt.'

'The Game Master's a big bloke with cropped hair . . . fair. He wore a checked shirt.'

'Local accent?'

'He sounded quite posh.'

'What about the other man?'

'He didn't say much. And he didn't look too happy.'

'Description?'

'Average height. Ginger hair and freckles.' He thought for a moment. 'I think the Game Master called him Rich.'

'Did you see anybody with a firearm?'

Another shake of the head, more vigorous this time.

'What do you think happened, Dunstan?'

'I don't know. Maybe they were hiding in the trees and someone out shooting mistook them for animals.'

'But you said the people hunting you weren't armed?'

'They weren't, but there might have been other people about – out after vermin or – I don't know.'

The lad looked as if he was on the verge of tears.

'You're going to have to give us a proper statement, Dunstan. And my boss might want to speak to you. Is there anything else you can remember? Anything at all?'

'I've told you everything. I wish I knew what happened to them but I don't and all I keep thinking about is it could have been me. If whoever killed them had found me before that bloke on the quad bike did . . . '

When the tears began to stream down his face, Trish put a comforting hand on his bare arm, feeling an almost maternal urge to comfort him, which quite surprised her.

Wesley felt frustrated as he set out for Catton Hall to discover more about Dunstan Price's allegations. Until Keith Marsh regained consciousness, or Tessa Trencham got in touch, that particular inquiry had hit a dead end. But the mystery woman in Morbay was preying on his mind, just like the deaths of Barney and Sophie.

Gerry was in the passenger seat and, after a long wait for the car ferry, they eventually arrived at the entrance to Catton Hall Holiday Park. A sad place, Wesley thought, like a run-down seaside pier. All that fun; all those holiday memories turned to weeds and rotting wood. Catton Hall was also the home of Richard Catton, the man who'd neglected to call him as requested. Perhaps he'd forgotten; or perhaps he had a more sinister reason for avoiding the police. Dunstan Price had told Trish about a 'Rich' who was the Game Master's right-hand man. Richard Catton fitted the bill perfectly.

He parked on an area of grass just inside the gates and walked slowly down the drive. They carried on past the trees until they reached the field where Neil and his team were working away in a long trench. The artists were still there watching the scene with earnest faces, almost as though they hadn't moved since Wesley had seen them last, frozen in time and concentration. As the two policemen walked towards the trench, the artists didn't appear to notice, absorbed as they were in their own small world, unlike the archaeologists who all raised their heads to watch the newcomers. Neil gave a cheerful wave as Wesley made his way over the field and called out a greeting.

'How's it going?'

Neil nodded towards the artists and lowered his voice. 'This set-up gives me the creeps, it really does. Dave's gone back to the fort and I can't say I blame him.'

'Are you down to the picnic level yet?'

'We're nearly there but Orford won't let us take any short cuts. He wants the whole excavation experience.' He rolled his eyes.

'We could take part if you like,' said Gerry who had walked over to stand beside Wesley. 'I could take off my clothes and strike an artistic pose in your trench.'

'I think that'd be a step too far even for Orford,' Neil said with a smirk.

'We're on our way to Catton Hall to have a word with Richard Catton,' said Wesley.

'He rang you then?'

'Not yet. And we need a word.'

Neil suddenly frowned as though there was something on his mind. 'Er ... this might be nothing but I saw Richard with a carrier bag full of clothes. He said they belonged to some backpackers who'd been staying in one of the old chalets but ... Those kids were found naked, weren't they?'

'One of their mates told us they got changed in a chalet,' said Wesley.

Neil raised his eyebrows. 'I think Richard dropped a piece of underwear. It's still there if you want to have a look.' He began to climb out of the trench. 'If Orford says anything, I'll tell him I'm helping the police with their inquiries.'

He led the way across the field to the disintegrating wire fence, erected to keep stray balls and wandering children out of the Cattons' private estate. They stepped through a broken-down section into that other, neglected world.

When they reached the chalet in question, Neil took a furtive look around before giving the door a violent push. It flew open and Neil hesitated for a moment before stepping inside.

'It's in there,' he said, opening one of the doors at the back and stepping aside to give the two policeman a better view.

Wesley stepped into the room and squatted down. The bra lay on the dusty floor, lacy, pink and fairly new. He took a pen from his pocket, picked it up and dropped it into a plastic evidence bag. 'If it's Sophie's we'll know for sure where they got undressed. And if it is hers, it looks as though Catton's been trying to get rid of the evidence.'

Gerry's phone rang and he fumbled to answer it. Wesley and Neil watched, listening to the brief, one-sided conversation and trying to work out whether the news that had just been imparted was good or bad.

Eventually Gerry ended the call. 'Our search team's found bloodstains in the woods and some shot embedded in a tree trunk, but there's no sign of any empty cartridges so the murderer must have taken them with him. Very inconsiderate. We could have done with some nice finger-prints.'

Neil looked at his watch. 'I'd better get back before Orford starts complaining,' he said. 'And, boy, does he complain if things aren't done exactly as he wants them.'

The three men stepped outside the chalet, closing the door behind them and Neil hurried off, back to his trench and his strict taskmaster.

'We need to see Catton. We'll try the hall first.'

'If he has something to hide he won't have gone far. He'll be like a nervous hen, wondering when someone's going to uncover his little secret.'

Wesley knew Gerry was probably right. They made their way back past the chalets and through the gap in the fence, skirted the edge of the field where the strange dig was taking place, and walked along the potholed driveway to Catton Hall.

This time their luck was in. Catton himself answered the door and Wesley held up his ID. 'I left a message for you to call me, Mr Catton.'

The man looked nervous. 'I've been meaning to but ... er, I've been busy.'

'Well, we're here now,' said Gerry with a grim smile. 'Can we come in?'

'Nice house,' Wesley said as they were led into the hall.

Catton turned. 'The bloody roof leaks. And it's Grade Two listed so I can't touch the place without being watched by an army of conservation officers,' he said with a hint of bitterness.

'It belongs to your father?'

'Yes.'

'Is he in?'

'He's having one of his bad days. He's upstairs in bed.'

'Sorry to hear that. I believe you only moved back here recently.'

'Someone needs to take charge of the place.'

'Your family owns the holiday park?'

'The freehold yes. The company who used to run it didn't want to renew the lease so I'm going to knock the chalets down and replace them with something more up to date. People want a bit of luxury nowadays. They won't put up with "cheap and cheerful". I've got a mate in marketing who thinks it's a winning idea so ... It should keep this place afloat anyway,' he said looking round. 'And perhaps I'll open the house to the public, once I've had a chance to make it look decent.'

'I hear you've been letting some of the chalets out to backpackers.'

Suddenly the man's eyes flickered towards the door, as though he was searching for an escape route. 'Yeah. I can't charge them much but at least something's coming in.'

'What about the artists in your field?'

'Kevin Orford's high profile so the publicity he generates can't do the place any harm. And he's paying handsomely, although I can't quite work out why.'

Catton led them into a library with a low-beamed ceiling and shelves packed with ancient, leather-bound volumes around all four walls, punctuated only by a huge stone fireplace carved with a coat of arms. It smelled of musty books, and close to the fireplace a pair of threadbare brown velvet sofas stood on a fraying rug of indeterminate pattern. A massive oak desk in the corner stood laden with files, papers and old books, as though someone had been working there and had just stepped out for a moment.

'This is one of the few decent rooms, I'm afraid. My father's let the place go. Lack of funds.'

Wesley caught Gerry's eyes as he sat down and the DCI gave him a small nod. It was up to him to do the talking.

'We had a look inside one of your chalets.'

'Did you have a warrant?' It was hard to tell whether Catton was joking.

'We can get one if you like,' Gerry growled. 'In view of the two murders that occurred on this property—'

'Those bodies weren't found on this estate. That coastline belongs to the National Trust.' Catton was sounding worried now.

'Oh, didn't I say? Our search team's found the place where the two youngsters were killed ... and they died on this estate.'

Wesley saw fear in Catton's eyes as he sat there frozen, lost for words. 'You were seen coming out of one of the chalets with a bag full of clothes.' He took the evidence bag containing the bra from his pocket. 'I think you dropped this.'

Catton stared at him for a few seconds. Then he spoke. 'I was checking the chalet out and I found some clothes in one of the bedrooms. The last people who stayed there must have left them.'

'Where are these clothes now?'

Catton swallowed hard. 'I burned them ... in the garden.'

'Bit drastic. They might have come back for them. There was a hunt on your land on Thursday night.'

'Hunting's illegal,' Catton said quickly.

'I'm not talking about hunting foxes. I'm talking about hunting human beings.'

There was no mistaking the flash of alarm on Catton's face, there for a moment, then swiftly hidden.

'I understand quad bikes were used. And bloodhounds.'

There was a long silence; the silence of a man who knows he's cornered and who's trying desperately to think up a way out.

'What is it about these hunts that you don't want to become common knowledge? What goes on?'

There was a long silence. Gerry was about to speak but Wesley caught his eye and shook his head. In his experience if there was a silence, people could never resist the temptation to fill it.

Eventually Catton bowed his head as though he was ashamed of what he was about to say.

'The hares run naked.'

'Hares?'

'Kids who act as the quarry.'

'I take it they get paid for being chased round naked in the dark?'

Catton swallowed. 'A hundred quid a time.'

'Nice little earner for your average teenager then. Have any of them ever been injured . . . or harmed in any way?'

Catton shook his head vigorously. 'Absolutely not.'

'Until two of them ended up dead at the foot of a cliff,' said Wesley quietly.

'That was nothing to do with the hunt. They were shot and we never use guns. The dogs trail them, then the hunter puts his tag on them and gets the collar they wear as a trophy.'

Wesley looked at Gerry. 'Collar and tag? Explain that to us.'

'The hares are naked apart from a leather collar – like a dog collar. The huntsmen remove the collars and keep them as trophies.'

'And the tag?'

Catton blushed. 'The winner writes his initials on the hare's backside with a felt-tip pen. It's another proof of victory.'

159

Wesley said nothing for a while. He couldn't help visualising the type of person who would get a kick out of hunting a naked adolescent and subjecting him or her to the humiliation of putting his mark on their backside. Perhaps he was old-fashioned – Pam often told him he was – but the thought of Sophie submitting herself to this treatment made him uncomfortable.

'So how many hares were caught on the night of the murders?'

'Just the one. Dun, I think his name was.'

'And three set out?'

'Two weren't caught.'

'So why weren't they wearing these leather collars when they were found?'

'Maybe whoever killed them took them off? I don't know.'

'We were told they were allowed to keep their trainers on.'

'I don't know anything about that.'

Wesley could see beads of sweat forming on Catton's forehead.

'What did you think had happened to the kids?'

'I thought they'd got away.'

'Without claiming their hundred quid apiece?' Gerry asked.

'I thought they'd had second thoughts. I thought they must have doubled back and gone home.'

'Naked?'

Catton looked away.

'Those clothes you burned belonged the dead kids, didn't they? We've got the bra so we can match the DNA on it with the dead girl's.'

Richard bowed his head. 'OK. I found their clothes in the chalet and when I heard they were dead I panicked and thought I'd better get rid of them. It was a stupid thing to do. I realise that now.'

'Yes,' Gerry growled. 'It was stupid. You could face charges for tampering with evidence; perverting the course of justice.'

'I panicked.'

'They had other things with them, I believe,' said Wesley. 'Rucksacks and mobile phones?'

'I burned the rucksacks in the garden incinerator when I got rid of the clothes and I chucked the phones into the sea. I just wanted to get rid of everything.'

Wesley sensed he was telling the truth. But they needed to know more. 'How did the murdered kids get here? Did they come in a car?'

'I don't know. There were no cars there after everyone had left so . . . '

'Who's the Game Master?'

He hesitated. 'His name's Carl Heckerty. The hunts were his idea. He owns a paintball centre near Dukesbridge, and he's wanted to organise them ever since he learned that one of my ancestors used to have them here a couple of hundred years ago. He got in contact with one of the local hunts who lent us some bloodhounds, so that was no problem, and someone he knew provided the quad bikes. He thought it was a great idea. There's no harm in it. It's not illegal.'

'But murder is, Mr Catton,' said Wesley. 'I need you to come with us to Tradmouth Police Station. Do feel free to bring along your solicitor. We want to do everything by the book.'

Wesley saw a look of sheer terror in Richard Catton's

161

eyes. But somehow he couldn't conjure up much sympathy for the man.

When one of the PhD students began to uncover what appeared to be a wine bottle, Orford and his companions moved their seats closer to the action. But their expressions remained impassive, as if they were trying hard not to display any interest or excitement.

Neil knew that some of his colleagues were uncomfortable about the constant scrutiny, but when he caught their eye he winked and mouthed the word 'money' – it seemed to work wonders.

It made it worse that the deadpan watchers never spoke or communicated with them. They seemed to be taking it all so seriously, and it was only Kevin Orford who showed anything approaching emotion. He seemed nervous, on edge, and when his PR man appeared – which he did most days – Neil could sense his anxiety, as though he was discussing a matter of life and death.

Neil adjusted his kneeling mat and started to scrape away at the earth, relieved that they appeared to have hit the picnic level. He had just found the edge of what looked like a white china plate, filthy with caked soil but otherwise intact, when he heard a voice.

'What's this?'

He turned his head and saw one of the students sitting back on his heels, poking at something with his trowel.

'Not sure what it is yet. Looks like plastic – remnants of a rubbish bag maybe.'

The student had been speaking in a low voice but the operator of the video camera must have heard because he had moved along the trench, edging towards them.

The student continued what he was doing, trying to ignore the prying lens. He scraped the earth away carefully from the brittle, shredded plastic. Then he suddenly stopped, his hand froze in mid-air, and called Neil over in an urgent whisper.

'Have a look at this,' he said quietly, shifting his body round to hide his discovery from the camera.

Neil straightened himself up and picked his way carefully across the trench, trying to look casual. He crouched next to the student and scraped away some soil.

'I see what you mean,' he whispered after a few moments. 'That looks like bone.'

'Maybe they had a big joint of meat,' the student suggested hopefully.

'It looks to me like the top of a skull.'

The student swore under his breath. 'Could it be a boar's head or something? They might have had some sort of medieval banquet.'

Neil removed some more soil. The camera had now reached the other side of the trench so their discovery was no longer hidden.

And as Neil and his colleague scraped the soil away carefully from the grinning human skull, their every move was recorded for posterity.

Chapter 20

The Steward's Journal

17 June 1815

I fear the Squire and Henry Catton are arranging another entertainment. For two days now they have been huddled together with John Tandy, laughing and whispering. In my presence they are silent, but I have ears to hear by doors.

I was outside the stables yesterday when I saw Tandy with two lads who work in the garden here. They were listening to his words most attentively and I watched as he handed them some coins.

I spoke to the Head Gardener and told him of my fears. He too is of the Methodist persuasion and he spoke to the lads most firmly, but this was to no avail for they denied any dealings with Tandy. I feel there is nothing more I can do but pray for their safety.

This morning I saw a man in the garden, but I did not recognise him as a worker on the estate. When I approached him to ask his business he told me some tale about looking for his sister. I told him that no new maid-servant had come to work at the house and that he must seek his sister elsewhere. He said he would do so and fled into the trees. Perhaps he is a thief. Or someone connected to Henry Catton, which I think more likely, for he has all manner of undesirable acquaintances.

Today the Squire received an invitation from Lord Townstall to bring the Lady Pegassa to a soirée at his grand house in Tradmouth. Perhaps if she were to go into society she would be safer. I am concerned about the way she is kept here like some wild and exotic pet.

I feel it my duty, humble though I am, to be that lady's protector, for in a strange country she will be innocent in certain matters. I have seen the way Henry looks at her – with lust in his eyes – so it might be as well that I should seek out another home for her with ladies who would ensure that she comes to no harm.

Chapter 21

'I'm calling the police in.'

Kevin Orford stared at Neil as though he'd just uttered an obscenity. 'I can't allow that.'

'We've no choice. When human remains are found unexpectedly, we have to report it.'

When the bones were first unearthed, Neil had half suspected that they were part of the artwork – after all, he'd read on the Internet that one of Orford's aims was to 'shake people out of their complacency'. But the artist's shocked reaction seemed genuine enough ... unless it was all part of an elaborate charade.

Orford's colleagues, who had been watching so assiduously all day, had now made their excuses and vanished, leaving him to face the fallout alone. But the PR man remained and he was watching the proceedings with interest.

'It will destroy the whole artwork.' Orford sounded peevish, like a child refused an expected treat.

'Oh I don't know,' said the PR man who was standing there, arms folded. 'It might get us more press attention. How did the skeleton get in there? Who could it be? The story could run and run.'

'You're sure it isn't someone who ate the picnic?' one of the students chipped in. 'Nasty case of food poisoning?'

As Orford gave him a withering look, Neil took out his phone and selected Wesley's number. When he'd made the call he turned to the artist.

'We've only just reached the level of the picnic, so it looks like the skeleton was placed on top.' He looked at Orford accusingly. 'I take it you were here when that trench was filled in?'

Orford shot a desperate glance at the PR man. 'Yes, but I don't know anything about it. This whole thing's a nightmare,' he shouted before striding away.

Carl Heckerty had already come to their attention because he'd provided Tessa Trencham with a reference for her rented house. But now they knew he'd sent the two teenagers off into the woods, naked and vulnerable, to their deaths, so he'd just shot to the top of the list of people they wanted to speak to.

Wesley parked the car in front of the paintball centre when his phone rang. He was aware of Gerry watching him, probably hoping it was good news, and when he looked at the caller display, and saw that the call was from Neil, he was almost tempted to let his friend leave a message. But as Neil was working near Catton Hall, there was a chance he might have something relevant to report, so he held the phone to his ear and said 'hello'.

'We've found a skeleton in our trench.' Neil had always believed in coming straight to the point.

'The picnic? Can you tell if it's recent or—'

'It was wrapped in a black bin bag and placed just above the picnic so it must have been buried sixteen years ago or later.'

Wesley sat there for a few moments. He could see the hopeful look on Gerry's face and he wondered how he was going to break the news. They had enough to deal with at that moment without this new development. 'Orford must have been there when the trench was filled in. What does he say?'

'He threw a hissy fit when I told him the police had to be notified and I've not seen him since.'

'Did he seem surprised when it was found?'

'Yes, I'd say so. However, I could be wrong. He's been really jumpy since we started – like something's on his mind – but he might always be like that, for all I know. I can't see him going to all this trouble to reopen the trench if he knew it was there, can you? It wouldn't make sense. Unless it's all part of his artwork.'

'Is that likely?'

'I wouldn't rule it out.'

'Is the skeleton male or female?'

'Definitely male. Are you coming over?'

'Yes, but there's something I have to do first.'

'OK. We've stopped digging and sealed off the trench.'

'Let me know when Orford shows up again, won't you. I'll need to talk to him.'

'What's up?' Gerry's voice made him jump.

'Neil's found a skeleton in that trench he's digging at Catton Hall. He's sealed off the area so I'll get a crime scene team over and give Colin a call too.'

Gerry looked as though he didn't know whether to laugh or curse. 'That's all we need.'

As soon as they emerged from the car, they heard a volley of shots and loud whoops of triumph coming from the building.

'That must be the paintballers. Rachel said there was a big area out at the back of the building where they did whatever it is they do. Ever tried it, Wes?'

'Not really my style.'

Gerry grinned. 'Nor mine. I used to enjoy a good game of Cowboys and Indians when I was a nipper, but I grew out of all that as soon as I discovered girls.'

Gerry began to make for the entrance and Wesley followed.

They found Carl Heckerty in his office, which came as a relief as neither man fancied an encounter with a couple of paintballing teams high on adrenalin and testosterone.

Heckerty stood up as they entered, and from the worried look on his face, Wesley suspected that Richard Catton had already been in touch to warn him of their visit. But Gerry usually liked to have his suspects in a state of dread. He reckoned it helped loosen their tongues.

Heckerty's manner was casual as he invited them to sit, but the clenched fists and darting eyes betrayed his nervousness. 'Have you any news of Tessa?'

'Only that she's not the dead woman.'

Heckerty put his hand to his chest. 'That's a relief. Do you know who—?'

'Not yet. We haven't come about Ms Trencham. We've been speaking to Richard Catton. He tells us you've been organising hunts of his land.'

'Only instead of foxes you use kids,' Gerry chipped in. 'Naked apart from a pair of trainers and a leather collar.'

'It's not illegal and nobody comes to any harm. It's just

something a bit different, that's all. Since the ban some hunts have started using human quarry – hunting the clean boot, it's called – so I decided to add my own twist to make it a bit more exciting. I wanted something that would appeal to people like my customers here who aren't part of the hunting, shooting and fishing brigade. Something . . . in tune with nature.'

'Like chasing naked kids to their death,' Wesley said softly.

Heckerty stood up. His face had turned red. 'If those kids met up with poachers and got themselves shot that's hardly my fault . . . or Rich's. We didn't know what had happened to them. We thought they'd just chickened out and gone home.'

'Without their clothes?'

'I don't know anything about that. One lad stayed – he was caught by Bob, one of my regulars, and he picked up his pay and went home, none the worse for the experience. If you think those dead kids had anything to do with me, you're mistaken.'

'Do you organise a similar game online?'

'I might do.'

Gerry leaned forward. 'Do you? Are you the Game Master?'

'Yeah. So what.'

'And you decided to branch out and do it for real?'

'Rich gave me the idea. An ancestor of his was one of these so called "wicked squires" who seemed to be so popular in these parts. He kept a jester who used to release a couple of naked men into the woods for the squire and his mates to hunt on horseback with a pack of hounds. The jester's diary's up at the hall; that's how Rich found out. His

170

dad's writing a book about it. If the hares – that's what he called them – survived, they got paid handsomely.'

'If they survived? They were hunted to the death?'

'You can't risk that sort of thing nowadays with Health and Safety and all that. We look after our quarry. They have a cushy time.'

'How much do the hunters pay to take part?'

'Five hundred quid a time. We keep it exclusive. We like to attract local businessmen and the like . . . The last thing we want is a load of drunken louts.'

'We'll need the names and addresses of everyone who took part on Thursday night.'

Heckerty nodded meekly. 'I'll get them for you.'

'How did you feel about Sophie taking part?'

'She was up for it. And it gave my punters a bit of a kick, chasing a naked girl,' he added, with a smile which verged on a leer.

'She died, Mr Heckerty.'

'But it wasn't the hunt that killed her, was it. It was poachers. Rich's dad's had problems on his land before.'

'There's no record of any complaints.'

'He's never bothered reporting it. He didn't think anything like this was going to happen, did he?'

'We need to locate those collars the victims were wearing. Have we your permission to search these premises?'

'We can get a warrant if you refuse,' Gerry added, a threat in his voice.

Heckerty's bravado suddenly vanished and he looked frightened.

'Is there something you want to tell us, Mr Heckerty?'

'Look, we had nothing to do with their deaths. But one of the dogs found them in the woods and the bloke panicked.'

'Which bloke? We need a name.'

'I only knew him as Fred. He's a mate of one of my regular punters here. He was in a right state when he found them. Lying together like the babes in the wood, he said they were. He rang me on his mobile and me and Rich went straight over there on quad bikes.'

'What time was this?'

'Late. Most people had gone by then, including the other lad – Dun, I think his name is – so he knew nothing about it. I wondered why the other kids hadn't been caught.'

'What happened after you found them?' Wesley asked quietly. Heckerty was in confessional mode and he didn't want to break the spell.

'We tried to revive them, but it was obvious they were dead.' He swallowed hard. 'Fred said we should call an ambulance but I knew from the look of them that it was too late. Then Fred got really scared. He's a solicitor with a reputation to keep up and he didn't want to get involved, so I told him to go home and forget about it. I said we'd deal with everything; our punters expect us to be in control and we need to keep them happy. When he'd gone I took the collars off – it didn't seem right to ...'

'Did you find any shotgun cartridges at the scene?'

'No. Nothing like that.'

'Where are the collars now?'

He nodded in the direction of a large cupboard by the window. 'In there.'

'Were they wearing trainers?'

'Yeah. We threw them into the sea.'

'How did the bodies end up at the foot of the cliff?'

'Rich said we needed to put them somewhere where they couldn't be linked to us. What happened had nothing to do

172

with the hunt. Nobody had firearms and it wasn't our fault if the kids ran into poachers. We panicked, that's all. Rich said if we pushed the bodies off the cliff the sea would take them away and they'd be found miles away. But there's a little beach under there where the tide doesn't reach so . . . '

Gerry stood up. 'We need you to come down to the station and make a statement. And if I were you, I'd get your solicitor down there too.'

Carl Heckerty went with them, as meek as any lamb.

Exhaustion had crept up on Anne Marsh and, in spite of the loud bleeps from the various machines that were keeping her husband in the land of the living, she had fallen asleep on the chair beside his bed in the Intensive Care Unit of Morbay Hospital.

As she slept, she dreamed. She was in an undulating field, the sort she'd seen in the nearby countryside and she could see her husband, Keith, in the distance. She was trying to get to him, but he was surrounded by a pack of dogs with women's faces, barking and snarling as she approached with leaden feet.

Then something jolted her awake and she opened her eyes, blinking in the brightness of the overhead lights. Her husband was lying supine on the bed, tied down with tubes and wires like a balding, middle-aged Gulliver, and she stared at him for a few seconds in disbelief.

Keith Marsh's eyes were open and he was mouthing something that she couldn't make out. He was back. And now the questions would begin.

Chapter 22

The Jester's Journal

22 June 1815

Napoleon Bonaparte is defeated at a place called Waterloo and, after this great victory, word has it that he has been taken prisoner once more. Now Boney would have made an excellent hare, for he has proved a slippery rogue, escaping as he did from Elba and setting himself up as Emperor again in Paris.

Our hunt is arranged for tomorrow and my hares are ready. The gardener, however, has spoken to them of the matter and now they are afraid that he will judge them ill. I told them to pay the interfering man no heed, for it is the Squire who rules here, not some pious fool who digs the soil. They are to come to the stables at ten o'clock and then I will instruct them how to proceed.

Henry boasts how he has taken Mistress Howe, the

Squire's housekeeper, to his bed. He has persuaded her with honeyed words to work upon the Lady Pegassa so that she may be recruited into our games.

24 June 1815

Last night three of Henry's gaming friends took part in the evening's entertainment and they wagered much upon who would be the first to capture a hare and lead it back to the house, bound by the neck behind his steed.

At midnight we set out and all was well. However, I fear that later on matters became somewhat out of my control for Henry Catton had taken too much drink and whipped the hounds into a frenzy. The Squire had words with him about riding his horse too hard, but to no avail. He would hunt and he would have blood.

I had sent the hares off into the woods with words of encouragement, and promises that they should reap a great reward when the night was done and they ran off, vulnerable in their nakedness. For in dark garments they would have melted into the night like wild beasts.

As the riders departed I looked back at the house and saw a pale face hovering at the window like a phantom from an old tale. I recognised the Lady Pegassa by the strange headdress she habitually wears and I was glad she was taking an interest in our entertainment, for her curiosity might, in the future, entice her to join us. And yet if she learned of last night's events, I fear she would most likely flee the house.

I did not discover the lad, Robert, until this morning when I walked out to find him, as he had not come forward after the hunt to claim his money. His companion had reported to me that they had become separated and he had assumed that Robert had found his way home and would claim his reward in the morning, although his clothes still lay in the stables where the boys had changed.

I found Robert's body amongst the trees, his face a mass of congealed blood, crawling with buzzing flies. His naked body bore the marks of the whip and he had been slashed with a blade so that, in places, the white of his bones showed through the dead flesh. This had been done by no earthly hound. It looked as though Satan himself had used the lad's body for his violent pleasure. I brought him back to the stables to await the Squire's instructions, and when Henry found me his eyes shone as he gazed upon the corpse. I knew that soon more blood will be shed. And how I long to be part of the game.

Chapter 23

Gerry put his phone down and looked up at Wesley. 'Keith Marsh has regained consciousness but the quacks say it'll be a while before he's capable of answering questions. They're going to let us know as soon as he's up to it.'

Wesley suddenly felt impatient. 'Let's hope it's soon. We need to find out what he's got to say for himself.'

Gerry's phone rang again and after a brief conversation he ended the call.

'Trish has spoken to this bloke Fred and he confirms Heckerty's story.' Gerry sat back, and his executive leather chair sighed under his weight. 'It turns out Fred's a solicitor in Exeter. Specialises in criminal law. Wonder how he'll enjoy being on the receiving end. His version of the story is that he was there when the kids were found but he thought they were still alive, so he went home and left the others to deal with it. He says he thought Heckerty had called an ambulance and he swears he had nothing to do with disposing of the bodies. He said he asked Heckerty to let him know how the kids were but he never called him.'

'So he claims his hands are clean?'

'He'll know how to twist a story to make him look like a knight in shining armour rather than a toe-rag who gets his kicks out of hunting naked kids.'

'Have all the others on the list been contacted?'

'Yes, but they're all telling the same story. Nobody saw or heard anything suspicious apart from a few shots, which they put down to the usual poachers or farmers.'

'Have those collars been sent off to the lab?'

'Yes. I suppose it's too much to hope the killer's prints will be on them.'

'Far too much, Wes. Whoever did this will have shot the kids and run – not forgetting to pick up the cartridges as they went.'

Wesley began to sift through the file he'd brought into the office to show the boss. 'Trish took a statement from Dunstan Price – he's the boy who was with Barney and Sophie on the night they died. I'd like to speak to the lad myself, clarify a few things. Fancy coming?'

Gerry began to lever himself out of his seat. 'Sure. Any news on that skeleton at Neil's dig?'

'Colin's gone to have a look so we'll know more soon. I called Neil a few minutes ago and Orford's still not come back.'

'It's hard to believe he doesn't know how a body came to be lying on top of his precious picnic,' said Gerry. 'Let's go and have a word with Dunstan Price, eh.'

As they drove out to Dunstan's place, Wesley noticed that the DCI seemed to be in a remarkably good mood, considering their workload. But the lack of progress on both their cases was beginning to frustrate Wesley. And as for Neil's skeleton, that was something he could really do without.

According to Trish, Dunstan's father hadn't been home when she'd talked to the lad; he'd been off in some distant field tending to his livestock, a farmer's work – like a woman's or a police officer's – never being done. But this time Len Price was home and he greeted them at the door, telling them his son was upstairs playing on his computer.

'I couldn't believe it when he told me what he'd been up to,' Price said as he led them through to the living room of the farmhouse. 'If I'd known about these hunts I would have put a stop to it. He could have got himself killed. If that lunatic had found him—'

'Yes, Mr Price,' said Wesley. 'We just have to be thankful that he came to no harm. I expect his mother's worried too . . . ' There was no sign of a Mrs Price and Wesley didn't like to ask directly.

'Yes. She's very upset about it.'

'Is she about?'

'She's at work at the moment. Sit down, won't you.'

Wesley looked around at the shabby room. From the state of the farm, he'd been wondering how Price could afford private education and now he had the chance to satisfy his curiosity.

'What made you decide to send Dunstan to Corley Grange?' he asked, his interest not entirely confined to the case. Since Michael was almost at the age when they had to consider his future education, he was keen to glean any information he could about local secondary schools – although he suspected Corley Grange might be way beyond his and Pam's budget.

'Dun was getting in with the wrong crowd at the

179

comprehensive and his grandparents offered to pay for the school fees.' Somehow he didn't look too happy about the older generation's generosity.

'Has he been happy there?'

Price shrugged. 'It's hard to tell.'

'Is he going to university in September?'

'He's got a place at Southampton and I want him to go straight there, but all his mates are having gap years, travelling round the world, so he wants to do the same. The grandparents have stumped up the cash again. I really wish they wouldn't. The lad needs a dose of reality.'

Gerry nodded earnestly, as though he agreed with every word. But before he could say anything, the door opened and Dunstan walked in.

Wesley made the introductions and the boy studied their warrant cards carefully, as though he suspected they might be impostors.

'I've already given a statement,' he said as he sat down.

'I know but DC Walton must have told you that we'd probably need to speak to you again.' Wesley gave the boy an encouraging smile and received a solemn nod in return.

They began by going over his statement and he repeated the story, adding a few more trivial details as he went along. But Wesley had other avenues he wanted to explore. They'd heard the authorised version from their classmates at Corley Grange but now it was time they tried to find out more about Barney and Sophie. Get to know the victim and you get to know the killer: that was something that had been instilled into Wesley from the very first day he'd started in CID at the Met.

'I'd like to talk about Barney,' he said, watching the boy's face closely.

'What about him?'

'Did he have any mates who went shooting?'

Dunstan suddenly looked wary. 'A few.'

'Any who went lamping? You know what I'm talking about, don't you?'

'You can't live around here without knowing what lamping means. Some people at school did it from time to time.'

'Have you ever been lamping?' He saw Dunstan glance at his father before answering.

'I don't like guns much. I use them around the farm of course. Dad taught me to shoot, didn't you Dad? I sometimes go out after pigeons or rabbits but it's not something I particularly enjoy.'

'But Barney did?'

'Oh yeah.'

'And he went shooting with his mates? Lamping?'

Dunstan looked uncomfortable, as though he feared he was about to betray the dead boy's secrets. 'Suppose so.'

'When did you last use a gun, Dunstan?' Gerry asked.

It was the father who answered. 'I asked you to take a few shots at those bloody crows in the top field yesterday, didn't I?'

'That's right.'

'How well do you know Carl Heckerty?'

'I've played the Blood Hunt computer game, and I've done a few hunts but I wouldn't say I know him that well.'

'I believe it was Sophie and Barney's first one?'

'Yeah. But they knew what to expect; the stripping off and everything.'

Price half rose out of his seat and glowered at his son. 'You never mentioned . . .'

Dunstan rolled his eyes. 'It's no big deal, Dad.' He looked

at Wesley. 'A few of my other mates did it too. I mean a hundred quid – easy money.'

'Which mates are you talking about?'

'Jodie and a couple of others. But it was mainly Marcus. I think he did every hunt, apart from the one last week.'

'So Marcus must know Carl Heckerty quite well?'

Dunstan leaned forward. 'He first met him at a paint-balling party. I wasn't there 'cause I was ill, but when Marcus came into school he was full of it; how he'd met this cool guy who ran the place. Then the game started up –on the computer – and a few months later Carl started organising it for real.'

'What about Sophie?'

'Barney was up for it and she went along with anything he did.'

'Do you know what she thought of Carl?'

'She'd played online for a while but that night was the first time she'd met him. I think she seemed a bit scared of him, but that's just the impression I got. I can't be sure.'

Wesley sensed that Dunstan was getting bored with their questions. But he had one more thing to ask. 'You say you borrowed your dad's Land Rover to get there?'

'That's right. He did,' said Price, sounding a little defensive.

'How did Barney and Sophie get there? No car was found near the scene and neither of their families are missing a vehicle. Did you give them a lift?'

Dunstan shook his head. Then he looked up, as though he'd suddenly remembered something.

'I think Sophie said they'd got a lift from one of their mates.'

'Which mate?'

'I don't know.'

'Which of your mates knew where they'd be that night?'

Dunstan shrugged. 'Anyone could have known. It was no big secret.'

Wesley stood up and handed the boy his card. 'If you remember anything, however small, please call me.'

'He will,' Price said, taking the card from his son's fingers. 'I'll make sure of that.'

Wesley wanted to revisit Catton Hall and have a look at Neil's discovery, but his workload seemed to thwart his plans at every turn. They had to find out how Barney and Sophie got to Catton Hall that night, and the Lister Cottage case was always there in his mind, tantalising and frustrating.

At last, he managed to get away. As he was leaving the office, he passed Paul in the corridor and asked him how things were going at his aunt's place.

'Not good,' Paul replied. 'My aunt's in pieces and I can tell my Uncle Brian's on the verge of losing it.' He paused. 'It's hit my cousin Jack badly too. He won't come out of his room. I've been trying to spend some time with him but ...'

Wesley looked at his colleague's forlorn face and felt a pang of sympathy, so strong that it almost hit him like a punch in the stomach. 'The poor lad's probably in shock,' he said.

'I've left them with the family liaison officer. Thought I'd do a stint back in the incident room. I want to do something to find out what happened.'

Wesley let him go. Paul's dark-ringed eyes were fixed ahead, determined to achieve his goal. At least there'd be one more officer on the team now – and with Paul's drive to catch the culprit, he'd probably be as effective as two.

Just as he was about to set off for Catton Hall, Gerry burst out of his office, a wide smile of triumph on his face. 'I've just been speaking to Tessa Trencham. She's got our messages at last – very apologetic.'

Everybody in the incident room looked round, he had their attention.

'Have we got a name for the dead woman?' Wesley asked.

'Tessa let someone called Evie Smith house-sit while she was away, and Evie fits the description of the dead woman. She doesn't know of any jealous husband, in fact, she wasn't able to tell me that much because she kept losing the phone signal. Anyway, she's driving straight back and coming here as soon as she arrives. I had to break the news that her house has been sealed off as a crime scene. And with the body having been there so long there'll be a fair amount of work to do in that bedroom. What a homecoming, eh?'

Wesley didn't answer. Soon the Lister Cottage case would become red-hot again. And he just hoped that Neil's bones wouldn't add to their workload.

The field where Neil was working was crawling with crime scene officers, aided by archaeologists dressed in matching crime scene suits. Neil was amongst them but he was deep in concentration and he didn't look up as Wesley approached.

Colin Bowman stood on the edge of the trench, watching the activity, and he turned to greet Wesley, smiling broadly.

'Wesley. It's good to see you. We've got a bit of a puzzle here. Neil, says the skeleton was lying just above the remains of a picnic that was buried sixteen years ago. Apparently, to an archaeologist, context is everything, so he says the bones must have been buried around or just after the time of the picnic, which means that our man died sixteen years ago or possibly later.'

'You don't sound convinced.'

Colin shook his head. 'I'm not. And neither is Neil, or Dr Spender, the forensic anthropologist he called in. It had been placed in a plastic bag – the plain black sort you put your rubbish out in every week – and it has no modern dental work. To be honest, without further tests we can't confirm how old it is. Do you want to have a look?' He nodded towards a white tent. 'I'll take the bones back to the mortuary later for closer examination and the archaeologists are checking whether there's anything in the ground that might be related to the burial.'

He led Wesley towards the tent where a photographer was snapping away, taking pictures of the bones from different angles.

'The skeleton doesn't appear to be articulated and it's missing a few tiny bones from the hands and feet, the sort that often get lost in old burials. If a body had been put into the bag prior to decomposition, I would really have expected them to be there.'

'So someone might have dug up an old skeleton and reburied it here?' Wesley said as he stared down at the bones.

'That would be my guess, but of course I could be wrong.'

'What can you tell me about our skeleton?'

'According to Dr Spender, he was in his mid to late twenties, around five foot nine, and he was strong, possibly used to manual labour.' He smiled. 'Or of course he might have worked out in the gym. Neil and Dr Spender have suggested radiocarbon dating and I think that's the only way we're going to get a definitive answer.'

'That takes time.'

'Indeed it does. But it's the best option in the circumstances.'

'What about the cause of death?'

'There appears to be a rather nasty skull fracture and some broken bones, all of which were probably acquired around the time of death, but I'll know more once I've had a chance to conduct a proper examination.'

Wesley thought for a few moments. 'Is it likely that he's been dead for more than seventy years?'

Colin smiled. 'So it wouldn't be your problem?'

'You've read my mind, Colin.'

Colin squatted down and picked up one of the larger leg bones. From his days studying archaeology, Wesley recognised it as the tibia. 'Our man here broke his leg at one time, probably in childhood. You can see for yourself that it wasn't set very well. This doesn't suggest a trip to a modern A & E to me, but on the other hand he could have broken it when he was travelling and found himself in a country without access to good health care.'

'Or he might date from a time when only the rich could afford a proper doctor.'

Colin pondered the possibility for a few seconds. 'My instincts tell me this skeleton is old, but I'm not sure, and neither is Dr Spender.' He gave Wesley a rueful smile. 'Thankfully it's your problem, not mine.'

Wesley took his leave, glancing at the skull that was grinning up at him from the plastic sheet. If Colin's instincts were proved right, there would be one less thing for him to worry about. But as he made his way over to where Neil was working, he knew that things rarely turned out to be that simple.

'How's it going?' he asked.

Neil had been concentrating so hard on his task that the sound of Wesley's voice made him jump. 'You've seen our bones?'

'Colin thinks they might be old.'

Neil shrugged. 'But why would someone stuff an old skeleton into a bin bag and put it in a newly dug trench?'

'Someone who'd found it somewhere and didn't know what to do with it?'

'Perhaps. But I wouldn't put money on it.'

'Any sign of Orford?'

Neil sat back on his heels and shook his head. Then he focused his gaze beyond Wesley's face and swore under his breath. 'Talk of the devil . . . '

Wesley looked round and saw Kevin Orford marching straight towards them. He looked agitated, as though he was carrying the weight of the artistic world on his shoulders and this latest outrage was about to break him.

'Neil. What's going on? I never expected all this . . . '

Neil stood up. This is DI Peterson – he's with Tradmouth CID.'

Orford gave Wesley a wary look.

'I need to ask you a few questions, sir,' said Wesley, showing his warrant card and keeping it formal. 'I believe you were here when the trench was filled in sixteen years ago. Can you throw any light on how these bones got here?'

'Of course not. How can you think I've got anything to do with this? I'm an artist.'

'I'll need the names of the people who were with you at the time the trench was filled in.'

Orford took a deep breath. 'OK. Three other artists were working with me at the time. My publicity people were there too but—'

'Names?'

'The artists were Ralph Button, Bobby-Jo Henchard and Daniel Parsland. The first two are still about on the art scene, but Daniel seems to have disappeared off the face of the earth. As for the locals who helped out with the digging, I can't tell you their names, but I remember Richard Catton was there. I had a PR girl called Cassandra at the time but I've no idea what became of her.'

'Thanks. I'll need the contact details for your artist colleagues.'

'My PR people will find them for you. I'll get them to email them through.'

As Wesley handed Orford his card, he noticed that the artist's hand was shaking a little and beads of sweat were forming on his forehead.

When Wesley's phone rang, Orford looked relieved, as though he'd been let off some imaginary hook. He hurried away, almost breaking into a run, in his desire to put some distance between him and the police. Wesley answered his phone and heard Gerry's voice.

'There's been a development.'

Wesley saw that Neil was watching him intently. He turned away. 'What sort of development?'

'Scientific support have got into this Blood Hunt the kids were playing and you'll never guess what.'

'Surprise me.'

'One of the scenarios in the game has a naked kid being chased by hunters around a wood. And when they catch him, he gets blasted with a shotgun and fails to reach the next level. Sound familiar?'

It sounded familiar all right. Perhaps Barney and Sophie had just failed to reach the next level in Carl Heckerty's game.

Chapter 24

The Jester's Journal

26 June 1815

Yesterday morning, before dawn, we buried Robert in a small clearing in the woods. It is strange to think that he will lie there in the cold earth and nobody will ever know of his fate.

The heat affects me sorely, so that I can do nothing but lie beneath a tree and dream of novel ways to entertain my master and his cousin. However, I fear the Squire has lost interest in my antics as he now simpers after my Lady Pegassa, as though he would like to pull her strange and colourful plumage from her body. I tell him that she teases him and takes him for a fool, and that it is only I who am permitted to be a Fool at Catton Hall. Yet he ignores my warnings and continues to dote upon his prodigy.

Robert's brother called upon the Squire today, demanding to know the lad's whereabouts. He says he will not rest until he has found his brother and if the clod is bent on causing trouble, he must be dealt with.

There are many ways to silence a man. It is merely a matter of selecting the correct method for the occasion.

The Steward's Journal

30 June 1815

I tried to communicate with the Lady Pegassa today, but her inability to converse in the English tongue rendered the task impossible. She seems afraid of someone or something and I must endeavour to discover the cause of her trepidation.

The parson, a scholarly man who knows much of geography and nature, has attempted to discover where she is from, but to no avail. In the Squire's absence he has visited often with maps and illustrations of strange tribes and artefacts, but none seem familiar to the lady. His latest theory is that she is from some ship that sailed to the port of Tradmouth from the East Indies. He believes that she came ashore and became lost, finding herself somehow on the wrong side of the River Trad. He believes she is a highborn lady of her people, but who her people may be, he cannot say.

I think often of that kiss she gave me. Perhaps it is a custom of her tribe – a display of gratitude perhaps? Yet, as I lie in bed, I think of her lips and I am unable to sleep for the anticipation of sin. I must be strong.

The gardener tells me that Robert has absented himself

from his labours since the night of the hunt. I made enquiries of his friend Nathaniel but he is afraid to speak openly, saying only that Robert has gone away to the house of Henry Catton to tend his garden there. I saw the Squire's cousin leave on horseback, but I did not see Robert go with him.

There seems to be much fear in this house, and I feel it my duty to discover its true cause.

Chapter 25

First thing on Wednesday morning, Richard Catton bent down to pick up the letter that lay on the fraying coir door mat. It was a bill. It was always bills these days, and the old man was oblivious to it all.

Getting the holiday park up and running again was all that stood between the Cattons and bankruptcy. If it didn't happen, they wouldn't survive. And now the discovery in the field had thrown Richard's unsettled world into further turmoil.

His father was still in bed. Later he'd be in the library surrounded by his old documents, working on the book that had become his obsession. If he'd put half the effort into running Catton Hall that he put into his writing and research, the estate might not be in such dire straits. But to Alfred Catton, the past was a friendlier place: a time when the Squire was ruler of his domain and banks and taxmen knew their place.

Richard looked at the letter in his hand; a plain brown envelope with a window for the address, so unlike the brief messages of affection he'd received during his relationship with Daniel. Those envelopes had been deckle-edged and the colour of Devon cream, and his name had been inscribed in beautiful calligraphy because Daniel was an artist whose talent had governed everything he did. Daniel had told him that Kevin Orford was a fraud, a con-man with scant talent and an eye on the bottom line. He had claimed that Orford was jealous, and that was why he'd edged him out of the project. At the time the fact that he'd walked out of the situation had made complete sense. But Richard had always wondered why he hadn't confided in him, and why he'd gone without saying goodbye.

When Richard learned that Orford was returning, he'd hoped for news of Daniel. But although Orford swore he knew nothing, Richard could tell he was on edge, as though he was in possession of some terrible secret.

Since the discovery of the skeleton, he'd lain awake each night going over the events of that distant summer in his mind – every moment, every word. Daniel had vanished around the time the picnic had been buried in the ground and he hadn't heard from him since.

Now he needed to know what had happened to him. And why the man who'd introduced him to love had abandoned him without a word.

At the morning briefing, Gerry said they needed to speak to Sophie and Barney's friends again – the ones who'd played Blood Hunt on their computers.

Rachel and Trish had already visited Marcus Dexter, and they knew each other well enough to sit in amicable silence during the journey to Jodie Carter's house on the outskirts of Neston. They drew up outside a large stone building that had once been a farmhouse but, unlike at the farm where Rachel had grown up, there was no muddy machinery on display, no pervasive smell of slurry and no sound of lowing cows, clucking chickens and barking sheep dogs. This place smelled of money rather than muck.

The only concession to rural living seemed to be the new-looking stable block that stood to one side of the house. Rachel could also see a paddock and a large ménage, set with jumps of varying height and difficulty. Rachel had ridden when she was younger – she had even been a regular at local gymkhanas – but the facilities at her parents' farm were nothing like the ones she saw here. Her jumps had been cobbled together in one of the meadows out of wood and old tractor tyres found lying around the farm.

Trish rang the doorbell, pressing it three times as if to emphasise the importance of their visit, and the door was opened by a girl with a pixie face, poker-straight dark hair and tight jeans which emphasised her thinness. She looked at the newcomers with studied boredom for a few seconds before standing aside to let them in.

It was Trish who did the talking while Rachel took in her surroundings. The floor was marble and the sweeping stair-case was thickly carpeted. Jodie led them through to a palatial kitchen where a large shocking-pink Aga occupied what had once been a fireplace, and invited them to sit on a pair of tall bar stools by the granite counter.

'I've already told the police everything I know.' Jodie folded her arms and looked Rachel in the eye, daring her to contradict.

But Rachel wasn't going to be put off by a kid with attitude. 'I know, but we need to talk to you again.'

'You've been to see Marcus, haven't you?'

'You've spoken to him?'

Jodie glanced at the tiny mobile phone she'd placed on the counter in front of her. 'Yeah.'

Rachel knew that in the age of instant communication it was too much to hope that their visit would take Jodie by surprise. 'So you'll know what we're going to ask.'

'About the hunt.'

'That's right. I believe you've taken part in the hunts at Catton Hall yourself?'

'Yeah.'

'You didn't mind being chased around with no clothes on?' said Trish.

'It was a bit scary at first, but it was a laugh. We got a hundred quid a time and the dogs who hunted us were really cute. I love dogs.'

'What about the men who hunted you?'

'The Game Master made sure none of them stepped over the line, if you know what I mean. And I was with Marcus and Dun.'

'You play Blood Hunt on your computer?'

'It's just a game.' She sounded a little unsure of herself.

'In the game a character is shot exactly like your friends were.'

For a split second a flash of panic appeared in Jodie's eyes. 'So?'

'We think their deaths might be connected with the game.'

'I don't know anything about how they died. I wasn't there.'

'We never said you were,' said Trish. She allowed a moment of silence before she asked her next question. 'Could any of your other friends have gone there that night?'

'What did Marcus say?' The question was cautious.

'He said he was in his room all night. His parents were out so he's got nobody to vouch for him.'

When they'd spoken to Marcus, Rachel had known he was lying because he'd changed his story rapidly as soon as Trish mentioned that they were able to trace what websites he'd been using. Rather than being on his computer all evening, he'd claimed he'd spent the time reading. She hadn't believed a word of it, and now they needed Jodie to fill in the blanks.

She held her breath and waited, watching Jodie fidget with her phone. 'Two of your friends have been killed. Don't you want whoever did it to face justice?'

'You don't rat on mates,' Jodie said, pressing her lips together in a stubborn line.

'Not ratting on your mates is OK at school, Jodie. But this is different. This is murder.'

Jodie's hand went to her throat and suddenly the confident young woman became a frightened little girl. 'I don't want to have to say anything in court.'

'I'm sure it won't come to that,' Rachel said, rather surprised at the smooth way she was able to bend the truth. 'Why don't you tell us what you know?'

Jodie breathed deeply, staring at her phone. Rachel waited for the decision to be made, hoping it would be the one she wanted.

'Marcus fancied Sophie. More than fancied, he was obsessed with her. He used to follow her round, but she

197

wasn't interested. Then she started going out with Barney and . . .'

'And what?'

'Him and Barney had a fight. Marcus just went for Barney and a couple of the other lads had to pull them apart.'

'When was this?'

'The last week at school, just before we finished for the summer. Look, I don't want to get Marcus into trouble. He's a bit hot-headed but he wouldn't actually—'

'You're probably right,' said Rachel with a reassuring smile. 'But we'll still have to speak to him about it. Do you know if Marcus has ever used a shotgun?'

Rachel saw the colour drain from the girl's face. 'His dad has an estate near Dukesbridge and he runs shooting weekends for people from London – business people. Marcus helps out and teaches them how to shoot and all that. He says some of them are really useless, haven't a clue.'

Rachel slid off the stool and slung her bag over her shoulder. 'Thanks, Jodie, you've been a great help. You weren't in touch with Marcus on the night Sophie and Barney died, by any chance?'

Jodie shook her head. 'I was talking to another mate on Facebook, but when I tried Marcus he wasn't there.'

Rachel saw Trish give the girl a sympathetic look.

'We'll be in touch,' she said.

And as she left, Rachel felt she'd just been party to a betrayal.

'We've finished all the crime scene stuff and the police have given us the go-ahead to continue the dig.'

Neil thought the news would cheer Kevin Orford up, but

the artist's face remained solemn and it was a while before he broke his silence. 'Have they any idea who it is?'

'We know it's a male and he was probably in his mid to late twenties when he died.' He paused, watching Orford's face and wondering why he looked so uneasy. 'You were here when the trench was filled in. You must have some idea how he got there.'

Orford looked away and shook his head.

'You disappeared sharpish when it was found.'

'I . . . I was in shock.'

'Your colleagues, were they in shock as well?'

Orford looked up at Neil, as though he'd just realised he was being gently mocked. 'Anybody who isn't in the habit of digging up human remains would have found the whole business disturbing.'

Neil could see Orford's fellow artists approaching over the field, each carrying a folding chair that they set down in silence. They sat in a row, almost in the same position they had occupied before the discovery of the bones had upset their carefully staged tableau. When the cameras came out again, Neil straightened himself up. He was on show.

He was about to resume digging when he saw Richard Catton approaching across the grass, making straight for Orford and his seated line of friends with a look of intense determination on his face.

'Kevin. I need to speak to you – urgently,' said Catton as soon as he was within earshot.

Neil saw Orford's face turn as pale as his wild shock of hair. He then hurried over to Catton who grabbed his elbow and led him across to the other side of the field. Neil strained to hear what they were saying, but failed. Then the conversation became more animated and Neil could make out every word.

'Where's Daniel?'

'He went away.'

'Why hasn't he been in touch?'

He couldn't make out Orford's reply.

Carl Heckerty had been brought in late the previous afternoon. When Wesley and Gerry had questioned him, his solicitor had been present, intervening every now and then when he felt boundaries were being overstepped.

Heckerty claimed that he hadn't noticed any resemblance between the deaths of Sophie and Barney and the incident in the Blood Hunt level where the losing player was shot dead. Game over. Wesley didn't believe a word of it. And yet he kept asking himself why the man would emulate a game of his own devising. It had only drawn attention to him. Unless it was some clever double bluff.

He had an uneasy feeling that there was something he was missing about Carl Heckerty, a question he needed to ask. And halfway through the interview, he'd suddenly realised what it was. 'Did the kids have anything on you?'

Heckerty had pretended not to understand the question and Wesley had rephrased it several times before he finally got an answer.

'No way,' he'd said. 'Those kids looked up to me. I'm their Game Master and we're all good mates.' Then a wary expression had passed across his face. 'Have any of them said anything?'

Wesley hadn't answered. None of the kids involved in the games either online or in real life had said anything to incriminate Heckerty in any way. On the contrary, they'd spoken of him as some kind of hero.

However, in his opinion, there was bound to be something dodgy about a man who encouraged young girls to prance naked through woods, pursued by a gang of testosterone-filled males. But maybe he was allowing his own prejudices to cloud his judgement. They had nothing on Heckerty apart from vague suspicions, and as he'd met all the conditions of his bail they'd had to let him go.

The next morning Wesley sat in Gerry's office picking over the details of Heckerty's statement and examining the pictures of Orford's original Feast of Life which had been emailed through, as promised, when Gerry's phone rang. Gerry looked tired – more than tired, despondent – but the call from the constable on duty at Morbay Hospital brought a fresh sparkle to his eyes. Keith Marsh was finally fit to talk to them.

During the long drive to Morbay Hospital, their spirits were buoyed up by the prospect of learning the truth about the dead woman in Lister Cottage. She had remained an enigma for too long.

Marsh had been moved from Intensive Care to a High Dependency ward, a step in the right direction towards recovery. They were relieved to find that Anne Marsh had gone out for some fresh air, as they knew Marsh would probably talk more freely if his wife wasn't there to hear. When they walked into the ward the patient was dozing, but as they dragged seats over and sat themselves down by the bed, his eyes slowly opened.

'Do I know you?' The patient spoke in a hoarse, puzzled whisper.

It was Gerry who made the introductions and asked how

the patient was feeling. Then, when the niceties were over, he came to the point of their visit.

'Last Friday you reported the death of a woman at an address in Morbay. This was a few hours before your accident. You didn't give your name but we traced the call to your mobile phone.' Marsh lay there, staring up at the ceiling and Wesley could see a tear creep out of the corner of his eye and trickle down past his ear onto the white hospital pillow, leaving a small wet patch. 'When our officers went to the address on St Marks Road they found a woman's body. She'd been dead about a week and, because of the warm weather, the body had decomposed, so identification's been a problem. We were hoping you could help us.'

They waited for what seemed like an age then Gerry spoke again. 'Did you hear me, Mr Marsh? We need to know about the woman you found.'

Marsh turned his head, slowly and painfully. 'Her name was Evie.' He spoke in a rasping croak as if each word was an effort.

'Evie Smith?'

'You don't get to know their surnames.'

Wesley looked at Gerry. 'You mean she was a working girl?'

'For God's sake, don't tell my wife. She has no idea that I . . .'

When all those condoms were found in the bedside drawer, Wesley had suspected that their victim had been in the throes of a passionate relationship. But now they knew that the passion had been purely professional. He wondered if Tessa Trencham knew how her house-sitter made a living.

'Can you tell us what happened?'

'I told my wife I was flying to Germany from Manchester Airport the Friday before last, but instead I drove down here to see Evie.'

'How long have you known her?' Gerry asked.

'About six months. Barry, one of my colleagues who'd been down here on business, recommended her. I got in touch with her when I had to spend a week down in Plymouth.'

He began to cough a little. Wesley helped him to sit up and poured him a glass of water from the jug on the bed-side trolley. Marsh took it gratefully and sipped the liquid until he was ready to start again.

'Evie listened to me ... took an interest. I suppose I fell in love with her a bit, and I started visiting her whenever I could. Anne's busy with her own life and Evie became a habit I couldn't break.'

'So what happened when you visited her the Friday before last?'

There was a long silence before he answered. 'We spent that Friday night together, and early the next morning I drove over to Heathrow to catch my flight and left the car in the airport car park. I'd promised to visit her again on my way back from Germany – I was going to drive up the M4, make a detour to Morbay, then drive back up north. Last Friday I went to the house, as arranged, and when I couldn't get an answer I was a bit worried – I mean, you hear of all sorts of things happening to women in her line of business, don't you?'

'How did you get into the house?' Wesley asked.

'I knew she kept a spare key under the flower pot by the front door and when I got inside, the smell hit me. And when I heard the flies, I knew something was terribly wrong.' Another tear trickled down his cheek. 'I went upstairs and found her ... like that ... and I called the police to say she was there, but I didn't leave my name because I didn't want to get involved. Then I went to the pub and had a few drinks to steady my nerves. I shouldn't have driven, of course I shouldn't. But then I had the accident, and you know the rest.'

'We need you to tell us everything you know about Evie,' said Gerry. 'Did she ever talk about herself? Did she ever mention her children at all?'

'Children? No. Did she have children?' Marsh sounded quite shocked, as though the thought that his lady of the night could be a mother was quite alien to him.

'The house was rented by a Tessa Trencham. Did Evie ever mention her?'

'She never mentioned anybody. She was a good listener and we talked about me most of the time. But she had only just started to use that house and she said it was temporary. When I first met her she was living in another place nearby.'

'We'll need that address,' said Wesley. He needed something – anything – that might give them access to the secret that was Evie's life.

'Twenty-three Roly Walk. It was a two bedroomed town house. Nice little place. Very quiet street.'

'Did she tell you why she left that address?'

'Something about the lease running out.'

Marsh lay back on his pillow and turned his head away.

'Did you kill her, Mr Marsh?' Gerry asked. 'Did it finally dawn on you that you weren't the only one enjoying her services? Did the thought of other men in her bed make

204

you lose control? She was strangled. Typical crime of passion, I'd say.'

'You don't understand. It wasn't like that.'

At the sound of his raised voice a nurse appeared from nowhere, bearing down on them with an avenging fury. But before she could scold them for disturbing her patient, the two policemen stood up.

'We'll be in touch, Mr Marsh,' said Gerry as they left the ward.

Chapter 26

The Jester's Journal

23 July 1815

The Lady Pegassa is still with us, pampered and ogled by local society. When I suggested she should take part in our entertainments, the Squire boxed my ears. How I long for the day when my master tires of the novelty and turns her out to shift for herself, but I must be patient and bide my time.

   This day I observed the Lady out walking in the gardens and watched from behind a bush as she issued forth a scream and ran back to the house, as though the devil himself was after her. My curiosity aroused, I made haste to discover what had so alarmed her and I came upon a man lurking in the trees. He was a handsome, dark-haired man of some twenty-five summers – hardly the sort to inspire fear in the heart of a woman – but I thought he might be some thief come to rob us, so when he hurried away I followed him, moving with great stealth.

He came to the stream and as he bent down to take a drink I saw that his clothes were dirty and ragged, as though he had been sleeping out of doors. After a time I revealed myself, and he seemed most shocked for he had thought himself alone and unobserved. He gazed upon me with terror, but when I assured him that it was not my intention to betray his presence to my master, his fear diminished and I ventured to ask him his business.

At first his manner was guarded, but soon he began to talk freely, revealing that Pegassa was his stepsister – the daughter of the man his mother had wed some two years since – and the girl was, as I suspected, no foreign princess, but a stonemason's daughter from Exeter. This man had, he claimed, visited Catton Hall some weeks ago but had been told that his stepsister was not here. Then he searched the country round about and received word of a young foreign lady at the hall who matched his stepsister's description precisely. According to this stepbrother, her name is plain Peggy and she has always been in possession of an adventurous spirit. How I laughed at her bold deception. I believed the truth of his tale, but there would be no entertainment in a simple reunion between brother and wayward sister. Perhaps I will persuade him to stay, for Henry returns tomorrow and, while we are blessed with fine nights, he is keen to hunt again and if one of our hares was to stumble, it would be as well to have a ready replacement to hand.

When I gave the man leave to sleep in the stables, he asked me to say nothing of our conversation to Pegassa. Perhaps I do not believe his story after all.

Chapter 27

Wesley had obtained the address of the anonymous caller who reported the shooting of Jimmy Yates. The phone was registered to a Craig Walker who lived near Jimmy on the Winterham Estate.

Even police dogs were known to patrol in pairs on that particular estate, but as everyone in the incident room was busy with their investigations, he had no choice but to go alone.

Walker lived in a small pebble-dashed council semi with a dirty white UPVC front door. An old Land Rover with a spotlight fixed to the back stood in a paved front garden where the weeds poking up between the concrete slabs provided the only hint of greenery.

It was the school holidays and a gang of hooded kids was hanging around the patch of sparse grass opposite Walker's house. Wesley could almost feel their eyes watching him. A well-dressed black man was a rarity in their part of the world. From the hostile stares, he guessed that they knew he was police. He just hoped all his tyres would still be inflated when his visit was over.

He knocked on the door and after half a minute it opened to reveal a small man, thick-set, like a pit bull terrier, with a shaved head and an entertaining array of tattoos.

'Mr Walker?' Wesley held out his warrant card for the man to inspect.

Walker didn't answer. He just stood aside to let him in, looking like a man who was resigned to his fate, whatever that was. He led Wesley through to a small room with the sort of busy floral wallpaper that was the height of chic back in the 1980s and a pair of cream leather sofas too large for their surroundings. The effect was claustrophobic and the decor did nothing to relieve Wesley's incipient headache. But he took out his notebook and sat down when invited.

'We're here about a call we received reporting the shooting of Jimmy Yates. It came from a phone registered to you.'

Walker sat down on the sofa opposite, head bowed, the picture of repentance. Wesley waited for the man to speak and after a while his patience was rewarded.

'Look, I admit I made the call. But I never shot him.'

'Tell me exactly what happened?'

Walker leaned towards him like a penitent making his confession. 'Me and Jimmy were out that night doing a bit of lamping, shooting vermin and that. Just for a laugh. Just for sport.'

'Do you do this often?'

'Oh yeah. And before you ask, I've got a licence for my gun. Proper cabinet and all that.'

'I'm sure you have,' said Wesley soothingly. 'Go on.'

'Well Jimmy had already bagged a couple of rabbits and put them in the Land Rover, and he'd just wandered off for a piss when I spotted a fox and fired, but I reckon I missed and it got away. I knew Jimmy was somewhere nearby but I couldn't see him 'cause he'd gone into the trees. I think I might have heard him say something but I can't be sure about that. Then I saw the fox again. It was limping, so I must have winged it. Anyway, I shot at it again and then I heard this sort of yelp. I thought it was the fox at first but when I looked it wasn't there, so it must have got away again. I've been going over and over what happened in my head and now I reckon I might have heard a second shot – like someone had fired a moment after I did. You see, at first I thought I'd shot Jimmy by accident, but when I saw the state of him ... I was using a .22 rifle and I could tell he'd been killed with a shotgun, so there was no way it could have been me.'

'You think there was someone else there in the trees – someone he spoke to before he was shot?'

'I can't be sure. It could have been the wind in the trees because it was pretty breezy that night, but now I think about it, it could have been a voice.'

'Did you see anybody else? Hear footsteps?'

He shook his head. 'It was very dark, not much moon. And when you're lamping you can't see anything outside the range of your beam.'

'You'll have to come to the station to make a full statement. And we'll need to examine your gun.'

'No problem.' He looked Wesley in the eye. 'I was going to come forward right away, but I thought I might get the blame. It's been eating me up, like, that I was there when it

210

happened and I couldn't stop it. I feel so bad 'cause Jimmy was just a kid. His mum must be in pieces.'

'If what you say is true, Mr Walker, you weren't responsible for his death. But you really should have stayed there until the emergency services arrived.'

'Do you think I don't regret doing a runner? I'd do anything to turn the clock back.'

Wesley led Walker out to the car, carrying the rifle, unloaded and well concealed from the watching eyes of the hooded youths who were still hanging around like wasps at a picnic.

Who was Evie? And was Evie even her real name? Where had she come from? Who were her next of kin? How did a woman who was clearly on the game come to be using a house belonging to an apparently respectable woman who ran a jewellery business in a craft centre? The questions swirled around Gerry's head as he sat at his desk. He'd had officers trying to trace her through the usual official records but they'd had no luck. It was almost as though she had never existed.

The officer who'd visited the address Marsh had mentioned, 23 Roly Walk, had drawn a blank. The new tenants knew nothing about Evie and no trace of her remained there. Although, a couple of weeks ago, the new tenants had received a visit from a well-dressed man in a business suit, who had asked for Evie and had seemed rather disappointed not to find her there. The new people also provided the information that the letting of their town house was handled by Morbay Properties and the name made Gerry's heart beat a little faster. Morbay Properties had let out Lister Cottage as well. He'd thought that the manager, Kris

Kettering, had been hiding something and he had always prided himself on being a good judge of these things.

He had just been upstairs to brief Chief Superintendent Nutter on the latest developments in the case, and his frustration at the way bureaucracy, form-filling and covering your back could hamper a murder inquiry kept bubbling to the surface. It had been many years since Nutter had led a major criminal investigation and Gerry imagined he'd probably forgotten what it was like sifting through evidence, knocking on doors and interviewing suspects in windowless rooms.

And Nutter wasn't the only source of Gerry's frustration. The local vice squad had never heard of Evie at either her old or her new address. Sometimes Gerry wondered what they did with themselves all day.

He stood up and wandered out into the main incident room. He knew Wesley was downstairs taking a statement from the man who'd been with Jimmy Yates on the night he died, so he looked around for someone reliable who would fancy a trip out to Morbay.

Paul was sitting at his desk, staring at his computer with an intensity that suggested he didn't want to be disturbed. Gerry knew that Sophie's death was still at the forefront of his mind and, although he thought that a trip out might do him good, he was reluctant to divert him from his work. At least if he was helping to investigate his cousin's murder, he'd feel as though he was doing something constructive.

He saw that Trish had just put her phone down so he bore down on her, beaming like a benevolent uncle.

'Evie's old address and Lister Cottage were let by the same company – Morbay Properties – and I don't believe in coincidences. Fancy paying them a visit?'

Trish didn't need asking twice. She picked up her handbag and as she slung it over her shoulder her phone began to ring again. When she answered it, she turned away, and Gerry noticed that she was blushing. He heard the words 'Hi Steven,' but he couldn't make out the rest of the hushed conversation, even though his natural curiosity meant that he was straining to hear.

'Want me to drive, sir?' she said when the call was finished.

Gerry nodded. Driving was something he always left to others. 'Who was that on the phone?'

She hesitated before replying. 'Tessa Trencham's dentist. He just wanted to know if she'd turned up yet.'

Trish was a good officer, but she was a bad liar. However, Gerry said nothing.

The journey was impeded by the thickening tourist traffic and when they finally reached Morbay Properties, Gerry pushed the door open, warrant card at the ready. The plump receptionist was wearing the same black trouser suit she'd worn the other day, and as soon as she recognised the DCI, her expression changed from mildly welcoming to wary.

'I'll get Kris,' she said, as though she was anxious to shift the responsibility onto someone else.

'In a minute, love. Maybe you can help us. Do you know the woman who lived at this address until a couple of weeks ago? Her name was Evie Smith.' He passed her a slip of paper bearing Evie's old address.

'Twenty-three Roly Walk. Is this to do with the ... with the woman who died ... Ms Trencham?'

Gerry didn't answer the question. 'If you could just look the address up in your records.'

As the woman rose and walked over to the filing cabinet in the corner, Kettering emerged from his office. At first only Trish was in his line of vision and he made straight for her, wearing a cocky smile on his face as he looked her up and down appraisingly. When he spotted Gerry the smile vanished.

'Hello, Mr Kettering. Remember me? DCI Heffernan. And this is my colleague DC Walton. We're after your help again, I'm afraid.'

'I've already told you everything I know,' Kettering sounded defensive. 'I hardly had anything to do with Ms Trencham.'

'Oh, didn't I say? The body in Lister Cottage wasn't Tessa Trencham. She's in France and the dead woman was house-sitting for her.'

'Has Ms Trencham told you who the—?'

'Her name was Evie Smith and she lived in another of your properties until recently. Roly Walk. Number twenty-three.'

'I don't remember anyone of that name renting that particular property.' The answer came too quickly and Gerry had a sneaking suspicion that he was lying.

Kettering's receptionist had been rooting through the filing cabinet, but now she turned to Gerry with a puzzled frown on her face. 'I've found the file on Roly Walk and it contains the details of the people who are in there now but there's nothing about the previous tenant.' She passed the file to Kettering. 'Do you know anything about the last tenant, Kris?'

'No.' He didn't sound too convincing. 'Maybe someone's filed the papers somewhere else by accident.' He looked at the woman accusingly.

214

She looked a little sheepish and it occurred to Gerry that filing might not be her strong point. 'Not to worry, love. If you find it, give me a ring.' He handed her his card. 'It could be important.'

Gerry glanced back over his shoulder as they left Morbay Properties and saw that Kettering was standing, fists clenched, with a blank expression on his face. Poker face, he'd heard it called. Only the police held most of the good cards.

'Did you believe him, sir?' Trish asked as they were walking to the car.

'Not a chance. If anybody mislaid that file, I bet it was him.'

'Maybe he saw Evie in a professional capacity,' she said with a knowing smile.

'You could be right. It's just a matter of getting him to admit it.'

'Are we taking him in for questioning?'

Gerry shook his head. 'We'll let him stew for a while. In the meantime I might get a search warrant and get someone to go through the office for those missing details. That should soften him up nicely.' He hesitated for a moment. 'Are you and Paul still OK? I reckon he needs a bit of support at the moment.'

'I know, sir.'

They spent the rest of the journey back to Tradmouth in silence.

Kevin Orford had vanished for a while after his spat with Richard Catton, then he returned half an hour later as though nothing had happened.

From what Neil knew of Orford, he imagined the

argument could have been about something trivial, but he didn't bother to ask because he couldn't whip up the necessary interest. He just wanted to get this project finished, receive the cheque and then move onto something more interesting, like the investigation of the Napoleonic fort at Fortress Point.

The most fascinating aspect of the dig so far had been the discovery of the skeleton. However, although the police had gone through the motions, they were dealing with the shooting of the two teenagers and the murder in Morbay, so the bones didn't seem to be top of their priority list.

Now that they were able to resume digging they'd reached the level of the sixteen-year-old picnic. The state of preservation of the various items was mildly interesting from a professional point of view, although it wasn't really his specialism. However, some of his colleagues, those with a more scientific bent, seemed to be in a state of high excitement.

Orford had asked for the individual items to remain *in situ* rather than being lifted and placed in trays, so the remains lying in the bottom of the trench looked as if someone had just abandoned the feast to nature. The food on the plates had long rotted away into the earth but the crockery, glasses and bottles still lay grubby but intact on the filthy, shredded fragments of a patterned tablecloth.

The artists kept up their strange surveillance regime and the archaeologists' every action was photographed and videoed. Orford had told him that a video of the excavation would be played on large screens at the exhibition, which was to be held at Tate Modern. It was some kind of immortality, Neil supposed. Although he would have preferred something a little more conventional and less pretentious. A portrait above a fireplace in the Council for British Archaeology headquarters perhaps, casually posed with trowel in one hand and some impressive find in the other.

His reverie was interrupted by the sound of a voice saying 'hello' and when he looked up he saw Richard Catton had returned and was standing at the edge of the trench watching him.

'I want to ask you a question.' He spoke quietly as if he didn't want Neil's fellow diggers to overhear.

'Fire away,' Neil said, immediately regretting his choice of words when he recalled the double murder nearby.

'Those bones you found.'

'What about them?'

'I've heard they're male.'

'That's right.'

'Can you tell how old the person was when he died?'

'Late twenties we think.'

'And was he tall or short?'

'Around five nine. Why?'

'Do you know how old the bones are yet?' Something told Neil that the question was more than a casual enquiry.

'A sample's been sent away for dating but it'll be a couple of weeks before we get the results. Our expert thinks they're probably old but they were found in a bin bag which suggests—'

'What?'

'Well, we can't be sure, but I'll know for certain when we get the test results. You seem very interested.'

The man didn't speak for a few moments. 'I was here when they filled in the trench. I'd like to know how the skeleton got there.'

'You and me both. Have you any ideas?'

Catton stood in silence for a while, staring at the earth. Neil sensed he still had more to say, so he waited. Eventually his patience was rewarded.

'Have you heard Kevin Orford mention someone called Daniel?'

'I don't think so. Who's Daniel?' The man's vague hints at something amiss were beginning to annoy him.

'A friend,' he said with a secretive smile. 'A lost soul.'

Then Richard Catton turned slowly and walked away.

'Wesley, can I have a word?'

Rachel was standing by his desk and from the determined expression on her face, he sensed she was about to tell him something important.

'What is it?'

'I've been to see Sophie and Barney's school friends, the ones who played that Blood Hunt game with them online.'

'Learn anything interesting?'

'As a matter of fact, I did. A girl called Jodie said that Marcus was obsessed with Sophie. He had a fight with Barney over her.'

'Remind me, what's his alibi for the time of their deaths?'

'He claims he spent the evening at home, but his family were out so they can't vouch for him. At first he said that he was on his computer, but when I told him that Internet use can be traced, he changed his story and said that he was reading. He's going to study English at Cambridge and he said he has a lot of reading to do before the course starts.'

'He will have but it's strange that he changed his story.'

'And there's something else. Marcus's dad owns one of these estates that runs shooting weekends for townies and he helps out. He knows how to handle a gun and apparently he's a good shot.'

Wesley sat back in his seat, considering the implications. 'So he had a grudge against Barney, he knew where they'd be that night, and he has access to firearms. We need to bring him in.'

When Rachel didn't move he knew there was more to come.

'I asked Paul if Sophie's parents could give him the names of some of the teachers at Corley Grange. When I got back here there was a list on my desk and I contacted the headmaster for their details. When I rang them most just came out with the usual stuff about how tragic it was et cetera, but there was one – a Mr Dickens – who mentioned a piece of creative writing Marcus did a few months ago. He said it was quite remarkable and extremely well-written, but the subject matter was pretty violent and disturbing. It was about this boy stalking people who'd offended him and ...'

'And what?'

'And blasting them in the chest with a shotgun.'

Chapter 28

The Steward's Journal

24 July 1815

Oh, what excitement there is in the district! Bonaparte himself has come amongst us. HMS *Bellerophon* has dropped anchor off Morbay, and as soon as word spread, numerous boats conveyed people out to the ship to view that formidable man.

I had it from a man of the village, who met with a sailor, that Bonaparte walked above an hour on deck so that people would have the opportunity of seeing him, and whenever he observed a lady he would remove his hat and bow. How remarkable that such a man would behave thus like a true gentleman.

I came upon the Lady Pegassa with a large portmanteau, which I recognised as belonging to the Squire. She appeared to be struggling under its weight and when she saw me, she looked most afraid, as though I had caught her in some shameful act. I forgot that she spoke no English and I found myself asking her what she was doing. To my astonishment, she took my arm and led me into her bedchamber. The action was so unexpected that I found that I was struck quite dumb for a few moments. Could it be that she desired me? And if this was the case, what was I to do?

She closed the door and stood before me, the portmanteau at her feet. Then she spoke in a whisper.

'I am afraid,' she said.

I gaped at her for a while, amazed to hear her speak in my native tongue. And she sounded for all the world like a Devonshire girl rather than some princess from across the seas.

Chapter 29

Before they questioned Marcus Dexter, Wesley wanted to read the piece he had written for himself. According to Rachel, his teacher, Mr Dickens, had kept hold of it, maybe as an example to future students of vivid prose. Dickens lived nearby in Tradmouth, so Wesley thought that having a civilised chat with the teacher before confronting the boy might be the best way forward. It was best to be armed with all the facts. And besides, it was always possible that Dickens was being over-imaginative, that the piece Marcus had written bore no real resemblance to the deaths of Sophie and Barney.

Wesley left the police station and walked to Dickens's address on Albany Street. Once the main street into Tradmouth, Albany Street rose upwards towards Wesley's own house in a series of wide, cobbled steps, fine for the packhorses and donkeys who'd brought goods in and out of the port in days gone by but useless for anything with an internal combustion engine. It was narrow, precipitously steep, and the subject of many a picture postcard with its crooked pastel-painted houses and window boxes filled with bright, scented flowers.

Dickens's small cottage stood at the end of a row next to a flight of stone steps leading to a street below. The cottage was pristine white with a glossy black front door, which bore a plaque with the name 'Bookman's Cottage' painted in decorative gold letters. The owner hadn't chosen the usual Tradmouth maritime theme for his house name, rather he had selected something to reflect his own interest in literature. Wesley felt rather keen to make the acquaintance of this English teacher with the literary name that no doubt caused some mirth amongst his students.

The door was answered almost immediately, as though the occupant of the house had been waiting on the other side for Wesley's knock.

Dickens was a small, round man whose long, grey hair was gathered back in a pony tail. His face was smooth and it was hard to guess his age, but his bow tie and brightly coloured waistcoat, gave Wesley the impression of an actor playing the part of the absent-minded academic. He led Wesley into a room lined from floor to ceiling with books and invited him to sit on a sagging antique sofa. The room too had the look of a stage set: the unworldly professor's natural habitat.

'What can I do for you, Inspector?'

'You told my colleague DS Tracey that your student, Marcus Dexter, wrote something about a shooting.'

Dickens began to fidget with the corner of his waistcoat. 'So I did. I rather wish I hadn't.'

'Why is that?'

'He is my student and I feel I've betrayed his trust, that's why. Can you understand that?'

'I can, Mr Dickens. But if Marcus hasn't done anything wrong he has nothing to fear.'

Dickens snorted. 'Now where have I heard that one before? Our great British police aren't always renowned for getting it right, are they?' He studied Wesley for a minute. 'But I suppose you look slightly more intelligent than most of the Neanderthals they seem to select for the force.'

'You sound as though you've had a bad experience with the police.'

'When you've been arrested like I have for exercising your democratic right to demonstrate against oppressive government policy, you tend not to have too high an opinion of the boys in blue. I expect you've had a hard time, being black.'

'There have been moments – especially when I was working in London.' Wesley knew he needed to gain the man's trust. 'Look, I sympathise with your point of view but two of your students have been murdered so—'

'Barney wasn't my student. He was one of the scientific brigade. All facts and no imagination.'

'That doesn't mean he deserved to die like that.'

There was an awkward silence and Wesley hoped his last words hadn't created a barrier between them. Dickens was staring at a picture hanging above the fireplace; a long, framed school photograph in black and white.

'How long have you taught at Corley Grange?' he asked.

'Thirty years. I've seen a lot of students come and go. Some have been successful and others have dropped by the wayside. I count two cabinet ministers, a celebrity chef and the youngest ever master of an Oxford college among my successes. My failures one doesn't tend to hear about. But, as far as I'm aware, I've never taught a murderer and I don't think that situation has changed during the past few weeks.'

'But you told my colleague about the piece Marcus Dexter wrote so it must have worried you.'

Dickens looked Wesley in the eye. 'In view of what happened to Barney and Sophie, it did worry me, you're right. That's why I mentioned it.'

'We can't turn the clock back, you realise that. We can't just ignore it and pretend we don't know.'

Dickens didn't reply.

'May I see the piece Marcus wrote? Do you have it here?'

Dickens let out a long sigh. 'Yes. After your colleague's call I drove over to school and picked it up. I didn't want it to get lost or cleared away by an over-zealous cleaner.' He stood up and walked a few paces to the bookshelves to the right of the fireplace, opened a large rosewood box and took out a sheaf of A4 papers, stapled together in the top left hand corner.

He held it out to Wesley, who thanked him as he took it from his outstretched hand. Wesley began to read it through carefully, absorbing every description, every nuance of emotion.

'I am the hunter,' it began. *'I hunt to the death. My ears are tuned to the sound of my prey. Every breath, every sigh. Every squeak of exhaled air, as the exertion of running forces the breath out of my victims' gasping lungs. The weapon I carry is heavy, weighing me down and impeding my progress. Shall I abandon it and kill with my bare hands? If I were a stronger man, that would be my aim but, as it is, I cannot end two lives cleanly and without detection unless I make those preparations so necessary for one in my trade. For death is a trade, like*

whoring or selling your mind and most cherished ideas to the highest bidder.'

Wesley read on, fascinated. The boy had written a vivid description of the pursuit of two fleeing victims. And at the end of the third page, those victims met their deaths. The hunter came on them in a clearing and shone a light into their eyes, dazzling them like cornered beasts – lamping only with human quarry. The victims in Marcus's story were naked and they were both women who'd rejected the hunter, which Wesley found somewhat disturbing. He stared down at the text. There was no escaping the fact that the similarities to the double murder were remarkable.

'May I keep this?' he asked. 'I'll let you have it back as soon as possible.'

'If you must.'

As Wesley placed the story carefully in a plastic folder, Dickens didn't look too happy. But there was nothing he could do about it.

'What can you tell me about Marcus? What sort of boy is he?'

He was prepared to hear a eulogy, a defence of one of the teacher's top pupils. But it seemed Dickens had decided on the truthful approach.

'He has a brilliant mind, Inspector. But that doesn't make him a particularly likeable person. A few months ago he called me an old queen, implying that I had a penchant for getting inappropriately close to the younger boys. It isn't true, of course: I'm always careful to keep a professional distance – you have to in the present climate – but the fact that it was Marcus who said it, someone I've tried so hard to encourage . . . I found that hurtful.' He paused, as though he was making a decision. 'Recently I've sensed bad feeling between him and Barney, although I can't be certain of that. It was just one of those things one picks up on the ether, as it were.'

Wesley already knew that Barney and Marcus had had a fight but he wanted Dickens's angle on it. Jodie, after all, might have been bending the truth for some reason of her own. 'What was the bad feeling about?'

'I'm sure Marcus is resolutely heterosexual so I would think it would be about a girl, wouldn't you? The perils of co-education. In the days when the school was boys only, one didn't have to worry about these things.'

'You think the girl was Sophie?'

'Now that I can't say. Contrary to my reputation, I don't know everything that goes on at Corley Grange.'

'What about Barney and Sophie? What were they like?' Wesley thought it was time Dickens was reminded that the matter was serious – that two young people had died.

'In a word, they were unremarkable. Run of the mill. Neither was going to set the world on fire.'

'Unlike Marcus?'

'Unlike Marcus. And Dunstan too is a bright lad, although he may never reach his full potential. I don't know all the gory details, of course but I've heard that there are financial problems, and others for all I know. Hardship can be a spur to greater things for some people, but for poor Dunstan, I fear it has proved an unfortunate distraction to his studies.' He hesitated for a moment. 'If you speak to Marcus, please don't mention that it was me who told you about the story. After all, nobody likes a Judas.'

Wesley stood up. 'You did the right thing, Mr Dickens. In the circumstances there was no way you could have kept quiet about that story. Thank you.'

'Will you interview him? Take him to your cells and—'

'We'll speak to him.'

'He really is a most remarkable boy, you know,' were the last words Dickens said before Wesley left him alone with his books.

Wesley walked back to the police station, his progress impeded by groups of tourists, lingering to point their cameras at Tradmouth's prettier views.

As he walked, he thought about what Dickens had told him. Marcus had written the story; Marcus had known where the victims would be; Marcus had no alibi for the time of the murders. He had also fallen out with Barney, possibly about Sophie. It fitted so well that they had no choice. They needed to bring the boy in for questioning and they had to do it soon, before Dickens had a fit of conscience and took it into his head to warn him that the police had been sniffing around. However, Dickens could have called Marcus as soon as Wesley had left his cottage so they might already be too late to have the advantage of surprise.

When he reached the incident room, he found Gerry holding an earnest conversation with Rachel. When he spotted Wesley, he raised a hand to greet him. From the expression on his face, Wesley knew that there had been a development in his absence.

'We had another call from Tessa Trencham while you were out, Wes. She's about to catch the ferry. Should be back tomorrow.'

'Did she tell you any more?'

'She confirmed that the lease ran out on Evie Smith's house in Roly Walk and she told her she could stay at her place while she was away. Evie was waiting to move into another place that wasn't ready yet, and Tessa didn't want to leave her place empty, so the arrangement suited both of them fine.'

'How does Tessa know her?'

'That's on the long list of questions I'll be asking her as soon as she arrives, but I get the impression she didn't know her that well. We've had no luck tracing Evie through official records yet, which is a bit odd, don't you think? You look like you're in a good mood, Wes. Did you get anything out of that teacher?'

'As a matter of fact my visit proved quite interesting,' he said before revealing everything he'd learned. He had Marcus's story in a plastic folder and he passed it over.

Gerry scanned it and handed it back. 'Do you think this Mr Dickens will take it into his head to warn Marcus of our interest?'

'It wouldn't surprise me. He seems to think a lot of him . . . academically.'

'Any other way?'

'He did imply that he's not a very nice person, so I think he's just impressed with his talent. Pam's the same. If you have an outstanding pupil you do tend to feel they're your protégé.'

'And he might not want his precious protégé's future ruined by a murder charge.' He glanced at his watch. 'I don't think we should waste any more time.'

Marcus Dexter lived outside the village of Balwell, just off the main road from Tradmouth to Neston, in an elegant double-fronted Regency house built out of mellow stone. The sort sometimes referred to as a 'gentleman's residence' and a setting any of Jane Austen's heroines would have felt at home in.

Wesley swung the car into the gravel drive, his tyres crunching loud enough to announce their arrival. He parked at the end of a row of other vehicles, mostly expensive four by fours, and when they emerged from the car he could hear the sound of conversation punctuated by the occasional hoot of laughter. The noise was coming from the back of the house so, after ringing the doorbell and getting no reply, Gerry led the way through a pretty side-garden towards the rear of the house. They could smell something delicious – the tempting aroma of cooking meat – and when they reached the corner of the house they stood for a while watching.

There were twenty or so people at the barbecue, mostly middle aged; Marcus's parents and their friends. At one end of a large patio a long table stood laden with food, and a tall man with steel-grey hair was tending the barbecue, wearing an apron bearing the words 'Danger. Head chef at work'. The cook was tanned and handsome, and something in his manner suggested that he was used to being in charge.

Sitting on a sunlounger, eating a piece of steak without the benefit of cutlery, was a young man who bore a strong resemblance to the self-appointed head chef. The boy looked bored, as though he'd rather be somewhere else. Even the proximity of a swimming pool a few yards away from the patio did nothing to relieve his ennui. A couple of children were splashing each other in the bright-blue water, but in spite of the heat, nobody else had ventured in.

Taking a suspect in for questioning in front of his family

and their guests wasn't ideal but they'd probably have no choice. Wesley braced himself and emerged from the cover of the house, making for the barbecue, because manners dictated that the suspect's father should be informed of their intentions. Gerry, meanwhile, approached the boy they assumed was Marcus and squatted down to have a word in his ear. If possible, they wanted to keep everything discreet.

Wesley saw the boy's expression change from boredom to horror. 'I haven't done anything,' he said loudly, drawing stares from the guests. 'Dad!' he called out like a frightened child.

The chef had emerged from behind his barbecue before Wesley could reach him and he was bearing down on Gerry with a face like thunder. Wesley managed to come between them, apologising for the disturbance and assuring the father that they just needed to ask Marcus some questions. But before the man could answer, he was joined by a woman in diaphanous red who seemed a little unsteady on her stilettos.

'What's going on, Peter? Who's that man with Marcus?' Her words were a little slurred.

'We need to talk to your son, Mrs Dexter,' said Wesley, summoning all the charm he could muster. The situation could so easily turn bad.

'The police have already spoken to him,' said the protective mother.

'There are a couple of things we need to check. I realise it isn't convenient to speak to him here because you've got guests, so it would be best if he came with us to Tradmouth police station to have a chat. Just routine.' He saw Mr Dexter put a reassuring hand on his wife's shoulder. 'It shouldn't take long and a car will bring Marcus back afterwards,' he added, thinking that if the interview went badly for Marcus, there might not be an afterwards for quite a while. But there was no point in making waves.

The parents looked at each other. In view of Wesley's manner, it would have seemed almost churlish of them to object, which was his intention.

'I'm coming with him,' the chef said, discarding his apron. He looked at Gerry, a challenge in his eyes. 'I'm over the limit so you'd better be right about the lift.'

'Of course, sir,' said Wesley.

The father barked orders at his wife to call their solicitor and one of the guests sidled towards the barbecue, preparing to take over.

Marcus sat silently next to his father in the back of the car during the journey back to Tradmouth and Wesley made no attempt to speak to either of them. He could see Marcus through the rear-view mirror and Wesley could tell that he was trying his best to look unconcerned, as though being carted off to the police station was an everyday occurrence. But something in Marcus's eyes betrayed his nervousness.

Interview room three was vacant. It was the smallest of the interview rooms, windowless and claustrophobic. The table top was dented and stained and the paint on one wall was peeling. Either Marcus would find these surroundings intimidating, Wesley thought, or he would brazen it out and claim that the place was some kind of breach of his human rights, he wasn't sure which. Contrary to his expectations, the boy said nothing but sat staring ahead, possibly psyching himself up for a series of 'No comments'.

Wesley sat down beside Gerry and switched on the tape

machine, facing the boy, his father and the family solicitor, who had been waiting for them in the station reception. The story Marcus had written had been placed in a clear plastic evidence bag and Wesley slid it over the table towards him.

'Do you recognise this?'

Marcus took it and studied it closely for a while. Then he looked up. 'It's a piece of creative writing I did. Charles thought a bit of storytelling would be good for our souls or something – that's Mr Dickens; it's not his name but that's what we call him. English teacher – Charles Dickens – get it?'

'I get it,' said Wesley, resisting the urge to roll his eyes at the feeble witticism. 'Why did you choose this particular subject?'

'Felt like it.'

'Why did you feel like it?' Gerry chipped in.

'I don't know. Just did.'

'You had an argument with Barney not long before he died.'

'Lots of people have rows.' He suddenly sounded a little unsure of himself.

Wesley watched the boy's face closely. 'You argue with someone and then they die in exactly the same way as you describe in your story. Surely you can see why we need to question you?'

'I told that woman where I was that night.'

'You mean Detective Sergeant Tracey?' Wesley took Marcus's statement out of the file in front of him. 'You say you spent the evening reading but your parents were out so you have no witnesses. That's not really much of an alibi, is it?'

'It's the only one I've got. And it happens to be true.'

'Did Carl Heckerty ask you to take part in the hunt that night?'

'He was looking for volunteers but I didn't fancy it, and I had a lot of reading to catch up on for uni. That's what I was doing, catching up on my reading. Coleridge and Wordsworth if you want the sordid details.'

'You've taken part in the hunts before?'

'It's an easy way to make a hundred quid but, like I said, I had other things to do that night.'

'What's this about a hunt?' Marcus's father was leaning forward now, suddenly alert.

'It's no big deal, Dad. Nothing to worry about.'

This seemed to satisfy the father who sat back and folded his arms.

'You have a car of your own, Marcus?'

'Yeah. Why?'

'If your car was out that night we can find out from our number plate recognition cameras. They're dotted all around – most people don't realise that.' Wesley was exaggerating the power of the police's technology a little but he thought it was worth a try. 'We're trying to find out how Sophie and Barney got to the hunt that night. We think somebody gave them a lift to Catton Hall but we don't know who it was yet.'

Marcus's studied nonchalance suddenly vanished. He started to fidget with the empty plastic cup in front of him and he shot a nervous glance at his father. 'Er, can I have a word with my dad and Mr Dennis in private?' he asked Wesley with a new humility in his voice.

'Of course.'

Wesley and Gerry left the room and stood in the corridor.

'Think he's going to confess?' Gerry said in a loud whisper.

'I think he's going to confess to something. But I'm not sure that something'll be murder.'

They left it another couple of minutes then re-entered the room. Marcus was sitting with his head bowed and his father's protective hand on his shoulder.

The solicitor wore an expression of exasperated resignation. 'My client wishes to change his statement,' he said.

The two policemen sat down and Gerry flicked the switch to re-start the tape recorder.

'I wasn't reading all night,' Marcus began. 'Sophie rang me and asked if I could give her a lift. She said her car was in for a service and she needed to get to Catton Hall 'cause she'd told Heckerty she'd do the hunt. Honestly, I thought I was on a promise. She never mentioned Barney would be with her.'

'What did you feel when you found out?'

'I was pissed off, but anyone would have been. She'd made a fool of me – not for the first time.'

'But you still took her to Catton Hall?'

'Yeah. She had the cheek to ask if I could wait and give her a lift back but I told her to get lost. I knew she was just using me.'

'And you didn't like it.'

'No, I didn't. But I didn't kill her.' He shot a pleading look at his father. 'I went straight home after I'd dropped them off. Look, I've decided to tell you the whole story 'cause it's the right thing to do.'

'And because I mentioned our number plate recognition cameras, so you think we might have discovered your car was out that night and thought the worst.'

Marcus didn't answer and after a few seconds of silence, the solicitor enquired whether they were going to charge his client or release him. This time it was Wesley's turn to be evasive. He had another question to ask.

'Are you a good shot, Marcus?'

The boy looked wary. 'What do you mean?'

When Wesley repeated the question Marcus's eyes flickered as though he was seeking an escape route.

'I believe you help out with your father's shooting weekends,' said Gerry. 'Helping all the townies get their aims straight so that they don't go back to London with their backsides peppered with shot. You must be an expert. Learn to shoot when you were a nipper, did you?'

Marcus nodded reluctantly. 'Yeah. But I never shot Sophie and Barney. I'm going up to Cambridge soon. Why would I risk everything for them?'

'Good point,' the father muttered, only to be silenced by a look from Gerry.

'Spur of the moment thing, was it?' Gerry continued. 'You saw them together and you realised Sophie was just using you, so you lost your temper. Or did you plan it? You must have had the gun with you—'

The father spoke. 'All our guns are locked away safely in cabinets and I keep the key. My son couldn't have got hold of one even if he'd wanted to.'

'There must be spare keys for the cabinets?'

The father produced a key from his trouser pocket. 'I keep the key with me at all times and there's a spare in the safe in my Neston office. And before you ask, Marcus doesn't have access to the office and he doesn't know the combination of the safe. You'll find no irregularities in our safety procedures. Ask any of my employees.'

'Can my client make a fresh statement and leave?' the solicitor asked wearily.

'OK. But don't leave the country will you, Mr Dexter,' said Gerry, favouring Marcus with a smile that would grace a crocodile.

Paul returned to his aunt and uncle's place. DCI Heffernan reckoned that under the circumstances it was helpful for them to have a family member around to share the duties of the family liaison officer who, however well intentioned, was a stranger. But now Paul was longing to be back to the incident room again. Although he was calling in at Tradmouth police station for a few hours each day he felt that he was losing touch with the inquiry. And he wanted more than anything to get Sophie's killer put away. He had never before felt this strong, almost primitive desire for vengeance. But Sophie had been his cousin; one of his own.

He hated it when Carole vanished up to Sophie's room. He knew she sat there on his cousin's bed, nursing Sophie's clothes and soft toys to her chest like precious babies, rocking to and fro, crooning the lullaby she used to sing to Sophie when she was small. It broke his heart to see her like that and know that there was nothing he or anybody else could do to ease her pain. His uncle busied himself with practical things and his own mother, Carole's sister, bustled around making sure there was always tea in the mugs and food on the table. But nothing could bring Sophie back.

It was coming up to five o'clock and his mother was in the kitchen preparing a salad for their evening meal. Whatever horrors they had to face, they still had to eat, she said. Food had always been high up on his mother's agenda.

He looked at his watch. It wasn't too late to go back to the station, just to see if anything new had come in, and to see Trish. He'd been disappointed that she hadn't called him. For the past few days she'd seemed rather distant. Perhaps she didn't know what to say – some people were like that around death. Or perhaps she was reluctant to intrude on his family's grief.

He was about to make his excuses to his mum when Carole appeared at the living room door. She looked pale and haggard, and from the puffy redness of her eyes, he knew she'd been crying again. He stood up, took her arm gently and began to lead her to the sofa. But she shook her head and handed him a DVD that she'd been clutching in her hand.

'It's Sophie's party ... her eighteenth,' she said. 'You remember?'

Paul nodded. He'd been there with Trish and he suddenly realised that some of their suspects must have been there too. Not that he'd really been aware of them. Being so much younger, Sophie's friends had kept to the large conservatory. His only impression of them was the loud braying of the boys and the giggly drunkenness of the girls. Now he wished he'd taken more interest. Hindsight is a wonderful thing.

'I want to watch it.'

'Are you sure?' All Paul's instincts told him that this was a bad idea; picking at scabs so they became raw and painful again.

Carole gave a firm nod so he took the disc from her and put it in the machine. The TV screen flickered into life and he found himself looking at the faces he'd seen pinned up on the notice board in the incident room – the witnesses, the suspects and the victims – as they pulled faces and performed for the camera.

There was Barney, kissing Sophie enthusiastically and when he spotted the camera he gave it a sly sideways look and waved it away. There was Jodie Carter looking bored and downing a blue drink while talking to Dunstan Price, who was taking occasional swigs from a bottle of lager. Marcus Dexter was sitting on the stairs with a brightly coloured drink in his hand and, from the speed he was downing it, he seemed to be intent on inebriation.

Paul saw fat tears rolling down Carole's cheeks. 'Are you sure you want to go on with this?' he asked.

'Yes. Leave it,' she said in a hoarse whisper.

Paul had no choice; he sat back and watched the moving images on the screen. Now Barney was deep in conversation with Dunstan. They seemed to be sharing some sort of secret. They were too far away from the camera for Paul to make out what they were saying but it all seemed so normal; just two lads sharing information. A new nightclub perhaps or a cheap drinks offer. Oh, to be young again.

Then the camera focused on Marcus Dexter again. He was making a bee line for Sophie who was talking to a couple of female friends, and when he reached her he grabbed her by the arm, tight enough to cause bruising in Paul's opinion.

This time he could hear what was being said. Marcus's face was close to Sophie's and she was backing away. 'I'll fucking kill you,' he was saying. 'If you don't ditch that loser, I'll fucking kill you.'

He looked at Carole. She was sitting upright on the edge of the sofa, her eyes wide with shock.

'I didn't like that boy,' she said, staring at the screen.

*

In a small house on the Winterham, estate Jackie Yates had finally summoned the strength to go through her late son's earthly possessions. Jimmy Yates hadn't had much. Just the usual things. iPod, mobile phone and a selection of posters Blu-tacked to the wall: Morbay United and a bevy of well-endowed women in various states of undress.

Every few days Jackie had ventured into her son's room to harvest dirty clothes and food-encrusted crockery from the floor. But since his death the door had remained shut and each time she'd passed it she'd tried to imagine that Jimmy was still in there, doing whatever it was he did. She'd been tempted to call out to him. 'Your tea's ready,' or 'have you got any washing?' Instead she'd stared at the wooden barrier between her and the domain of the dead, unable to cross that boundary.

But now, she placed her hand on the doorknob and twisted it until the door swung open with a creak – she'd been on at Jimmy to oil it for weeks because every time he'd go to the bathroom in the middle of the night it had woken her up. Recently, as she lay in bed she'd found herself listening for that creak and hating the silence.

The room was revealed in all its squalor. The grubby unmade bed; the clothes and underwear hanging like ripe fruit on the chairs and chests of drawers; the mugs containing something furry and pale green; the pornographic magazines strewn across a carpet dotted with crumbs. Stinging tears sprung into her eyes, blurring the scene, and it was some time before she gathered the courage to cross the threshold. The room still smelled of him and she found some comfort in that as she began to strip the bed. Some people would have left the room just as it was, as a shrine to the dead. But her house was too small for such an indulgence. Besides, her new partner wanted to move in and he had two kids in tow so the room would be needed. Life went on.

She threw the duvet to one side and when she stripped the flattened pillow, something fell out of it. The envelope lay on top of the rumpled pillowcase, standing out bright white against the dove-grey cloth, which, once upon a time, had been the same colour. The envelope looked well-stuffed and she stared at it for a while before picking it up.

It wasn't sealed and when she lifted the flap she was surprised to see a wad of ten pound notes inside. She took them out and counted them. A hundred pounds exactly and no explanatory note. She counted it again, relishing the feel of the notes between her fingers. A hundred quid. Where did Jimmy get that sort of cash from when he was on benefits and claimed he couldn't give her anything towards the housekeeping?

Finders keepers. Jimmy wouldn't be needing it now, so it was hers. She stuffed it into the pocket of her jeans and hauled the sheet off the stained mattress.

Chapter 30

The Steward's Journal

24 July 1815

She took both my hands. 'The pretence is ended,' she said, her dark eyes looking into mine. 'I am no foreign lady, but my father is a stonemason in Exeter and there was one in that city I feared. So I fled and rode on a carrier's cart all the way down to these parts. I amused myself by dressing in scraps of the brightly coloured cloth he carried and fell upon the notion that I should pretend to be some great lady from the East.'

'You were most convincing,' I said to her. I could not help but admire her spirit and resourcefulness.

She smiled and I saw that the smile was merry, creasing the tender flesh around her eyes.

'What is your name?' I asked.

'Peggy.' The smile vanished in an instant as though a

sudden disturbing thought had crossed her mind. 'Will you inform Squire Catton of my deception?'

'It cannot go on. And if it does, I cannot be a party to it.' I saw a look of distress pass across her face and I knew I had to give her some assurance of my friendship. 'However, I will not betray your secret.'

'I think Silly John suspects that I am not what I seem, and I am sure he wishes me ill.'

'That man wishes many ill,' I said. 'But the Squire will hear no word against him. John Tandy and Henry Catton have brought much evil into this house.'

'I know of the hunts. I know it is innocent souls they hunt, not wild beasts. After that last time, I saw them digging in the woods. I have seen and heard much, but they think I speak no English so I do not understand. If they knew . . . '

'What will you do?' At that moment I was reluctant to say farewell to her and yet I knew, for her own safety, it would be better for her to leave this place.

She shook her head, her eyes filled with sadness. 'I would return to Exeter but I am afraid.'

'Of your father?'

She shook her head vigorously and a lock of dark hair escaped the confines of her bright headdress. 'No, he is a good man and I regret that I have caused him much worry.' She fell silent, watching my face, as though she was wondering how far she could trust me. After a while she stepped closer to me so that when she spoke, almost in a whisper, I could feel her breath on my cheek. 'It is another I fear and I have seen him hereabouts. He has come here to find me.'

I took her hand. I would be her protector, her defender

from all enemies. 'Tell me his name and I will ensure your safety.'

'It is no matter. I must leave this place, for I fear Silly John and Henry Catton will use me ill should they discover that I am no lady. I have heard them speak of their hunts and how they yearn for female quarry. My lowly standing and the untruths I have told the Squire will leave me at their mercy. I must go.'

'Stay for a while longer. I will guard your secret well.'

She stared at me. Her eyes were large and beautiful and I felt that she was no stonemason's daughter. Perhaps her mother had betrayed him with some Indian prince for the woman was indeed a rare and exotic jewel.

'Why should you do such a thing for me?'

I was tempted to confess my feelings but I stayed silent.

The Jester's Journal

24 July 1815

Oh, what joy! What entertainment we shall have – even better than Boney's antics aboard the *Bellerophon*.

I always find that listening at doors brings great rewards, and today I have reaped the greatest one of all. I was unsure whether to trust the word of the man I encountered in the gardens, but now I have heard the truth from her own lips and I know also of our pious steward's complicity in her secret. I shall stay silent and await the opportunity to use my knowledge. How I shall enjoy plotting her destruction. That sly little deceiver with the dark, fiery eyes.

Chapter 31

Richard Catton had just received a call to say that full approval had been granted by the Council planning authorities, so the builders could begin work on the holiday park next week.

It should have been a time of celebration, but he didn't feel much like rejoicing as he stood in the entrance hall, preparing for a meeting with the surveyor down at the chalets. The business of the dead kids hung over him like a curse, it was only a matter of time before the police came asking questions again. And now he had a nagging fear that the name of Catton Hall would forever be associated with the double murder. What if parents wouldn't wish to bring their precious offspring to the newly rebuilt holiday park because of its link in the public imagination with violent death? Perhaps it would be wise to change the name of the place – if only he could come up with something appropriate.

Then there was that skeleton buried with the picnic. Nobody had yet explained how it came to be there, but it was male and it belonged to someone who'd been around Daniel's age and height.

He had vivid memories of that original picnic because it had been a turning point in his life – one of those times when something happens to change all your assumptions of how the world works. He had been home from boarding school that summer and the artists taking part had seemed so exciting with their confident voices and colourful clothes. Daniel had been one of them, but somehow he had been different from the rest. Daniel had charisma. He'd charmed Richard's mother but it had been the son who'd received most of his attention. He'd been with Daniel at every opportunity, spending time with him in the library at Catton Hall, amongst the old family records – those same records that now claimed his father's every waking thought. Daniel had spoken to him of jesters and hunts and how he longed to recreate the past. His ideas had seemed magical, like chasing unicorns through golden glades.

Nothing Daniel said or did ever seemed mundane or ridiculous. He was from a sophisticated world and Richard had been seventeen, emerging into adulthood. With Daniel, he had enjoyed the first rapture of love. Until he had abandoned him and vanished from his life for ever.

That summer he had been just a year younger than the kids who'd died in the woods; the kids whose bodies he and Heckerty had desecrated by throwing them over the cliff. The thought of the charges he would have to face because of this thoughtless, panicked act meant that he didn't feel inclined to celebrate the planning approval. There was too much that was wrong in his world. And those bones found in that trench didn't make things any easier.

*

246

They weren't having much luck with CCTV footage from the Lister Cottage area. There was a convenience shop with a camera outside further down St Marks Road, but going through all the footage was taking time, and it wouldn't be much help if the murderer had approached from the other direction.

'At least we have some idea of the time frame now,' said Wesley, trying to sound optimistic.

'If Keith Marsh is telling the truth – we only have his word for it that he left Evie alive and well first thing that Saturday morning.'

Wesley knew Gerry was right. They still couldn't pinpoint the exact time of the woman's death.

Gerry sat down heavily on his swivel chair. 'If only we'd been able to talk to that Marcus without his dad and his brief breathing down our necks. I'm sure he's hiding something.'

'We've got to do things by the book, Gerry.' He handed a sheet of paper to the DCI. 'This has just arrived from ballistics. Barney and Sophie were killed by exactly the same kind of shot as Jimmy Yates. It's a very common make, mind you.'

Gerry read the verdict and handed the paper back.

'Are we missing something, Gerry? Could there be a link between Sophie and Barney and Jimmy Yates?'

'I can't see it myself. They moved in different worlds.'

'Perhaps Jimmy took part in the hunts. Perhaps he got to know Heckerty somehow – at the paintball centre, maybe?'

'We can ask his mother, and his mate, Craig Walker. They might know.'

'We need to find the weapon.'

'There are lots of shotguns around here – licensed and

otherwise. Let's face it, Wes, the countryside's bristling with firearms. It's like the ruddy Wild West round here. The wild south-west.' He chuckled at his own joke.

Wesley was about to leave the office when Paul Johnson appeared at the door. He was holding a DVD and he looked as though he was bursting with important news.

'I think you should see this. It's a video of Sophie's eighteenth birthday party.'

They followed Paul into the small room where the AV equipment was kept. Some screens were occupied by officers given the mind-numbing task of watching CCTV footage. They looked up as they walked in as though they were glad of a distraction. Paul sat down, slid the disc into the machine while Wesley and Gerry stood behind him, fixed their eyes on the screen and waited.

There was nothing sadder than watching somebody who'd met a violent death on film, full of joy and blissfully unaware of the fate that would shortly overtake them. If you looked for signs and omens of doom they weren't there. It reminded Wesley that life was fragile and precious: you never know when it's going to come to an abrupt end.

Paul turned the sound up. 'This is the bit I want you to see. Just listen.'

They sat staring at the screen and they saw Marcus grab Sophie's arms roughly and put his face close to hers. Then they heard his words, spat out as if this was no idle threat. 'I'll fucking kill you.'

Wesley sat back and looked at Gerry. 'Do we get him in again? Confront him with this?'

'I don't think we've got much choice, Wes. And we'll get his premises searched too. We can't ignore a death threat.'

'What about Jimmy Yates?'

248

'We need someone to visit Carl Heckerty to find out if he knew him.'

Paul stood up. 'I'll go, should I, sir?'

'Thanks. How's your aunty?'

'As you'd expect,' Paul said before hurrying from the room, leaving Wesley and Gerry staring at the footage of the party.

'Let's see how our Marcus explains this one away,' Gerry said as he removed the disc from the machine.

Neil and his colleagues stood at the edge of the trench and looked down at the Feast of Life, lying there in all its rotting glory.

The feast had been laid out on a trestle table: Neil had seen the photographs of the artists sitting on folding wooden stools, tucking into the chicken legs and wine. The table and stools had collapsed and all but perished, leaving only rusty screws and fragments of spongy wood behind, but now that the ceramics, wine bottles, cutlery, chicken bones and plastic cups had been brushed free of earth, it was easy to make out where the guests at that strange meal had sat.

'It's been an interesting exercise,' he said with a sigh to nobody in particular. The artists were about to take a cast of the remains which would later be exhibited at Tate Modern along with the video of the dig. Orford seemed to assume that Neil would be thrilled about featuring in an art installation and he'd been rather disappointed at his lack of enthusiasm. But the truth was Neil couldn't wait to return to some proper archaeology.

It was just coming up to five but the sun was still strong and he shielded his eyes as he looked around.

Earlier Richard Catton had disappeared between the

chalets for another meeting with some planner or surveyor. Rumour was that work would begin soon on the new, improved holiday park, but Richard was looking more worried than triumphant. Neil couldn't help wondering about his father up at Catton Hall. According to Richard, he spent all his time working on a book about his family's history, but he was surprised that he hadn't been down to the field to see what was going on. Perhaps the old man was ill? Perhaps Richard looked haggard because he'd been up with him all night? Who knows what goes on in other people's lives.

He was about to help himself to a coffee from the flask he'd brought with him when he saw Orford approaching. He braced himself for some complaint, but the artist's brittle bluster seemed to have disappeared as he sidled up to Neil and shot a glance at the side of the trench where his colleagues were standing watching, waiting for the fun to begin.

'Have you had the results of those tests on those bones yet?'

'Not yet.' He looked Orford in the eye. 'You sure you don't know anything about them? They weren't chucked in as some kind of artistic statement?'

'Don't be ridiculous.' Orford almost spat out the words. Then he stared at the ground in silence for a few moments before speaking again. 'I heard on the radio that they'd found a woman's body in a house in Morbay.'

Neil wondered where the conversation was going. 'Yeah. My friend's working on the case. Why?'

'I'm contemplating some sort of study of violent death, that's all. Just looking for inspiration.'

Neil watched his face. Somehow his tasteless, unfeeling

words didn't quite ring true, and he had a gut feeling that his interest was more than academic. But he could be wrong. What did he know of the art world?

'Do you know if the police have made any progress?'

'I've no idea,' said Neil.

Neil stood quite still and watched, puzzled, as Orford turned and walked slowly back to the decaying feast.

Rachel looked round and saw Paul standing by Trish's desk. He'd had no luck at the paintball centre. Heckerty had never heard the name Jimmy Yates before he'd read about his death in the local paper, and he certainly hadn't been one of his select band of hares. They all came from Corley Grange – the game, online and real, was quite a craze amongst the sixth-formers there. Heckerty said that Yates might have taken part in one of his paintballing sessions at some time but he didn't keep records of everybody's name, and he certainly didn't recognise his photograph.

It might have been her imagination but Trish looked a little awkward, but then she'd been quiet of late, almost as though she was harbouring a secret. Or perhaps Paul's bereavement had affected her more than she was letting on. As Rachel watched them she felt a twinge of envy. Work meant that she hadn't seen her boyfriend, Nigel, for almost a week now, murder enquiries always wrecked your social life, and now she was involved in three separate investigations she was starting to feel that no life existed outside the walls of Tradmouth police station. There were times when she wondered whether the job was getting too much for her, and this was one of them.

When Trish stood up and walked over to her desk, Rachel forced out a welcoming smile. 'Anything new?'

'The offices of Morbay Properties have been searched but they didn't find anything, although the boss still thinks the manager knows more than he's telling.' Her eyes lit up. 'However, we've had more luck with the house-to-house interviews with Evie's former neighbours at Roly Walk. A couple of them mentioned that she had a lot of male visitors.'

'Did they know anything about her?'

'No. They said she kept herself to herself. But I've just found out that a few months ago there was a complaint from an old lady who lived opposite. It seems she was sharp enough to suspect what Evie's line of business was and she started taking down registration numbers and giving them to the local police like a good citizen.'

'A busybody.'

'Mmm. I wonder if she was one of the reasons Evie moved out. Maybe things got too hot for her once somebody cottoned on to what she was up to. Anyway, one of Evie's regular callers had a black BMW with blacked-out windows.'

'Did she get the number?'

'She certainly did. The letters spelled 'GAP'.'

'And?' She knew Trish was stringing it out, keeping the best till last.

'The car belongs to George Anthony Pickard – the father of Barney Pickard. We've found a connection between the murders. I'd better tell the boss.'

As Trish hurried away, Rachel felt another twinge of envy. Not only did Trish have a lover on the premises, but now she was going to get all the credit for this new discovery. She put her head in her hands and told herself not to be such a stupid bitch. But she felt too tired to take any notice of her own advice.

Chapter 32

The Steward's Journal

26 July 1815

A most dreadful thing has happened and, in my shock and grief, I am at a loss to know how I should proceed.

This morning, Peggy was found dead in the woods by the Squire himself as he was exercising his hounds. She lay amongst the trees and she was brought back to the house on a shutter by two of the menservants. Now she lies coffined in the dining room. The Lady Pegassa. And it is said that she will have a grand funeral paid for by the Squire as befits a princess.

The Squire is adamant that she met with an unfortunate accident and has forbidden any examination of her body, so the manner of her death is unclear. I, however, knowing of her true identity, fear that some foul play has taken place.

Today I walked through the estate, hoping to see the young man of whom she was so afraid, but there was no sign of him. I returned to the house, and as I did so, saw John Tandy in deep conversation with the Squire. The so-called jester looked afraid, as though he was fearful of being caught at some mischief or other. Perhaps with this tragedy, Henry Catton's cruel entertainments might cease.

I will try to find a way of examining Peggy's poor dead body. For I was truly fond of her, in spite of her deception. I fear that her death might have been caused by one of the evil persons hereabouts. There has been much wickedness in this house of late.

The Jester's Journal

26 July 1815

The matter of Pegassa's death has even distracted the busy-bodies hereabouts from talk of Boney's visit, and what lamentations there have been for this stonemason's daughter. I confided my knowledge to the Squire but he boxed my ears for slandering the dead, thinking it some jest of mine. Sometimes the mask of Silly John means that my words are treated as mere foolery.

The Squire will give her a princess's funeral at our little parish church. I told him that we do not know if she is a Christian, but he responded that in death she must have the best and most dignified obsequies that our community can provide, whatever faith she followed in life. Where Pegassa is concerned it is the Squire who wears the jester's cap and bells. How a lovely woman can turn a man's mind to broth in the flash of a pair of dark eyes.

I came upon the steward in the hall just before dinner and he says he has examined the lady's body against the master's wishes. He claims he saw bruising around her neck and he will not believe that her death was an accident. Knowing how I resented the Squire's interest in the girl, he made accusations against me and claimed that my murderous envy caused me to kill her when I came upon her alone and unprotected. This I denied. But I fear my words were unconvincing, for he spoke the truth. I did hate the woman's growing influence over my master. What is an aging jester, a relic from a bygone age, compared with an exotic beauty who knows how to flatter an old man.

I rejoice that she is dead.

Chapter 33

The previous evening Neil had called Wesley to say that Kevin Orford had been asking about the inquiry into Evie's death. But Wesley had dismissed this as a case of natural curiosity: it's said that many people enjoy a murder mystery and there was no reason why a well-known conceptual artist shouldn't be one of them. Besides, he had more urgent matters to deal with. And speaking to Barney Pickard's father was top of his list.

It was 8.15 a.m. and somebody had already called Pickard to make sure he'd be at home. As Wesley and Gerry drove into Morbay everything seemed quiet. Hardly surprising, Wesley thought, as the holidaymakers would still be enjoying their full English breakfasts in the town's hotels and guest houses. A couple of hours later, when they'd organised themselves to enjoy a day in the sunshine, the seafront and the sandy beach would be packed.

Pickard lived at one of Morbay's more exclusive

addresses; a modern penthouse overlooking the little harbour where an array of white boats bobbed at anchor. Wesley thought of the beautiful house occupied by Barney and his mother: there was certainly money in this family and he couldn't help wondering where it came from. Then he remembered that the mother, Patsy Lowther, had once been a top model, and he imagined that there was probably a lot of money in standing around being photographed looking lovely. Nice work if you could get it.

Wesley, with Gerry standing by his side, pushed the buzzer in the glass entrance hall and a disembodied voice told them to come up. The voice sounded casual, quite unworried. Wesley wondered whether Pickard would sound the same once they told him they knew of his connection with the dead Evie.

Gerry insisted they took the stairs because Joyce had been nagging him about his fitness again. Besides, he'd just been notified that he was due for a routine medical and this always seemed to spur him into activity. When they reached the top they paused for Gerry to get his breath back before ringing Pickard's door bell. The door was opened almost immediately by a small, bald man whose rotund middle was well camouflaged by the expensive cut of his dark suit. Somehow Wesley had expected someone tall and distinguished, someone who matched up to Patsy Lowther's beauty. Perhaps George Pickard had an attractive bank balance.

Pickard looked impatient as he closed the door and shook their hands. 'I have to catch the train to London for a business meeting in an hour, so I can't spare you much time. What can I do for you?'

Gerry caught Wesley's eye. Pickard obviously had no notion of what was coming and Wesley almost found himself feeling sorry for the man.

'First of all let me say how sorry we are about your son.'

Pickard's face clouded. 'Yes. We were close in spite of ... in spite of his mother. I tried my best with him, even though it wasn't easy.'

'I'm sure you did, Mr Pickard,' said Wesley. 'But we haven't come about your son. We need to talk to you about another matter.'

Pickard still didn't seem particularly worried, only mildly curious. 'What's that then?' he asked, glancing at the large Rolex watch on his left wrist, as he led them into a huge lounge with windows that filled one wall, giving a panoramic view of the sea.

They sat down on an uncomfortable black leather sofa before Wesley asked the first question. 'A few months ago you were a regular visitor to an address in the St Marks district of Morbay. Number twenty-three Roly Walk.'

The blood drained from Pickard's cheeks and he hesitated for a few moments, gathering his thoughts, before answering. 'I might have been there a few times but I don't see what—'

'You visited a woman called Evie.'

'How do you know that?' His eyes darted to and fro as though searching for an escape route.

'One of the neighbours kept a note of all the cars that visited the address and their registration numbers.'

'Why?'

'Because—'

'She thought it was a knocking shop,' Gerry's interruption earned him a look of astonishment from Pickard.

There was a lengthy silence before Pickard spoke again. His cheeks had reddened but he was bluffing it out. 'Well, I don't suppose there's any point in denying it, and I'm sure we're all men of the world.'

'We are indeed,' said Gerry.

The man paused for a few moments before continuing. He was sitting in an armchair opposite, his fingers arched in a confessional pose. He lowered his voice. 'I did visit a lady at that address. Her name was Evie but I haven't seen her for a couple of months.'

'She was murdered a fortnight ago,' said Gerry. 'Her body was found last week.'

Pickard sat back suddenly, as though he'd been hit. 'I . . . I had no idea she was dead. I . . . I don't know what to say.' He looked at Wesley as though he judged him to be the more sympathetic of the pair. 'Was she that woman who was murdered in St Marks Road? On the news they just said an unidentified woman. I didn't even know she'd moved house.'

'If you contacted her on her mobile I don't suppose a change of address would have mattered,' said Wesley.

'Yes, I always called her mobile.' He stood up. 'I've got her card here somewhere.' He began a frantic search of the wallet he'd taken from his inside pocket and when he had no luck he turned his attention to the desk in the corner of the large airy room. Wesley noticed that his hands were shaking.

'I'm sorry. I can't find it.'

'If you do, will you let us know,' said Wesley. 'It could be useful.'

'Of course.' Pickard had regained his composure. But his fists were clenched tight.

'What can you tell us about Evie?'

'I didn't ask too many questions. She was attractive, discreet, and our relationship was purely professional. She'd been recommended by a business associate. She catered for the higher end of the market.'

'You mean she was expensive? How much did she charge?'

When Pickard named a figure, Wesley saw Gerry's eyebrows shoot up.

'You always went to her place?' said Gerry.

'I preferred it that way. What is it they say? "Don't piss in your own backyard".'

This comment made Wesley a little uneasy. But he carried on with the questions. 'So you were one of her regulars?'

'I suppose so.'

'But you say you haven't seen her for a couple of months. Why was that?'

'I've been busy. Problems at work and I've had to spend time in Prague sorting it out.'

'Where were you the weekend before last?'

'Prague. Giving my suppliers a hard time. The factory was manufacturing vital components and they got the specification wrong and—'

'I get the picture,' said Gerry before the man went into too much detail. 'Why didn't you call her when you got back?'

'I tried but her phone was switched off.' He looked at Wesley and frowned. 'I'm surprised you didn't trace me before through her incoming phone calls.'

'We think her killer took her phone.'

Pickard swallowed hard and said nothing.

'Perhaps you can give us her number.'

Pickard picked up his BlackBerry, which was lying on the coffee table in front of him and selected a number. He scribbled it down on a scrap of paper and handed it to Wesley.

'When you were with her did she mention anybody else?'

Pickard shook his head. Then he looked up as though he had suddenly remembered something. 'On one occasion when she was unavailable she recommended a friend. A woman called Penny. I visited her a couple of times, but I preferred Evie. She was more my type.'

'Do you have Penny's number?'

He consulted his BlackBerry again and scribbled Penny's number underneath Evie's.

'Did Evie say why she was moving out of Roly Walk?'

'Like I said, she never talked about herself and I liked it that way. Ours was a business transaction. She supplied a service.'

Gerry tilted his head to one side. 'Like the factory in Prague?'

For the first time Pickard managed a weak smile. 'Something like that. Only the service Evie provided was far superior.'

They needed to see Marcus Dexter again, to ask him about the threats he'd made to Sophie. But when they returned to the incident room at 9.30 a.m. Rachel told them that there had been a call while they were out. Jimmy Yates's mother had called with some information. Wesley said he'd deal with it.

As Gerry vanished into his office, Rachel spoke again. 'How was Morbay?'

'Productive. We've found out that Evie was a very professional kind of professional lady, and she charged a fortune for her services.'

'How much?' asked Rachel, almost as though she was considering a change of career.

'Well, I think she had a sliding scale of charges but a figure of four hundred pounds was mentioned.'

Rachel shuddered. 'I still wouldn't fancy it. All those old men ...'

'You said there'd been a call from Jimmy's mum.'

'Yes. She's found some money under his mattress. A hundred quid, she said.'

'Why's she telling us?'

'I'm not sure really. She just said he was on benefits and he was always broke, so she wondered whether it could have something to do with why he was killed.'

Wesley thought for a few moments. 'He could have got it anywhere. He could have sold something, or been dealing drugs. But it might be worth having a word with her. Maybe she has her suspicions and she doesn't want to discuss it over the phone.'

'A hundred quid. That's what those kids who took part in the hunts at Catton Hall were paid.'

'That's what I was thinking. If Carl Heckerty hadn't been so adamant that only Corley Grange kids took part ... Tell you what, you go and see her, just for a chat.' He smiled at her and the sudden memory of the time they'd almost become too close gave him an unexpected feeling of guilty discomfort. But he told himself he'd moved on since then. Things had changed.

'OK,' she said as she stood up. She seemed eager to be out of the office and he couldn't blame her.

He looked round the office. 'Take Paul with you – he looks as if he needs to get out of the office.'

'Sure you don't want to come.' She almost made it sound like a proposition

Wesley looked away. 'The boss and I are going to have another word with Marcus Dexter.'

The phone on his desk began to ring and he rushed over to answer it. Then, as soon as the brief conversation had ended, he rushed to Gerry's office and flung open the door, feeling quite excited. This was something they'd been waiting for.

'Tessa Trencham's arrived. She's downstairs in the interview room.'

'About time too,' said Gerry as he stood up and sent a file plunging to the floor.

Five minutes later they were in interview room two, armed with coffee and questions.

Tessa looked up as they walked in. Someone had already given her a coffee from the machine in the corridor and she was fidgeting nervously with the empty plastic cup. They had never managed to get a proper photograph of Evie's face – the only certain image they had of her was of a rotting, discoloured corpse, which they couldn't have circulated to a sensitive public – but Tessa certainly bore some resemblance to the E-fit picture of the victim. Similar build, similar colouring and a similar hairstyle. They could have been sisters. He wondered if they were and she'd been reluctant to mention it for some reason. Perhaps that was why Tessa had been so ready to lend Evie her home while she was away?

'Ms Trencham. Good of you to come and see us,' said Gerry. 'How was France?'

She ignored the question. 'I can't believe Evie's dead. It's come as such a shock.'

He watched her face. Either her shock was genuine or she was a very good actress. 'At one stage we thought she was you.'

'We are fairly alike.'

'Are you related?'

'No. we're not. She's just one of my most regular customers. I suppose we hit it off and we became friends.'

'You knew what she did for a living?'

'Of course. She worked at Morbay University – something in admin, I think.'

Wesley and Gerry looked at each other. Evie had lied to Tessa – unless the story about the university was true and her other occupation was a way of supplementing her income to make ends meet. Gerry left the room for a few minutes to call the incident room and get the university angle checked out. But they both suspected the story had been a smokescreen to convince Tessa of her respectability.

'We need you to tell us everything you know about her. You said her name was Evie Smith?'

'That's right.'

'And she was a customer of yours?'

'Yes. Whenever she came to the shop we always used to have a good long chat. She loved jewellery – always said it was her one weakness.'

'How come she was at your house?'

'She told me the lease was running out on the house she was renting. She'd found somewhere else but it wasn't ready yet and she had to find somewhere to stay in the meantime. I was going to France for a few weeks so she asked if she could stay there while I was away. I took her up on the offer; to be honest I was glad to have someone in there looking after the place.'

'You must have trusted her.'

'Like I said, we got on well. And she worked at the University, so . . .'

'You didn't let your landlord know?'

'Why should I? She wasn't paying rent. She was just house-sitting.'

'What was she like?'

Tessa gave a sad smile and Wesley could see tears brimming in her eyes. 'Really nice. I just can't believe what happened to her. Have you any idea who did it?'

'We were hoping you'd be able to help us with that. I'm sorry to ask this but have you any enemies? Anyone who might want you dead?' Mistaken identity was a possibility they had to consider.

Tessa snorted. 'I don't think I'm the sort of person who makes enemies.'

'Any abandoned ex-boyfriends who might have mistaken Evie for you in the dark?'

Tessa shook her head vigorously.

'Can you tell us about her relationships? She must have talked about men in her life. Kids?'

'She never mentioned any kids, so I assumed she didn't have any. People like to talk about their kids, don't they? There was a friend she sometimes mentioned – someone called Penny. She worked with her at the University.'

'We already know about Penny. Is there anything else you can tell us about Evie?' Wesley paused. 'Did she have anything to do with your friend Carl Heckerty, for instance?'

Tessa frowned. 'I don't think so.'

The interview lasted another twenty minutes or so, but they

didn't learn anything more. On their return to the incident room they found out that Evie had been lying about working at the University and Wesley had suspected that all along. Evie seemed as elusive as ever. But at least now they had Penny, and maybe she would be the answer to their prayers.

When they arrived at Penny's address, Wesley pressed her entry phone key. As soon as they announced that they were police, there was a long silence, as though she was thinking up some excuse why she couldn't see them. But eventually she told them to come up to the first floor in a voice that sounded less than enthusiastic. When they arrived at her flat she was waiting in the open doorway, arms folded: Penny who didn't work in the offices at the University of Morbay, but rather worked on a self-employed basis in an expensive flat with a balcony overlooking the seafront, not too far from Pickard's penthouse.

She was tall, slender, black and stunning and, if she'd set her mind to it, Wesley was sure she could have rivalled Patsy Lowther in the supermodel stakes. For a few seconds he felt a little intimidated by her beauty and self-confidence. Then he reminded himself that she shared the same profession as Evie and, however high class, hers was a risky and precarious existence. Unless, like some of the famous courtesans of old, she managed to hook herself a wealthy client and go respectable.

She invited them inside, leading the way, her hips swaying with a natural grace that isn't given to many women. Wesley looked around as they followed her and saw that the apartment – the word 'flat' somehow seemed inadequate – was immaculately furnished and decorated in good taste with the most costly materials.

As soon as they'd made themselves comfortable on the soft tan-coloured leather sofa Gerry came straight to the point. 'We've come to talk to you about Evie. I take it you know Evie?'

Penny sat down in the chair opposite. 'Why are you asking? Has something happened to her?' She was looking worried now. Worried and a little puzzled. It was obvious she hadn't heard the bad news.

'How did you meet her?'

'A few years ago we both rented flats in the same house. I tried to call her the other day but her phone was switched off. Is she OK?'

Wesley hated breaking news like this. 'I'm afraid she was found dead a week ago. It's taken us a while to identify her. We still don't know much about her life, and we're hoping you can help us.'

Penny clamped her hand over her mouth and stared at Wesley, wide-eyed with horror. 'Oh God,' she said after a while. 'How did she . . . ?'

'She was murdered,' said Gerry. 'Her body wasn't found for a week and the weather's hot. That's why she's been hard to identify.'

Wesley thought that Gerry was being too brutal. Penny was finding the simple fact of her friend's death hard to come to terms with, never mind the gruesome details. She sat there, too stunned to utter a word.

Wesley took over and Gerry sat back and left him to it. 'I'm sorry we've been the bearers of bad news but we really need to find out who killed her,' he said gently. 'We know what you and Evie do for a living, by the way, so don't be embarrassed.'

She looked at him, her eyes moist with tears and long,

damp streaks of mascara forming on her cheeks. 'There's always a risk in this game, however careful you are,' she said softly. 'However strict you are about applying the rules.'

'What rules are they?'

Penny took a deep, shuddering breath, wiping a tear off her cheek with the back of a beautifully manicured hand. 'Oh, there are rules you have to follow if you want to stay in one piece, believe me. I call them the rules of the Game.'

'Go on,' said Wesley.

'Well, first of all, you never have sex with anybody, even if they're a regular, without using a condom. Then there are the safety precautions. My first ever client told me that I was asking to get myself murdered. When I asked him what he meant, he told me . . . Number one.' She began to count the rules off on her fingers. 'Never accept a drink – it might be spiked. Two; jewellery – never wear hoop earrings that can be ripped off in a struggle or anything round your neck that can be used to strangle you. Three; never wear anything that personalises you – a cross, or a locket, or anything with your name on. Four; don't wear shoes you can't easily run in. Five; plan your escape route in case things go wrong. Watch the door and make sure it's not locked – if it is, make any excuse to get out fast.'

'Did Evie know these rules?' Wesley asked.

'Oh yes. I made sure of that. She was very particular – even changed the sheets after each client. She was always careful.'

'Not careful enough,' Gerry muttered. 'What did you mean, you made sure of it?'

Penny looked down. 'It was me who suggested she became an escort. Her kid was having trouble at school – got in with this boy who was bad news. The job she was in didn't pay much and she wanted money to send the kid to private school – to get a good education and have the chances she never got.'

'Do you know which school?'

'I don't know, sorry.'

'What else can you tell us about Evie?'

'She'd been married, but her husband had someone else. Anyway she went off with another man but it didn't work out. After that she found it hard to make ends meet. The kid was still living with her ex, but she was worried about this boy.'

'Her child was a girl?'

Penny shook her head. 'She always called it "my kid" like she didn't want to give too much away. I think there was a lot she kept back, if you know what I mean. I only thought the kid was a girl because she mentioned a boy who was a bad influence.'

'So it could have been a boy?'

'It could have been. I don't know.'

'What job was Evie doing when you first met her?'

'Working in a pub, I think. She got married early and she wasn't qualified to do much else.'

'Did she want her child to live with her?'

'She said the kid was better off staying with her ex rather than being dragged round cheap bedsits, because that's how she was living at the time. Like I said, she was desperate. The husband married his other woman and claimed he was broke so he didn't give her any money, but she said he was lying.'

'Did the kid go to private school?'

'Once Evie started working she was able to pay the fees. I asked her why she didn't have her kid live with her but she said she didn't want to, not with the job. It's not right for a kid to see . . . You know what I mean. And there was no way she wanted the kid to know where the money for the school fees came from. I can understand that, can't you?'

'We need to contact her ex-husband,' said Wesley.

Penny sighed. 'I can't help you there, I'm afraid. One thing you should know about Evie is that she wasn't one for talking about her life and I'm sure half of what she told me was made up, to protect her family maybe. I never even knew her husband's name, or the kid's. She just referred to them as "my ex" and "my kid".'

'What about the man she left her husband for?'

'She never said much about him either. I think he was from London and he may have been a writer or something, but she was vague about everything. She liked to keep her life a mystery.'

'Even to you?' said Gerry. 'You were her friend.'

'But she knew what I did from the start. I reckon she was trying to protect herself. It was like that fairy tale, "Rumplestiltskin". Never let anyone know your real identity – if they know the truth about you, they have power over your soul.' She hesitated for a while before she asked the next question. 'How exactly did she die?'

'She was strangled,' Wesley said. He saw her nod slowly. 'Have you any idea at all who might have done it?'

'If you mean did she have a client who liked using violence, if she did, I wasn't aware of it. We compared notes sometimes, maybe shared clients if one of us couldn't keep an appointment or was double-booked. I certainly can't think of any regulars who'd do anything like that.'

'It might not be a regular. Someone new?'

'We don't walk the streets, Inspector. We only take on

270

someone new if they're recommended by one of our existing clients.'

'Do you know a man called Keith Marsh? He's a businessman from up North. Had quite a crush on Evie by all accounts.'

'She mentioned him a few times. He wanted to leave his wife for her but she reckoned he was harmless. I told her to be careful. If punters get obsessed with you it can turn nasty.' She sat forward. 'Do you think it was him?'

'We don't know. But he was the one who found her and reported her death anonymously.' He suddenly remembered Kris Kettering's reaction when they'd asked him about Evie. 'Do you know a man called Kris Kettering? Manager at Morbay Properties?'

'Oh yes, I know Kris. I rent this place through his company. I think he helped Evie out as well. The lease on her old place was running out and she said he was going to find something else for her.'

'And is he a client of yours or Evie's?'

'We've both seen him professionally from time to time. But I don't see him as a murderer. He doesn't seem the obsessive type.'

Wesley was about to point out that sometimes appearances can deceive but he had more questions to ask. 'Do you know George Pickard? He was one of Evie's regulars.'

'That's right. I sometimes saw him when she was busy.'

'His son was murdered a few days ago.'

Her eyes widened.

'He was one of those kids who were shot up at Catton Hall.'

She bowed her head. 'That's awful.'

271

'Look,' said Wesley. 'Is there anything else you can tell us about Evie? Anything at all?'

She shook her head. 'Like I said, she was a very private person. We were friends but I always knew there were parts of her life she kept hidden from me. But I can tell you something for nothing.'

'What's that?' From the expression on her face Wesley had a feeling that he was about to learn something vital.

'I'm sure Evie wasn't her real name. And before you ask, I have no idea what she was really called. She said Evie was a name she'd always liked and it went with the new life she was going to lead.'

Eve – the new creation, Wesley thought. Eve the mother.

Their visit to Marcus Dexter had been postponed because of developments in the Evie case, but Gerry reckoned this would have its advantages. The longer the lad was kept waiting, the more he'd think he'd got away with whatever it was he'd done. And a cocky suspect ends up making mistakes.

After sending Trish and Paul over to Morbay to pay Kris Kettering another visit to find out about his association with Evie, Wesley and Gerry set off for the Dexter place with a trio of detective constables and a search warrant.

When they arrived, Marcus's father greeted them, his face red with barely suppressed fury, and followed the search team around the house, protesting his son's innocence and complaining loudly about the incompetence of the police. For Marcus, it meant another trip to Tradmouth police station to be interviewed under caution. And, although he did his best to hide it, there was no mistaking that this time he looked terrified at the prospect.

Now they had evidence that Marcus had issued death threats against Sophie, Wesley felt more optimistic. And they also knew he was a crack shot, used to firearms since he was big enough to handle a gun. Killing Barney and Sophie would have been easy for him, and however much his father insisted on his safety procedures, there are always ways around the rules. Marcus had probably practised the shooting over and over in his head and online many times; rehearsed that moment of horrified astonishment when he appeared in front of them with the gun raised, pointing at their bodies, and they finally realised that his threats were no joke. That what he said had to be taken deadly seriously.

This time Wesley was relieved that the father was tied up with work because he knew Marcus would talk more freely in his absence. At first they made him go over the story he'd already told them. It was only when the boy started to look comfortable, assuming that they had nothing new on him, that Wesley switched on the laptop that was sitting in front of him on the table and played the DVD of Sophie's party. He watched Marcus's face for any giveaway sign of guilt but the boy's expression remained neutral, as if he was being shown something vaguely interesting that was really none of his concern. However, there was no mistaking the alarm in his solicitor's eyes, which wasn't a good sign.

When the video was finished, Wesley and Gerry waited for him to speak. There was a long silence but Wesley knew that the guilty, like nature, deplore a vacuum. Marcus, however, held out longer than most before he spoke.

'It was a joke,' he said, glancing at the solicitor. 'I didn't mean it.'

'Then why say it?'

'I fancied Sophie and she went off with Barney. I would have got over it. In fact I have.'

'You seemed pretty angry,' said Wesley. 'She'd let you down, betrayed you with your friend. Believe me, men have killed for less.'

Marcus moved his seat back so that the legs scraped loudly on the floor. 'You don't want to be questioning me. What about Jodie? She's really hated Sophie ever since they had a row over Barney.'

Wesley and Gerry exchanged looks.

'Tell us more,' said Wesley, folding his arms.

'Like I said, they couldn't stand each other. There'd been this thing between them, ever since Sophie had started going out with Barney. He used to go out with Jodie and they split up because of Sophie.'

Wesley didn't respond for a few moments, as he tried to get the teenage relationships, complex as any soap opera plot, straight in his head.

'Sophie used to spread stories about her – that she'd slept with people – screwed around. Some of the stories weren't nice.'

'Or true?'

Marcus shrugged.

'Can Jodie use a gun?'

Marcus smiled. 'Oh yes. She learned to shoot years ago and she helped out on one of my parents' shooting weekends last year. Dad said she was a natural. Can I go now?'

'Sorry,' said Gerry. 'We've not finished with you yet. Are you telling the truth about Jodie? You're not just trying to distract us from your fight with Barney?'

Marcus put his head in his hands. 'Believe what you like, but I'm telling the truth. Ask Jodie.'

'We will. And we might ask her about your death threat to Sophie while we're at it.'

The sunshine shone dimly through windows clouded with years of accumulated dirt. Alfred Catton had always been too mean to pay for anything but the most basic of cleaning, and as Richard watched his father sitting at his dusty desk with his beloved old letters and documents strewn chaotically around him, he longed for the day when he would be in charge. Once the holiday park was up and running and the money was coming in, he'd have the hall cleaned and restored to its former glory.

'I told you about the skeleton they found in the field while they were digging up that picnic. You remember the picnic?'

His father was reading an old, leather-bound book containing pages of slanting handwriting in faded brown ink and he looked up, impatient at the interruption. 'Of course I remember. I'm not senile yet.' He waved his son away as if he was shooing a fly. 'Now let me get on.'

'What is it?'

Alfred's expression changed. 'Glad you're taking an interest. It's the journal of Christopher Wells who was steward to Squire Edward Catton who was my . . . ' He paused to make a calculation. 'Great, great, great uncle. On his death the estate was inherited by his cousin, my great, great grandfather, Henry – the one they buried in a caged tomb so that he could never rise again.'

'And hunt through the woods with his ghostly whisht hounds. It's all crap. Ghost stories of old Devon to entertain the tourists.'

'It's not "crap" as you so elegantly put it. Read in conjunction with John Tandy's account I'm getting a far clearer picture of what happened when Pegassa died.'

'Pegassa. You're obsessed with that woman.'

Alfred looked hurt. 'This is our family's past, your past, Richard. Squire Henry had a reputation for evil and history repeats itself, don't you think?'

'So you keep on saying. But this story about Pegassa has nothing to do with us. It might not even be true.'

'It's definitely true. Her grave's in Queenswear churchyard.' He paused, his hand shaking slightly. Then he lowered his voice as though he was afraid of being overheard. 'She's still here in this house. Sometimes I almost feel as if I can talk to her.'

Richard felt his fists clenching with frustration as he resisted the temptation to haul the old man to his feet and shake the truth out of him, to bring him hurtling back to the present. But he breathed deeply and tried to keep his voice calm and reasonable. 'Look, I need to know why Daniel left so suddenly. Do you know anything about it?'

The old man looked startled. Then he sat for a few moments, turning his pen over and over in his fingers before answering. 'Why should it be anything to do with me?'

Richard slumped down on a chair and put his head in his hands, going over and over the time when he had last seen Daniel. He had just lost Ursula, his precious black Labrador, who'd been his faithful, uncritical companion whenever he'd come home from school in the holidays. His father had buried the dog because he'd been too upset to do the job himself, and now she lay in the little pets' cemetery at the back of the house, sleeping in the cold ground. He was rather ashamed to realise that he hadn't felt his own mother's loss as keenly as Ursula's, but she'd been a distant figure, subcontracting his early upbringing to a young nanny while she busied herself with her own concerns and sent him off to boarding school at the age of seven.

Then Daniel had vanished one day without saying goodbye. Richard had thought of him over the years, he'd even tried to contact him with no success, but now a terrible possibility suddenly entered his head.

'You hated Daniel. You hated what we had together.'

The old man began to turn the pages of the journal, a small, maddening smile on his lips. 'You were seventeen and he took advantage of your inexperience. I admit I didn't like the man, but he was a predator, and he moved on, as predators do.' Richard leapt up and his father started at the unexpected movement. 'Where are you going?'

'I've got an appointment.'

'Is it with that dreadful Heckerty man? A date is it?' His lips twitched upwards in an unpleasant smirk. 'This place needs an heir. It needs to be passed on to the next generation when the time comes. When are you going to understand that?'

Richard rushed from the room, his feet clattering on the old oak floorboards as he hurtled down the staircase.

Chapter 34

The Steward's Journal

27 July 1815

One of the women from the village came to prepare Pegassa's body for burial and she now lies in her coffin which has been set upon the long table in the dining room. I gaze on her pale, dead face and marvel at her loveliness, even in death.

If her claim to be an Exeter maid is true, her family must be told the tragic news. Perhaps it will be my sad duty to enlighten them, although I dread the task of telling her kindred that she has met with such a terrible end.

I have been thinking much upon her murder, for murder it was, and I am certain of her killer's identity. I witnessed the depth of John Tandy's jealousy and I know that on the night of her death there was a hunt, although little was spoken of it.

I saw Tandy that night and he certainly lacked the usual

278

bravado that befits a Master of Ceremonies on such an occasion. Rather he appeared most furtive, as though he was committing some shameful act. And there is no act more shameful than murder.

The Jester's Journal

27 July 1815

There has been talk that Pegassa was killed during one of our hunts, that one of the huntsmen came upon her and when she refused his advances, he put his hands around her neck and strangled her. It is true that a hunt was held that night, the quarry being two lads from the household of Henry Catton, but I suspect the real truth will never be known. The Squire himself did not attend, for he has lost his appetite for the chase after the death of Robert on the last occasion. However, I am of the opinion that the death of the quarry added much excitement to the proceedings. I had not thought the Squire so lily-livered.

Our sober steward stopped me today and said he was making enquiries of his own into Pegassa's death. Perhaps I will seek Henry's advice as to how we should rid ourselves of the troublesome meddler. I would create some tale for the Squire that would bring about his dismissal, but I know he will not hear of it. With Christopher Wells having charge of the mundane and tiresome running of the estate, he can dedicate himself solely to pleasure and the welfare of his beloved hounds.

But our steward, Wells, and his Methodist cronies threaten our liberty so somehow he must be silenced. I will think upon the problem.

Chapter 35

The cast had been taken of the remnants of the Feast of Life with much fuss and ceremony. Neil and his colleagues watched as latex was poured into the trench, and when the cast was set, it was prised off to be taken back to Orford's London studio and filled with plaster so that the form of the rotting meal could be preserved.

The archaeologists had been promised an invitation to the opening of the exhibition at Tate Modern. Neil wasn't sure whether he'd accept and the others hadn't displayed much enthusiasm either. They'd had enough of Orford and the thought of going all the way to London to sip a complimentary glass of wine in his company hardly appealed. Although, Neil was mildly curious to see the film of the dig. We all like to see ourselves as others see us from time to time.

Orford mentioned that he wanted to speak to Richard Catton before he left, so Neil, bored and in need of a walk, volunteered to pass on the message. He left his colleagues backfilling the trench, covering the picnic up again for future generations, and made his way towards Catton Hall. Being polite to Orford, a man he considered to be a fool and pretentious buffoon, was a strain and he wanted time to think.

When he reached the hall and knocked on the front door there was no answer. He knew Richard's father would probably be in, immersed in his documents, but as the old man was unlikely to answer the door, he decided to try the kitchen entrance. As he walked to the rear of the house, he was surprised to see Richard Catton emerging from the back door, his face red and a haunted look in his eyes. He looked like a man who'd just had a bad shock.

When he saw Neil, he came to a sudden halt and stared at him for a moment. Then, after a few seconds he broke his silence. 'That skeleton you found. I think I know who it is. He disappeared around the time the trench was filled in.'

'Who did?'

'Daniel. Daniel Parsland. My lover.'

Jodie sat in the kitchen where she'd last been interviewed by Rachel and Trish. Wesley had wondered whether they should take her down to the police station to emphasise the seriousness of the situation, but Gerry reckoned they'd get more out of her in her home environment. And it seemed now that he was right.

'Yes, I admit I didn't like Sophie. I used to go out with Barney and she pinched him off me.'

'You were jealous of her?'

Jodie didn't answer.

'We've heard that she said some cruel things about you ... spread stories,' said Wesley gently.

Jodie lit a cigarette and took a first, greedy puff before pursing her lips and exhaling a neat plume of smoke. 'Who told you that?'

'Marcus.'

Jodie looked away. 'That figures. Yeah, she said some things. She could be a real cow at times, but it was no big deal.'

This last statement didn't sound convincing. Wesley guessed that Jodie had been hurt by Sophie's allegations, and she wasn't particularly good at hiding it. He had only heard Paul's version of his cousin's nature and that had been rosy. But either Paul had been deceived or he was protecting family sensibilities by ignoring the shortcomings of the dead. From what Jodie was saying, the real Sophie wasn't the sweet-natured lass that they'd assumed she was.

'Look, Marcus fancied Sophie. More than fancied – he was obsessed with her. If you're looking for whoever killed her and Barney, he should be at the top of your list.'

'Funny, love. He said the same about you.'

'Then he's a fucking liar.'

'You knew where Barney and Sophie would be that night. You know how to handle a shotgun.'

'So?' She put the cigarette to her lips again and inhaled deeply. Her hand was trembling.

'Did you kill her?' Gerry asked with his usual bluntness.

The girl looked up horrified. 'Of course I didn't.'

'Marcus said you were quite capable.'

She stood up, sending her chair flying. 'If anyone hated Sophie and Barney it was Marcus. I heard him threatening to kill Sophie at her party. And he's got a foul temper. It's him you should be looking at. Dun can't stand him either. He's always having a go at him – makes jokes about him living in a pigsty, just 'cause he hasn't got a nice house like the rest of us. You ask Dun about Marcus and he'll tell you the same as me. He's bad news. And he likes shooting things.'

'People?' Wesley asked.

'Wouldn't surprise me.'

Jodie had spoken with sincerity and somehow they couldn't see her driving out to Catton Hall with a shotgun and stalking Sophie and Barney through the woods. But they'd been wrong before.

Gerry left the kitchen but Wesley hung back and handed the girl his card. 'Look, if you think of anything else, give me a call.'

She took the card from him and stared at it. 'OK,' she said before stuffing it into the pocket of her jeans.

They were driving back to the police station when Wesley's phone rang and he looked at the display; he saw Neil's name. He answered it, hoping that Neil had some relevant news – perhaps something about Carl Heckerty. It wasn't the right time for social chat.

It was then that Neil informed Wesley that if, contrary to expectations, the dating tests turned out to say the bones he'd found were recent, he had a possible name for the skeleton.

'He says he knows who it is,' Neil said softly, nodding towards Richard Catton who was sitting on a garden bench, head in hands. He looked as if he could do with something stronger than hot, sweet tea. When Wesley had first started at the Met as a callow young graduate, his DCI had always carried a hip flask of single malt in his pocket. But in these days of political correctness, he had nothing to offer but a few comforting words. And he doubted whether these would have any effect.

'Are you going to let me in on the secret?' Wesley asked. He'd left Gerry in Tradmouth and come straight over, hoping it wouldn't be a wasted journey.

'He keeps saying it's someone called Daniel. We're still waiting for those dating results to come back. All the indications are that they're old but our expert's admitted she could be wrong.'

Wesley looked at his watch. The skeleton wasn't at the top of his priority list just at that moment, but this was something he couldn't ignore, especially when it was so closely connected with Catton Hall, the site of the shootings.

'I think it's time I had a word with Mr Catton.'

Neil put a soil-stained hand on his arm. 'Go easy, Wes. I think he's in shock.'

Wesley approached Catton slowly and squatted down by his side. 'Let's go somewhere we can talk,' he said.

Richard offered no resistance and allowed himself to be led towards the house, Wesley's guiding hand at his back.

Soon they were in the kitchen with its low ceiling and sage-green walls, and even though the room was large, it felt claustrophobic. He looked round for a kettle. Pam had trained him well in the early days of their marriage and he quickly found the kettle, tea bags, milk and a couple of chipped and stained mugs.

'Now, who's Daniel?' he asked as he set the steaming tea down on the scrubbed pine table and pulled up a chair.

Richard stared at the mug and Wesley waited in silence

for him to speak. Eventually his patience was rewarded.
'His name was Daniel Parsland and he was an artist taking
part in the original Feast of Life with Kevin Orford. I was
seventeen at the time and I was helping out at the holiday
park for a bit of extra cash. Even though my family own the
land we had nothing to do with running the park because
that was leased to a separate company. Anyway, I used to
hang about and watch the artists preparing everything. I'd
never come across people like that before and . . . '

He paused. The memory had brought a small, sad smile
to his lips. Wesley waited for him to continue.

'I'd suspected for a long time that I found men more
attractive than women and when I met Daniel, I knew for
sure. He was in his late twenties, a lot older than me. I asked
him to stay here in the hall and my father assumed he was
just a friend.'

'But he was more than that?'

'I didn't think my father knew. Daniel was very discreet,
and he even made a point of spending time with my
mother to throw my father off the scent. Then one day he
left and I never saw or heard from him again.'

'Your mother's not around?'

'She walked out on us years ago. Her and dad led separate lives and her relationship with me was always rather
distant.' He said the words matter of factly, as though his
mother's lack of interest hadn't really bothered him. 'She
went off to Spain to live with some man she'd met.
According to my father, it had been coming on for quite a
while, but I'd been away at boarding school so I hadn't
realised what was happening. She was there that summer,
bored out of her head. She was always restless; that's how
I remember her.'

'Have you heard from her recently? If the bones do turn out to date from the time of the picnic, we may have to talk to her.'

Richard turned his head away. 'I haven't seen her since she left. Apart from the occasional postcard there's been no contact. But then she was never very good at the whole "mother" thing.'

'And we might have to question your father too if—'

Richard snorted. 'If those bones are Daniel's and my father was responsible for his death in any way, help yourself. I hope he rots in jail.'

'Why would your father have killed him?'

'Because of his relationship with me. My father's very big on family and inheritance. If I had a relationship with a man it would prevent me giving him an heir. I'm his only family, so if I don't have children, the whole Catton Hall thing stops with me. The more I think about it, the more it makes sense.'

'But I still don't see—'

'You don't know him.' Richard had raised his voice. 'You haven't had to live with his obsessions,' he said as tears began to well up in his eyes.

Trish watched Paul's fingers moving on the computer keyboard. He'd hardly said a word to anybody since his return from his daily visit to his aunt's. There'd been a time when they had shared everything and she felt sad, and a little hurt, that he'd become so distant and morose since Sophie's death. But when violent death comes close to home, the world becomes a different and less friendly place.

And his sadness did nothing to alleviate her uneasy conscience. She'd met Steven Bowles twice now, just for a quick drink when she'd managed to get away from work. But she told herself that it meant nothing. She hadn't even bothered to tell Rachel where she was going because it wasn't important, was it?

She thought about what DCI Heffernan had just told her about his meeting with Jodie Carter, out of Paul's hearing of course. The DCI had learned from Jodie that Sophie hadn't been the angel everyone assumed she was: she'd been cruel and bitchy to a girl who'd been her rival in love. She only hoped this information wouldn't filter back to Paul: there was no point in ruining his rosy memories of his cousin, even if they were an illusion.

She watched Paul stand up and make for the door, wondering whether to call after him to ask if there'd been some new development, but somehow she couldn't bring herself to do it.

As Paul left the room, he passed a young woman who was standing in the doorway looking a little lost. She looked around and when she made eye contact with Trish she made straight for her desk, as though she'd spotted a friendly face in a room full of strangers.

'I'm looking for a DI Peterson. Do you know where I can find him?'

'I think he's downstairs in the interview room at the moment. Can I help?'

'I'm from scientific support. These have finally come through from the phone company,' she said, laying a folder on top of Trish's computer keyboard. 'DI Peterson requested a breakdown of all the calls made and received from the murder victim's mobile number – Evie Smith, is it?'

'Thanks. We've been waiting for these.'

'Sorry they've taken so long,' she said as Trish began to open the folder, suddenly impatient to get down to some serious work.

As soon as the woman had gone, she began to go through the list of numbers. Evie had received a call shortly before the estimated time of her death and she made a frantic search of her desk for the list of numbers they had for some of the lead characters in their real-life drama.

Eventually she found it and, for the first time since Sophie's death, she felt as if she was on the verge of a breakthrough. She stood up and hurried over to Wesley's desk. When he returned to the office the news that Evie had received a call from Barney Pickard shortly before she died would cheer him up no end.

Chapter 36

The Steward's Journal

30 July 1815

There was much pomp at Pegassa's funeral, and it was pleasing to see that she received a good Christian burial in the churchyard at Queenswear. The Squire is to erect a memorial to her bearing the words 'The Lady Pegassa, princess of her tribe who died far from her home and people. Cruelly done to death. God grant her rest.'

I know that any lies and falsehoods should meet with my disapproval, but the knowledge that her deception had been perpetuated in death made me smile. For she was a remarkable woman, such as I had never encountered before.

Today at the funeral I observed the man who claims to be Pegassa's stepbrother. He wept but, recalling her account of how he used her, his tears left me unmoved. The Lord forgive my bitter hatred of that man. For love makes us mad and the only fruit of madness is pain.

The Jester's Journal

30 July 1815

Our hunt is fixed for tonight and I have made the stranger who is said to be Pegassa's stepbrother an offer of money that he, in his need and poverty, cannot refuse. Desperation leads us to many a foolish risk. He has been told to report to the stables just before midnight when he will be given his instructions.

The Squire will join the hunt tonight and I rejoice that his spirits are restored. Henry told me that he desires a hunt to the death.

Chapter 37

Alfred Catton had arrived at the police station of his own volition, saying he wished to make a statement. And now he sat on the hard, wooden chair in the interview room, looking so frail that Wesley was concerned for him. But there was a fierce determination in his rheumy eyes. His body was weak but there was strength in his soul.

'Are you sure you're up to this?' Wesley said gently.

Alfred nodded. 'Of course. I want to get it all off my chest. But if you're going to arrest me, I'll need my papers from my library. I'd like to continue my work.'

'What work is that?'

'I'm writing a book about an incident in my family's history.'

'You said you wanted to make a statement,' Wesley said.

The duty solicitor had been summoned, Richard having declined to arrange for the family lawyer to be called, and he was sitting beside Alfred, looking as though he'd rather be somewhere else.

Gerry too had decided to sit in on the interview, saying he needed a break from his other enquiries.

Alfred sat up, ramrod straight. 'I wish to make a full confession,' he said in a strong voice that didn't match his bird-like frame.

'Very well. We're listening,' he said, shooting a glance at Gerry who was listening intently.

Alfred cleared his throat, as if he was preparing to make a long speech. 'Daniel Parsland was a so-called artist taking part in that ridiculous picnic up by the holiday park. When he came up to the hall and made himself known to me, I confess I found him charming and urbane. I must have longed for sophisticated company back then because I ended up inviting him into my home, not suspecting for one moment that he would abuse my trust by seducing my only son. Richard was just seventeen and Parsland was at least ten years older, and experienced in the ways of the world. I hope you're not going to accuse me of prejudice: if Richard had been my daughter I would still have felt the same.'

'So what happened,' Gerry asked.

'I caught them together and there was a scene. I told Parsland to leave my house immediately. He laughed at me. That was the worst thing, that mocking laughter. He said he would do whatever he pleased and there was nothing I could do about it. I tell you his arrogance was breathtaking. To him I was a narrow-minded little man who had no comprehension of the modern world. As it happens, I'm not at all narrow-minded and I would have accepted any decision Richard made in that direction. It was the age

292

difference and the exploitative nature of the man I objected to. He said he intended to ask Richard to go to London with him, to throw up his place at Cambridge and live in some sort of artistic commune. I'm afraid I lost my temper and hit him on the nose, causing it to bleed. After that, he left rather abruptly, and neither I, nor Richard, ever heard from him again. When the artists returned I thought he might be with them, and when he didn't appear I was rather relieved.'

'So you deny having anything to do with his disappearance?'

'Of course I do but . . .'

'But what?'

'I do have a confession to make – something that's been on my conscience.'

Wesley sat forward, suddenly curious. 'Go on.'

'Ursula, Richard's dog, died around the time all this happened and when I dug her grave in our pets' cemetery, I encountered an unexpected problem.'

'What was that?' asked Gerry who appeared to be fascinated by the tale.

'I came across a skeleton. A human skeleton. It was a shock and, in the circumstances, I didn't know what to do. After the nasty incident with Daniel, I couldn't face calling in the police and having to answer God knows how many intrusive questions, so I did something rather foolish.' He paused for a while, studying his fingernails. 'Somehow it seemed the right thing to do to take the bones out of there – to clear the ground for Ursula's grave. But now I had the problem of what to do with the skeleton. Then the solution presented itself quite nicely, as it happens. The so-called artists had dug a large trench and had buried their ridiculous picnic. They'd left by then, but the soil was still soft so it took very little effort for me to put the bones in a bin bag from the kitchen, dig a fresh hole and throw them in.'

'I expect you had a hell of a shock when Orford came back and wanted to reopen the trench,' said Gerry.

Alfred gave him a rueful smile. 'The worry and the stress of it all has made me quite ill. And my heart . . . '

'You've seen our doctor?' asked Gerry. He sounded concerned. The last thing he wanted was for the man to die on him.

Alfred bowed his head. 'Thank you. I've been very well-treated here.' He hesitated. 'Now I've told you everything, are you going to arrest me?'

'I don't see why you shouldn't go home after you've signed a formal statement,' said Gerry. 'The results of the dating tests on the bones should be back soon to confirm your story.'

The old man looked relieved. 'Oh, that is good news. I need to get back to work.'

'What period are you researching?' Wesley asked.

'I'm particularly interested in the events of 1815. The year of Waterloo when HMS *Bellerophon*, with Napoleon Bonaparte himself on board, anchored off Morbay. Bonaparte was an amiable man, by all accounts, and he spoke quite openly with Captain Maitland of the *Bellerophon* about the activities of the seafarers hereabouts. He suggested that many local fishermen were smugglers, which may have been true. But he set the cat amongst the pigeons by claiming that many were in his pay and acted as French spies, although I suspect this was brave talk.'

Wesley listened politely. He could see the passion blazing in the man's eyes and he hardly liked to interrupt.

'On a more personal note, I have recently discovered

some fascinating documents in the muniment room of the hall – a journal written by my ancestor, Sir Edward's steward, a man called Christopher Wells, and also his jester's account of events.'

'Jester?' Gerry sounded surprised.

'Sir Edward was the last squire in the county to keep one. I've also managed to acquire a diary kept at that time by the Vicar of Queenswear.'

Wesley smiled. Alfred Catton, it seemed, lived in another time. And, interesting though it was, unless the bones turned out to be recent, they had to allow him to return to his own private world.

They had no more time for distractions.

Barney Pickard had rung Evie shortly before her estimated time of death and the call had lasted two minutes. It was just a pity, Wesley thought, that there was no way of knowing what had been said.

News of another development was waiting for him in the office as well. A woman had called in at Reception and had left a brown envelope addressed to DI Peterson. Now it was lying there in the middle of his desk and he stared at it for a few seconds before opening it.

He found a note inside, written on pale-blue notepaper in a small neat hand. 'I found this and thought you might be interested. It's of me and Evie and it was taken recently.' It was signed Penny and there was a kiss by the name.

It struck him that he had never actually seen Evie's living face before. All he'd seen was a rotting head with bloated features, and the electronic image of how an artist had imagined she had looked in life. But now he had the real woman in front of him, and he felt rather excited.

295

Evie was slim with full breasts, shoulder-length, dark hair and a pretty smile. She was wearing a low-cut red dress with narrow straps and one hand was resting on Penny's shoulder. Wesley recognised the jewellery she was wearing at once as Tessa Trencham's work – a necklace, two rings and a bracelet. She'd been wearing the same rings when they'd found her dead, but the necklace and bracelet had been shut securely in the dressing table drawer. He recalled Penny's words: don't wear a necklace because it might be used to strangle you; and don't wear anything personal that might reveal who you really are. Apart from the rings, Evie had stuck to those rules on the day she died. But somebody had still killed her.

Clutching the precious photograph, he made his way to Gerry's office where the DCI was sitting, staring into space. As soon as Wesley entered the room, he looked up.

'I take it Alfred Catton got home OK?' he said.

'I organised a car to take him back. Are we going to charge him with concealing a burial?'

Gerry shrugged. 'I'm reluctant to press charges, but I suppose we'll have to do things by the book.'

'It bothers me a bit that this Daniel still appears to be missing.'

'He could be anywhere in the world, Wes. People go off all the time for one reason or another. What have you got there?'

'Evie.' He placed the photograph on Gerry's desk.

He picked it up and stared at it for a few moments. 'Pretty woman. We still don't really know her story, do we? All we know is that Evie Smith probably wasn't her real name.'

'Now we've got this, we can put out an appeal.'

'It didn't work with the E-fit.'

Wesley laughed. 'That's not surprising. It hardly did her justice. I'll get this photo enhanced. I want it shown on the local news bulletin as soon as possible.' Wesley checked his watch. 'Although it might have to be tomorrow. There's something else too.'

'What's that? Give me some good news, Wes. I need it.'

'The details of Evie's mobile calls have come through and the last call she received was from Barney Pickard.'

Gerry gaped at him. 'Barney Pickard? The kid who was shot?'

'Bit of a turn up, eh.'

'What was Barney doing ringing a lady of the night?'

'Maybe his friends will know.'

'Marcus Dexter is still top of our suspect list. We can bring him in again and ask him.'

'There's something I want to check first, Gerry. Come to the AV room with me. I want your opinion.'

'That's an offer I can't refuse.' Gerry stood up and followed Wesley out.

Five minutes later they were watching a re-run of Sophie's party but there was one incident Wesley kept winding back and watching again and again.

'That white thing in Barney's hand – does that look like a business card to you?'

'You could be right, Wes.'

'Perhaps we should have another word with George Pickard before we talk to Marcus again. Remember he couldn't find Evie's card. What if his son took it?'

'Sophie was gorgeous. Why would he need to?'

'A bet? A dare? A way to get back at his dad? Let's go and find out.'

*

It was almost seven o'clock in the evening by the time they reached George Pickard's penthouse. He had just returned from his office and he looked worn out. The loose flesh of his face had a grey tinge and there were dark semi-circles beneath his bloodshot eyes. Wesley wondered whether he had been spending much time with his ex-wife. It certainly didn't look that way. The split, he thought, must have been pretty acrimonious for such bad feeling to trump their united grief at the murder of a child.

'What do you want now?' he asked as he opened the door. Wesley detected a slight slurring of speech. The man had been drinking, but that was hardly surprising. His week must have been unusually tough.

'Just a quick word, Mr Pickard,' said Wesley. 'We won't keep you long.'

Pickard stood aside to let them in. 'Have you found out who shot my boy yet?' There was aggression in his voice and a whiff of whisky on his breath.

'We think we're getting closer to making an arrest,' he said. It sounded better than a stark 'no'.

Pickard walked ahead of them into his lounge.

'We've got hold of Evie's phone records,' Wesley said as they took a seat.

Pickard waved a bottle in their direction. 'I suppose you're going to say "not while I'm on duty" like they do in the cop shows,' he said, pouring himself a generous measure into a crystal glass.

'Thanks, but we have to keep a clear head,' Wesley answered quickly. 'Did you know Barney had Evie's number?'

Pickard's head jerked up sharply. He suddenly looked sober. 'What do you mean? Of course he didn't have her number. How could he?'

'We were hoping you could tell us. When we were here before you were looking for her business card. You couldn't find it. Barney spent some time here, didn't he?'

'Yes but . . . Oh, I see what you're getting at. He found the card and his curiosity got the better of him. It's possible, I suppose, but he never mentioned anything to me.'

'Did you ever talk to him about Evie?' Gerry asked. 'Man-to-man stuff?'

Pickard frowned. 'I might have let something slip; made some remark. He wasn't a kid. He was eighteen. But I certainly didn't give him her address and tell him to give her a call if that's what you're thinking.'

'You wouldn't have to if he'd found her card. He might have used his initiative.'

'Like I said, he never mentioned it. And neither did Evie. She was picky. High class.'

'If Barney told her he was your son . . .'

Pickard shrugged. 'It's possible. But we can't ask them now, can we?'

Wesley produced a still from the party video, blown up so the card was plain to see. 'It looks as if Barney's showing a card to one of his friends. We've had it enhanced but it's still not clear. Look carefully. Could it be Evie's card? The one you lost?'

Pickard took the picture and studied it carefully. 'It's hard to tell.'

'Evie received a call from Barney shortly before the estimated time of her death.'

Pickard put down his glass. 'What are you suggesting?'

'Nothing,' said Wesley. 'I'm just stating a fact.'

The man rose from his seat like an avenging fury. 'Then

you can keep your facts to yourself. My boy's dead and he can't defend himself. You can't go accusing him of—'

Gerry raised a calming hand. 'We're not making any accusations here. We're just trying to get to the truth.'

'Then do it somewhere else.' He was shouting now. 'My son's dead and you're trying to smear his memory instead of getting out there and finding his killer.'

Wesley felt Gerry's hand on his arm and, reluctantly, he turned to go.

Wesley was in low spirits when they returned to the incident room. It was almost half eight now and he just wanted to get home. He wanted to spend what was left of the evening with Pam: he wanted to see the kids, maybe read them a bedtime story. But when Gerry ordered a Chinese takeaway to be delivered to the office, he knew the night was still young.

'Who's your money on for Evie's murder, Wes?' Gerry said as he tucked into a spring roll.

Wesley stared into space for a few moments. From where he was sitting he had a good view of the noticeboard in the incident room with pictures of all the dramatis personae of their particular pair of dramas pinned on, with Gerry's comments scrawled beneath each image. 'I'm not sure,' he said. 'Maybe one of her clients; we're tracing them from the incoming calls on her mobile phone, but it might take time.' He thought for a moment. 'How about Kris Kettering from Morbay Properties? He admitted he was a client of Evie's. He even let her rent Twenty-three Roly Walk without the usual references.'

'And his motive is?'

Wesley shook his head. He couldn't think of one.

'What about Keith Marsh?'

'He's up there with the best. He was obsessed with her so the psychology's right, and he could have reported her death because he couldn't bear the thought of her lying there undiscovered. She was laid out respectfully, and that shows love in my book.'

'But is he our man?' Gerry issued a theatrical sigh and helped himself to another spring roll. They were almost gone and Wesley had only managed to have two. 'What about the two kids? Why would someone kill them? Stalk them like that then blast them both with a shotgun?'

'It's a scene from that game.'

'So someone didn't want them to reach the next level?'

Wesley tilted his head to one side. 'What did that next level involve?'

'Being together? Making the killer feel jealous?'

'That would cover Marcus and Jodie. Or maybe the next level was about achieving something? Or revenge of some kind? We're going round in circles here.' He sighed as he began to open a container of egg fried rice.

'What about Jimmy Yates?'

'Maybe he knew something. Or maybe his death's unconnected after all.'

'At least we've got that skeleton out of the way now. Full confession. Good for the clear up rate, unless those test results come back and say he died recently. And what was a human skeleton doing in a pets' cemetery anyway?

'It's not like you to look for complications, Gerry. That's usually my job.'

'I just feel there's more to it than meets the eye, that's all.'

There was a bold knock on the open door and when Wesley looked up, he saw Trish standing on the threshold.

She had the satisfied look of a hunter who'd just run the quarry to earth. Wesley suddenly felt hopeful.

'Can I have a word?' She stepped into the DCI's office, carrying a file in her left hand, half hidden behind her back. 'You know you've had someone going through all the available CCTV footage from the area around Lister Cottage for the estimated time of the murder.'

Gerry rolled his eyes. 'I know most of it had been wiped and reused by the time we got round to making the request.'

She held out the file. 'We've had a bit of luck. These are from the convenience store down the road taken on the Saturday we think she died. They don't cover Lister Cottage, but they do show some of the street nearby. I've had some still photographs printed out. They're timed and dated.'

Wesley took the file from her and emptied the contents onto Gerry's cluttered desk. Both men grabbed at the photographs, studying them closely. Eventually Gerry gathered them up and favoured Trish with a beaming smile.

'You did well, Trish.'

'It wasn't me, it was Paul.'

'Then tell him well done,' said Wesley.

'But we could have done with them a bit earlier,' Gerry added under his breath as they began to sift through them.

'Oh, this is good,' said Gerry, rubbing his hands together with glee. 'Isn't that Carl Heckerty large as life and walking towards the crime scene just before midday.'

Wesley picked up the photograph and examined it. 'All it proves is that he was on St Marks Road. It doesn't prove he called at Lister Cottage,' he said, introducing a note of caution.

'He won't know that. We'll have a word with him anyway.'

Trish selected another picture and passed it to him. 'This was taken an hour later. This kid's walking towards the convenience store. Then in this one he comes out with a carrier bag and walks off down the road.'

Wesley stared at the picture. 'It's Barney.'

He handed it to Gerry who opened his desk drawer and took out a pair of reading glasses, which he perched on the end of his nose. 'So it is.'

'There is something else I'd like your opinion on,' said Trish as she began to sift through the pictures again, eventually selecting another and presenting it to Gerry. 'That boy at the bus stop over there looks as though he's watching him. Could it be Jimmy Yates?'

Trish was right. The figure leaning on the bus stop, looking in the direction of Lister cottage, did bear a strong resemblance to the dead boy. She was on a roll. She pushed another picture towards him. 'There's this one too. It was taken a bit earlier . . . just before eleven. That man's walking towards Lister Cottage. You can only see his back view but . . . '

Wesley obediently stared at the picture. The man in question had a shaved head and he wore combat trousers and a white, sleeveless vest. There was something familiar about the distinctive tattoos on the man's bare arms but he couldn't think where he'd seen them before. Maybe it would come to him.

He peered at the photograph, taking in every detail. 'That looks like a Land Rover parked there. Pity we can't see the registration number.'

Gerry pushed his glasses up his nose and examined the

image closely. 'They're common as seagull shit in this part of the world.' He looked at his watch. 'We'll put Heckerty and Marcus on our visiting list. There's nothing much more we can do tonight, Wes. Why don't you get home.'

'Pam's invited our new neighbours round for a barbecue tonight.'

'Then with any luck you'll be too late for burger duty,' said Gerry with a grin.

Wesley stood up. He needed to get out of there. He needed a break from the case.

Chapter 38

The Jester's Journal

31 July 1815

Our hare was released at twenty minutes to midnight, stripped naked, his pale flesh glowing in the moonlight against the darkness of the foliage.

The man had little to say for himself and there was a recklessness about him, as though he cared not whether he lived or died. Perhaps it was grief at his stepsister's passing – if indeed she was his stepsister. Or perhaps there was another reason for his rash and bold demeanour. But it was of no matter, for the hunter takes no account of the fox's humour.

It set my heart racing to see the Squire mount his horse and raise his cup in a toast to the hare and all who hunt him, as the hounds bayed for blood. There were four huntsman on this occasion: myself, Henry Catton, the Squire and one Humphrey, a friend of Henry's and an officer at the nearby fort. Humphrey hunts with the relish his men hunted Bonaparte before his recent defeat, and Henry urges him on.

Just after midnight, we set off, the hounds running ahead after the hare. We followed at a good pace across the fields, then we entered the woods and our sport began in earnest.

We followed for what seemed like miles and when we were out of the trees, Humphrey halted his steed and said that if the hare went much further we should reach the boundaries of the fort and all would be lost, for he would be seen by the sentries and shot on sight as a French spy still loyal to his deposed Emperor. I thought this unlikely as French spies would hardly go about their business naked. But Humphrey said that a spy might swim ashore from a boat and discard his wet clothing. I hoped our hare had chosen a different course.

In the event, he was scented at the edge of the estate, attempting to double back to the hall. We were soon in hot pursuit. The Squire and I rode ahead after the pale figure flitting through the dark trees. We would have him soon, I knew it.

Chapter 39

The previous night had been fine and warm, the sort of balmy, breezeless evening that lures the British into their gardens for a spot of alfresco dining. As Wesley had walked home at nine thirty he'd felt guilty about missing Pam's planned barbecue. However Neil had been invited, along with their new next door neighbours – an accountant and his wife who had a daughter the same age as Amelia – so he'd told himself his absence wouldn't have made that much difference.

When he'd arrived home the neighbours had long gone, but Neil was waiting for him, armed with a glass of wine, sitting opposite Pam at the wooden table just outside the back door. He was keen to recount how he'd done the honours with the charcoal and burned sausages, and for a few short moments Wesley felt an unexpected prickle of envy that another man, even though that man was his best friend, should have assumed his role at what should have been a family occasion. But his head told him that he should have been grateful that Neil had stepped in to save the evening and, by the time the morning came, all the misgivings conjured by his tired brain had vanished. He put them down to frustration – rarely had the solution to a case seemed so elusive.

Neil had spent the night on the Petersons' sofa and early on Saturday morning Wesley crept downstairs and found him fast asleep and gently snoring. It wouldn't be long before the children woke up and shattered his peaceful slumbers so he decided not to disturb him. But as he tiptoed out of the room, making for the kitchen, he heard Neil's voice.

'What time is it?'

'Half seven. I've got to go into work.'

Neil sat up and stretched. 'I'll have a shower, then I'll head back to Exeter. Good of you and Pam to put me up.'

'No problem.'

Neil looked at his watch. 'I'm back at the fort on Monday, thank God. I've had just about enough of Orford and the art world, but I'm putting the whole thing down to experience.' He shrugged. 'The only bright spot was that skeleton. You should have seen their faces when it turned up. I can't believe Richard's dad buried it.'

'It came as a surprise to us too.'

They chatted as Wesley grabbed a hurried breakfast and steered the conversation round to the excavation of the fort, because he wanted to put Catton Hall and its related murders out of his mind until he was forced to face it at work. The thought of Barney and Sophie being hunted naked through the trees and finally coming face to face with a gunman haunted him. He kept imagining their final

308

moments; the sudden realisation that they were about to die as they looked down the barrel of the shotgun. He hadn't slept well, and probably wouldn't, until the killer was safely in the cells.

After breakfast he left the house and made his way down into the town. As he walked down Albany Street, he glanced at Dickens's cottage and the sight of it reminded him of Marcus Dexter and the piece he had written.

He hadn't forgotten those words. They echoed in his head whenever he thought of Sophie and Barney dying there in that wood, shot like vermin. *'I am the hunter. I hunt to the death. My ears are tuned to the sound of my prey. Every breath, every sigh. Every squeak of exhaled air, as the exertion of running forces the breath out of my victim's gasping lungs.'*

Was it a coincidence that Marcus had described the murder scene so well? Or was it something he'd dreamed of doing for a long time? An itch that had to be scratched? Had he regarded hunting fellow human beings to the death as the ultimate thrill? If he had, he needed to be stopped before he decided to repeat the experience. Murder can be addictive. And easier second time around.

When he arrived in the incident room he found Gerry leafing through statements, frowning with concentration. He looked up as Wesley walked in. 'Richard Catton called. He wanted to know if his dad's going to be charged.'

'What did you tell him?'

Gerry shrugged. 'That it's up to the CPS to decide what's going to happen. He told me they're starting work on the holiday park on Monday. Him and Heckerty are going to be up there today getting things ready.'

'I take it we're going to ask Heckerty what he was doing near Lister Cottage around the time Evie was murdered?'

'There might be an innocent explanation, but let's go and have a word.' He stretched and Wesley saw his shirt straining dangerously over his stomach. 'The Nutter said he wants to be brought up to date with developments, but he can wait.'

They took the stairs down to the reception and picked up a pool car to drive over the river. There was no queue for the car ferry and they made it to Catton Hall in record time.

Just after nine o'clock they parked next to what Wesley now thought of as the picnic field. The place was empty now, the only sign of all that artistic activity being a long strip of bare, red earth scarring the expanse of rough pasture. Orford and his colleagues had gone, probably back to London. Last night Neil had been wondering whether to travel to London to see the fruits of his labours when Orford's work was exhibited at Tate Modern. But, from his lack of enthusiasm, Wesley thought, it was far more likely that he'd just take the cheque for the Archaeological Unit and put the experience behind him.

They crossed the field and stepped through the broken-down fence into that other world of crumbling holiday memories. As they made for the chalets, they looked around for signs of life, and it wasn't long before they saw Richard Catton and Carl Heckerty deep in conversation with a man whose hard hat and clipboard marked him out as something to do with the building work.

Gerry had brought along the still photo of Heckerty walking in the direction of Lister Cottage and, as he approached the three men, he took it from his jacket pocket.

'Can we have a word in private, Mr Heckerty?'

For a split second a flash of panic appeared on Heckerty's face, but he swiftly composed himself and forced out a weak smile. 'Of course. The old site reception is fairly comfortable. We can talk there.'

Heckerty led them between the empty chalets and when he arrived at the reception office he took a huge bunch of keys from his pocket, trying several in the lock before he found the right one. Wesley had heard it said that the more keys a man possesses, the more cares he has. If this was the case, Heckerty was bearing a lot of burdens. And things might be about to get worse for him.

They stepped into an office strewn with litter, mostly old leaflets about tourist attractions, at least a decade out of date. But there were several usable chairs and Heckerty invited them to sit, the perfect host in his tattered domain.

'What can I do for you *this time*?' Heckerty began, emphasising the last two words. 'I've admitted that Richard and I moved the bodies and there's really nothing more I can add.' He leaned forward, taking them into his confidence. 'Look, you can see why we did it. We couldn't afford to have the work on this place held up. Time is money and budgets are tight.'

'We're aware of that, sir,' said Wesley. 'The CPS is looking at the charges and you'll be hearing in due course. However, something else has come up.'

On cue, Gerry handed the photograph to Heckerty. 'This was taken around the time we estimate the woman at Lister Cottage was murdered, the woman we thought at one time was your former employee, Tessa Trencham.'

Heckerty stared at the picture for a while before handing it back to Gerry as though it was contaminated. 'There's a

311

simple explanation,' he said. 'I didn't tell you before because I didn't want to get involved.'

'And what's that?'

Heckerty took a deep breath. 'I went to see Tessa that Saturday morning, but she wasn't in.'

'You told us you hadn't seen her for a while.'

'I was telling the truth, I hadn't. But I wanted to ask her if she'd come back and work for me when the holiday park's up and running. To be honest I didn't reckon her jewellery business would be going that well and I thought she might be glad of a job with a regular income. I'd tried to call her but there'd been no answer – she has an annoying habit of switching her phone off. Anyway, I happened to be in Morbay that morning so I thought I'd call in. No harm in that.'

'No harm at all,' said Gerry. 'If it's true. What happened?'

'A woman answered the door. I'd never seen her before. I said something like "Hi, is Tessa in?" and she told me Tessa was away in France and she wouldn't be back for a while. I said I'd catch her when she got back, then I went away. That's it.'

'Did this woman say who she was?'

'No. Actually she was a bit short with me, as if she was disappointed that I wasn't after her, if you know what I mean.'

Wesley caught Gerry's eye. If Evie had been expecting a client, a caller looking for somebody else might have been a little irksome, especially if she had to summon up fresh courage for each encounter. Perhaps Evie hadn't been so cool and professional after all.

'What time was this?'

'Around midday.'

'You should have told us this before,' Gerry growled. 'It would have saved us a lot of wasted time.'

'I'm sorry. When I heard about the murder I thought it was best to keep quiet. After what happened here I didn't want to be a suspect, did I?'

There was no way of proving Heckerty was lying. In fact Wesley had the impression that he was telling the truth. But there was something he needed to ask.

'While you were there, did you see anybody hanging around?'

Heckerty's lips twitched upwards in a knowing smile. 'Now you come to mention it, I did see someone walking away from Tessa's place. I was really surprised because I didn't expect to see him there.'

'Who was it?'

'Kevin Orford. He wasn't wearing his wig and his clothes were pretty normal – perhaps he always dresses like that when he's off duty.'

'You mean that hair's a wig?' Gerry sounded astonished.

'You can tell if you look carefully. I believe it's part of his "artistic persona".'

'Did you actually see him come out of Lister Cottage?' Wesley asked.

'I can't say for certain, but he was certainly walking away from there. I don't think he saw me.'

Wesley produced the remainder of the pictures and handed them to Heckerty. 'Can you see him on these?'

Heckerty examined the pictures and handed one back to Wesley. 'That's him.'

Wesley studied the picture. He'd wondered where he'd seen those tattoos before, and now he knew. The shaved head and the clothes had fooled him.

313

'Do you know where we can find him?'

'Rich might know. Is Kevin a suspect?'

Wesley didn't answer. If he'd left the house before Heckerty saw Evie alive, he was probably in the clear. But he might still be an important witness. 'We'd like you to make a statement, at the police station.'

Heckerty nodded meekly. Wesley suspected, in view of the pending decision about his prosecution, he didn't want to make things worse for himself by protesting.

Gerry said he'd wait in the car and Wesley went off in search of Richard. He found him talking to the surveyor and, when he interrupted, the man seemed to welcome the distraction. He excused himself before asking Wesley to walk with him towards the hall.

'How's your dad?' Wesley asked as they walked.

'OK.'

Something in Richard's voice told Wesley that the subject of Alfred Catton was off limits, so he came straight to the purpose of his visit. 'At least you've got rid of the artists now.'

'Yes. I thought it would be easy money having them here, but it only opened up things that should have been forgotten long ago.'

'You mean Daniel?'

Richard didn't reply.

'Has Orford gone back to London?'

'No, he's still around. He's asked to see me. I hope he doesn't want to get out of paying me what he promised.'

'Do you know where we can find him?'

'He's staying in Morbay – the Riviera Towers, no less.' He sighed. 'There must be money in bullshit.'

Wesley left a few moments of silence before he spoke again. 'Your friend, Daniel, was an artist.'

314

'Yes. But he had talent.'

Wesley watched his expression and saw pain there. Orford's return must have been an unwelcome reminder of his loss. 'I hope your holiday park's a success,' he said with some sincerity.

'If it isn't I'm in the shit. Look, do you think there's a chance I'll go to prison for moving those bodies?'

'That's not up to me.'

'I didn't kill them and neither did Carl. You do believe me?' The man looked at Wesley with pleading eyes as though his whole future was hanging on the reply.

But Wesley could offer him no reassurance. He had to play this by the book and Richard and Heckerty were still on the suspect list.

Catton suddenly stopped walking and turned to face Wesley. 'Do you believe my father's story about the bones?'

'Don't you?'

'I still can't get the fact that Daniel disappeared out of my head.'

'You really think that skeleton is Daniel?'

'I can't understand why he hasn't been in touch.'

'Maybe he didn't want commitment? Some people don't.'

'But he wanted me to go to London with him.'

'People change their minds,' said Wesley, wondering how he'd come to be acting as relationship counsellor to one of his suspects. But it was part of his job to listen in the hope that some secret would be betrayed.

'If he changed his mind, I blame my father. He drove my mother away with his manic fixations and he drove Daniel away too. I shouldn't be able to forgive him for that.'

Wesley stared down at the ground. 'Maybe life would be easier if we were quicker to forgive people.'

'That's an odd thing for a policeman to say.'

'It's what my brother-in-law says. He's a vicar.'

'That's his job. Yours is putting away the bad guys.'

'I don't think your father's a bad guy. He was probably trying to look out for you in his own clumsy way. Look, I've got to go.'

'Will you come back? Will you need to ask me any more questions?' Wesley could hear a note of desperation in his voice.

'I'm not sure. Good luck with the holiday park.' He turned and walked quickly back to the car, aware that Richard was watching him. As soon as the car was in sight he took out his phone and made a quick call the Riviera Towers, to ensure that their journey wouldn't be wasted, and he was told that Orford was still in residence.

He couldn't wait to see what Orford had to say about why he was on St Marks Road around the time of Evie Smith's murder.

The Riviera Towers was one of Morbay's more upmarket establishments and the automatic doors swished open as they walked in.

Gerry looked round. 'Nice place, if you can afford it.'

Behind a polished mahogany reception desk stood a young woman with scraped back, dark hair and an immaculate black suit. She fixed a smile of cold greeting to her face and asked how she could help them. But when they showed their ID, the smile immediately vanished and she picked up a telephone to call up to the room. But Gerry stopped her in time.

'Just give us the room number, love. We want it to be a surprise.'

After a brief show of reluctance, the woman mumbled the number and Gerry bounded towards the lift, Wesley following.

'It's only one floor; we should have taken the stairs,' he said.

'I'm conserving my energy,' the DCI replied as they stepped out into a thickly carpeted corridor lined with doors.

Eventually they found the room and Gerry tapped on the door, calling out 'Room service'. When the door opened a crack, Gerry stuck his foot in the gap with the deftness of a seasoned door-to-door salesman and pushed until the room beyond came into view. Orford was standing there, shaven headed, wearing a snowy T-shirt and well-cut chinos. His white hair was draped over a wig stand on the dressing table, like a small abandoned animal. Wesley found the sight of it rather disconcerting.

'We'd like a word, Mr Orford,' said Gerry.

'As far as I'm aware I've committed no crime, but do sit down.' The voice was confident but the man's restless fingers plucked nervously at the T-shirt.

'You've changed a bit since I last saw you.'

Orford glanced at the wig. 'I suppose you could call that my stage persona – my mask, if you like.'

Wesley and Gerry said nothing. They made themselves comfortable on the sofa by the window and Orford sat down in an armchair opposite. He appeared relaxed, but Wesley knew he was putting on a show for their benefit. He was used to living a lie so it probably came easily to him.

'You were seen on St Marks Road here in Morbay a week last Saturday around eleven thirty in the morning,' Wesley began, handing over the still photograph taken from the CCTV footage.

Orford stared at the picture and it was a while before he spoke. 'I was calling on an old friend.'

'Name?'

'Karen. She'd read about the Catton Hall art project in the local paper and contacted me.'

'Where does she live?'

'St Marks Road.'

'What number?'

'It had a name. Something Cottage, I think.'

'Had she lived there long?'

'She was looking after the place for a friend.'

Up until that moment they'd had nothing but nebulous suspicions, but now it seemed they might be in luck.

'Was that friend called Tessa?'

'She never mentioned her name.'

Wesley knew evasion when he saw it. He took the photograph of Evie and Penny out of his pocket and handed it to Orford. 'Is this Karen?'

It was a few seconds before he spoke. 'Yes, that's her.'

'How do you know her?'

'When I was down here sixteen years ago we had a thing going. She left her husband and we lived together in London for a while, then we split up. It was all quite amicable. No big deal.'

Perhaps it wasn't a big deal on Orford's part, but Wesley suspected the consequences had been more serious for Karen, if that was her real name. 'Did you know she was working as a prostitute?'

Orford looked shocked. 'You're joking aren't you?'

'Why would we joke about something like that?' Gerry asked.

'I'm amazed. She was always quite ... bourgeois.

318

Perhaps that's why we split up – she didn't fit in with my lifestyle.'

'Ordinary people can be driven to extraordinary lengths by necessity,' said Wesley. 'Maybe she had it tough after you'd broken up with her. You wouldn't know. Why should you?'

Orford turned his palms upwards in an appeasing gesture. 'All right, I was immersed in my work so I never contacted her to see how she was. But we didn't owe each other anything. We were both free agents and whatever decisions she made after we'd parted had nothing to do with me.' He had raised his voice a few decibels, as though he was anxious to convince them of something. Maybe that he had nothing to do with her life . . . or her death.

'Did you see her that Saturday?'

'I paid her a visit. I stayed for about an hour.'

'What time was this?'

'In the morning. About half ten, quarter to eleven maybe. It was the only time I had free.'

'What happened?'

'She asked me for money and I gave her a hundred quid.'

'Why?'

'If you must know, I felt sorry for her. She said she'd lost her job and she needed some cash. I had a feeling it was a sob story, but I gave her the money, like I said, but I told her there would be no more where that came from.'

'Did you have sex?'

'For old times' sake. Nothing wrong in that.'

'You got it cheap,' said Gerry bluntly. 'Her usual rate was four hundred. Mate's rates, I believe the Aussies call it.'

'Look, I'd no idea she was on the game. She never said.'

'How would you have reacted if you'd known?'

'I would have told her to be careful, to think very hard about what she was doing.'

'That's very conventional of you, Mr Orford,' said Gerry. 'Very bourgeois.'

'It just seems wrong for her, that's all.' He sounded defensive, as though the accusation of being bourgeois had rattled him.

'How did you find out about her death?'

'I heard that some woman had been murdered in Morbay, but that was about a week after we'd met so I didn't associate it with Karen.'

'Didn't the address make you wonder? Didn't you want to check if Karen was OK?'

'We'd started the project then and I spent every waking hour with my colleagues. You've no idea how intensely we work.'

'The thing is, Mr Orford, she wasn't strangled a week after you'd met. She died around the time you say you were with her. She just wasn't found till a week later.'

Wesley waited for Orford to speak but he just studied his fingernails, avoiding their gaze.

'Did you go back later and kill her, Mr Orford?'

'Of course not. Why should I?'

'If she was making demands on you. If she threatened to make life awkward.'

'I swear she was fine when I left her.'

'Did you see anyone else around her house at the time?'

'Actually I did. I'd just come out when I saw Carl Heckerty. I'd met him when I had to gain permission for the project and I didn't particularly want to make small talk, so I hurried off in the other direction.'

'Did you see him go into Lister Cottage by any chance?'

320

'I looked back and I saw him standing on the doorstep. Karen opened the door and they had a brief conversation – just a few words – and then he walked away and got back into his car.'

Wesley saw Gerry nod. Without knowing it, Orford had just put Heckerty in the clear as regards Evie's – or Karen's – murder. Orford's account matched his exactly and both men had put Keith Marsh in the clear. Two witnesses had spoken to the victim after he'd set off for Heathrow to take his flight to Germany.

'Tell us more about Karen?' said Wesley. The life of the murdered woman had remained an enigma until that moment. He just prayed that Orford would be able to fill in the many gaps.

'When I first met her she was in a boring marriage. It was stifling her. She reckoned her husband had a bit on the side and she wanted some excitement too.'

'Where did you meet?'

'I was down here creating the first Feast of Life and we had a drinks reception at Catton Hall to thank the Cattons for their co-operation.'

'You knew Mrs Catton?'

Orford nodded. 'Now there was an unhappy woman if ever I saw one.' He fell silent.

'You were telling me about Karen.'

'She was a waitress with the outside caterers we brought in. I spotted her and . . . ' He snapped his fingers and Wesley found the gesture profoundly irritating. 'Her simplicity appealed to me, and I engineered a couple of meetings. She didn't take much persuading to come to live with me in London.'

'Did she have a child?'

321

'The kid stayed with its father. It was all rather boring.'

'Was it a girl?'

Orford shrugged. 'I thought it was a boy but she never spoke about it when we were together, which suited me fine. Look, she'd led a dull existence in some godforsaken place in the middle of nowhere before she met me. She said her husband had someone else, and was the most boring man in the universe to boot. In the circumstances you can hardly blame her for wanting to break out of her cage, can you?'

Gerry looked affronted. 'Since when has being boring been a criminal offence? If it was, our cells would be full to bursting. We all have our boring moments. Even artists, I don't doubt.'

Orford looked away.

'What was her surname?'

When Orford said the name, Wesley caught Gerry's eye. It could be a coincidence. But on the other hand, it had to be checked out.

'We'll need you to come down to the station and make a statement. I'll get a car to pick you up. Don't leave town, will you, Mr Orford,' Gerry said before sweeping out of the room with Wesley following in his wake.

'That man is a pretentious shit,' he hissed as they hurried down the stairs. 'Come on, Wes, we've got another visit to make.'

Bidwell Farm looked good in the sunshine. The weather even lent the shabby corrugated-iron cow sheds and the rusting tractors a degree of rural charm. As Wesley brought the car to a halt in front of the house, Dunstan Price emerged from the front door, his mother hovering behind him.

When they showed their identity Mrs Price seemed to relax. She'd obviously thought they were somebody else. Debt collectors, Wesley wondered. The place certainly looked run-down. Or perhaps a pair of DEFRA officials come to pull them up on some breach of regulations.

'Do you need to speak to Dunstan again? She placed a hand on the lad's arm but, unlike many teenagers with an over-protective mother, he made no move to shake it off.

'It's your husband we need to see,' said Gerry. 'Is he around?'

'He's up in the top field,' said Dunstan. 'I'll show you the way.'

'Just point us in the right direction,' said Gerry with avuncular jollity. 'We'll find our way. Not taken part in any more hunts, have you?'

Dunstan shook his head.

'Don't blame you.'

The boy opened his mouth as though he wanted to say something else. Wesley waited for him to gather his thoughts and speak.

'I heard you've spoken to Marcus about . . . '

He took a step towards the boy and lowered his voice. 'Is there something you want to tell me?'

'It's just that he wrote this story at school about . . . hunting someone and killing them.' Dunstan gazed down at his feet, embarrassed. 'Look, I don't want to grass on a mate or anything but . . . '

'We already know about the story. But if there's anything else you know that might help us, call me any time and I'll check it out.' He handed the boy his card and watched as he shoved it into his pocket.

Gerry had already stridden away across the farmyard

and, as Wesley followed, he suddenly realised that his footwear was hardly suitable for the terrain.

It was quite a trek to the top field and when they got there, shoes and trouser bottoms splattered with mud, they found Price examining the hoof of a large ewe who seemed to be taking the invasion of her privacy philosophically. Price spotted them and hesitated before releasing the ewe and sending her on her way with a pat on her woolly backside.

'We'd like a word, Mr Price,' said Gerry.

'What about?'

'About your former wife, Karen,' said Wesley. It was a pure guess. For all they knew Karen Price had been his sister-in-law, or no relation whatsoever. But anything was worth a try.

Price's expression gave nothing away. 'What about her? I haven't seen her in years.'

'When did she leave?'

He shrugged. 'Eighteen, nineteen years ago, something like that.'

'So she's not Dunstan's mum?'

'Pat's Dunstan's mum.' There was a determination in his voice that didn't encourage argument.

'Why did Karen leave?'

'Went off with another bloke.'

'An artist? Was his name Kevin Orford?'

The answer was another shrug, as though the events of the past held no interest for him.

Wesley produced the only picture they had of Evie. It was getting a little dog-eared now but it was still clearly recognisable. 'Is this your ex-wife?'

Price took it in his soiled hands, holding it by the edge, as though he didn't want to get it dirty. He studied it for a while and then nodded slowly.

'I'm afraid she was found dead in Morbay. She was looking after a house in the St Marks area for a friend and someone strangled her. She wasn't found for a week. It's been on the news and in all the local papers.'

The farmer stood for a while staring at the grass. 'I don't have time to watch the news,' he said, looking up at Wesley. 'I've got a farm to run. And I only read the papers for the football scores. But I'm sorry to hear about Karen. Whatever she'd done, she didn't deserve that.'

'The man she went off with said she had a child.'

'I wouldn't trust anything he says.'

'We've spoken to him and he says it's only sixteen years since Karen went off to London, so by my reckoning she must be Dunstan's mother.'

'Pat's his mum.'

'So he's not yours?'

'Yes, he's mine. Me and Pat . . . Maybe that's one of the reasons Karen left.' He pressed his lips together as if he'd said all he was going to say on the subject.

'You don't seem very upset about this.'

'Why should I be? She walked out on me years ago. Past history. Is that all? I've got work to do.'

Wesley wasn't usually a gambler but on this occasion he decided it was worth a shot. 'Were you in St Marks Road around the time your ex-wife was killed?'

To his surprise he saw a flicker of panic pass across Price's face. 'Of course I wasn't.'

Wesley handed him the grainy photo from the shop's CCTV. 'This is your Land Rover in the corner of the picture.'

He saw Gerry looking on with approval. There was absolutely no evidence that it was Price's Land Rover, but Wesley knew that if you say something with enough conviction, people tend to believe it.

For a few moments Price stared at it in silence. 'I was just passing. That's not a crime is it?'

Wesley felt a thrill of triumph. His gamble had paid off.

'I parked there and I went into Morbay because I had some shopping to do.'

'It's a long way to walk to the shops.'

Price didn't answer.

'So your car happened to be parked on that particular street around the time your ex-wife was murdered?' said Gerry. 'I don't believe in coincidences like that. Besides, our forensic people are wonderful these days. If you stick to your story we'll run all the tests and if you were inside that house where Karen died we'll find out.'

'OK, I went inside to have a word with her. But I didn't kill her.'

'We'd like you to come to Tradmouth Police Station to answer some more questions,' said Wesley before reciting the familiar words of the caution.

Gerry had been hoping that it would be a night of celebration, because it was traditional for the team to have a drink once a suspect had been charged. Price, however, was sticking to his story. And even if he'd made a full confession Wesley would have had misgivings about celebrating before they'd cleared up the murders of Barney, Sophie and Jimmy Yates, especially with Paul's forlorn presence in the incident room.

Price had made a statement. He'd had a call from Karen

asking to see him and he'd gone round that Saturday just after twelve thirty. He'd sat in the Land Rover for a while, mustering the courage to face her, and when he'd called at the house she'd been in an argumentative mood.

Then she'd asked him for money. She reckoned he owed her because they'd been married and she should have had her fair share of the farm when they'd split up. She'd even suggested that he take out a further mortgage on the place to make up for the fact that he'd been too mean to give her any financial support all those years ago.

They'd quarrelled, but, according to Price, she'd been alive when he'd walked out, slamming the door behind him.

When Wesley asked whether he knew anything about the deaths of Sophie and Barney, or whether he'd ever heard of Jimmy Yates, he shook his head. He'd admitted he'd seen Karen and that was all he was admitting.

Perhaps the death of Karen Price, alias Evie Smith, would turn out to be a simple domestic matter: a greedy ex-wife threatening the financial stability of a man's family. Maybe she hated the life she was living and wanted the money she thought was due to her in order to give it up? It certainly made sense, but Wesley knew that it was danger-ous to leap to conclusions.

He was about to sit down when Rachel walked into the incident room. He caught her eye and she hurried over to his desk. Her expression was serious as she pulled up a chair and sat down. He could smell her perfume, the one she always wore. He had bought Pam a bottle for her birthday.

'Pat Price knows her husband's here being questioned,' he said. 'But I think someone should speak to her, see if she knows anything. Do your parents know the family?' The

Traceys, having farmed in the area for generations, had an encyclopaedic knowledge of the local farming community and it occurred to Wesley that it might come in useful.

'I've never heard them mentioned. Maybe they keep themselves to themselves. Some people do. Do you believe Price's story?'

Wesley sighed. 'I don't know. He swears he didn't kill her.'

'But someone did. And she could have made big trouble for him.'

'When we asked him if he knew what she did for a living he denied it. In fact, he seemed genuinely shocked.'

'Maybe he found out and that's when he lost it.' She gave him a mischievous smile. 'Hurry up and get him charged, won't you. I could do with a drink tonight.'

'Even if he admits everything it's a bit early to be celebrating, and we mustn't forget that Paul's lost his cousin.'

Rachel looked a little guilty. She wasn't usually so thoughtless but the workload was getting to them all. 'I'll go and have that word with Pat Price,' she said.

He watched as she hurried out of the incident room. When he looked round he saw Paul sitting at his desk. He appeared to be engrossed in some paperwork but Wesley sensed that his mind was elsewhere.

'Paul, I've got a job for you.' He scribbled something down on a piece of paper and passed it over to him. 'Can you check this out for me?'

Paul took it and gave an earnest nod. 'OK.'

'How's your aunt?'

Paul shook his head. Wesley knew it had been a stupid question. He heard Trish's voice just behind him. He hadn't heard her approaching and the sound made him jump.

'Sir, I've been checking out that artist, Kevin Orford, like the boss asked,' she said. 'It turns out he's got form. Assaulted a woman five years ago. Domestic. She was his girlfriend and they had a row. She ended up with two cracked ribs. Think it might be important?'

'Thanks, Trish. Let the boss know, will you.' He watched as she walked over to Gerry's office and knocked tentatively on the open door, as if she feared some frightful beast might emerge from behind the desk and devour her. Then he began to consider the implications of what he'd just learned. Orford had a record for violence and if he'd approached the house from the other direction, away from the CCTV camera's intrusive gaze, there was a chance he could have gone back. But, on the other hand, all his instincts told him that something about Price's story didn't add up, and he had the best motive of all to murder his ex-wife.

The phone on his desk began to ring, so he answered it, hoping it was good news. But it turned out to be someone from Uniform, reporting that there had been a break-in at Jimmy Yates's house. It had been treated as a routine matter but, in view of Jimmy's recent murder, the constable thought that the investigation team should be informed, just in case. Wesley thanked him and put the phone down, grateful that somebody had used their initiative and made the connection.

He told himself the break-in probably meant nothing. Burglary was a regular occurrence on the Winterham Estate – almost like postal deliveries and a visit from the bin men. However he decided to send Trish to have a re-assuring word with Mrs Yates. He could rely on her to be sympathetic.

No sooner had Trish left the office than his phone rang again. He took a deep breath and picked up the receiver.

'Incident room. DI Peterson speaking.'

There was a long silence and he waited patiently. It took some people a while to pluck up the necessary courage to speak to a police officer. He could hear Gerry's voice in the background, complaining about somebody's incompetence. He pressed the phone closer to his ear and listened.

Eventually his patience was rewarded and he heard a breathless female voice. 'This is Jodie Carter ... Sophie's friend. I've got something to tell you.'

'What is it, Jodie?'

'Sorry, I've made a mistake. It's nothing.'

He heard the dialling tone and stared at the instrument for a while before trying to return the call. But Jodie wasn't answering.

Whatever had been bothering her, she had lied when she'd told him it was nothing. She'd sounded frightened.

They'd been granted more time to question Len Price and Gerry planned to resume first thing the next morning. The suspect needed a break, and so did they.

Wesley left for home at eight thirty, but before leaving the station he went down to the custody suite and peeped into Price's cell. The man was lying on his mattress with his eyes shut but Wesley had sensed that he wasn't asleep. If he was charged with murder he'd have to face the ordeal of the trial and possible life imprisonment for his single act of madness. The sight of him lying there made Wesley sad.

He left the police station and the town centre, now packed with tourists roaming the streets in search of a restaurant, and walked back home up Albany Street. When he passed Dickens's cottage the lights were on and the blinds were open, but there was no sign of the man; if there had been, he might have been tempted to stop for another word. He passed that cottage twice a day and each time he was reminded of Marcus Dexter's story. But all the evidence against him was circumstantial: they needed something solid if they were to going to make an arrest. He hoped their luck would begin to change soon.

His walk home in the evening sun gave him a chance to go over the events of the day in his mind. Trish had seemed troubled when she returned from visiting Mrs Yates. The house had been broken into all right. Mrs Yates had returned from the supermarket to find a broken back window and a mess upstairs, but as far as she could tell, nothing had been taken. Jimmy's room had appeared to be the burglar's main target. It had been turned upside down; the drawers had been emptied onto the floor, and the contents of the wardrobe scattered about. Even the mattress had been thrown to one side. If the place hadn't already been tidied to within an inch of its life, the chaos would have been a lot worse. But as it was, there hadn't been much of Jimmy's left in there.

Mrs Yates had blamed kids. But Trish could tell that the room had been systematically searched. Somebody had been after something. Perhaps it was time they had another look through Jimmy's meagre possessions, Wesley thought. However, that would have to wait till tomorrow.

The break-in apart, Trish had seemed a little concerned about Mrs Yates's mental state. She had gone on about her Jimmy being a good lad – it wasn't true what some people said about him. When Trish had asked her to explain, Mrs Yates had shaken her head and said it didn't matter. But,

Trish knew it mattered deeply to her, because it was at the forefront of her mind at her time of grief.

Rachel too had been rather subdued when she'd returned from Bidwell Farm. Pat Price hadn't said much. In fact she'd sat there in silence, giving monosyllabic answers to Rachel's gently probing questions. Rachel thought that she'd seemed more angry than distraught, as though Price had gone off to visit his ex-wife just to irritate her. It was hard to predict how people would react under stress, and having your husband arrested on suspicion of murdering your predecessor must be up there on the list of all-time stressful experiences. But Pat had been firm about one thing: Len Price might have had a heated quarrel with Karen, but he wasn't capable of murder, no matter what the provocation. Rachel hadn't been sure whether she was trying to convince the police, or herself.

Dunstan had stayed with his mother throughout her visit, a quiet, watchful presence, and Rachel had been struck by his sudden maturity, as though he'd realised that Pat might need him now. If Price's guilt was proved, Dunstan would have to assume the mantle of 'man of the house', which on a farm is an onerous role to fall on young shoulders. Perhaps all his plans to go to university would have to be put on hold. If so, Wesley couldn't help feeling sorry for the lad.

And then there were the annoying loose ends. Jodie Carter had sounded frightened when she'd called him and he'd half expected her to ring back, but there'd been no word. On top of that, Paul hadn't yet come up with the information he'd asked him to check out. And that was something he needed to know.

He reached the cul-de-sac of modern detached houses at

the top of the town, all with shiny cars parked in their neat front drives. Kevin Orford would have despised the suburban scene, he thought, as his own house came into view. But he tried to put work out of his head for the time being. Tomorrow he would sacrifice his Sunday and return to the incident room, so he resolved to make the most of his leisure time while he could, even though Jimmy Yates and the two teenagers who'd died at Catton Hall kept intruding into his mind.

Pam came out into the hall to greet him and stood on tiptoe to give him an absent-minded peck on the cheek. 'How's it going?' she asked, a note of anxiety in her voice.

But before he could answer Michael and Amelia burst into the hall.

'Moriarty's caught a mouse,' Amelia announced proudly as he put his arm round Pam and led her back into the living room.

'It's what cats do. They're natural hunters,' Michael said philosophically. Wesley told him he was right. Sometimes you couldn't fight against nature.

The young cat was lying on the sofa, exhausted by her murderous efforts. He picked her up and when he sat down in the space she'd warmed for him, she punished him for the disturbance by sinking her claws into his leg and purring loudly.

The remainder of their evening was uneventful apart from a drunken phone call from Pam's mother, Della, saying how much she was missing the children. Pam had taken the call and Wesley had watched her listen to her mother's excuses, her face expressionless. Pam wouldn't back down. She didn't want her children exposed to her wayward mother's influence any more; to her unsuitable boyfriends and her habit of downing a full bottle of wine while babysitting. She'd overstepped the mark on too many occasions and Pam's patience was exhausted. When she'd finished the call he said nothing. It was up to mother and daughter to be reconciled in their own time – but Wesley felt a small pang of guilt that he wasn't in any hurry for that to happen.

By half past ten he was completely relaxed and anticipating a good night's sleep. But the insistent ringing of his mobile phone put paid to all that and he sat up straight, suddenly alert.

'It's Jodie Carter,' said a breathless voice on the other end of the line. 'Sophie's friend.' The explanation was unnecessary. Wesley remembered all too well who she was – and he thought the use of the word 'friend' wasn't entirely accurate: there hadn't been much love lost between the two girls.

'I was expecting you to call back earlier,' he said. 'Look, can this wait till tomorrow?' He looked at Pam and saw that she was frowning with disapproval.

'No. I think he's going to do something stupid.'

'Who?'

Silence.

'If it's important, tell me now and maybe I can do something about it.'

Another long silence followed and he was afraid she'd changed her mind. Perhaps he shouldn't have tried to put her off. He was relieved when he heard her voice again.

'Marcus said he wasn't up at Fortress Point on the night Sophie and Barney were killed, but now he's admitted he was. It's not far from Catton Hall.'

'OK. Slow down. What was he doing at Fortress Point?'

'He sometimes takes one of his dad's guns up there to do

some target practice. He told me he's going up there again tonight. I thought you should know.'

'Why's that?' Wesley's heart was beating a little faster.

Jodie hesitated, then the words came out in a rush. 'He had that big bust up with Barney and . . . I think he killed them.'

'You've done the right thing telling me, Jodie,' he said. 'Leave it with me. And Jodie?'

'What?'

'Don't get it into your head to go up there, will you?'

The line went dead, and Wesley stared at the phone for a few moments before replacing the receiver. Then he made another call. He needed to speak to Gerry.

Chapter 40

The Jester's Journal

31 July 1815

He was making for the hall, and we ran him to earth by the wall that separates the rose garden from the wilder parts of the Squire's land. I surmised that he was heading for the stables to fetch his clothes and flee, but now the hounds had him trapped as he searched for the gate that would lead to freedom.

We had him there at bay, the hounds barking and baring their teeth, awaiting their master's orders. Our hare cowered at the foot of the wall, breathless and exhausted, shielding his face as though he expected blows to rain down upon him. I dismounted and shooed the hounds away before stepping forward to grab the man's hair, and when I looked up at Henry I saw his eyes shining with anticipation.

'Shall he be shown mercy?' I called out.

'No mercy,' the Squire cried.

Humphrey had been hanging back but now he brought his horse nearer. 'We have had our sport. I say mercy.' There was a tremor in his voice, as though, despite his war-like occupation, he had no stomach for what was to come.

Henry grabbed the reins of his mount and began to lead him away as the Squire signalled me to take the cudgel from my belt and prepare for the climax of our entertainment.

As I brought the instrument down on our quarry's trembling limbs, his screams pierced the night air, mingling with Henry's laughter as he drew his sword and made deep cuts in the pale flesh while his victim squealed for mercy. And as I raised my cudgel to dash out our quarry's brains, I heard the voice of the Squire urging me on. He was not to be denied his vengeance.

Chapter 41

The light had faded by the time Wesley met Gerry and the others in the car park some distance from Fortress Point. On a summer day the place was usually packed, but now the only vehicles there belonged to the police.

The Armed Response Unit vehicles made him uneasy. But if Marcus was in possession of a shotgun they had no choice. The boy was a crack shot, who had played Blood Hunt with enthusiasm and poured out his murderous fantasies on paper. It was hardly surprising that Marcus had eventually chosen to play the game for real.

After telling the ARU officers to keep out of sight until they were needed, Gerry led the way down the track to the fort. Wesley walked beside him, cursing the fact that the gravel on the path crunched loudly beneath their feet. They didn't want to alert Marcus and alarm him into doing something stupid. They needed to keep things calm and make a quiet arrest.

Keeping their eyes focused ahead, they walked on briskly towards the shadowy, half-ruined buildings perched on the headland. There was no sign of a vehicle parked near the entrance and Wesley hoped they had arrived first so they would have the advantage of surprise. But he knew there were plenty of places nearby where a vehicle could be hidden from view.

They crossed the wooden bridge into the fort, passing the fenced-off area where Neil's team were excavating, but Wesley didn't even give it a cursory glance.

A few hundred yards away, beyond a group of low stone buildings – some collapsed shells, others still roofed – the lighthouse perched on the headland, sent out its bright, pulsing signal to unseen ships, and the beam lit up the fort for a few seconds before it was plunged into darkness again. It also made them sitting targets for any lone sniper until they took cover.

To their left they could see the distant lights of Morbay glittering across the bay, all that brightness a world away from this silent, ruined place.

The hollow click of a gun being loaded echoed through the quiet night air. Unmistakable. He was out there. And that place of shadows would provide abundant shelter for the gunman. They pressed their backs against the rough stonework of the perimeter wall and moved on further into the heart of the fort. Wesley could hear his heart thumping, sure they were being watched; or, worse still, stalked by an unseen hunter.

They heard a shot cracking like a whip through the darkness. Wesley couldn't tell where it came from, but the sound reverberated around the walls. After a few seconds Gerry grasped his arm. They had to find Marcus but they couldn't risk becoming his quarry.

Wesley heard a second shot followed by the sound of reloading. By his reckoning, it came from the roofless building near the centre of the fort. From a previous visit he knew that it had once been an artillery store, and he wondered if the gunman realised how appropriate his choice of shelter was. They moved closer, keeping to the shelter of the ruined walls and after another shot rang through the night air, Wesley saw the brief flare of a match or lighter through one of the glassless windows. He nudged Gerry and pointed at the flitting shadows of the ARU officers who were moving fast to surround the building. Wesley edged his way along the wall until the doorway came into view.

Then he shouted Marcus's name.

There was a long silence then the words 'Piss off,' drifted over the night air.

'Come out slowly and put your gun down on the ground. There are armed officers surrounding the building so you've got no choice.'

'Ooh, I'm scared.' The voice was slurred. The boy was under the influence of something – and that made him unpredictable.

'Why don't you come out? We just want to talk to you.'

'What about?'

'Barney and Sophie.'

There was another lengthy silence before they heard the boy's voice again. 'Do you want to know who killed them?'

'Why don't you tell us?'

'They deserved everything they got. Now go away and let me get on with my target practice.'

'What do you mean, they deserved everything they got?' They needed to keep him talking, to establish some sort of rapport.

There was a lengthy silence before the answer came. Wesley could hear the gentle sound of the waves lapping at the base of the nearby cliff as he held his breath and waited.

'Barney was going to betray me and I wasn't going to let him do that.'

'What about Sophie?'

'Collateral damage. It happens.'

The words chilled Wesley's heart. 'You mean she got in the way.'

There was another long pause. 'I couldn't afford a witness, could I?' The boy's voice faltered and he suddenly sounded unsure of himself, a lonely boy cornered like a huntsman's prey.

'Why don't you come with us and we'll call your father and your solicitor—'

'I don't want my father.'

'Your mother then.'

The next words came out as a raw, primeval cry piercing the darkness. A statement of terrifying pain. 'My mother's dead.'

'What does he mean?' the DCI whispered, nudging him in the ribs.

Wesley didn't answer. His eyes were fixed on the roofless building where the boy was hiding, cowering from the armed, black-clad huntsmen who were closing in, their rifles aimed at their target.

All of a sudden another gunshot tore through the night and Wesley was aware of the ARU officers edging forward.

'Go to hell,' the boy yelled before he let off another shot.

Wesley heard the shotgun being reloaded, then everything went quiet. They stayed quite still, hoping desperately that he would tire of this game. A match flared again and Wesley caught a whiff of cannabis in the air.

He could hear Gerry breathing beside him, forcing himself to conquer his natural impatience and wait. But it was the only choice they had if they were all going to come out of this alive.

He saw a sudden movement and a dark figure appeared in the shadow of the artillery store entrance. He could make out the long shape of a shotgun sweeping round to encompass the ARU officers. He heard the hollow click of weapons being readied and held his breath, praying that the boy wouldn't do something stupid.

An ARU officer barked the order. 'Put your weapon on the floor and come out with your hands up.'

After a brief hesitation the boy let off another shot. Then a second shot followed, almost like an echo, and Wesley watched as the boy collapsed to his knees and his gun clattered to the floor.

Wesley rushed forward and when he reached the boy who lay still and prone on the cobbled ground, he kicked the weapon out of his reach, uncomfortably aware that the ARU weapons were trained on him.

He knelt and felt for a pulse. It was there all right but he could see a dark pool of blood on the ground, glistening in the moonlight. 'Someone call an ambulance,' he shouted.

'Already done,' Gerry answered, approaching slowly. 'Is he . . . ?'

Before Wesley could answer, he heard a metallic clatter of something being thrown on the ground followed by frantic shouts and the sound of running feet. He looked up and, in the lighthouse beam, he saw a figure dodging with the skill of an experienced rugby player past the ARU officers who were shouting and trying to block the way. The figure was making straight for them.

'You've fucking killed him,' it screeched.

Wesley struggled to his feet. 'Hello, Marcus,' he said. Then he took his torch from his pocket and squatted down again, turning the injured boy over to get a proper look at his face.

They walked down the corridor towards the Intensive Care Unit at Morbay Hospital. It was a familiar route, one they'd travelled many times before when Keith Marsh had lain there, hovering between life and death.

'He might have been making it all up. He might just be upset about his dad,' said Gerry.

'Then why did he fire at us? And what did he mean about his mother being dead?'

'Hopefully we'll find out. They say he'll live. He was lucky they didn't shoot to kill.'

'And Marcus was lucky that he dropped his shotgun before the ARU saw it or he might have been shot too.'

When they arrived at the entrance to the ward, they were told that Dunstan Price was unconscious. There was no way he was up to receiving visitors apart from close family and he was certainly in no state to face police questioning.

His mother, they were told, was at his bedside. The mother who he claimed was dead.

It was Monday morning and Dunstan was stable after undergoing surgery. Wesley and Gerry hoped they'd be able to get past the protective cordon of medical staff and speak to him, but they'd been told he was still unconscious.

In the meantime Len Price was still in custody, being

given updates on his son's condition while his wife, Pat, kept her quiet vigil at the bedside.

All they could do for the moment was ensure all their paperwork was in order, and Wesley felt restless. The only items of interest that had landed on his desk that day were a final confirmation from the lab that the bones in the picnic trench dated from the early years of the nineteenth century and a notification from the CPS that Alfred Catton wasn't going to face prosecution for moving them. For some reason he was relieved that the old man wouldn't have to undergo the stress of appearing in court. After all, he hadn't really done anyone any harm.

The office was hot and stifling and he needed some fresh air, so breaking the good news to Alfred gave him the perfect excuse.

The skeleton's identity still remained a mystery, but he hoped that Alfred's researches might provide the answer. He'd wondered whether to call in at the fort to see Neil while he was over on that side of the river. But when he recalled the events of Saturday night – the sound of shots bursting through the darkness and the boy collapsed and bleeding on the ground, fighting for his life – he knew he couldn't face returning to the place just yet.

When he reached Catton Hall Alfred himself answered the door. He was wearing reading glasses perched on the end of his nose.

As soon as he was inside, Wesley broke the news of the CPS's decision and he saw a look of relief pass across the old man's face.

'That is good news. Thank you for coming in person. I'm sure you must be so busy.' He paused. 'I heard there was an incident up at the fort on Saturday night.'

Wesley gave him an apologetic smile. 'It's not something I can discuss just yet, I'm afraid, but you might be able to cast some light on the identity of that skeleton that caused you all the trouble. Our tests have confirmed that it dates from the early nineteenth century, and I know you've been researching the history of this place.'

As Alfred ushered him along the dimly lit panelled hall, his expression was almost gleeful as though he'd been transfigured by the prospect of sharing his knowledge with a kindred spirit.

When they reached the library, Wesley perched himself on a rather uncomfortable chair and waited while Alfred rummaged through a heap of books and papers. Eventually the old man's lips formed a triumphant smile and he sat back, his hands clasped behind his head.

'Imagine yourself back in the time of the Napoleonic wars,' he began. 'The owner of Catton Hall in those days lived in his own little fiefdom, unaware of the Enlightenment and much else that was going on at the time. He even kept a jester.'

Wesley raised his eyebrows.

'Known as Silly John. According to the vicar of the day he was a nasty piece of work and he organised hunts for his master. Only the Squire and his cousin, Henry – who is my direct ancestor, by the way – considered hunting foxes rather old hat; they preferred to hunt human beings. Naked human beings. Usually workers from the estate. There were one or two fatalities, but because of his almost feudal status nobody dared to complain. In a way it must be rather nice to have that sort of power,' he added wistfully.

'Is that where your son and Carl Heckerty got the idea for their hunts from?'

'Oh, the story of the hunts has been common knowledge around these parts for many years. Henry Catton was reputed to have made a pact with the devil. He was buried in a caged tomb so that his spirit couldn't escape, and it's still said that he hunts with his pack of ghostly whisht hounds on All Hallows Eve. All rubbish of course and there are enough ghostly hounds in Devon to fill Battersea Dogs Home three times over. But I digress. The trouble started when a young woman turned up unexpectedly at Catton Hall. She spoke no English and she was taken for a foreign princess. But it turned out she was just a Devon girl with a vivid imagination and a lot of chutzpah.' He chuckled. 'She had them all fooled. Then one day she was found murdered and the jester, Silly John, got the blame.'

'Was he guilty?'

Catton raised a hand. 'I'll come to that. The girl's step-brother had turned up a few days earlier and shortly after her death he was killed in one of the hunts.' He handed an old, leather-bound book to Wesley. 'After the hunt, the Squire died as a result of a fall from his horse and he made a full confession. This is the Vicar's account of events.' Alfred pointed to the book. 'If you're wondering where that body I found in the pets' cemetery came from, the answer's in here. Please take it and see if you come to the same conclusion. But do make sure you return it, won't you.'

'Richard says you're writing a book on the subject.'

'Yes. A local publisher's shown an interest. I've recently found another volume of the Jester's journal in the muni-ment room. I haven't read it yet but when I do . . . '

'I'd be interested to read your book when it comes out.'

Alfred looked rather gratified. 'I'm not sure when I'll get

346

round to finishing it, but when I do, I'll make sure you get a copy.'

Wesley thanked him and picked up the old volume carefully. He stood up to go and turned to face Alfred who still sat, half hidden by his papers. 'We never did manage to trace Daniel Parsland, you know.'

'He was a free spirit. He could be anywhere. But it's all ancient history. Dead and buried.' He stood up and shook Wesley's hand before showing him off the premises, shuffling slowly ahead, chattering inconsequentially.

Wesley tucked the book under his arm and said goodbye before making his way back to the incident room, glad of the temporary distraction of the past. It was only a matter of time now before Dunstan Price regained consciousness and then all hell would break loose.

Chapter 42

Journal of the Rev. Octavius Quilly, Vicar of Queenswear

31 July 1815

An hour before dawn this morning, my servants were awoken by a frantic beating upon my door, as though Satan himself had come to claim our immortal souls. Our insistent visitor was Christopher Wells, steward to Squire Catton; who urged me to attend his master at once, as he had fallen from his horse after a night-time hunt and was not expected to live till morning.

When I reached Catton Hall, I was shown to the Squire's chamber which was a dank, dull room with little modern comfort. Lying there upon the bed was the Squire, and I could see at once his injuries were most grievous. The doctor had left the house shortly before my arrival, saying there was little more he could do. Wells told me that the

Squire had requested my presence, which caused me much amazement, but miracles do happen even in this age of war and reason.

The Squire opened his eyes wide as I knelt beside the bed to pray and he clutched at my sleeve with a strength that I would not have expected from a man so close to death.

'I must confess all,' he said. 'I have sinned grievously and I have lived a life of wickedness, but the one time I willingly took a human life, it was so that justice would be done.'

I told him to remain calm and confide all to me, for God is quick to forgive those who truly repent. He began to speak and his words astounded me.

He confessed that his jester had overheard the Lady Pegassa talking with his steward and to his astonishment, they conversed in English. Later that day the Squire had challenged her and she admitted all to him, throwing herself on his mercy. She claimed she was an honest girl with a taste for adventure and a desire to separate herself from her older stepbrother who used her like a chattel and insisted that she obeyed him in all things. He would not allow her to venture out alone and offered violence to any young man who paid her any attention. When she left her home, she knew he would seek her out, so she hit upon a plan to utilise her dark and exotic looks to alter her person and her nationality so that no trace of the simple Devon maid would remain.

For a while her deception succeeded, and she came to relish the role of princess from the Orient, even though she feared her stepbrother would hear of the attention she received from local society and track her down. And so it did prove. The man enquired in the district and received word of a young maiden of foreign appearance who, having convinced all that she was some eastern princess, resided at Catton Hall as guest of the Squire. He knew his stepsister's playful nature and that she would relish the pretence, so he travelled to Catton Hall to confirm his suspicions.

Now this man had always had a strange affection for his stepsister that many would say was contrary to nature, and his anger was more that of a betrayed lover than a fond brother, and when he came upon Peggy – for that was her real name – alone and unprotected, they quarrelled and he put his hands around her throat and killed her. When she was found, it was assumed that the jester, Silly John, who envied the esteem in which his master held her, was responsible for her demise, but the Squire soon sought out the truth of the matter and offered the stepbrother a choice. Either he could be handed over to the magistrate, or he could take the part of the hare in one of the Squire's hunts. Thinking the second choice would allow him to gain his freedom, he set off, naked and vulnerable, with the hounds baying for his blood, quite unaware that the Squire had arranged for this particular hunt to result in the death of the quarry.

And on that moonlit night, the woods at Catton Hall became the scene of brutal, vengeful murder when the quarry was run to ground and summary justice dispensed with John Tandy's cudgel.

The naked, bleeding corpse was brought back to Catton Hall, slung across a horse and, at Tandy's suggestion, a hasty burial was arranged in the place where the Squire's beloved dogs are interred. The grave was dug swiftly by moonlight and the cadaver rolled in to lie there without the benefit of a Christian burial.

Once the Squire had made his confession to me, he

grasped my hand and asked me to pray for him. This I did as he passed from this life, and yet I could not ignore what I had learned. It is necessary for me to notify the relevant authorities so that Tandy may be brought to justice for his crime, and the dead man, guilty though he was of his step-sister's murder, might be buried in accordance with the law of the land and of God. When I left the Squire's bed-chamber I came upon Tandy loitering on the landing. I pray that he had not been eavesdropping. I left the house with a heavy heart, careful to avoid Henry Catton, whom I knew to be in his cups downstairs, no doubt awaiting his inheritance for he is the Squire's only heir.

And now I write this account in the privacy of my study, preparing for what I must do.

The Steward's Journal

1 August 1815

The Squire has embarked on his long journey to meet his Maker – or, as some say hereabouts, to sup with Satan. The parson was with him at the end, so I pray that his soul was saved, albeit at the final moment.

I thought it strange when I heard the news that the parson himself was found dead this morning. Word has it that he fell in his study and that he hit his head on the fire-place causing most terrible injuries.

I heard somebody leave the hall last night in the early hours and, unable to sleep at the thought of the Squire lying dead and cold in his chamber awaiting his coffin, I looked out of the window and saw John Tandy hurrying away down the drive towards the village.

2 August 1815

Today Tandy was in the Squire's chamber, weeping over his corpse, while I endeavour to keep the household running smoothly. Henry is gone to the attorney in Tradmouth to discuss the business of his inheritance and I took advantage of his absence to examine Tandy's chamber. There I found a book, bound in the finest leather, hidden beneath the Fool's mattress and, upon examination, I discovered it to be the parson's journal.

When I read it, I became privy to the dreadful secret that the Squire confided to the parson before his death and I understood the significance of my discovery. For this journal was filched from the parson somehow on the night of his death. And I am determined that the man who took the unhappy clergyman's life shall face the gallows.

Chapter 43

Gerry's phone rang and, after a brief conversation, he looked up at Wesley. 'Dunstan Price has come round. They say he's up to questioning.'

Without a word they both stood up and made for the door, but before they could leave the office Paul Johnson bore down on them, holding a sheet of paper. There was a grim expression on his face. Since his cousin's death, the old, easy-going Paul had vanished somewhere, lost in the land of unpleasant experience. The man who'd replaced him was serious and determined; bent on justice – or maybe on retribution. Wesley had noticed that he and Trish hardly communicated these days, although she looked happy enough, as though she'd found something to distract her.

'I've found that information you were after, sir.' He handed the paper to Wesley who studied it for a few seconds and passed it to Gerry who nodded solemnly and made no comment.

An hour later they were at Morbay Hospital. On their way to the Intensive Care Unit they called in on Keith Marsh, who was due to be discharged in the next few days. His wife was nowhere to be seen and Wesley guessed that this was a bad sign.

Marsh asked them how the investigation was progressing, but Wesley's reply was noncommittal. At that point he wasn't exactly sure of the whole truth himself but he hoped that once they'd spoken to Dunstan, things would become clearer.

When they reached Intensive Care, they met Pat Price in the visitors' waiting room. They'd wanted to see her before they tried to talk to Dunstan because they needed some explanations, and now she sat down opposite them, twisting a tissue in her hands.

She looked up, her expression a blend of anxiety and defiance. 'Are you going to release my husband? Surely you can't keep him in custody while his son's—'

'We've got hold of a copy of Dunstan's birth certificate,' Wesley interrupted.

He let the statement hang in the air for a while until Pat looked up at him with terrified eyes.

'Why has everyone been lying to us? Why have we been led to believe that you're Dunstan's mother?'

'When I moved in with Len after Karen left, Dunstan was just two, so I was the only mother he ever knew. Karen walked out on him to live with some artist. She abandoned him.'

'That wasn't quite true, was it? You and Len had been in a relationship before she left. Your affair might even have been driven her into the arms of the first man who showed a bit of interest – only that man wouldn't have looked at her twice with a toddler in tow.'

Pat looked away.

'I think Karen began to see quite a bit of her son once he was old enough to lead his own life. And she paid his school fees. That's another thing we've checked. They've always been paid by cheque. Her cheque. The wealthy grandparents don't exist, do they?'

Pat bowed her head. 'Dunstan got in with a bad crowd at the local school. He was going off the rails and when Karen found out she said she'd pay for him to go to private school.'

'How did she find out?'

'She contacted Len for updates from time to time, to see how Dunstan was, so he must have told her. I wasn't happy about it, but Len said if that's how she wanted to spend her money ...'

'Was one of his undesirable friends called Jimmy Yates?'

She nodded. 'Yes, he was one of them. The lads Dun hung round with were always in trouble and Len was scared that he was going to go the same way.'

'Do you know how Karen got the money?' Wesley asked.

'No, and I didn't ask.'

'Do you think Len killed her to stop her seeing Dunstan?'

She didn't answer.

'Is Dunstan up to talking to us?'

The answer was a reluctant nod and they left her there, sitting alone staring at a pile of six-month-old gossip magazines.

When they reached the ward, Dunstan was wide awake and, when he saw them approaching, he struggled to raise himself upright, but because of the tubes and monitors attached to his body, he had to abandon his efforts and he flopped back, exhausted, on the pillows.

Gerry sat down on a pink plastic chair by the bed, but Wesley preferred to stand.

'Are you up to talking to us, son?' Gerry asked.

'Don't call me son,' the boy hissed with venom. Then Wesley realised that the very word probably had painful associations.

'You said you killed Barney and Sophie. Is that true?'

'I was stoned. I didn't know what I was saying.'

Wesley caught Gerry's eye and the DCI gave him an almost imperceptible nod. It was his turn to try. And Wesley knew what questions to ask.

'Evie was your real mum, wasn't she?'

'My mum's name was Karen.'

'Of course it was. Did your dad know you'd been seeing her?'

'He knew she paid my school fees. But that's about all he knew.'

'Did you meet her at her house?'

'We always met in cafes and places like that. She never wanted me to go to her house.'

'Why did she pay your school fees?'

'Cause Dad couldn't afford it.'

'I don't mean that. Why did she want you to leave your old school?'

'Cause of Jimmy. We were best mates and he was always getting me into trouble. I started smoking dope and we robbed an off licence.'

'You were never charged.'

'Jimmy got the blame. I was there but he didn't grass.'

'And your real mother, Karen, heard about all this and paid for you to go to Corley Grange? Corley Grange doesn't come cheap. Where did she get the money from?'

'I never asked.'

'When you eventually found out, it came as a shock,

didn't it? Did Barney pinch Evie's card from his father?'

Tears began to form in the boy's bloodshot eyes and he made a noise which sounded like a sob.

Wesley edged closer to the bed. 'Let me tell you what I think happened, Dunstan. Tell me if I'm wrong, won't you?'

The boy gave a small, painful nod.

'I don't think you had any idea about your mother's double life or where that money came from,' he began. 'You saw her occasionally and you got on quite well, but it must have been hard for you. I expect you felt you were betraying Pat, because she'd brought you up. And your father must have told you how your mother ran off and left you when you were a baby. I expect you had mixed feelings . . . confusing feelings.'

'Yeah. But she said she was sorry. She wanted us to be closer.'

'I'm sure she did. Then one day Barney suggested visiting the prostitute his father had been seeing regularly. Is that right?'

Dunstan nodded again and Wesley could tell the movement caused him pain. 'We'd had a bit to drink and he dared me. He'd rung her and she said she could see him at one on Saturday afternoon. He'd pinched his dad's credit card and got some money from a cash machine. He said it'd be a laugh. Barney went in first and I hung back while he was talking, so I couldn't see her, and by the time I went inside she'd already gone upstairs to . . . to get ready. Then Barney said he'd changed his mind; he didn't fancy it 'cause he had Sophie, so he told me to go on upstairs and enjoy myself while he went across the road to get come cider. He said he'd pay. His treat, he said.'

357

'You must have had a hell of a shock when you saw her. Your own mother.'

Dunstan gave a sob that jerked through his whole body. 'She looked so ... so cold ... so hard. She stared at me like she'd seen a ghost and asked me what the fuck I was doing there. Then she yelled at me to get out and she started to cry. I lost it and all I remember is squeezing her neck and wishing she was dead. She didn't fight back; she just looked ... I don't know ... sad. When I came to my senses she was lying there on the floor, and I realised what I'd done.' Tears were rolling down his cheeks now. 'She shouldn't have been there like that. She shouldn't have done it. She was my mum.'

He flung his head back and issued a primitive howl that brought a nurse hurrying to the bedside. Wesley knew she was about to order them out but, as Dunstan sobbed, Gerry took her to one side and promised they'd try not to upset her patient further. She hovered at the end of the bed for a while watching, making sure they didn't overstep the mark.

It was a minute or so before they were able to continue and Wesley tried to keep the questioning gentle.

'You say she was on the floor? You moved her on to the bed later?'

'I didn't touch her – I couldn't. I just ran out and threw up in the loo. Then I remembered Barney was waiting for me, and I knew I had to cover up what I'd done somehow. I knew I had to try and act normal.'

'So you pulled yourself together and tidied up a bit. You'd watched cop shows so you knew you mustn't leave any trace. You searched the place and took her phone and anything else that might identify her as Karen Price. Is that right?'

358

'Yes,' he whispered.

'What happened when you met Barney again?'

'He asked me how it went and I just said "OK". I told him I had to go 'cause I found it hard to act normal after . . . I went home and sat out in the top field till it was dark, and after a while it just seemed like a bad dream – like it had never happened. And when there was nothing about it on the news, I thought maybe I hadn't killed her, that maybe she'd just been unconscious.'

'So let's move on a week. Karen's body was found and there was a lot of publicity. Then Barney puts two and two together and says "Hey, that sounds like the woman we visited. You were acting a bit oddly when you came out. Did you kill her?" He was joking, of course, but you were terrified he was going to tell the police, so he had to be silenced. Only the one chance you had was at the hunt when Sophie was with him. Did you think he'd told her your secret? Was that it?'

'Something like that.'

'What the jury will find so hard to take is the way you must have planned it all. Did you take the shotgun in the Land Rover and double back to get it? Maybe a torch to shine in their eyes? You've been lamping, haven't you, Dun?'

He gave a small nod.

'Now we come to your old mate, Jimmy Yates. We've got him on CCTV hanging round the bus stop down the road at the time you killed Karen?'

'I saw him afterwards, when I met up with Barney again. He called out to me but I pretended not to hear him.'

'He'd followed the news about Evie's murder and he knew it must have taken place around the time he saw you in St Marks Road. Did you know he'd seen you coming out of the house?'

'Not till he got in touch.'

'And he tried to blackmail you?'

'He said he'd had a good view from the bus stop and he asked for a hundred quid to keep quiet. He said he'd taken a picture of me with his mobile.'

'And you paid up?'

'I had to.'

Wesley nodded, a little surprised that he'd hit the target so many times. 'You followed him one night when he went out lamping and shot him just like you had Barney and Sophie. It was becoming easy now. They say murder does. Jimmy was lying about the photograph, by the way. But you had to make sure so you broke into his house. Only we had his mobile down at the station. I bet you were worried when you couldn't find it. Easy to break-in, was it? Did you remember everything Jimmy taught you back in the days you were at school together? Were you hoping to get the money back too? Only his mum found it, and I reckon her need is greater than yours.'

'Piss off.' Dunstan's spirit seemed to be returning.

'Then we found out who the dead woman was, and we arrested your dad. Bet that came as another shock. When we told him we could ID his Land Rover parked near Karen's house from a CCTV picture, he must have guessed the truth so he made up a story about being there and having a row with her. But that was to protect you, wasn't it? I don't think your father was there at all. But when we arrested him on suspicion you felt you had to do something about it, so you thought of Marcus. You don't particularly like him, do you, and you thought he'd make the perfect scapegoat. You arranged to meet him at the fort for a bit of target practice, and I guess he was going to go the same way as Barney and Sophie. Were you going to make it look like suicide?'

There was no answer.

'You got high to give yourself a bit of extra courage and waited for him. Only Jodie misread the situation and told us where Marcus was going. She thought *he'd* killed Barney and Sophie. Luckily for Marcus, as it happens.' He paused. 'Have I got all this right, Dunstan?'

Again he didn't answer. But Wesley knew the answer was 'yes'.

The next day, Wesley worked all morning, clearing his paperwork, and as he filed away statements and cleared up loose ends, the thought of Dunstan Price, who'd looked so unexceptional, just like thousands of other teenagers in schools, colleges and universities throughout the country, harbouring that terrible, festering secret, disturbed him more than he expected.

It raised uncomfortable questions in his mind. Are we all capable of evil given the right triggers? How can we ever know that what is going on in somebody else's head isn't some perverted version of reality? How can some people wear such an innocent, amiable mask to hide a stinking corruption within? But he knew these questions were more his brother-in-law's province than his. His job was to get to the truth and hand the guilty party over to the courts.

He needed to talk to somebody, to exorcise the demons in his head, so he strolled over to Gerry's office. But Gerry was due to attend a meeting with Chief Superintendent Nutter and the CPS, so he seemed rather preoccupied.

Wesley glanced at his watch. It was almost lunchtime and the sunshine was streaming in through the office window. He wanted to be out there in the open air. He'd earned a break.

He left the station and as he walked past the Memorial Gardens and the boat float to the High Street, he felt comforted by the normality of the busy scene; proof that life went on. After queuing for a vegetable pasty he strolled to Baynards Quay where he found a vacant bench and ate, surrounded by seagulls and holiday makers, watching the yachts and pleasure craft gliding up and down the river on the high tide, and the steam train chugging out of Queenswear station on the far bank; sending cotton wool clouds of smoke up into the clear blue sky. When he'd finished eating he decided to take the ferry over the river and he made a call to Neil, asking his friend to meet him at Queenswear church. There was something there he wanted to see.

It was good to feel the cooling river breeze on his face as he leaned on the rail, looking down into the sparkling grey water. And when the ferry docked, he strolled off first with the rest of the foot passengers, feeling the thrill of freedom, like a child released from school after a particularly harsh exam.

He climbed the steep road to the old stone church with its squat tower and opened the gate to the churchyard. Once inside, he began to look around, studying the names on the gravestones, searching for three in particular. The first was easy to locate. It was a rather grand table tomb on the north side of the church by the wall. There was another similar tomb next to it, contained in an iron cage. Wesley picked his way through the overgrown headstones to get a

362

closer look, and when he got there he found that the inscriptions on both tombs were still quite clear.

The first read 'Here lies the body of Edward Catton of Catton Hall. Died 31st July 1815 aged 64.'

He turned his attention to the caged tomb. The inscription on this one was simple. 'Henry Catton of Catton Hall. 1787 – 1839. Deliver us from evil, oh Lord.'

Wesley stood for a while staring at the graves. There was no mention of murder or the events leading up to Edward's death. Just that brief, tantalising mention of evil on Henry's memorial.

It took him a further ten minutes to discover the third grave, but he'd guessed that it might be harder to find. This time the memorial was a flat slab and the words were worn and difficult to make out.

'The Lady Pegassa, princess of her tribe, who died far from her home and people. Cruelly done to death. God grant her rest.' The date of death was given but no age. He supposed the inscription said it all.

There was, of course, no memorial to her killer – the stepbrother who had driven her from home and ultimately brought about her death. He had lain all those years amongst the Catton family pets, unmourned and unremarked, until his bones were discovered by Alfred Catton and deposited unceremoniously in a bin bag, to take his place with the remnants of Kevin Orford's Feast of Life.

Near to Pegassa's tomb, Wesley discovered a humbler headstone and he recognised the name at once. 'Here lies Christopher Wells, Steward of Catton Hall. Died 3rd August 1815 aged 28. Called suddenly to his Maker.'

He thought for a moment. It was too great a coincidence that the steward, John Tandy's sworn enemy, should have died so suddenly after the demise of his master. But he told himself it wasn't his problem.

'What's up?'

Neil's voice made Wesley jump. He swung round to see his friend watching him, arms folded.

'Nothing's up.'

'Pam said you've cleared up the case. Shouldn't you be celebrating?'

'I had to charge an eighteen-year-old lad with the murder of his mother and three of his mates, so I've not really felt like it.'

Neil said nothing for a few moments and Wesley guessed he was lost for words.

'But on a more cheerful note, I've solved the mystery of your skeleton in the picnic trench. And if you're interested in the story of how it came to be there, I suggest you call at Catton Hall and have a word with Richard Catton's father.'

'I always knew those bones were old. That badly healed leg fracture ...'

'Easy to say with hindsight, but we had to be sure.' Richard Catton's insistence that his lover, Daniel, had vanished around that time had always nagged at the back of his mind. But now it looked as if Daniel had just chosen to leave Devon and he was probably somewhere out there in the world, doing whatever it is that free spirits do.

'Well now we know. Want to come and see how the dig's going?'

Wesley forced out a smile. 'Why not?'

They drove to the fort in Neil's yellow Mini. It was time he got a new car, Wesley observed, but Neil pleaded poverty, as usual.

When they reached the fort, Neil led him to a newly dug

trench a couple of hundred yards from where Dunstan Price had made his last pathetic attempt to secure his freedom.

Once Wesley had made admiring noises and asked a few intelligent questions, Neil spoke again. 'I heard from Kevin Orford this morning. The exhibition at Tate Modern is at the end of August.'

'Are you going?'

Neil shook his head. 'I doubt it. But the powers that be are pleased with his contribution to the Unit's coffers, so I suppose I should be grateful to him, even though he was a pretentious wanker.'

They stood for a while in amicable silence, enjoying the warmth of the morning sun on their faces. Wesley gazed out to sea where a pair of container ships chugged at snail's pace across the distant, hazy horizon.

'Are you doing anything tonight? Thought I might pop round seeing as I'm in the area.'

'Gerry's organised one of his case clear-up parties. He thinks it's good for morale. Truth is I'd rather get home, so I'll probably slip away early.' Wesley hesitated. 'I'm going to London to visit my parents at the end of August. Maybe I'll go along to Tate Modern to witness your moment of glory. It's not every day someone becomes part of an art installation.'

Neil smiled ruefully and shook his head. 'Now if they offered to show a film of one of my excavations in the British Museum ... I suppose you want a lift back to Queenswear?'

Wesley nodded and turned to go. He still had work to do.

Chapter 44

The Jester's Journal – Volume II

1 August 1815

How easy it is to end a man's life and release his soul to hell.

I followed the parson to his lair and gained access through an open window. I stalked him to his study and hid in the shadows, waiting for him to settle to his writing.

I moved silently. And when I struck, his skull cracked beneath the weight of my cudgel like an uncooked egg.

3 August 1815

I had thought my secret safe but there was more work to do. The steward is a young man, and strong, but he was no match for me when I came upon him in his bedchamber and thrust my knife between his ribs.

For I am death. Death the hunter who stalks his quarry behind the mask of a fool. And there is no escape from my cunning.

How well I will serve my new Squire. What sport we shall have.

Chapter 45

The old holiday park had been demolished, leaving a scarred, barren landscape of broken concrete and weeds. But construction was starting today, the realisation of all Richard's plans and dreams. He talked of little else these days, and Alfred was starting to find his single-minded enthusiasm slightly tedious.

He had no liking for his son's business partner – that vulgar man called Heckerty who ran the paintballing centre. They'd both been charged with moving the murdered teenagers' bodies, but the lenient judge had punished them with a suspended sentence. Alfred was sure it had all been Heckerty's idea, but he seemed to have the business acumen the Cattons lacked, and money was money: it would make a pleasant change to have some flowing into Catton Hall after all these years.

Now that Richard was fully occupied, and the police were no longer sniffing about, Alfred knew he had to do some clearing up of his own. If the holiday park generated enough money to make all the much needed improvements to the hall's decaying fabric, there was something that had to be done before the place began crawling with curious tradesmen interfering with all those buried pipes and cables.

The police had been perfectly satisfied that he'd found the bones he'd deposited in the picnic trench when he'd been digging Ursula's grave in the pets' cemetery. And there had been no reason why they shouldn't have believed him, because that particular story had been true.

He had brought the spade indoors from one of the crumbling outhouses and now he carried it stiffly down the cellar steps. He'd already placed the other things down there – the trowel and the plastic bin liners – and when he reached the spot, he began to dig, feverishly at first, then more slowly as exhaustion overtook his ageing body.

As he dug, the events of the past flashed through his mind as vividly as though they had happened yesterday.

He'd known they were meeting in the woods; he'd heard them arranging it. No doubt Daniel Parsland had enjoyed destroying Richard's innocence and initiating him into the pleasures of physical love. But that particular flirtation had been a sideshow, because Richard's mother, Selena, had been his target from the first. It had been an unforgivable thing to do, to use the son as a smokescreen to mask his true intentions; to hurt the boy's tender adolescent feelings like that. Parsland had been an odious, amoral man, but he had paid the price for his sins and received his due punishment. And as for Selena, she had disappointed and disgusted him.

Alfred had taken the shotgun from the locked cupboard,

as he often did at night when he went out to hunt vermin. It had seemed like a game in the pallid light of the full moon, with everything seen in silver shadows: owls swooping from the sheltering trees and frightened woodland creatures scurrying in the undergrowth. Then that magical landscape changed, and play became terror, as it dawned on Daniel that they were being hunted. As Alfred approached, gun loaded and ready, he'd started to run, dragging Selena behind him.

He'd closed in on them by stealth. From his childhood he'd explored those woods and he knew every clearing and every track. They had thought they were safe until he appeared there in front of them and levelled the gun carefully at Daniel's chest. He would never forget the terror in the voices of his cornered quarry as they squealed and pleaded for mercy.

But he had hardened his heart, squeezed the trigger twice and watched the life depart from their earthly bodies. Then there had been the deception; the carefully altered postcards dating from Selena's early travels before Richard's birth – the smudged postmarks and the greeting 'Dear Alfred' changed to 'Dear Alfred and Rich'. She had never written more than a few words: 'Everything fine', 'Enjoying myself'. Her casual brevity had made it so easy to convince Richard that she was still alive.

He continued to dig, taking frequent rests to catch his breath, and it was half an hour before he saw the tell-tale white of bone against the dark earth of the cellar floor. Two skulls, side by side as though in conversation.

After all those years his wife, Selena, and her lover, Daniel, were about to leave Catton Hall.

*

370

Pam was keen to see the exhibition at Tate Modern, although Wesley, after having had the dubious pleasure of meeting Kevin Orford, had his reservations.

Wesley's mother had taken some leave and seized the chance to entertain her grandchildren, so they travelled from the Petersons' home in Dulwich and arrived at the gallery just before lunch.

The red-brick power station beside the Thames, which had metamorphosised into Tate Modern, looked magnificent in the sunlight, and Wesley wasn't sure why he felt apprehensive as he approached the gallery housing Orford's exhibition. Perhaps he was associating the picnic with the horror of Dunstan Price's crimes that had been there at the back of his mind all summer, tainting everything however hard he tried to forget.

And now he was face to face with one of the witnesses. Kevin Orford, resplendent in an orange sleeveless vest, particoloured baggy trousers and wild, white wig, was holding court with a glass of red wine in his hand, surrounded by an adoring group of earnest young people. More than ever now, he reminded Wesley of a jester – one who lacked the knack of amusing an audience.

The installation filled the entire gallery – a huge plaster cast of the rotting picnic, left ghostly white. On each wall, large screens played footage of the excavation and Pam nudged him and pointed at Neil's moving image.

'Fame at last,' she whispered. It didn't seem appropriate to make comments out loud in that church-like atmosphere.

To Wesley's surprise, Orford spotted him, said a word to his rapt audience and hurried towards him with the determination of a guided missile. For a split second, Wesley toyed with the idea of turning on his heels and fleeing, but he stood his ground and waited.

'I'm so glad you could make it to my little exhibition,' said Orford. 'Impressive, isn't it?'

'Yes,' said Wesley, unsure what to say next. Pam was hovering by his side, her curiosity palpable, so he made the introductions and Orford took Pam's hand and kissed it in what Wesley thought was a remarkably affected manner. But she seemed to be enjoying herself, so he smiled and said nothing.

Orford leaned forward and whispered in Wesley's ear confidentially. 'I'd like to have a word in private if that's OK. There's an office we can use just over there.' He turned to Pam. 'I'm sure your lovely partner will excuse us. Do help yourself to more wine.' He clicked his finger at an underling who scurried over and, after whispered instructions, Pam's glass was refilled and she was led towards the canapés arrayed on a trestle table at the end of the room. Wesley had wondered whether it was part of the installation – a feast within a feast – but it seemed its purpose was purely functional.

Wesley followed Orford into a mundane office behind the artistic scenes. Once the door was closed, the artist removed the wig to reveal his shiny scalp and wiped his brow, like an actor arriving back in the wings after delivering a gruelling Shakespearian soliloquy.

Wesley was intrigued now. 'What did you want to talk to me about?'

'Something's been on my mind. I know I should have told you at the time and it probably won't make any difference but ...' He paused and Wesley waited patiently for him to continue. 'My statement, as far as it went, was true.

I did see Karen and I did give her money that Saturday morning but ... to tell you the truth, I went back later – around one thirty or maybe two, I can't be sure of the exact time. I was worried about her and I wanted to make sure she was all right. When I didn't get an answer I pushed the door and it wasn't locked. I found her ... she was still warm.'

'You should have told us this before.'

'I didn't want to incriminate myself. But now someone's been charged ... When I found her, she was on the floor but ... well, I couldn't leave her like that, so I laid her out properly on the bed. I felt she deserved some respect. I know I should have told you but ... '

'Her killer said he left her on the floor so we were wondering how ... ' The prosecution had been sure that Dun was lying, but Wesley had never been convinced. And now he knew the truth.

'And there's something else.' Orford focused his eyes on the floor and breathed deeply, as though he was about to make some dreadful revelation.

'When I got to the house, I saw a kid dashing out and his eyes ... they were sort of wild, as though he'd just seen a vision of hell – that's the only way I can describe it. I don't think he saw me. He didn't look as if he was in a fit state to notice anything. It was the same kid whose picture was in the paper – the one who killed her. It said he was her estranged son.' Orford began to edge towards the door.

'Why didn't you tell us this earlier?'

Orford looked Wesley in the eye. 'Because he was just a kid. I knew that once you lot got your claws into him he'd be locked away and labelled for life, and I thought he deserved a chance – an opportunity for his spirit to soar.

And who knows, perhaps he just thought he'd killed her and someone else finished off the dirty deed. Maybe he didn't do it.'

The artist gave Wesley an enigmatic smile, replaced the wig and opened the door.

'I'll be in your part of the world again next summer. I'm returning to Catton Hall to create a piece of performance art. It'll take the form of a hunt in period costume.'

Wesley followed him from the room and went in search of Pam. He'd had enough of games.

Historical Note

As Devon is a county rich in history and legend, it's hard to resist taking inspiration from some of its fascinating stories.

There are many eerie tales of ghostly whisht hounds, which are said to roam the countryside, particularly around Dartmoor. In Buckfastleigh, a squire called Richard Cabell, who died in 1677, was reputed to have been so wicked that his tomb had to be enclosed in an iron grille so that his spirit couldn't escape and terrorise the living – this grille can still be seen to this day. It is said that he was chased to his death by a pack of phantom hounds and this legend was possibly the inspiration for one of Sir Arthur Conan Doyle's most famous Sherlock Holmes stories, *The Hound of the Baskervilles*.

Devon was notable hunting country (although, as far as I am aware, the kind of manhunts described in this book exist only in my imagination). In the eighteenth and nineteenth centuries, many squires and clergymen kept packs of hounds, the most famous of the 'sporting parsons' being the Rev Jack Russell who was born in Dartmouth in 1795.

The county is dotted with many small manor houses, and in times gone by, some squires lived untouched by the elegant manners adopted by most gentry of the time. At the end of the eighteenth century, a Squire Arscott of Tetcott in North Devon kept a jester who used to swallow live mice to entertain his master's guests.

In 1817, a young woman of exotic appearance who apparently didn't speak a word of English (or any other known language for that matter) turned up in Gloucestershire where she intrigued and enchanted the local gentry and convinced them she was a 'Princess of Javasu' called Caraboo. She became quite a celebrity, but the wide circulation of her story led to her being unmasked as Mary Baker, a young woman from a poor Devon family who had developed a mischievous taste for adventure. Fortunately, she did not meet Pegassa's fate, and it is believed that she ended up in America (although what became of her there isn't known).

Napoleon Bonaparte did indeed visit South Devon when HMS *Bellerophon* dropped anchor in Tor Bay (in view of the fortress at Berry Head near Brixham, which had been built to defend the coast against French invasion) on 24th July 1815 to await instructions regarding his final destination.

During his visit, he displayed composure and great charm, praising the beauty of the Devon countryside. He remained on deck, attracting many sightseers in small vessels and the sea was said to have been so crowded with boats during his visit that it resembled dry land. Sailors aboard the *Bellerophon* even used blackboards to keep the crowds informed of the imperial passenger's movements. The *Bellerophon* eventually received instructions to sail to Plymouth where Bonaparte was transferred to the *Northumberland* for his final journey to St. Helena in the South Atlantic where he died six years later.